Books by Jo-Ann Mapson

Fault Line *(stories)*
Hank & Chloe
Blue Rodeo
Shadow Ranch
Loving Chloe
The Wilder Sisters

The Bad Girl Creek Trilogy
Bad Girl Creek
Along Came Mary
Goodbye, Earl

THE OWL & MOON CAFÉ

A NOVEL

Jo-Ann Mapson

SIMON & SCHUSTER PAPERBACKS

NEW YORK • LONDON • TORONTO • SYDNEY

SIMON & SCHUSTER PAPERBACKS
Rockefeller Center
1230 Avenue of the Americas
New York, NY 10020

First Simon & Schuster paperback edition 2006

SIMON & SCHUSTER PAPERBACKS and colophon are registered trademarks of Simon & Schuster, Inc.

Manufactured in the United States of America

ISBN-13: 978-0-7394-7156-2
ISBN-10   0-7394-7156-2

To my husband, Stewart, with love:
Thirty-two years, five dogs, two horses,
and one great son. Every moment astonishing.

I

Tell me what you eat and I will tell you
who you are.

—ANTHELME BRILLAT-SAVARIN,
Physiologie du goût, 1825

1

Mariah

"HALLELUJAH," MARIAH MOON said as the endless line of cars began moving forward. Twenty feet away, the Monterey exit shimmered like a desert mirage. She flipped on her blinker and waited impatiently to turn into traffic, brave the tunnel, and make her way to Lighthouse Avenue, where her mother was no doubt already preparing for the lunch crowd. Her grandmother, bless her heart for trying, was either filling salt-shakers or replacing sugar packets, stopping to rest when her legs ached. If the café was slow, she might be saying novenas for Simon, the gay cook she was certain she could get to defect to the other side. To Gammy, success hinged on bolstering his spiritual life. God and beauty products were what she believed in, which was why creams and abandoned potions cluttered the upstairs apartment. She wanted to turn back the clock, not just on her face but on the varicose veins that plagued her legs as well. To say it was hard watching someone you loved grow old didn't begin to cover it.

Traffic stopped again. Mariah rested her forehead on the steering wheel and sighed. Highway One, the two-lane scenic byway on California's Monterey coast, was two lanes too narrow to accommodate the tourists and commuters. A person could waste a whole morning here, breathing exhaust fumes and getting exposed to God knows what. And time was money. From now on every tick of the clock would remind her of that. This morning at six forty-five she had awakened as a thirty-three-year-old term assistant professor of sociology about to start the fall quarter. She had her master's, and fully intended to finish her doctoral dissertation, as soon as a chunk of time came her way—coinciding with a blue moon, or a four-leaf clover, or a flying pig. By ten-fifteen AM she was another unemployment statistic due to budget cuts. Her checking account was in the dismally low three figures. Of course it was. All summer she waitressed at her mother's café and lived on tips. When fall rolled around, the coffers were low.

And then this morning the dean had called her in and explained that the term post she'd held for eight years was being phased out. Michael Howarth, Ph.D., freshly graduated from the University of Louisiana, would now cover her classes. He was twenty-eight years old and had already published a book. After eight years of promises that her job would be made permanent as soon as they got more funding, Mariah wanted to call Michael up and tell him not to get too cozy, not to hang any pictures on the walls until he got tenure.

If Mariah were to make the monthly car payment on the Subaru, the condo she and her daughter, Lindsay, rented would have to go. She could COBRA their insurance benefits— that is, if she could find a way to pay for them. At the heart of her worries was Lindsay's tuition for Country Day Academy for Girls.

Her twelve-year-old daughter's I.Q. tested at 175. That kind of intelligence was as much a burden as a gift. Mariah was determined to provide the right environment for her daughter's intelligence to flourish, meaning public school was not an option. The stress would be traumatic, and such a drastic change had the potential to seal Lindsay's fate as the too-smart geek girl to be avoided at all costs. Mariah knew that popularity was based on nothing more than the callow whim of youth. Other twelve-year-olds went to the movies, played soccer, slathered on fruit-scented lip gloss, and begged for trendy clothes. Not her daughter. Lindsay lived, breathed, and ate science. Quantum theory science. Bioethics science. Science fiction. Scientific essays with words longer than most sentences. The kinds of science a normal person could go a whole life without understanding and get along just fine.

The driver behind her leaned on the horn, startling her out of her daydream to pull forward maybe six inches. Since when did a measly half-foot merit blasting your horn? Control freak. Without even looking she knew it was a man at the wheel, ramming the palm of his hand into the horn. Just for that she'd drive slower.

Lindsay had her father's strawberry blond, curly hair. She was four feet five inches and had not grown in almost a year. At her checkup, the doctor joked that maybe Lindsay's intellectual growth had stunted her body's progress, but Mariah didn't think that was funny. Lindsay had skipped grades four and seven, and now she was in eighth. No way was she ready for high school, Mariah thought, picturing Lindsay's beloved posters of Carl Sagan and Lewis Thomas. Lindsay so often asked to be quizzed on the periodic table of the elements that Mariah had the poster laminated. Then there was the Darwinian theory poster, and her two-by-three-foot print of the saltwater fishes of Monterey County. When they left the condo, where would the posters go? For that matter, where would she and Lindsay go?

The condo and the car were expendable—things—not vital. In the immediate future she would temporarily return to waiting tables at her mother's café, The Owl & Moon. The restaurant was a Pacific Grove landmark. Francis Moon, 1883, read the painted marker on the front wall, a distant relative on her grandmother's side. The exterior was weathered cedar and peeling paint, and all summer the window boxes spilled over with geraniums, pansies, phlox, and Cecil Brunner minia-ture roses. The Owl & Moon Café offered a wide variety of soups, all organic. Their pastries were baked on-site, daily. On Saturday mornings, the line of people waiting for a table could spill halfway down the block, even though Pacific Grove was prone to fog year-round, even when just a few blocks up the sun was shining. Mariah hated waitressing. She looked at every customer and couldn't help placing him or her in a soci-ological context—this one an upper-socioeconomic misogy-nist, that one an abandoned wife when her husband hit his mid-fifties. But she could keep her head down and do it until she found a better-paying job. She'd given up a lot more to meet Lindsay's needs. Men, movies, manicures; it did no good to think about it.

How could the university do that to her after eight years? How dare they wait until the last minute to tell her? Each year Mariah felt she was that much closer to a permanent hire. It was too late to apply for a teaching job anywhere else. The adjunct positions had already been snapped up. She would gather her family together and tell them . . . and then what? Try not to choke on her broken heart. She had sacrificed hav-ing a social life, given up time with her daughter because working hard now allowed her to invest in Lindsay's future. Mariah was a product of public schools, marking time until she could get to college. She was determined to give Lindsay the best of the best despite having no father in the picture. Gammy Bess and Mariah's mother had worked hard for Mariah to rise above their stations. And now she had failed.

Breathing car fumes was muddling her thinking. What she needed was a lemon tart and a cup of coffee. She'd tell Gammy the news first, grateful for any homespun wisdom her grand-mother might have. "God shuts doors right and left, Mariah. I won't tell you He doesn't. But somewhere you least expect it, a little mouse is gnawing a hole, and right there's the gateway to freedom." Gammy was straitlaced and old-fashioned, but protective as a mother tiger.

Mariah's mother was a different story.

Mariah's head was filled with memories of her mother's embarrassing escapades. The opposite of Gammy in every way, she was a professional protester. Sit-ins, gay pride parades, testifying before the city council on chemical runoff into the bay, defending trees slated for removal. She even fought the initiative to eradicate the deer that roamed the El Carmelo cemetery, although they were truly nuisances, causing car accidents and ruining landscapes. Though she supported causes Mariah herself believed in, such as the homeless shelter and the no-kill animal shelter, Mariah still couldn't get over the way her mother told dirty jokes in the café. She'd gone topless on the beach and was issued a ticket for it—which she fought and won—after she pulled up her shirt to show the court that her tiny bosoms could not possibly be offensive. Later, the judge had asked her out. Her mother, in her fifties now, was moored in the "Hey, babe, what's happenin'" way of speaking. Every Friday night she went dancing, whooped it up and closed down the bars when other women her age were taking up knitting.

Her mother's name was actually Alice, but she insisted everyone call her Allegra, including Lindsay. "Gammy's the only grandmother around here," she'd said. In music, the term *allegro* meant quick, lively, and she was that. She didn't wear a bra. She didn't shave in any of the conventional places. "I'm a peace-loving, left-leaning hippie," she'd proudly tell anyone who asked about her political affiliation. But while hippies had a reputation for being laid-back and accepting, Allegra was bossy and loud. She drove Mariah crazy with her advice. On more than one occasion, she'd told Mariah to "loosen up, and have more sex." As if sex was nothing more than jogging, or painting your nails, and something you couldn't wait to discuss with your mother.

When Mariah was seven years old, her mother had leaned a ladder against the café building in order to reach the sign. "All the way to the top, babe," she said, and Mariah, who'd never been scared of heights, did as she was told, with her mother climbing up after her. But once up there, the world looked different. Cars on Ocean Avenue hurtled by so fast Mariah was sure they could never stop in time for a pedestrian. The cemetery across the street looked huge, dotted with dozens of gravestones that stuck up out of the earth like dead men's tongues. Just to think there was a corpse under each grave made her light-headed. What if a sudden wind came up, or an earthquake knocked her off the ladder? Mariah's stomach tied itself into a Gordian knot, but did Allegra notice? Of course not.

Her mother painted "sizing," a substance that looked like glue, all over the carved wooden moon in the café sign. Then Allegra took from her apron pocket a perfectly ordinary package, and peeled away the tissue paper to reveal what must have been the thinnest sheet of gold in the world.

Mariah remembered thinking that her mother must have found the treasure at the end of the rainbow. Gold was the stuff of pirates, Spanish doubloons, or the queen of England's crown. Allegra showed her how to brush gently over the fragile gold paper, teasing it away from the package, and then lightly laying it down on the now sticky wooden moon. "Go on, babe," she said. "Paint."

Mariah hesitated. "What if I make a mistake?"

"You can't make a mistake," Allegra told her. "There are no mistakes in art, just unplanned outcomes."

Mariah painted, watching the gold catch the light. Its wrinkles disappeared as they melded with the sizing. Down on the sidewalk, the café sign had looked like a wooden plank with a badly painted owl. Up on the ladder, however, Mariah saw that the owl's feathers were individually carved, and all together they made up the outstretched wing.

Her mother hugged her from behind, and Mariah felt the ladder wobble. "Whoops!" Allegra said, and wiggled it a second time just for fun. "Mariah Janis Joplin Moon," she said, "you just gave that old moon a second life!"

Except Mariah had done nothing of the sort. Things weathered quickly in the beach climate, and every six months the sign required maintenance.

Her mother was open and easy with everyone else, but from Mariah she kept secrets. How many times had Mariah asked her who her father was—just his name—and each time Allegra gave a different answer. He was a vagabond sailor. An Irish traveler hiking his way across Europe. And when Mariah pushed too hard, her mother said, "He was the man in the moon! Now stop with the questions before I lose my temper." And do what? Mariah wanted to ask. Punish me by making me listen to another *Grateful Dead Live* bootleg?

Her heart heavy, Mariah parked in the slot behind the café next to her mother's ancient VW bus. Gardener's Alley was narrow and cobbled, and fragrant with garbage. As she walked around front she looked up at the sign. It was eye-catching. Decorative, like the window boxes stuffed with miniature meadow grasses that defined Pacific Grove and its neighbor, Carmel-by-the-Sea. But The Owl & Moon wasn't like any other place. Inside it became its own little country.

Like the kitchen of an Iowa farmhouse, the bead board walls had been painted over so many times that they looked doused with cream. The floor was old planked pine stained the color of chestnuts, and deeply distressed from years of foot traffic. On the street entrance threshold, Allegra had painted a mariner's compass in primary colors, its needle fixed on true north. Mariah walked inside and slipped behind the counter where two customers sat on stools.

Gammy was deep in conversation with one of them, a man in his forties. Mariah waved hello and went into the kitchen. Simon, in his chef's apron, held an industrial-size tin of ground cumin seed above a large soup vat. Yawning like he hadn't woken all the way up, he spilled some into the soup, not even bothering to measure.

"Hi, Simon," she said. "Where's Allegra?"

He nodded his head toward the stairway that led to the

upstairs apartment. "Catching a few z's before the lunch crowd arrives."

That seemed odd to Mariah, because Allegra rose with the sun and partied until last call. "Are you sure?"

Simon rolled his eyes. "Why on earth would I waste my time telling you a lie?"

"Forget I asked," she said, making her way upstairs. Snippy as usual. I'd be like that, too, she thought, if Gammy was on my case all day about sexual preferences. Ha. At least Simon had a sexual anything. Mariah began to count up the years since she'd had a romance and quickly stopped because it was too depressing. As usual, the door was unlocked. Monterey County's history was rich with trouble. Thieving pirates, Spanish invaders, and blatant abuse of migrant workers were a few of its more notable sins. But unlocked doors and helping strangers remained part of the town's charm.

"Mom?" she said as she closed the door behind her. "Everything okay?"

Her mother sat up on the sofa where she'd been sleeping, her cheek branded with the weave of a throw pillow. "Babe! What a nice surprise. I didn't expect to see you today. Let me give you a hug."

All in the same moment, Mariah endured the too-tight hug, worried what Allegra would say when she told her the bad news, and noticed how pale her mother's face was. "Are you catching a cold?" she asked.

"Of course not," Allegra said, grinning. "I stayed out too late last night, but let me tell you, it was worth it. Mm-mm, do I love a hunky fireman! Please tell me you came over here to help serve the lunch crowd. Your grandmother means well, but she just can't move all that fast anymore. We're going to have to hire a waitress."

Mariah bit her tongue before she told her maybe not. "As it happens, I can work the rest of the day."

"Hot damn!" Allegra said, twisting her long black hair into

a bun and securing it with chopsticks. "Let's haul our gorgeous asses downstairs and get to work."

Asses. Mariah winced at her mother's choice of words, and the scent of patchouli floating in Allegra's wake. Her thumping wooden clogs beat out a rhythm Mariah could never keep up with.

Growing up with twenty-four-hour access to food that regular mothers reserved for special occasions didn't rot Mariah's teeth. Before she was Lindsay's age, she'd tired of sugar. Her Achilles' heel, however, was her mother's lemon bars. Lemons are fruit, she told herself as she ate two, then three of the powdered sugar–topped delicacies. Between her schedule and Lindsay's, eating right came second to simply eating. Judge Judy, a sociological gold mine, had once publicly stated that "no child ever died from having McDonald's for dinner," and that was good enough for Mariah. Some days all Mariah managed was vending machine chips. And drinking eight glasses of water a day? No problem, if Diet Coke counted.

"How do the bakery cases look?" Allegra shouted out from the kitchen.

"Not bad," Mariah said. "We could stand a few more peanut butter cookies."

"A dozen Jumbo's coming right up."

The man at the counter smiled at Mariah. "I hate to bother," he said, "but could I possibly get a take-away tea?"

Take-away? Just when she thought she'd heard all the idioms, here was another. So many tourists visited the Monterey Coast that there really was no such thing as off-season. Mariah took a new tea bag from the box under the counter. "We don't get a lot of hot tea drinkers this time of year," she said as she filled a paper cup and fitted it with a cardboard sleeve.

"I see," he said. "I'm afraid Guinness was absent from your menu."

"Sorry to disappoint you," she said, thinking he was probably just another alcoholic fostered by the stress of working to afford living in one of the richest counties in America. "Anything else I can get you?"

He shook his head no, and then took out his wallet to pay. "Tea and scones have fortified me to go unto my day and slay whatever dragons await me."

Scottish, Mariah noted. A land whose history was written in war. "Dragons are in short supply around here, but come back and see us again."

He smiled once more, and she couldn't help thinking of Sean Connery, who looked attractive and dangerous all at the same time. "Count on it."

The unexpected thrill of a man flirting with her lifted her spirits. With that crooked smile she'd bet her last dime he was already in a relationship. In a week's time of asking customers she could find out everything about him from his marital status to his shoe size, if she cared to. A small town could triple in population, turn its Victorian houses into bed-and-breakfasts galore, but the core of people who lived there remained a merrily dysfunctional family. She filled napkin dispensers and monkeyed with the automatic dishwasher everyone knew was dying. Either they'd have to get a loan for a new one or hire someone to do the dishes by hand. Money. Why was it so hard to earn and so easily spent?

From years of teaching Mariah knew that when the economy faltered, families weakened, and sometimes split up. It was the twenty-first century. "Downsizing" had made it into the lexicon. Schools were overcrowded. In her *Intro to Sociology* text a map of the geometric increase in global population told the story: too many people, not enough space. In 1798, Thomas Malthus had predicted overpopulation would lead to social chaos. His theory was dismissed as flawed—failing to take into consideration medical advances and lower death rates—but just try to find a parking place in Pacific Grove and his point was clear.

Her mother, counting the register till, suddenly shrieked. "There are three one-dollar bills in here! How are we supposed to make it through lunch?"

Off she ran to the Bank of America on the corner, while Gammy watched the tail end of *All My Children* on the tiny counter television and complained it was high time they gave poor Bianca back her baby.

"That is an immoral story line," she said hotly. "I feel like writing ABC a letter."

"Soap operas are dripping with sin," Simon called out through the order bar.

"It's make-believe, you dodo," she said.

Simon laughed. "It's probably a sin to watch them."

Gammy huffed. "God and I have things all worked out. Can you say the same?"

Though in the pit of her belly the job news sat like a cold lump, Mariah's dysfunctional family was doing all right. She'd find a way through this.

"God better grant me a bale of patience this afternoon," Gammy said later that day, coming out from the kitchen with a tray full of bowls of artichoke soup. "If I make it through the day without killing Simon Huggins it will be a miracle."

"What did he do now?" Mariah asked, adding a handful of cracker packets to the tray.

Gammy sighed. "What he said doesn't bear repeating. He's just trying to get my goat."

Allegra slid by them toward the kitchen, throwing over her shoulder, "Then quit leaving your goat tied up where he can get to it!"

"Ha, ha," Gammy said, taking the tray to table four. "Mariah, your mother is as funny as a crutch."

"You'll get no arguments from me," Mariah said, then turned her attention to table two, where she opened her order pad. "Everyone decided?"

A middle-aged, brown-haired woman looked over her reading glasses. "I'd like a cup of artichoke soup, but not if it has MSG in it."

"All our soups are organic," Mariah said.

"So that means no MSG?"

"Correct."

The woman turned to the elderly man with her. He had to be at least eighty, Mariah thought. He was a sweet-looking old guy in his red shirt and blue suspenders. "Daddy, have you decided?"

"I want a bowl of artichoke soup."

"Daddy, you can't finish a whole bowl," the woman said.

"Don't you tell me what I can't do. I damn well want a bowl, and what's more, I want an oatmeal cookie to go with it."

Mariah waited while the argument ran its course. There it was, her future staring at her, the day when parent became child, and there was another lifetime of mothering to do. The definition of family was complex these days, what with blended families and single mothers galore. Gammy and Simon feuded constantly. What kind of soup to make, spotted owls, strip malls, gay rights, and Jesus. Except for each other, no one took them seriously. Mariah thought of her daughter, Lindsay, fortunately absent from this fray. She would be in art class about this time, the only class she detested. Just that morning, Mariah had listened to yet another plea.

"For example, while others are learning to throw pots, I could be memorizing the periodic table of the elements."

"I know you hate art, sweetie," Mariah had said. "Just try to hang in there this one last time and I promise I'll make a date to talk to Mrs. Shiasaka and see about getting you switched."

"Why can't you talk to her today?"

"Because today I have an appointment with the dean. We're already running so late I'm going to have to drive ninety miles an hour, and I have to sign my contract today or our benefits will lapse, and next week we start second quarter scheduling—"

Wow. Didn't all that feel like a lifetime ago? The father-daughter table was not making headway. It was time to step in. "How about I bring you a cup of soup, sir, and if you want more, then I bring you a refill?"

"Now that's the first intelligent thing I've heard all morning," the father said. "And don't forget my cookie."

"Daddy!" the woman said. "Here I am trying to help you watch your sugar—"

"Mariah! Where's my cinnamon roll?" one of the regulars asked, and she nodded and ran to fetch one hot from the baking tray.

"What good's a bagel without cream cheese," another customer announced as Mariah was trying to take a to-go order over the phone.

"Coming," she said, resisting the temptation to yell that if they wanted fast food, drive through Taco Bell. Running back and forth from the kitchen to the cold case, she had no time to think about her problems. When there was a lull, she looked to see what needed to be restocked. Among items in the glass cold case were cheesecake, marzipan candies, The Owl & Moon's famous Chocolate Cherry Thunder fudge, and a round of sharp cheddar for the apple tarts. The nonrefrigerated case held all manner of pastries, sweet rolls, and berry pies. When the buckwheat rolls came out of the oven they went directly into pink boxes tied with kite string.

Out of the corner of her eye she watched her mother answer the phone, tickle a customer's new baby, wrap fudge, and box up cookies like she was working every station on the assembly line. Her face looked drawn. Sometimes Mariah couldn't bear how hard Allegra and Gammy worked. The Owl & Moon was Faustian, ruling over their souls. Mariah had vowed never to let it take over hers, but the aroma in the café was comforting. The soup warmed you to the core. The pastry melted on your tongue. Conversation was always interesting. It was easy to become addicted, which meant regular customers eventually turned into demanding regular customers, and there you were, stuck in a loop of supply and demand with no time to rest.

From 11:40 until 2:25 she refilled coffees, emptied three pitchers of iced tea, and served artichoke soup until the last of it was gone. Her own stomach growled, her feet throbbed, and her arms ached. She couldn't wait to have a bowl of soup herself, even if all that was left was beef barley.

All afternoon Mariah replayed the brief moment with the dragon-slaying Mr. Tea-and-scones. Since she didn't date, she felt it was perfectly acceptable to indulge in fantasies. A real kiss would probably make her cry. Ever since Lindsay was born, she told herself she didn't have the time, the right clothes, but Lindsay was the reason she didn't date. What did men call the children of single women? Baggage. Lovely word. Spoiled rotten babies that men were, most of them wanted a mommy, and they wanted to be that mommy's only child.

"Attention, everybody!" Allegra called out, tapping a spoon against a glass. "Time for our daily joke. What did Confucius say when he saw the man standing on the toilet?" She waited a moment, and then finished with, "That man high on pot!"

The customers laughed, but Mariah found nothing humorous about marijuana. Working here permanently would drive her mad. She'd look for a job in an office, a research position, learn to write grants, substitute teach, anything but waitressing. But what skills did she have? A hunt-and-peck typist, she needed Lindsay's help to get anywhere on her computer. Decent jobs of any kind were hard to come by in Monterey County. The daily joke laughter was soon replaced by pleas—"I haven't been helped yet" and "What do you mean you're out of Chocolate Cherry Thunder fudge?" She edged by her mother to get to the cold case.

Allegra patted Mariah on the behind as she walked by with more cinnamon rolls. "Chill out," she said. "Take life a little less seriously and you'll have a lot more fun."

What do you get when you cross a hippie with a mother,

Mariah wanted to ask, and then let Allegra have it for every embarrassing comment since the day she was born.

A businesswoman tapped the counter. "Excuse me, I'm still waiting for my fudge."

"There's probably more in the back," Mariah said. "Let me ring up this check and then I'll go look."

The Owl & Moon would never lack for customers. If a person came in for Chocolate Bomb cookies for her daughter's birthday, while she waited to have them boxed she'd smell the paper-thin rosemary-garlic Cheese Pennies, and pick up two dozen. Then she'd ask for a taste of the gleaming slab of Chocolate Cherry Thunder fudge. She'd buy a small piece, unwrap it in the car, take one bite, and turn up Monterey Jack on KMPG, the drive-time radio DJ who played old Nat King Cole vocals and plenty of Ella. Pinch-by-pinch, the fudge would disappear.

Mariah knew firsthand how that fudge made for a moment of pleasure no one could take from you. When had her life come down to settling for moments? Why did she live at the beach when she had no time to swim, or sunbathe, or even take a walk? So eager to make a career, she'd spent the early years of her daughter's life reading student papers so late into the night that Lindsay had learned to put herself to bed.

Around two-thirty there was a lull, and Mariah noticed Gammy was limping. "Go sit down," she told her.

Gammy chose the same stool Mr. Tea-and-scones had inhabited. "Gammy," she said, wiping down the counter with their bleach-smelling cleaner, "who was the Scottish guy this morning?"

Her grandmother grinned. "Oh, you mean the one who looks like a movie star?"

"I really didn't notice."

"Careful, Pinocchio. Your nose is growing."

Mariah scrubbed hard at a stain. "Never mind."

Gammy clasped her hands to her chest. "Maybe he came all the way from Scotland to fall desperately in love with you and give me more great-grandchildren to spoil and Lindsay some siblings to play with."

"Stop it," Mariah said.

"A girl can hope."

"Gammy, the last thing I need in my life right now is a man."

Her grandmother untied her stained apron. As she brushed off crumbs, she said, "Dating wouldn't kill you. You could try that internet dating service. Who knows? You might make a friend. If you ever want to—"

"I lost my job!" Mariah blurted out, and there she stood, her last customers of the day sipping coffee with no idea that their waitress was on the verge of tears.

For a moment or two, Gammy's face looked every one of its sixty-eight years. Her snow-white hair was teased and sprayed into a proper old-lady helmet hairdo, but no amount of product could hide the baby-pink scalp peeking out.

"Go give that fellow his check," Gammy said, as if her granddaughter had told her nothing more important than the mail had arrived. "Go on, now. I'll make us some cocoa. Then we'll talk. You can tell me all about it."

Mariah composed herself, looking out the window as the fog started to roll in, erasing the sunny day that had begun so promisingly. There was a screech of brakes and a narrowly missed fender-bender that probably involved a protected deer with a mouthful of flowers, and someone started cussing. And then, just like she did at the end of every business day, Allegra started singing, "Come on people now, smile—" But she never finished the verse, because she fainted dead away behind the counter.

2
Lindsay

WEDNESDAYS WERE LINDSAY Moon's favorite day of the week because Wednesdays meant three whole uninterrupted hours of science. However, as Gammy Bess always said, anything you love is going to cost at least two days' tips, which in this case meant two hours of art, at which she hopelessly, terminally sucked. Standing on the school steps, she weighed her options. If she pleaded a stomachache, the school nurse would let her lie down for the time it took for art to be over. But would she buy it when Lindsay suddenly recovered in time for science? Lindsay got stomachaches a lot. This was only the fifth week of school and already she'd been to the nurse for a real stomachache. Would today's be the one that prompted the nurse to call her mother? Her mother would know if she was faking. She'd tell the nurse to send her back to art, or worse, make a doctor's appointment. Lindsay hated going to the doctor. The first thing they did was weigh you, and then they measured your height. She was so far behind in both categories that they made a huge deal out of it, and what was she supposed to do? Stretch herself on a rack? Eat Crisco out of the can?

You need art to become a fully rounded human being, her mother said when Lindsay begged her to drop the class. Art requires imagination. Think of it as exercise for your right frontal lobe.

Art was stupid. All the good art had been done hundreds of years ago. Lindsay could recognize Rembrandt, Picasso, and Van Gogh. Wasn't that enough? She could not paint. Every clay animal she sculpted looked like a dying snail. Her current project, a papier-mâché pelagic fish, looked like newsprint wrapped around a balloon. How did failing make her or anyone anything but sad?

She had just started up the steps when the fight broke out.

"Everybody look out!" Taylor Foster yelled as she stood on the grassy quad that led into Country Day Academy for Girls. "Here comes the Jolly Brown Giant!"

By giant, she meant Sally DeThomas, the girl who had won first prize in the previous year's Science Fair. Lindsay had come in second. Last year Taylor and Sally had been best friends, always giggling and whispering. This year they were mortal enemies. From the first day of school Taylor had been giving Sally the silent treatment. Soon after, all the Taylor clones started ignoring Sally. Now this.

"Shut up, Taylor," Sally said.

"You shut up," Taylor said back.

"You're a racist!"

"I am *so not* a racist! Can I help it if you're brown? What are you now, six-foot-twelve?"

Sally sighed, and shrugged the strap of her backpack up her shoulder. Lindsay could tell she didn't want to fight. "I'm five feet seven inches. You want to make something of it?"

The Taylor clones gathered round. "Taller is one thing, but you're freak-show tall. What did you do all summer? Climb Japanese skyscrapers?"

The lemmings waited until Taylor laughed, and then they laughed, too. Ha, ha, ha. The fake kind of laughing that felt like arrows in your face.

Lindsay watched Sally DeThomas, former leader of the popular kids, plant her feet like a gladiator. "Taylor, you think you're so great, but really you're not. Who beat you in the horse show? Ahem, I believe it was me."

"At least I'm not a dirty farm girl," Taylor said. "At least I have clean fingernails and don't smell like horse manure every day of my pathetic life."

Sally balled her hands into fists. "I'm Grand Champion Reserve Equestrian of this year's Strides and Tides, Taylor! Look 'champion' up in the dictionary, loser."

By now most of the other Country Day Academy girls were watching. Lindsay retreated to the school's oldest cypress tree, a gray giant that she particularly loved. The tree kept her company while she ate her lunch every day, except when it was raining. On rainy days teachers made everyone stay inside and eat at the table together, and play horrible, boring word games like hangman and Boggle.

"So what?" Taylor said. "It's just a piece of ribbon."

"It's a *gold* ribbon. What happened, Tay-tay? Couldn't your parents afford to buy you a decent horse? That old nag you ride is a bucket of glue waiting to happen."

Taylor blushed bright red. Lindsay's stomach clenched. She hoped a teacher would come out and make them stop before someone got hurt. Lindsay hated it when the students made fun of her, but truthfully, for a change, it was a relief having someone else in the crosshairs.

"At least I have normal teeth," Taylor continued. "How'd you break yours? Chewing on trees? God! Even poor people can afford porcelain veneers!"

Sally put her hand to her mouth, then quickly drew it away, but it was too late. Now everyone knew that mocking her teeth was a way to get to her.

Lindsay hoped Sally wouldn't cry. Taylor's real father—not the one her mom was currently married to—was a restorative dentist. Once he came to class and tried to get everyone excited about his career. Lindsay took a deep breath and walked past Taylor to Sally. "Um, Sally? Can you come inside for a second? I want to show you something." Summoning courage, she took hold of Sally's arm.

Sally looked at her arm like a bug had landed there. "What?"

"I can't describe it. You have to come inside to see. Please. It's really great."

"Fine, I'm coming." She looked back at Taylor. "Watch your mouth, Taylor."

"Ooh, I'm scared! Help, somebody call nine-one-one! Get animal control out here! Tell them to bring a truck for Queen Kong!"

As soon as they cleared the steps, Lindsay let go of her arm and said, "I lied. I hope you're not mad. It's not worth getting in trouble when you have the best grades in the class. Like my great-grandmother always says, 'In the eyes of the Lord everyone is naked and afraid and should be.' "

"Huh?"

"Basically it means everyone's equal, and you should never give people like Taylor Foster the satisfaction of seeing you cry."

"I wasn't going to *cry*," Sally said, her jaw trembling. "I was going to kick Taylor Foster's stupid ass from here to Modesto."

Lindsay nodded. "She deserves it, but not if it means you get expelled."

Sally smiled, revealing her chipped front teeth. She touched them with her tongue. "I did a back flip on this diving board at our vacation hotel and smacked them on the way down. I passed out and everything. The lifeguard had to save me. My stepdad called the paramedics."

"Wow, that must have hurt."

First bell rang, and girls from age six to thirteen began to pour down the corridor toward lockers and classrooms. Lindsay and Sally made their way to the eighth-grade lockers, which were painted apricot, a color that reminded Lindsay of a foul-tasting medicine she once had to take for bronchitis.

"I don't even remember it happening," Sally said. "They gave me a shot and pills to take after. I have to wait until I stop growing to get them capped. If Taylor wasn't so stupid she'd know porcelain veneers aren't permanent."

Lindsay wished she had been there. If Sally was her friend, and such an accident happened, Lindsay could have performed CPR or the Heimlich maneuver, or even R.I.C.E., which stood for rest, ice, compress, and elevate. She had her YWCA certification in first aid, a little white pin with a red cross on it, and a card to carry in her wallet, but who would ever call on someone four feet five inches tall for help? "Did you go to Taylor's dad?"

Sally made a face as she jostled her sticky locker door. "Are you serious? I made my mom find a dentist in Carmel-by-the-Sea. Considering how much it costs to live there, you know the dentists have to be the best."

"That makes sense," Lindsay said. Just the thought of exposed nerves made her stomach turn over. "Did you have root canals and titanium pins, or pulpectomies?"

Sally looked at her, surprised. "I had one root canal. They're supposed to hurt really bad but the dentist made me sniff laughing gas. It's a totally bogus name. It doesn't make you laugh at all. It kind of feels like dreaming."

Laughing gas sounded worrisome to Lindsay. Since reading *The Diary of Anne Frank* over the summer—it was on the Country Day Academy's summer reading list—she worried about gas. Take carbon monoxide. You couldn't see it, but if you didn't have an alarm, it could put you to sleep forever. The concentration camp stories stayed with her. And factor in the terrible true-life events, like anti-Semitism, yellow stars for Jews, pink triangles for homosexuals, all the families separated, people starving and put to death just because one man had megalomania. Stuff like that could happen again and you might not even see it coming until it was too late.

Sally pounded her locker door. "I don't even know why I bother with this lame ass thing," she said. "I spend half my freaking life trying to make it open or shut. I should just tear the freaking door off."

"You can put your stuff in my locker," Lindsay said. "I've never even had a filling. Sometimes I surf the net, though, just to look at medical stuff."

"No way! Me, too! There are so many cool surgery web-sites. No live feed, though. I would kill to watch a real live operation up close. Hey, have you ever been to my mom's website? Here, let me write down the address. You have to see it. There's a picture of me on my horse, Soul Man. With my gold ribbon, ha ha. Stick out your hand."

Lindsay held her hand out and Sally wrote the web address on it with a purple gel pen. "Thanks," Lindsay said, not quite believing that a girl like Sally was actually speaking to her without calling her Smurf or Munchkin or Thumbelina, thanks to the stupid folktales they had to read for Mrs. Potter's language arts class.

Second bell rang, and the girls bobbed their way through the sea of camel-colored blazers, crisp white blouses, and plaid skirts. At the door of Mrs. Shiasaka's classroom, their homeroom, Sally said, "You're all right, Lindsay. Here, have a pack of the cinnamon gum my dad brought back from Mexico. It's totally insane. If you put five pieces in your mouth at the same time, it gives you blisters."

The minute homeroom ended, Lindsay headed to the nurse's office. Her stomach actually did kind of hurt, not because of the gum—she was saving it—but the tension of watching Sally and Taylor fight had turned it sour. She let the nurse give her some Tums—orange flavor—and lay down on the cot, watching *Good Morning America* on the tiny television while the nurse knitted a purple scarf that had flecks of gold in it.

Dr. Ritchie stood at the whiteboard with her colored markers in her hand, going on and on about the first time ever Siemens Westinghouse award for middle school science projects.

"I realize this is short notice, it being September, and our projects are to be presented in December, but I want you girls to know what's at stake. If a student applies herself, goes the extra mile on a science project, this award is within reach. Awards accrue on a student's transcript. Consequently, by the time this student is a senior in high school, she just might win an academic scholarship that pays for everything."

"What do you mean by everything?" Sally asked.

"Not only tuition, but also textbooks, Bunsen burners, meals, and housing."

It sounded impossible to Lindsay, but she had to try for it. More than anything she wanted to go to a college with a first-rate science department, and she knew her mother wouldn't be able to pay for it all.

"This is why you girls need to take this year's Science Fair very seriously," Dr. Ritchie said, and turned to write potential topics on the board in her beautiful backhand script. Every girl at Country Day had tried to copy the elegant, spidery handwriting at one time or another. Lindsay was no exception. Dr. Ritchie was left-handed. Lindsay was right-handed. She knew for a fact that being left-handed automatically made you special.

Marie Curie, Albert Einstein, Linus Pauling, and Albert Schweitzer were all left-handed. Of course, no believable scientific theory could rest on such a small group of people. When Lindsay probed further, however, more proof emerged. Michelangelo, Leonardo da Vinci, M. C. Escher, Mark Twain, Hans Christian Andersen, Lewis Carroll, H. G. Wells, Eudora Welty, and Jessamyn West—all lefties. The lack of women in her research had initially bothered her until she mentioned it to Allegra. "Chalk that up to male chauvinism," she said. "Lots of left-handed women were geniuses. Janis Joplin was. All it means is that the macho-man researchers didn't bother asking."

"Do you think Dr. Ritchie wears granny undies?" Sally whispered to Lindsay.

Dr. Ritchie immediately looked their way. Lindsay, who had never gotten in trouble, looked back, smiling at her favorite teacher. Dr. Ritchie would stay after school if you needed help, but if you talked in her class during a lecture, it made her go postal. Stop it, she mouthed to Sally when Dr. Ritchie had turned around again.

"In addition," Dr. Ritchie enunciated sharply, "I'm pleased to announce that the NIH—National Institutes of Health—has allocated to California schools a stipend for studying science vis-à-vis . . ."

Vis-à-vis. In relation to, face-to-face, concerning, Lindsay thought. What a great term. She would try to use it in her lab notebook. If she ever got a B from Dr. Ritchie, she would throw herself off the Bixby Bridge.

"—our national epidemic of drug abuse," Dr. Ritchie finished. "Now, I want to be sure that you girls comprehend what I'm saying. If we were to study drug abuse properly, to take Country Day's holistic, interdisciplinary approach, it would quickly become obvious that there is more to the issue than mere science. As such, this would make a far too complex topic for your upcoming science projects, particularly within our short time frame. Let's brainstorm. . . ."

The room was warm, and Lindsay, having fallen asleep in the nurse's office, had awakened too late to get her lunch from her locker. She yawned, and let her mind wander, picturing a terrible storm with a blue-black sky and jagged yellow lightning moving through the lobes of her brain. Instead of rain, prize-worthy Science Fair ideas hailed down into her cluster diagram, a way of arranging your ideas nonlinearly, which Lindsay had learned in her second year at Country Day. Clusters weeded out the bad ideas, until all that remained was the best choice.

Last year, when Sally took the blue ribbon, Lindsay wondered where she'd gone wrong with "The Human Genome Project and Future Implications."

"Yours is nice, honey, but it lacks 'the wow factor,' " Gammy

Bess had said. "Just look at the cookies we sell at the café. People always reach for the one with the most chips first."

Sally's project was so great Lindsay couldn't find a single fault with it. "The Effects of Soil Rotation on Salinas County's Agribusiness." Since the migrant workers had struck, Sally even had a video loop of interviews in Spanish that she had translated herself.

Allegra had sniffed at it, saying, "Whatever happened to growing tomato plants to music?" and they went out for ice cream to soften the blow. Lindsay's mother had been teaching that night, so she missed it.

Lindsay clicked the lead mechanism on her mechanical pencil. She wondered whether her mother would be home that night, or stuck in faculty meetings she said she hated but Lindsay bet she secretly liked. Otherwise, why not get a job that allowed you to come home at the same time every night and read a book, or watch *NOVA*? Sometimes she pretended Dr. Ritchie was her mom. They both ate red licorice and drank Diet Coke first thing in the morning, but somehow Lindsay could tell that Dr. Ritchie's life was more interesting.

Lindsay imagined her peeling out of the parking lot on her orange moped, headed toward something better than teaching, like a boyfriend. Dr. Ritchie's boyfriend would look just like Carl Sagan, smart, kind of thin, and with a craggy face that was always smiling. He would have a cat named Stephen Hawking, or a big yellow dog named Marie Curie. They would stay up all night doing experiments. Lindsay wondered if they would have sex.

She knew all about sex, and it worried her. Sex sounded like a very tricky thing. First off, the diseases you might get could kill you. Just look at what was happening in Africa. Then there were accidents that resulted in pregnancy, and the pro-choice or pro-life question. Lindsay was pretty sure her mom had only had sex that one time, because she'd gotten pregnant with Lindsay when she was twenty-one years old, and as soon as Lindsay's father found out, he left to take a job in another state. She knew his name: Professor Ephraim Cantor. He didn't write or visit, send money or call. Her mom said that was fine with her; he didn't know what he was missing, so poop on him. Every once in a while Lindsay wanted to write him a letter, and maybe send him her school picture, but Gammy Bess always talked her out of it, saying "Let lying dogs sleep and you won't get bitten."

It wasn't like Lindsay missed having a dad. Pretty much all her mom did was work at The Owl & Moon when they needed her, teach classes, and stay up late correcting papers. After listening to her schoolmates talk, that sounded pretty much like a dad. Most nights her mom fell asleep on the couch. Lindsay would cover her with a blanket and she wouldn't even move, but she was always up early pouring out Lindsay's cereal.

Sally poked Lindsay with her shoe, then leaned her head back and pretend-snored. Lindsay smiled and turned away. No way was she getting in trouble in Dr. Ritchie's class.

"I want to see your précis next week, girls. More than two ideas, please. And girls? Please do not wait until the last minute and Google subjects you care nothing about in an effort to impress me. One must have passion for a project. It must *pertain*."

Out the corner of her eye Lindsay saw Sally finger spell the word *Y-A-W-N*. Students were required to study two languages at Country Day. French and Spanish were the most popular. Lindsay opted for Latin, which would help her in science. She also took American Sign Language, which she felt offered a view into another culture. Sally was in that class, too. ASL was valuable for lots of reasons. You could help a deaf person with it, and also pass a "note" that a teacher couldn't confiscate and read out loud. Cuss words were not so bad when you said them with your fingers.

"Sally?" Dr. Ritchie said. "I notice you're finger spelling. Is there something you want to share with the class?"

Sally folded her hands on top of her desk. "No, ma'am. I

was just stretching my fingers out. To become fluent in sign you pretty much have to stretch the muscles whenever the opportunity presents itself. I'll try to be less distracting."

"Do."

As soon as Dr. Ritchie turned her back, Sally rolled her eyes and finger spelled "E-P-I-C Y-A-W-N."

Lindsay smiled wider this time.

Pretty soon you could feel the tension in the air. Everyone's eyes were on the clock. Finally Dr. Ritchie gave up. "Go," she said, sighing. "I don't know why we bother to teach anything after lunch. Your circadian rhythms are at their lowest point. Go, you brilliant minds, brimming with potential. Go have a great afternoon and think about projects. Remember, every little thing that happens—autumn leaves turning, a dog barking, your very breath—occupies its own little niche in science."

"God, I thought she'd never shut her trap," Sally said as they lugged their backpacks outdoors into what was left of the dappled sunlight. Clouds were moving in, and the sun was moving on.

Lindsay didn't know what to say. "I like Dr. Ritchie. I could listen to her all day."

"Me, too. It's just that my butt was going to sleep. So, you want to do the science project together?"

"Do you mean it?"

"Of course I mean it. We both rock at science. You almost beat me last year. Why not work together on some really gnarly subject and get twice as much credit? Plus, the money! Start thinking about it. It has to be radical, and have social implications."

"Like what?"

"You know, the ethics factor. Stuff people argue about. Abortion, stem cell research, things that get people all whipped up." Sally peered around the tree they were standing under and groaned. "Oh, man. Here comes Taylor. I gotta run before she starts in on me or I just might clock her." Then she signed "E-mail me!" and turned away.

Lindsay watched Sally sprint toward the curb, where her stepdad was waiting in his red convertible. Taylor sniffed and said loudly, "Does anyone smell burritos?"

Lindsay began walking to the café. Whenever Gammy Bess and Lindsay went to the Del Monte mall, they saw Taylor and her friends there, roaming. Gammy said they dressed so alike they looked like a litter of pit bull puppies, but to Lindsay it looked like they were having fun. They wove into and out of places like The Body Shop, Victoria's Secret, Cinnabon, and Dillard's. They never seemed to stop laughing. Lindsay walked the last half block to The Owl & Moon in the rain.

"Gammy Bess," Lindsay called out.

Her great-grandmother was standing in the middle of the restaurant looking at nothing, holding Khan in her arms, petting the tiny black dog a lot harder than he liked, which wasn't a good idea. Khan had limits, and if you crossed them, he'd bite.

"What's the matter?" Lindsay said, scanning the room. There weren't any late customers, and apparently Simon had already gone home. She held out her arms for the dog, but Gammy hung on to him. That was weird. Every afternoon Lindsay and Allegra took Khan to Dog Beach for his run, well, for as much of a run as any six-pound dog required. If Khan didn't get his walk, he peed indoors, and then they had to listen to Gammy rant about the Health Department paying The Owl & Moon a surprise visit and shutting them down. "Where's Allegra?"

Gammy gave a quick smile, one Lindsay didn't buy for a minute. She lifted one of Khan's paws and made him wave. "Well, look who's here, Khannie. It's my little honey bun. Alice is out. A doctor's appointment. Totally routine. Nothing to concern yourself with. Your mother went with her. Just for the company. What do you want for your snack today? There's a bowl of beef barley soup with your name on it, and I set aside some oatmeal cookies. How about a nice slice of cheddar with that, and some cocoa?"

Lindsay, who never wanted anything for her afternoon

snack but carrot sticks, opted for the soup. While Gammy Bess fetched it, Lindsay took in the aspects of the environment like any good scientist. In times like this, when you clearly weren't getting the entire story, a person could use Carl Sagan's Baloney Detection kit.

Fact: Allegra hated Western medicine. When she felt sick, she went to see Krishna Dahvid, the acupuncturist. If she was at the doctor's, something could be seriously wrong. A broken bone, or maybe she needed stitches.

Query: Why keep that a secret? It wasn't like Lindsay would faint from hearing the news.

Invoking Occam's Razor: When a simple answer will do, a scientist has to go with it, even though other more complex answers are also true.

Conclusion: Allegra was sick-sick. Go-to-the-doctor sick. Scary sick.

Lindsay ate the vegetables out of her soup while sitting at the table by the window. "Why did Allegra have to get a ride to the doctor? Why not drive herself, in Cronkite?" That was what Allegra called her Volkswagen van.

"She just wanted company, that's all. Don't you like company when you go to the doctor?"

"Not really," Lindsay said. "Did she cut herself?"

"No," Gammy said. "It's just a checkup. She'll be fine."

Lindsay watched her great-grandmother start polishing salt and pepper shakers. That meant she was done talking. Lindsay set down her spoon. "Gammy, Khan likes his routine. If it's all right with you, I'll take him for his walk now."

"Honey, it's raining. Khan can miss his walk today."

"I'll put on his raincoat. We'll just go around the block."

Her great-grandmother nodded distractedly. "Okay, then. You be careful. Take an umbrella, and wear your rain boots."

Lindsay fastened on Khan's yellow slicker and harness. Allegra loved to dress him up. He had a cowboy outfit and also a Superman cape. At Halloween she made him a bumblebee costume and he won first prize in the Petco parade small dog division. "Bye, Gammy," Lindsay said, but her great-grandmother stayed right where she was, staring out the café windows as if she were waiting for Publishers Clearing House to show up with the oversized cardboard check. Allegra must be really, really sick.

Downtown Pacific Grove was a dog walker's heaven. From Lighthouse Produce to Tillie Gort's, there were dog biscuits for the asking. Even the bookstore set out a water bowl. Every other corner had a poop bag dispenser. Khan trotted from trash can to trash can, taking in the rainy world through his tiny nostrils. A dog's sense of smell was so far advanced that Lindsay could hardly imagine it. She unfurled the umbrella and sat down on a bus bench. Umbrellas were part of her world. In the summer she had to sit under one, otherwise she'd get sunburned. That was because of her father's genes, which included red hair and freckly skin. She wondered if Ephraim Cantor had any other kids, if somewhere out there in the world she had a half-brother or -sister. Did they also like vegetables more than pizza, and reading science fiction? Were they too short, like she was, and what did they think of the Human Genome Project?

Khan was Allegra's third Chihuahua. Allegra loved dogs more than she did cats, birds, dolphins, or horses. Lindsay liked Khan, but sometimes she imagined a longhaired orange cat curled up on her lap while she typed scientific findings into her computer. She imagined two tiny goldfish swimming in a bowl, waiting for the moment her fingers would release a pinch of flakes into the water. She imagined a cage with finches in it, too, with all their peeping and jumping, and then Khan whimpered for attention, so she stood up and started back toward the café. It was raining hard now, and her feet— she'd forgotten the boots—were soaking wet.

"We're having dinner here tonight," Lindsay's mother said as they set out the day's leftovers on the counter.

"Why?" Lindsay asked, her backpack in hand already for the usual rush home.

Her mother looked at her blankly. "What do you mean, why?"

Lindsay eyed the counter: a cinnamon bun that could feed a family of five, crumpets, almond horns, blackberry pie, and more beef barley soup. Reluctantly, she set her things on the floor, took a plate, and began filling it with two-day-old take-out salad. "It's the week before college classes start. Why aren't you meeting with students?"

Mariah looked at her mother and grandmother for help.

"Leave the fables to Aesop," Gammy Bess said. "The truth may sting a little, but in the long run it hurts less than deceit."

Lindsay watched her mom purse her lips in irritation. Who wasn't telling the truth? And about what? "Mom?" Lindsay said.

"Please," she said. "Just eat your dinner. We'll talk later."

"Allegra?" Lindsay said. "Want to hear my Science Fair project ideas?"

Allegra, Khan in her lap, looked very tired and did not answer.

"Do you want me to fix you a plate?" Lindsay asked. "I'll share my salad with you. It's really good, lots of ginger."

Allegra petted Khan the way he liked, which was gently and lightly, like a butterfly kiss. "That's all right, Lindsay. I'm not hungry."

The four of them sat at the table in the empty café, nobody talking. Lindsay looked from adult to adult. No one would meet her eye except for Khan, and that was because he was the all-time beggar of the world.

Later that night, home in their rented condo, Lindsay got into her pajamas and slid into her bed with her secondhand copy of *The Dragons of Eden*. A quote from Shakespeare started it: "What seest thou else in the dark backward and abysm of time?" The words gave Lindsay shivers. Until tonight, the first fifty pages had never failed to calm her. Her mind raced. A new friend. A science project partner. Allegra and her mom at the doctor. Everyone so quiet at dinner. What Gammy said about telling the truth.

Lindsay got up from her bed and looked across the hall. She saw light under her mother's door. No way she was sleeping. Lindsay got an antacid from the bathroom cabinet, chewed it up and swallowed, and then knocked at her mother's door. "Come in," her mother said.

Rather than propped up in bed with a dozen open books around her, her mom was just sitting there hugging her knees. When Lindsay looked at her, the tears began to fall.

"What's wrong?" Lindsay said.

Her mother shook her head.

"Mom, it can't be any worse than I imagined."

Her mother swiped at her cheek. "Yes, it can. I lost my job."

"Is that all? Mom! You can *get* another job. I thought it was much worse than that."

"Like what?" her mother said.

A prickly relief flooded Lindsay's skin. She held her arms out wide, gesturing. "End of the world stuff. Like maybe Allegra was dying, or there was going to be a tsunami, or we were going to have to move or something."

"You really are a genius," her mother said sadly. "You got two out of three right."

3
Allegra

ALLEGRA BEGAN HER MORNING in the usual way, pureeing wheatgrass in the blender and chugging it down in a single gulp. She ate a handful of almonds, and then an apple, and then drank a glass of water to swallow her vitamin supplements. Could a person eat any healthier? This fainting thing was probably something as simple as anemia. She'd given up beef years ago, doing her small part to save the rain forest. Then she'd given up chicken, too, because factory farming was evil and baby chicks were so adorable. Fish was full of mercury, so that left only tofu and veggies. Plenty of women lived with anemia. Menopause might be the culprit. She couldn't believe she was nearly fifty and in the dreaded "change of life" already. Cronedom. The Red Hat Society. What did that pipsqueak E.R. doctor know about women, anyway? Western medicine was jackrabbit-quick to jump to dire conclusions. Lots of people went their whole lives without seeing a doctor and did just fine.

Just to be safe, she telephoned Krishna Dahvid, her acupuncturist, and got his machine.

"You have reached Abalone Healing Arts and the home of

Krishna Dahvid. Please leave a message after the tone, and your call will be returned. Namaste."

Her acupuncturist didn't pick up when he was in session. "I need a tune-up ASAP," she said. "If you can fit me in this week I promise to bring you cookies." That did the trick. No matter how holy or faithful or devoted a person was, Allegra knew a recipe that would break their will. Krishna Dahvid's was Chocolate Bombs, a cocoa-meringue-powdered-sugar confection that melted on the tongue and had a sugar content high enough to shoot preschoolers to Jupiter.

She unbraided her waist-length hair and brushed it until it crackled. "Rapunzel ain't got nothing on me," she said, tossing it over her shoulders, then rebraiding it and pinning it up into the heavy bun she wore at work. A few gray hairs were beginning to show up at her temples, but mostly it remained the blue black that Gammy swore came from her late husband, Myron Moon, the father Allegra couldn't remember. The Moon family had been in lumber then. Bess's father was a church deacon. Her mother took in ironing. The way Gammy told the story sounded so romantic. Myron had been so taken with Bess that they'd eloped, and the Moon family, moneyed and high class, had not been pleased, but he loved her so much he defied their wishes.

Before Allegra's fourth birthday, the union abruptly ended. All it took was one tree falling the wrong way. Bess became a widow, and Allegra grew up fatherless. All that time was a fuzzy blur. She thought about doing rebirthing therapy to see if she could remember more, but it was so expensive only rich people could afford it. Just look at this hair, she thought. This is Moon hair. A person with leukemia would not have such healthy hair.

There. She'd let the L-word seep into her conscious thoughts. The E.R. doctor mentioned the possibility when he examined her and found the bruises on her abdomen. How did she get them? Allegra could think of lots of ways—bumping into the kitchen equipment, dancing at the bars, even during sex, which she considered a contact sport, she'd said. Or illness, he'd countered. Serious illness often begins subtly. Then he'd ordered more tests. Allegra had never done well on tests.

Krishna Dahvid had taught Allegra that once a fear was spoken, it was free to depart. Allegra imagined a giant letter *L* flapping its wings like a bat. "Go back to the dark and awful cave you came from," she said. "There's no room for you in my life." She'd cancel the follow-up appointment with the hematologist. It was a waste of time. Filling out insurance forms was pointless. The self-employed policy the restaurant paid through the nose for covered the absolute minimum. Every claim submitted was rejected on the first go-round. If you submitted the claim a second time, they'd reconsider, but the heartless freaks wouldn't part with a dime if they could get away with it. Besides, if her blood count was so dangerously out of whack, didn't it make sense to hang on to every drop? She skewered her bun with chopsticks, and looked out the window.

It was rainy again today. Overnight the brisk fall weather had vamoosed. Delivery trucks rumbled by in the fog. If a person had to live in a city, Pacific Grove was a good choice. Even in winter the beach had charm. After a storm, the tide delivered shells and beach glass by the handful. Allegra never grew tired of wading in the surf.

Gammy pounded on the bathroom door, startling Allegra, who dropped her hand cream into the sink. "Get a move on, Toots!"

"Give me a heart attack, why don't you?" she said to her mother, who was trying to make believe yesterday could be erased by prayer. Allegra had heard her last night, asking St. Jude to intervene on her daughter's behalf. That was Gammy's way. The doctor had wanted to give Allegra a transfusion. There are plenty of other ways to boost my red blood cells, she insisted. Give me an iron shot, or pills. I'll even eat liver, she'd said, though the thought made her shudder. She daubed her elbows with the cream, and rubbed in the scent of roses.

"Alice, I'm telling you, if you don't get your buns out here and start cooking, I'll have the heart attack. What in heck are you doing in there, anyway? Waxing your legs?"

Allegra capped the lotion and straightened her dress, a floor-length purple T-shirt. She tied her Guatemalan belt and smiled in the mirror at the healthy person smiling back. "Bring 'em on," she called down to Gammy. "I'm ready to feed the entire town." Then she let out her yip-yip-yip war cry, something she did on special occasions.

"God, grant me strength," Gammy said. "And while you're at it, can you please make her stop that awful racket?"

By nine, the place was packed with people wanting in out of the rain. Mostly the usuals, but a few new faces, like the man at the counter Allegra had been giving the eye. So what if he was fifteen years younger than she? Between that sexy five o'clock shadow, the broad hands, and the way he ate his breakfast, he looked like a man of large appetites. Allegra knew just what dish she'd like to fix him.

Mariah came in, her eyes red and swollen.

"Did you tell Lindsay you lost your job?" Allegra hollered over the din. "Is that why you've been crying?"

Mariah made the scowly face Allegra hated. "Mother, please! Do you have to announce my personal business to the entire town?"

"Well, pardon me! All I did was ask. I have to yell to be heard in here. It's noisy as hell, or didn't you notice?"

Mariah ramped down to bristling. "Yes, I told Lindsay and she's fine. Now will you please hand me my order pad so Gammy can take a break?"

"Here you go, princess." Allegra leaned in close to the cute guy at the counter. "That's my daughter," she said. "The branch of our family tree she fell off is as straight as a ruler."

The man looked up from his tea and scones. "She's lovely. You're both so lovely that I had you figured as sisters, actually."

Allegra boomed out her trademark laugh. "Any compliment you want to throw my way I gladly accept. So, what brings you all the way from the land of plaid and haggis to Pacific Grove? You're from Scotland, right?"

He folded his paper napkin, set it alongside his plate, and smiled a toothy grin. "I've never heard my homeland referred to in quite that way. How novel." He turned on the stool to watch Mariah take her first order of the day. "So what's the poor girl been weeping over? Jilted by a callous lover?"

Well, fine, then don't flirt with me, Allegra thought. There are plenty of other fish in the sea. "Oh, she lost a job," Allegra said. "But the way she's carrying on, you'd think her whole life had come to an end."

He looked up at Allegra. "Single?"

"As a matter of fact, I am, *and* I'm free tonight."

"Actually," he said, "I was inquiring about your daughter."

"Oh. She's unhitched, and a single mother, to boot."

He frowned. "What exactly does 'to boot' mean? I'm attempting to master your vernacular, but in Scotland, a 'boot' is the luggage compartment in the rear of an automobile."

Allegra cleared a customer's plate and folded the newspaper he'd left behind. She walked over to the magazine basket near the door and popped it inside, at the same time reaching down into Khan's bed to give him a pet. "A bonus. Something you don't have to pay for."

"If she has a child, then that makes you a granny, doesn't it?"

Well, wasn't this turning out to be quite the happy morning! Allegra tapped the counter with her order pad. "Watch it, buddy. You're treading on thin ice."

He smiled. "There you go again. The odd phrase. Although this one makes sense in metaphoric context."

"You're a smart one, aren't you? And by that I mean 'intelligent.' "

"Thank you," he said. "And I mean that from my heart. May I bother you for more hot water?"

"It's no bother." She moved away from the counter, trying

to get used to the idea that the man was more interested in
Mariah than he was in her. Maybe she did look sick. Maybe
she should use blusher. Burt's Bees made natural makeup.
God knows what went into the stuff they sold in department
stores. Whale fat, probably, and did anyone ask the whales'
permission?

"Alice!" Gammy called out. "Phone for you."

Allegra took the receiver. "Hello?"

"Am I speaking to Mrs. Alice Moon?"

Allegra sighed. "It's *Allegra* Moon, and not Mrs. Who's calling, please?"

"This is Dr. Goodnough's office. We've had a cancellation
and can work you in this afternoon."

"Dr. Good who?"

"Goodnough. Dr. Alvin Goodnough. The hematologist
your emergency room physician referred you to? You made an
appointment to see him next week?"

"Oh," Allegra said, twining the phone cord around her
hand. "Today's not really convenient for me. Actually, I'm
feeling so much better, let's cancel the original appointment,
too. Thanks for—"

The woman on the other end didn't let her finish. "Ms. Moon,
Dr. Goodnough reviewed the test results the hospital faxed us.
He told me to stress that it's imperative that he see you today,
not a month from now."

Allegra's heart took a leap. She pressed a hand to her
chest. "Why? What does he think is wrong?"

"I'm sorry, I'm not allowed to discuss your test results. The
doctor will go over them with you."

"That's crazy," Allegra said. "It's my body. Why can't I have
my test results?"

"You can. I'll make a copy for you when you come to the
office."

"Oh, for crying out loud, fine. What time? I work until three."

"Four o'clock."

"What's your address?"

She scribbled it on the back of the order pad, and then hung up the phone, trembling with fear. Yesterday, while she lay on the gurney feeling stupid—because by the time they'd gotten to the hospital she felt absolutely fine—she'd observed the medical world. Overworked nurses cleaning up kid barf. Mangled teenagers who'd driven drunk. The elderly clutching their chests because it was true, when your heart broke, it hurt. And all the lost souls who'd been turned out of institutions into the street when Reagan was in office, wandering, off their meds, ended up at CHOMP—the Community Hospital of the Monterey Peninsula—as if it was their Mecca. This was the world she tried to feed, not a population she belonged to. The test had to be a mistake. They'd repeat it and that would be the end of her big scare. She poured Scotland's hot water and smiled at Kiki Cooper, who was peering into the cold case. "Hi there, Kiki! What can I do you for on this soggy September day?"

"Cookies. Iced oatmeal raisin if you have them. I have bridge group this afternoon and they can't get enough of your baking. Better make it a dozen."

"Coming right up."

By ten the sleepy beachfront town fully roused itself. Shop doors unlocked. Compulsive shoppers cruised the wet streets. The bell on The Owl & Moon's door rang and rang, delivering Pacific Grove's population that needed a wake-up, a fill-up, or a cheer-up. Allegra loved all her customers, but she had a special spot in her heart for the seniors. They practiced tai chi in the park. They gave tours at the Monterey Bay Aquarium that Lindsay loved so much that Allegra had given her a membership for Christmas. They knew the steamy bits of Central Coast history. Where else could you find out that author Robert Louis Stevenson stayed here for three months to court the unhappily married Fanny Van de Grift Osbourne? The seniors were respected elders in Allegra's tribe. They kept in shape by walking, and The Owl & Moon was their in-town oasis.

But Allegra knew the sunny, happy stuff was only the town's outer fabric. Behind that façade were people who had worked all their lives here, and now were forced to sell their Victorian homes that lined Laurel Avenue to Ocean View Boulevard and move to where the cost of living wasn't so dear. It seemed like every six months another bed-and-breakfast conversion popped up. When she and Lindsay walked Khan, Allegra made sure to point out the widow's walks atop houses, and to explain to her granddaughter how the wife of a sailor would stand there watching for her husband's ship to return. That this town was once a fishing capital reaping huge profits from sardine and abalone sales must have sounded to Lindsay like a fairy tale, but Allegra wanted her to know more of the world than MTV and meth labs and astronomical housing prices.

Allegra wiped tables, cooed over customers' photos of new grandbabies, took phone orders, ran into the kitchen when she could to defrost cookie dough and get it into the oven.

"Last night I dreamt I found car keys under a giant redwood tree," Simon said as Allegra folded dried cherries into another batch of fudge. "What do you think that means, Allegra?"

Before she could answer, Gammy said, "That you have a hole in your pocket, you fool," as she harvested clean cups from the ailing dishwasher.

"Bess," he said, "you are the meanest old lady in this town."

Gammy didn't so much as twitch. "Maybe so, but I'm still the one who makes out your paycheck."

"Mama!" Allegra said.

"Mama what?" Gammy answered, walking away. "I'm only stating a fact."

"Simon, " Allegra apologized. "She can't help being cranky. Her legs hurt."

"I'm Teflon," he said. "Your mother's insults slide off me like a fried egg."

Allegra doubted that. She turned fudge onto the marble

counter to cool. Through the order cubby, she saw Mariah dart from table to table, unsmiling, but committed. Her daughter was like that from day one, putting the square peg in the square hole. Not what Allegra expected when she'd given birth to her at age sixteen. Why couldn't Mariah see that this job loss was a mere blip in her timeline? The reason this job had ended meant the universe had other plans for her daughter, and any minute now the universe would make those plans known. She sent up a good thought that something nice would happen to Mariah today. In the meantime, she and Gammy had some cash in the bank. Not a lot, but they could spare a bit.

"Half a pound of fudge to go," Mariah said at the counter, slipping in behind the Scotsman.

"Coming up," Allegra said, grabbing a pound of fudge on her way to Mariah, but suddenly she was so dizzy she had to grab hold of the counter. She felt Simon's hands on her shoulders.

"Mom, are you all right?" Mariah asked, throwing down her order pad and rushing to her side. Khan yipped from his basket.

"I'm fine, everyone," Allegra said. "Somebody comfort Khan, please?"

The Scotsman stood up. "Sit here," he said, and she did.

"You should be in bed," Simon told her. "You can't just go back into warp speed after something like that. You probably have a virus. Go upstairs and let Bess finish your shift."

"No fever," Gammy said, kissing Allegra's cheek. "You'd be fine if you ate a steak now and then. Vegetarian diet, my aunt Louise's garters. Look at the food pyramid if you don't believe me. A body can't get by without protein."

"I turned too fast," Allegra told them, standing up and returning to her proper place behind the counter, the exact spot where she'd fainted the day before. Maybe that patch of floor was the Bermuda triangle of the café. "I see the vampire doctor at four and he's going to prescribe iron medicine."

Simon returned to his kitchen to ladle up orders. Through the order window he called, "Get him to give you a vitamin B shot, too."

Allegra nodded, picked up the fudge, and brought it to Mariah. "Here you go," she said, handing her a plate with a half-pound chunk.

"Mom?"

"Yes?"

"They wanted it to go?"

"Of course they did," Allegra said, flustered and forgetting for a moment where they kept the waxed paper. "I'll get it."

A moment later, the telephone rang. Gammy was in the john. Mariah was arranging a tray of soups, and Allegra was making change with one hand and wrapping fudge with the other. So when the Scotsman got up and answered the phone, it seemed perfectly acceptable. "Owl & Moon Café eating establishment. Fergus Applecross, speaking. How may I help?"

Allegra finished wrapping the fudge and handed it over. She grinned at Mariah. "Not only drop-dead handsome, but a Boy Scout, too. I bet he's a good dancer. I might just have to ask him out."

Mariah took the fudge and the bill. "Please don't."

"Don't what?"

Mariah looked away. "He's too young for you. It's . . . it's embarrassing."

"You're *interested* in him? Well, how about that! Mariah has a crush. Any minute now I expect to see pigs hang gliding."

"Mom," Mariah said, "I am not interested in anyone. Just let him be a damn customer, will you?"

Fergus smiled, plunked down the money for his bill, and buttoned up his jacket. "Feels positively Baltic out there today. Thank you again for a wonderful repast. Tirrah until tomorrow, then."

Allegra smiled. Mariah frowned. Gammy waved happily, unaware of the catfight that simmered just beneath the surface. Handsome, the accent, the politeness factor, he would be good for Mariah, Allegra mused. God knows she could stand getting laid more than once every thirteen years.

"What does a man have to do to get a cup of coffee around here?" Kyle Cashin hollered out, and as if they had choreographed the response, all three Moon women turned and said, "Hold your horses, Kyle."

Allegra loved everything about her work. From the lawyers stopping in for lunch to the little kids she gave free sugar cookies, this was her world, and she adored every little nook and cranny of it.

At three o'clock, Allegra took her purse from under the counter and studied the directions on the back of her order pad. The café was officially closed, though a few people were still eating. Mariah could cash out the register. "I'm off to see the doctor," she said blithely, as if she were running to the market for carrots or brown rice.

"What doctor?" Gammy asked.

"The vampire doctor," Simon said. "Try to keep up."

"What in heaven's name is a vampire doctor?"

Allegra put a hand on each of their shoulders. "A doctor who takes your blood and tells you you're perfectly fine. Do not load the dishwasher until I get back, Mama. A dirty dish will be just as dirty an hour from now. You go sit down and put your feet up."

"I'm coming with you," Mariah said.

"That's not necessary."

"Mom, you fainted yesterday. No way are you driving yourself."

"Who's going to help me clean up this place?" Gammy said. "You know I can't do it on my own."

"I told you, just leave it and I'll do it when I get back."

"I'll stay late and help you," Simon said, taking the broom from her.

Gammy eyed him suspiciously. "Atoning for sins?"

"My conscience is squeaky clean. The fact that you will owe me is pleasure enough."

"You see? That's what your problem is, Simon. You can't do a good thing without thinking of yourself. In second Corinthians, chapter eight, verse nine . . ."

There was no point stepping between them when Gammy hauled out her Bible ammo. Mariah and Allegra left them arguing and got into the Subaru. The doctor's address was south of CHOMP, not a fun ride when the only way to get there was through clogged-up traffic. It was even less fun during the first big rain of the year, when everyone apparently needed to learn how to drive all over again. Allegra loved stormy weather. The rain washed a summer's worth of dust off the cypress trees, revealing a green so deep it made even the most ordinary of birds perching there seem tropical. "I wonder if we'll get an El Niño winter," she said.

"We might," Mariah answered, pulling into the doctor's parking lot. "Nervous?"

"Don't be silly. I'm a big strapping woman who cooks breakfast for a hundred six days a week. I hope the waiting room has lots of trashy magazines."

Allegra let Mariah hold her hand while the lab technician took her blood, but she wouldn't let Mariah come into the exam room. "Go read *People*," she said. "Find out who's sleeping with who and memorize all the juicy details."

"Mom, are you sure?"

"I'm sure," Allegra said. "I won't be able to relax if you're there."

The nurse showed her to a pale, blue room with a reclining chair, an exam table, and the kind of doctor's stool that made Allegra think of honky-tonk piano players. On one wall a magazine holder was filled with brochures on cancer, chemotherapy, bone marrow transplants, and pain management. Allegra had to look away. After she changed into the paper gown she peeked under the Band-Aid at the hole the technician had made in the fold of her elbow. Already a bruise was forming. Didn't anyone care about doing a good job anymore?

The nurse knocked, and then came in, opening a notebook computer. She began typing. "What medications are you on?" she asked.

"None."

Without looking up, she said, "By medications, I include nonprescription medicines, too. Do you take herbal supplements, vitamins, hormone therapy?"

"I take a daily vitamin C and, of course, E. I pop primrose oil now and then, and black cohosh when I get hot flashes."

The nurse continued typing. "You'll need to bring those in so we can get the exact ingredients and strengths. Do you drink alcohol?"

She was going to *be coming back*? "Of course I drink alcohol."

"Beer, wine, hard liquor?"

"All three, but never at the same time." She waited for a laugh, but this one was all business.

"How many drinks per week?"

"I have no idea. Ever since I turned twenty-one, I stopped counting."

"Would you say seven glasses of wine a week?"

Allegra bit her thumbnail. "Seven or eight sounds about right."

"And the hard liquor? More or less?"

This was awful. It made her sound like a lush. "On the weekends, I probably have four or five mixed drinks, but hey, I need a stress reliever after serving food all week to—"

"Do you smoke cigarettes?"

Now she was just being rude. "Of course not. Cigarettes are disgusting."

"Any recreational drug use, street drugs, or marijuana?"

Allegra took in a deep breath. "That's getting awfully damn personal."

The nurse didn't change expression as she looked up from

the computer screen. "Ms. Moon, it's vital that we know these things as they factor into your treatment. You signed the HIPPA form. I assure you, doctor-patient confidentiality is confidential. Nothing you tell Dr. Goodnough or me will leave this room. So, are you now or have you at any time in the past been a heavy marijuana user?"

She squeezed her hands until she could feel the nails dent her palms. "I grew up in the sixties! If you didn't smoke pot people thought you were a narc. I was stoned for years. How is that going to hurt my so-called treatment options, assuming that I need any?"

"You'd be surprised. It can make a big difference in drug regimens. Some experimental drug studies won't accept marijuana users. The same goes for certain organ transplants."

"That's ridiculous! What about the people who use it medically? Proposition two-fifteen made it legal for medical cases, didn't it?"

For the first time Allegra saw a trace of kindness in the nurse's face. "Ma'am, I never said it was fair."

"Fine. I used to smoke regularly, but I haven't for the longest time."

"Approximately how long is that, do you think?"

Allegra looked at the pamphlet wall again. She didn't buy for a second that the happy-go-lucky seniors pictured on the anemia pamphlet were one bit sick, or that the woman holding the tennis racket needed pain management. Mariah was thirty-three now. Twenty years ago, Mariah had been thirteen. "Twenty years."

The nurse closed her computer and stood up. "The doctor will be in to see you shortly. Would you like me to bring you some magazines?"

Allegra pointed to the pamphlets. "Yes. I sure as hell don't want to read those."

But the light reading she expected turned out to be some archaic woman's magazine with hamburger recipes—*ick*—and diets guaranteed to make you lose twenty pounds by Christmas.

The other was a *U.S. News & World Report*. Allegra flipped through its pages until she felt miserable at the state of the world, then laid it facedown on her lap and shut her eyes, practicing her yoga breathing. In one nostril, out the other. Mindful breathing lowered blood pressure, boosted the immune system, and released endorphins. It also made Allegra recall in painful clarity an incident that happened when Mariah was in junior high school.

Her eighth-grade class was raising money for a trip to the Steinhart Aquarium in San Francisco with a bake sale. Now *this* I can do, Allegra remembered thinking. She was a lousy field trip chaperone, because on the bus she'd taught the kids to sing "Ninety-nine Bottles of Beer on the Wall." Strike two was her failure as art project mom, when she tried to explain how making a sand mandala led to spiritual enlightenment. The teacher had shooed the kids outside. We have to remember separation of church and state, the teacher whispered in her ear, and Allegra had left, taking her colored sand and hurt feelings with her. But baking would be her coup, her chance to not only fit in with the uptight parents and snooty teachers, but also to sell the most, take in the most money, and for once make Mariah proud of her.

"Please don't make anything fancy," Mariah had pleaded. "Just cookies or brownies or banana bread."

"No problem, babe," Allegra said. In a double boiler she melted expensive bars of cocoa she'd splurged on, added raw sugar, the sweetest butter, and natural vanilla, ingredients that really made a difference. She'd filled two of the restaurant baking trays and kept an eye on them the whole time they cooked, so they would come out perfectly, with a nice crusty edge and a flaky top. As she was letting the trays cool before she cut them into squares, two old friends popped in. Reilly Wildflower and his old lady, Hannah. They made their living selling import jewelry, incense, and hemp products at the Farmer's Market.

They had just gotten in a shipment of Maui Gold. "Take a

hit," they urged her. "This stuff is incredible." Never one to turn down primo bud, Allegra had done just that, said good-bye to her friends, and then carefully cut the brownies into squares.

She loaded the brownies into her VW bus, stood up, and the world spun. Oh, no! She was lit up like a Christmas tree. They called it stoned for a good reason, because all she wanted to do was lie down on her bed and listen to "Sugar Magnolia" over and over again. She drove ten miles under the speed limit, arrived late, and nearly dropped the brownies as she stumbled through the cafeteria doors. "Whoa!" she cried out, maybe louder than she should have, but a clumsy move like that deserved an "oh, shit," and for Mariah's sake she'd held her tongue. "Who's got the munchies?" she called out, and Mariah, her little girl in knee socks, blazer, and a wrap-around skirt, looked at her, ashamed. Allegra was twenty-nine then, surrounded by parents who'd waited ten years longer than she had to give birth. She'd never cared what people thought of her, but she wanted her own flesh and blood to like her a little. By the end of the night, even the store-bought Chips Ahoy sold out, but no one had bought a single brownie. When the parents and kids started packing up, Mariah dropped both trays into the garbage can.

"What are you doing?" Allegra sputtered. "Those are perfectly good brownies. We can sell them in the café tomorrow."

Mariah turned to her. "Do you even *get* why nobody bought the brownies? Are you so stoned you can't see yourself in the mirror? Everyone in this room thought you put marijuana in the brownies. You reek of it. God, Mom! I might as well drop out of school."

"Honey, I swear I didn't put anything in them except chocolate and sugar—" Allegra had said, trying to put her arm around her daughter's shoulders. But Mariah shook her off, pulled on her jacket, and started walking home. Some free bud! Allegra's buzz was a distant memory, and now her daughter despised her. After a few blocks, Allegra convinced her to get in the car. "Mariah," she said, "what can I do to make this up to you?"

"Gee, I don't know. How about stop smoking pot? How about wearing normal clothes once in a while? How about wearing a bra?" And then she burst into sobs and rolled down the window as if breathing the same air as her mother was too awful.

Allegra thought of nothing else that night while Mariah cried herself to sleep. Gammy asked what was the matter. Cramps, Allegra said. Never again had she smoked pot. Allegra would have done anything to make up for it, but Mariah had turned away from her for good. Allegra concentrated on Lindsay. She'd sell her signed Janis Joplin poster on eBay to maintain that little girl's happiness. Allegra blinked back the tears that threatened to spill onto her cheeks.

The door opened, and the doctor, notebook computer in hand, said, "Good afternoon there, Alice Moo—"

And that was as far as he got before his face froze in surprise.

Allegra stared at the six-foot-tall bear of a man in a white coat that was one size too small for him. She'd know the curve of his jaw anywhere from all the times her fingers had traced it. He had the same toothy grin. He was simply an older version of the man she'd known thirty-four years ago. "Oh my God. Doc? Is that you?"

He looked at the computer screen and back at her. "Allegra? But it says here your name is Alice."

"Alice and Alvin. Remember? We sounded like the Bobbsey Twins so we made up nicknames that summer. I liked mine so much I kept it."

He took hold of her hands. "My God, Allegra. How long has it been? Come here and give me a hug."

Her paper gown rattled as she stood up. Doc embraced her. He smelled of sandalwood and cedar. It was warm inside his arms. They provided a perfect pocket of calm, something Allegra hadn't felt in a long time. "This is just incredible," she said.

Doc nodded. "What a coincidence."

"Coincidence?" Allegra said, pulling back to look at him. "I prefer to think of it as two people hiking a very long trail to arrive at this moment."

He chuckled. "You were New Age-y before the term was coined."

"Well, I wish to hell I'd copyrighted it." She gave him a frank appraisal. "At least I didn't sell out and cut my hair."

"Had to," he said. "It was starting to fall out. I looked like a demented monk."

She laughed. They stood there for a while, taking stock of each other. Then Alvin Goodnough, M.D., got down to business. He scrolled down the screen on the computer, examined a page of numbers, and Allegra nervously began to jabber. "Remember when we camped at Jedediah Smith?"

"I remember that we didn't get much sleep."

"When did you pop up here? I know everyone in this town and half the next."

"I only moved here a month ago."

"You live here now? Why all these years later . . ." She had no idea how to finish that sentence. She sat back down in the leather chair, wishing she'd brought a sweater. "Doc? Is it bad news? Please tell me it isn't."

He blinked his eyes several times, something Gammy always said was the mark of a person hiding the truth. "I understand that you're scared."

"I'm not scared. I'm just so glad to see you that I'd rather have a cup of coffee and talk over old times than blood tests. Let's give the exam the big mañana."

"Allegra," he said, and she could hear it in the tone of his voice—bad news.

She crossed her arms over her breasts and the paper crackled. "No. I mean it. I can't take it right now."

He looked at his watch. "Okay, we'll talk about me for a while. I bought a house, one of those enormous places on the golf course. Big enough to house Microsoft corporate headquarters, but inside it's cozy."

"You actually *play* golf?"

"Allegra, please. Golf's a game, not a political affiliation. I bought the house because it has a great view of the water."

"But golf? I can't believe it. So you're planning on staying?"

"Yes. Now it's time to talk about the blood tests."

That soon? It was the worst kind of news. "I'm thirsty. I need a drink." She tried to pace in the small room. "I have a café to run and a grandchild and my mother's getting old and she needs me. Please," she said. "Keep talking about yourself. Please? Just a little while longer."

He set the computer on the counter, and she saw him hesitate. "I'm planning on staying. The job is challenging, and it's a beautiful place to live—like you don't know that already. The house has beach access. You'll have to come by and enjoy the sunset with me sometime. We can catch up on everything else then. Now we need to talk about your condition, and how we can proceed to drive your leukemia into a nice, long remission."

"Leukemia?" Allegra said. "Are you sure?"

"I am."

How could her body betray her this way? Admittedly, she could have taken a little better care of it, not drank so much, or stayed up so late, but hard work deserved hard fun. As Gammy would say when she came into work hungover, "Apparently you're planning on sleeping when you're dead, but that isn't going to make the day pass any easier." Leukemia. It wasn't possible. Ali McGraw's character in *Love Story* had died of leukemia. That was dopey movie-star romance, *Romeo and Juliet* updated, not the same thing as real-life dying. Just because she and Doc had a past did not mean there would be a future. Of course not. After he dumped the bad news on her he'd walk back out to his perfect life in the ritzy part of town with his no doubt beautiful, young wife and the brilliant children who adored him.

He took hold of her hands. "Allegra? I know how to deal with this disease. Let me explain it to you."

"Why didn't you ever call me, Doc? Just one call all these years?"

He smiled gently. "We didn't tell each other our last names. I got married, had kids—"

"Of course," she said, pulling away. She could even see them, a son and a daughter, smart, successful, driving SUVs, graduated from Ivy League colleges their father could afford.

"—as I'm sure you did. But the kids are grown and gone, and I'm single now."

"Some stupid woman actually let you go?"

"My wife ran away with her gynecologist." He held up his hand. "Please, I've heard all the jokes. When I finished my residency, I worked overseas as part of a program to reduce my student loans, and for the chance to see how medicine is practiced in other countries."

She recalled him saying his family was wealthy. "Student loans?"

"Yes, Allegra. You probably don't remember what you said to me under the stars that night when we were baring our souls, but it sunk in. I paid for my schooling so I didn't have to do what Dad had planned. Worked out fine. I taught at U.C. Davis for a while. Great school and town. I was awarded a grant to do some research, but when the money ran out they cut the funding. It was disheartening, and I decided to make a life change. I thought about what would make me the happiest, and I realized I missed the day-to-day patient contact, so when this post opened up, I took it."

"Your kids?"

"My son Doug's an attorney in the San Francisco DA's office. My daughter Kaylie was born with cerebral palsy. Most of her life was spent in hospitals. She passed away fifteen years ago. I miss her, but it was a mercy all the way around."

"I'm so sorry."

"Thanks. Yours?"

"Only Mariah. She teaches college, or did until recently. My granddaughter, Lindsay, is so smart she corrects me all the time." Doc, she said in her head, is Alvin Goodnough. His only daughter died. How did he live with the loss? "What kind of last name is Goodnough?"

He shrugged. "The kind you get teased for all your life no matter how you pronounce it. My ancestors came through Ellis Island. It probably got abbreviated or misspelled or something along the way." He took a pen and a pad from his pocket. "You look fabulous. How'd you stay so young, Allegra? Did you find the fountain of youth? Did you marry rich and go to the spa every week?"

"Never got around to the marriage thing. I thought we'd decided that the fountain of youth was swimming naked in the Big Sur River."

His cheeks flushed, and she noticed how easily he slid back into his professional persona. "Okay, that's enough chat. I've got to examine you. If anything feels awkward, I can call the nurse in." He unwound his stethoscope and snaked it under her gown to listen to her heart and Allegra blanched at the touch of cold metal. "Alvin—"

"Just be quiet a minute so I can listen, will you? Remember the time we camped and saw that deer leap across the fire road."

How could she forget hiking Damnation Creek Trail all morning, making love all afternoon, sleeping under the stars, talking over dreams, eyes on the sky, watching for that rogue comet or falling star or UFO? Camped under a redwood tree, they had been heating water for cocoa following a lovely meal of pan-fried Spam. It seemed like magic, both of them looking up at the same time. Just the smallest sound of a leaf crushed under the stag's hoof. They saw his silhouette in the moonlight, the breath steaming from his nostrils. He leapt across the road so high it seemed like a trick. Why couldn't that be her last memory of Doc instead of this?

Alvin pulled the stethoscope out of his ears and hung it around his neck. "Your ticker is as strong as a horse's. Open your mouth and stick out your tongue."

"No," she said. "That feels too weird."

"It's nothing I haven't seen before. Open." Alvin peeked, typed some notes into her file, and then looked over at her. "Allegra, you can close your mouth now."

Allegra breathed a sigh of relief. "Won't it be fun to talk and open a bottle of good wine instead of the rotgut we used to drink?" She winked. "Play your cards right, you never know. You might get a free breakfast out of it."

He took her left hand, rubbed it between his, which were warm and big and made her feel like a child. Then he looked into her eyes. "Allegra, you're not going to be drinking alcohol for a while. In the early stages of leukemia like yours . . ."

She heard nothing beyond four syllables that hung in the air the way the Spanish moss drifted in the fog and wind from the cypress trees on Seventeen Mile Drive in wealthy Carmel-by-the-Sea. Some people loved Spanish moss, but Allegra thought the moss looked like the hair of a dead man. "It's a mistake," she said. "I am the healthiest person I know. I eat right, I examine my breasts monthly, and I have my yearly tests at the Women's Clinic—"

"That's why we repeated them."

"Run them a third time."

He took hold of her shoulders. "Allegra, listen to me. Leukemia's not the death sentence it used to be. There are treatments—"

"What? Chemotherapy? Poison myself so I can live long enough to feel horrible before I die? No way." She was trembling.

Alvin rolled his stool closer to her. He tore a page from the prescription pad he'd taken from his pocket, flipped it over, clicked his pen, and as if he was explaining to a child some troubling mathematical problem, began to draw Allegra a picture of her illness.

The words swam right over her. Chronic, acute. Chronic was the good kind. With the right management, potentially a normal lifespan. Acute was when the cells didn't mature.

Untreated, worst-case scenario, it could mean she had as little
as twelve weeks from this very moment to the funeral parlor.
It was September. That meant she could last until Thanksgiving, but she'd miss Christmas. Last Christmas could have been
her final holiday and she hadn't appreciated it enough. Oh,
God. She'd miss Lindsay's thirteenth birthday party.

Acute myelogenous—very bad. Chronic lymphocytic—
good survival rates. Treatment would begin at once. This was
the induction phase. They'd attempt to drive the disease into
"a durable remission." There would be chemotherapy. Way,
way, way down the line, there was a minute possibility of a
bone marrow transplant. Designer drugs. White blood cell
count high, red blood cell count low. Alvin spin-doctored the
horror of the whole thing by telling her how lucky she was to
faint and end up in an E.R. that took a thorough look at its
patients.

"I've talked for far too long," he said. "Surely you have
questions."

"Not really."

He handed the paper to her and closed her fingers around
it. "I know you're reeling, Allegra. But early intervention gives
us a chance to circle our wagons, to build out of your body
and available drugs a kind of fortress against the attacker."

Adrenaline flooded her skin. Her ears felt hot, and the
sides of things were going blurry. She'd never been a fainter
and refused to faint again. Fainting had caused this whole
problem. She opened her mouth, but no words came out, so
she shut it and tried not to cry. Then, as if directly from her
solar plexus, she blurted out, "I want Khan!"

"Who's Khan?"

"My dog," she sniffled. "You probably don't remember
Lieutenant Uhuru."

"The hell I don't. She peed on my hiking boots, and bit my
ankles whenever we had sex. I have scars."

She wiped at her tears and blew her nose. "I can't cry like
I used to. It's exhausting." She swiped at her cheeks. "And

Uhuru just wanted to protect me." Allegra remembered how badly she wanted to hear Doc say the same thing. "Uhuru lived nineteen years. Now she's—" She looked up at him and her eyes welled with fresh tears. "At the Rainbow Bridge, waiting for me to join her. If you won't release me this minute, I'll go AMA."

"You'll what?"

"Leave. You know, like they say on television, against medical advice."

Alvin shook his head and smiled. "Same old Allegra." He kissed her cheek, her forehead, and then, like in the old days, he saved the best kiss for last, delicate and noiseless and right on the tip of her nose. Doc's kisses used to be about life, but now, not only was she terminally ill, and that part of her life over, she probably grossed him out, which made needing Khan all the more pressing. She cried harder.

"Allegra," he said, "I won't insult you by telling you not to worry. But try not to let it consume you. I've had lots of patients sicker than you do just fine."

She breathed into his neck, and for a moment, lost herself in his scent. Too soon it was gone, and reality slapped her back to where she was and why. "Doc," she said, "would you ask my daughter to come in now?"

Our daughter, she didn't say, but that was the truth. He just didn't know it yet.

4
Mariah

MARIAH SET DOWN THE *People* she'd been reading and looked at the wall aquarium in the waiting room. It was filled with tiny, glittering fish. Lindsay would know their Latin names, but Mariah didn't. She sighed. Nothing with her mother could ever be simple. Allegra might telephone and say, "Why don't we go out to Point Lobos and watch the pelicans?" and Mariah would fill a bag with stale bread, get in Allegra's van, and boom, she'd find herself in a picket line for underpaid supermarket cashiers. Her mother loved to tell people that she had a "rap sheet." She was so pretty that several of the cops who arrested her ended up dating her, if you could call drinking and dancing and doing the horizontal mambo dating.

When the nurse called her name, Mariah looked up. "Yes?"

"Your mother's asking for you. Follow me, please."

They walked down a hall lined with colorful prints of the Carmel area. They passed a scale, a counter with various medical-looking items on it, cupboards above, and made a left to the exam room where Allegra sat crying and a bear of a man stood with his hand on her shoulder, rubbing.

"Mariah?" he said. "I'm Al Goodnough. Your mother and I

were friends a long time ago. I'm sorry to meet you under unpleasant circumstances."

In Allegra's shadow, all other women were plain. Everyone loved her. Everyone.

"Your mother has leukemia."

No, she didn't. Allegra was spontaneous. Passionate. Invincible. Healthy.

"Your mother and I were friends years ago," the doctor was saying. "While I wish the occasion were happier, I'm delighted to meet you nonetheless. We need to arrange for some tests and then your mother's chemotherapy schedule . . ."

Mariah had stopped listening and gone into college professor mode. Sociologically speaking, the best medical treatment was reserved for the wealthy. This balding, sandy-haired middle-aged man wore buttery soft Italian loafers. The gold pen sticking out of his coat pocket was a Mont Blanc. The watch on his furry wrist probably cost more than a down payment on a condo. She went to her mother's side and he moved away.

"The chemo clinic is at the hospital," he continued. "She'll need to be driven both ways. We'll begin with a five-week course, two days per week, and see how she tolerates it. Some people do just fine, no nausea at all . . ."

A fraction of one percent, Mariah figured. Her mother had slumped in the chair, shaking her head as if she couldn't believe it. Mariah had a hard time believing it herself. She patted her mother's back and handed her a new tissue and took the soggy one from her. The doctor seemed to have run out of things to say. "We need a little time by ourselves," she told the clod responsible for putting her mother in this state. "Can you please leave us alone for a while?"

He hovered in the doorway. "I'm not just a physician, I'm an old friend," he said. "Here's my home number. Please call, anytime. I truly mean that."

Mariah watched him gather up his notebook computer and stethoscope. She pegged him as in his fifties, wealthy, single—

she saw no ring. On the relative social prestige scale, he was an eighty-six, a bona fide member of the working rich. She'd forget his face the minute they left, but not the piped-in music in his office, the plushy chairs in the waiting room, or how he made her mother cry. "We're fine," she said flatly, as she took his card. "We need to go home now."

"Call the office tomorrow for the time we've set for her bone marrow biopsy."

Allegra let loose another sob.

"Will you just be quiet?" Mariah said, louder than she needed to, but his words rattled her down to her ribs. "What is the matter with you? Have you no consideration for the shock this terrible news has caused my mother? Did you skip the chapter on compassion in medical school? We'll be getting a second opinion."

This doctor put his hands into his slacks pockets and began nervously rattling his change. Mariah hated his belt buckle, one of those fancy silver ones you found at rodeos, or in some campy boutique on Melrose in Los Angeles.

"I'm happy to refer her to a colleague, but the diagnosis isn't going to change."

Mariah stuck out her chin. "You can't know that for certain."

"I'm afraid I can."

He looked at her mother, who was starting to calm down. "Allegra, forgive me for being such a clumsy ass about all this. I'm so sorry. I swear to you we can work on this, get you into remission. You'll have your regular life back in no time. But I can't help you unless you let me."

She buried her face in Mariah's shoulder.

"I'll wait to hear from you," he said, nodding sadly to Mariah, and finally exiting the room.

Mariah pressed her cheek to her mother's, which was hot and damp with tears. "Leukemia's just a medical term, Mom. One word doesn't mean you're going to die. You're going to be okay, I just know it. You're the strongest person I know."

While her mother's shoulders shook, Mariah tried to imagine a world without her. The Owl & Moon would shut down, or worse, turn ordinary. Gammy would have no one to argue with but Simon—for about a day, because Simon would quit without Allegra there to run interference. Gammy would get mad at God, and there would be endless railing about His mysterious ways. And what about Lindsay? Mariah didn't want to think about the hole this would leave in her daughter's heart. That she wanted to protect her mother wasn't surprising, because she loved her. So how could she expend so much effort on being annoyed with Allegra, when this terrible disease was lurking just around the corner? Oh, my God, she thought. I love my mother as much as I love Lindsay. It's true. I'd take her pain if only it would spare her.

That night, Mariah decided it was best to take Lindsay to dinner rather than stay at the café. Allegra was exhausted. She stopped long enough to pick up Khan and silently made her way upstairs. A minute later, Gammy walked down. Lindsay was at the counter doing her homework, looking engrossed, but Mariah knew nothing got by her daughter, the barometer of human emotions.

"Well, let's hear it," her grandmother said as they stood in the stairwell that led to the café kitchen.

Mariah tried to think how to word it. "It's not good. The doctor thinks she's developing leukemia."

Gammy's face paled. "What do you mean 'developing'? You either have something or you don't."

"I don't know any more than that, Gammy. You saw her. I don't know if you should try talking to her or not. I can stay the night if you want."

"Nonsense," Gammy said, taking hold of the small gold cross on her necklace. "I'm going to call to my prayer ladies, get a circle going for Alice. You've got enough on your plate with your little pitcher with the big ears over there. She's been asking a lot of questions. What will you say to her?"

Mariah considered that. She'd handle this better than she had losing her job. Straightforward, no deception or holding things in. "I'll figure something out. See you tomorrow morning, Gammy." She kissed her cheek, the skin there as soft as flower petals, and smelling faintly of Jean Naté.

Mariah wanted to come to Lindsay with tangible treatment options and facts. A mother was supposed to be hopeful, a life-affirming cheerleader during those windy spells when it felt as if the whole of your existence might blow away. When the obstetrician laid Lindsay on her breast, Mariah had pledged to be the kind of mother who would never be too busy to listen. What a ridiculous ambition, she scolded herself. You didn't fare any better than Allegra's catch-as-catch-can style of mothering. Maybe a person could only hope to redeem bad mothering by being a good grandmother. Maybe what Gammy was to her, she would become to Lindsay's child. Maybe that was all you could hope for.

A textbook she'd once used in class had a chapter devoted to the role illness played in society. Mariah could always get her intro students involved in a heated discussion when they talked over the sociological aspects of right-to-die issues, palliative care, and assisted suicide. But not once had Mariah imagined the words in her textbook applying to her own family. Suppose there was no remission? Suppose her mother's health only dwindled? If things got bad, would she be brave enough to help Allegra make a dignified exit?

As she and Lindsay drove toward Pier Two, Mariah noticed a docked sailboat with all its lights on, including a string of flickering Christmas lights that made the mast glitter like it was home to fireflies in the fog. She cracked her window **so she** could hear the wind-chime clanking of boats and lines **against** the moorings and tried to imagine living aboard a boat year-round. The kitchen would be no bigger than a breadbox. Damp would creep into everything. It had to be a man who lived there, like the jogger loping along the pier with his dog. What a huge dog. She couldn't imagine sharing living quarters with such a large animal. Maybe it was a rottweiler. Those were popular again.

"What do you feel like for dinner?" she asked Lindsay, who was counting her mother's tip money, separating coins.

She looked up. "Doesn't it depend on what we can afford?"

Mariah felt a pang in her heart. Too much was changing, and it was happening too fast. "We can spend a little money. How much do I have in tips?"

Lindsay flattened the dollar bills and quarters. "Forty-seven dollars and ninety-three cents. Is that a lot?"

That was all she'd earned in tips? Mariah pictured her university pay stub. Twice a month she checked it online, and transformed those numbers into the bills she had to pay. Now her pay would arrive in cash that came from the kindness of customers—or not. Suddenly dinner out seemed like splurging. "It's pretty good for a weekday. We're here at the wharf. How does chowder and crackers sound? I can get us a to-go order from The Sandbar Grill. It's too cold and wet to eat on the beach."

Lindsay shrugged. "Fine with me."

"Anything interesting happen in school today?"

"Not really."

"How's your week been so far?"

"Fine."

"Lindsay, cut me some slack. Can't you tell me a little bit of it?"

Lindsay dropped her mother's tips back into the peanut butter jar she kept them in. "Some girls got in a fight yesterday. We talked about Science Fair. In 'Life Paths, Life Questions' we saw a film about Christo, and art sucked."

"You know I don't like that word. It's ugly."

"Sorry."

But she didn't sound sorry, she sounded hopeless. Mariah scrambled. "Tell me about the Science Fair."

"Dr. Ritchie said we could partner up if we wanted to do something really hard, so my friend and I, we're brainstorming controversial topics so we can both get a good grade and maybe win a ribbon or, if we're lucky, the prize scholarship."

Mariah remained fixed on the "friend" part of the conversation. Lindsay had a friend? Thank God. "Sounds good," she said, deliberately keeping her reaction low-key. "So what did you do in art?"

"Worked on our projects." Lindsay pointed to a parking place only three spaces away from the wharf's boardwalk. "Empty spot. And it has time on the meter."

It was about damn time something good happened, Mariah thought, turning her car into it and noting the meter time remaining. "Okay, two chowders, oyster crackers, a Diet Coke for me and a water for you?"

Lindsay looked up. "Allegra's really sick, isn't she?"

Mariah sat back down in the driver's seat. "Yes."

"Does she have cancer?"

Mariah ran her finger over her purse strap. "That's what the doctor thinks."

"Will she die?"

Mariah stroked Lindsay's cheek, the pale, freckly skin so prone to blushing. "I don't know, sweetie. But she's tough. I'm betting she's going to make it."

"That all depends on what kind of cancer it is, doesn't it?" Lindsay blurted out. "Some brain tumors can't be removed. With cervical cancer you have a chance. Ovarian cancer, though, the odds aren't good. Is that what it is?"

Mariah tried to find the mother-words she would have wanted in Lindsay's place and came up short. The sad fact was that she didn't know what Lindsay needed. She only knew her own desires and low tolerance for half-truths. "Nothing like that. It's in her blood. Imagine if cancer had an opening act. That would be where she is. The doctor says she'll probably be back to her old life when they get her on the right treatment."

"So it's leukemia?" Lindsay asked.

"The doctor mentioned that word, yes."

"Chronic or acute?"

"Lindsay, I've told you all I know. They need to do more tests."

"Have they done a bone marrow biopsy?"

"Not yet."

Lindsay turned her head and looked out the window.

Was she crying? Mariah couldn't tell. "Honey, talk to me. I can't tell what you're thinking if you don't tell me." She touched her daughter's shoulder, a wing of sharp bone that could stand a little weight, if only Lindsay would eat more. But Lindsay was picky about food, and Mariah worried that if she made too big a fuss it could lead to anorexia or bulimia in this too-smart child who nevertheless was capable of only age-appropriate emotions. That was the thing about being a mother; you had to watch every word you said. "We'll look it up on the internet when we get home. You can print out whatever you think will help Allegra, okay?"

No answer.

"She has a highly respected doctor," Mariah said, though she could not imagine her mother ever having that insensitive oaf as a friend. "If a person has to get sick, California's a good place to do it. There are lots of great hospitals and different kinds of treatments. I know it's hard, but try to concentrate on the positive. Chances are—"

Lindsay turned to her, tears coursing down her cheeks. "This is just like what happened to Carl Sagan. He got the same thing and they did a bone marrow transplant from a close family member and he died anyway!"

Again with the Carl Sagan. Was this about not having a father? Mariah looked out the window as a couple holding hands made their way to the wharf. At the end of the wooden planks the seals were barking. The stresses of the day came down on Mariah like a shroud. She wanted to scream, she wanted someone to reassure her, but all she said was, "Why don't you sit here in the car while I get our order, I mean, our dinner?"

Lindsay nodded.

"I'll leave the radio on. Lock the door after me. No matter what Gammy says about Monterey being the safest place to live, there are still plenty of weirdos in the world."

The next morning, Mariah let Lindsay walk to school from the café. Gammy had packed her lunch, probably with a butter and sugar sandwich and a chocolate soda. She watched until Lindsay reached the corner, passing early-morning dog walkers and the power-walking teams in their neon-colored exercise clothes. Inside, she began folding silverware bundles into napkins, getting ready for the first customers of the day. "How's Mom?" she asked Gammy. "Did she sleep?"

Gammy shook her head no. "Alice spent most of the night crying. I sat up with her as long as I could, but I'm an old woman, Mariah. I worked ten hours yesterday, and over the past couple of days I have worried enough for six months. My legs were throbbing like wisdom teeth. I had to turn in. I told her not to come down today, that you and I could handle things. So I guess that means we'll have to."

She smiled her practical smile that tried its hardest to hide her disappointments, and Mariah vowed to move through this day at warp speed. "Let me give you a hug, Gammy. This feels so hard for me that I have to wonder how you're holding up. You're her mother. It must be a hundred times worse for you."

Her grandmother pulled away and began wiping the already clean counter. "Well, Mariah, what can you do? Deal with whatever life sends your way and leave the rest up to our Creator. All I can say is hold on to your hat, dearie, because I've got a hunch it's going to get a lot worse before it gets easier."

"What's going on here?" Allegra said from the stairwell. "It's past time to open. While you two are just standing there yakking we're losing money. Where in hell is Simon? Unlock the door and let's get to work."

All morning Mariah kept a close eye on her mother. Allegra zipped around the café as if this were any other day of the week. When Kiki Cooper came in for more cookies—it was mah-jongg day—Allegra talked to her for at least five minutes while Kiki related the latest news on her divorce. Mr. Cooper, the CEO of a software company who suddenly decided he wanted to marry a girl young enough to be his daughter, wouldn't know what hit him once Kiki was finished. Allegra had suggested Kiki contact N.O.W. for a good lawyer, and in no time Kiki'd gotten a really good haircut, and started taking Feldenkrais three times a week. Kiki's divorce was as dramatic as a prime-time reality show; something new happened every day, as the balance of power was constantly shifting.

Allegra filled cups, rang up the till, smiled, and laughed. Only Mariah and Gammy knew her well enough to see through the brave façade to the worry beneath.

Around ten, when the Scotsman came in, Mariah heard her mother shout, "Babe, Sean Connery Junior, twelve o'clock!"

Embarrassed once again by her mother's big mouth, Mariah walked up to the counter and turned the page on her order pad and stared at it, waiting. But even a sidelong glance at the thick black hair, ruddy complexion, and craggy face proved Allegra's words right. He did resemble the actor. Mariah wondered if he played that angle, saying "Bond, James Bond" at parties because it got him laughs. Allegra's humor was a safety valve, a way to defuse potentially disruptive situations, and to bring up taboos, but the only joke Mariah had ever found funny had been posted on the department bulletin board: "What do you get when you cross a mafioso with a sociologist? An offer you can't understand." She composed her workday smile. He was a customer, the same as anyone else, just easier to look at. "The usual, Mr. Appleton?" she asked, setting down a napkin bundled with silverware.

"Ah," he said, "'tis Applecross. The usual, yes, that'd be lovely."

"Sorry."

Mr. Applecross was wearing a dark blue rain slicker today, even though it wasn't raining yet. That indicated he was practical, planning for the future. Instead of yesterday's dress pants, he had on nicely faded denim jeans. One could speculate about that from several vantage points, not the least of which was what lay underneath. Mariah felt his shoes said it all: well-worn hiking boots. You didn't wear those unless you liked to walk long distances, no matter what the terrain. She set down his mug, the Earl Grey tea bag, and a metal pitcher of hot water. Gammy was all over her about making conversation with the customers. Make small talk, she said. Seem friendly even if you don't feel that way. Our off-season customers are the core of our apple, Mariah. It wouldn't kill you to ask how their day is or make a comment on the weather. Mariah thought of bagpipes, men in knee socks and kilts, and shortbread. Surely there was a subject to discuss in all that.

"So, Mr. Applecross. Is today casual Friday at your work?"

He smiled. "Please call me Fergus. Don't work on Fridays, generally."

"That sounds like a dream job."

"Afraid not," he said, "unless you enjoy fatally boring administrative tasks. Lots of time spent with paper, signing things, approving things, holding meetings. If I blethered on about it, you'd fall asleep on your feet."

Mariah wouldn't have minded a nap. She couldn't think of what else to say, so she stood there, her hand going numb from holding the metal pitcher.

"Tell me something, what do you recommend? The chocolate biscuits or the berry scones?"

"The scones," she answered.

"Such a quick decision. How did you arrive at it? Something off about the biscuits?"

"The biscuits are good. It's just that I can tell you're the kind of man who likes a routine."

He faked a gasp. "Well, this is a terrible turn. You make me sound as if I'm a crotchety old stick who always buys the same brand of tooth powder."

Mariah let out a nervous laugh. Gammy would not be happy if she drove this man from the counter. "Er—I didn't mean that the way it sounded. I just, well, correct me if I'm wrong, but you grew up in a monarchy, and a monarchy, with its sameness, has broad appeal. Using the powers of deduction from available evidence, scones seem the logical choice." She could feel the sweat start to gather on her back, right between her shoulder blades. "God, I'm sorry. I'll shut up now."

He handed her back the unopened teabag. "Now I'm appalled. I must do something about this stodgy persona you've formed of me. Not only will I have the croissants, but I'll challenge myself further with a different blend tea."

"A little help?" a customer said at the register. "I'm in a hurry."

Mariah set down the pitcher and quickly rang him up, feeling Fergus Applecross watching her every move. Unless she had all the academics surgically removed from her brain she would never have a boyfriend. But if she dumbed herself down, what would be left? A tabula rasa with no idea how to be a girly-girl, how to make men want her. All she really wanted was Allegra to get well. And to find a secure teaching job. Never mind. He'd duck out the second he'd finished, which was all for the best. Nobody could take away your fantasies.

He pulled the wicker basket full of tea bags toward himself and rubbed his hands together. Aside from Earl Grey, they had lemon pekoe, chamomile, and spice. Somehow it made her happy to see him reach for spice.

When Dr. Goodnough showed up, taking the seat at the counter that Fergus had only vacated an hour before, Mariah called her mother from the back of the café, where she had been happily chatting with customers as she replaced yesterday's carnations with daisies in the tabletop vases. Mariah pointed to the doctor, and when Allegra saw who it was, the joy went out of her so fast it felt as if the air had been vacuumed out of the room. Mariah went to her, cupping her mother's elbow. "Just say the word, Mom. I'll get rid of him."

Allegra looked grim. She set the handful of daisies down on the table. "Avoiding him isn't going to do anyone any good. We have to talk sooner or later."

"Why? There're other doctors out there. Surely one of them has a better bedside manner than the Hulk."

Allegra smiled. "He's not a hulk, Mariah. He's Alvin Goodnough. He's here, and in my life now. He's in all our lives, really. As Gammy would say, 'Here comes the organ grinder. Better have a penny for the monkey.' "

Mariah wondered where all that had come from. Was Allegra so afraid that she would die that she was making amends? Her entire life her mother appeared to take nothing seriously, including boyfriends. "Give me a sign if he's upsetting you, and I'll—"

"You'll what?" Gammy asked, walking by with two full plates. "Beat him to death with a soup ladle? Good Lord and little fishes, Alice. He took an oath to heal, not pester you to death. Go talk to him. Don't you want to get better?"

"Thanks, Mama," Allegra said. "No matter how shitty I feel I can always depend on you to throw a bucket of water on me so I can feel worse."

"That's my job, Alice. Now git. And go easy on the Anglo-Saxon. This is a family establishment."

Were it anyone else, Allegra would have her hand on his arm, or plant a smooch on his cheek. Mariah wondered what their past together had been like. The doctor said they were "friends." Had they done something that seemed "fun" at the time but in perspective was embarrassing, like group sex? No time for speculation. Booth two was filled with hungry lawyers, and she hurried off to take their order. What harm could come of Dr. Goodnough talking to her mother with a counter between them?

)

"Mariah!" Gammy called out as they were serving the last of the day's soup—cheddar-ale today, topped with popcorn—new to the menu—Simon's recipe—and a big hit. "Phone for you."

Mariah took the receiver, expecting Lindsay's homeroom teacher—she'd left her a message about the art class—or maybe her landlord, whom she'd left a fateful message: I'm giving notice. Take the rest of what I owe you out of the security deposit. She didn't have the cash to pay next month's rent. "Hello?"

"Fergus Applecross here."

She wiped her free hand on her apron. Now what? "Did the new tea not agree with you?"

He laughed. "The tea was lovely."

"Then what's up?" Mariah said. "Was it the croissants?"

"Curious expression, 'What is up?' The sky, for one. And the sun, though it appears to be making its hasty retreat. Stock market prices could be up as well. I suppose it's a good thing if one's suspenders are up. And one's spirits. I certainly hope yours are."

Mariah was happy to listen to his accent, but participate in an actual conversation? "I guess by spirits you mean physical exhaustion. If so, my spirits are tired, but they'll revive when I finish my shift. Why do you want to know?"

More laughing. "'Tis very good to hear you have a resilient spirit."

A what? Oh, he was *flirting* with her. She imagined him on the other end of the phone, playing with the cord, leaning into his words, that verifiable body language she'd seen exhibited in her students, in her mother, in everyone but herself. She decided to chat for another minute, to let him down easily. "How are your spirits? Are you one of those people who feel depressed when it rains? If so, be warned, it rains a lot here in the winter. And in the summer it mists. Full spectrum lights can help."

"I'm not worried. My spirits are definitely up."

Now that they'd settled that worry, she wondered what to say next. She was no good at this. "So, did you want to order something to go?"

"Actually, yes. Listen, Mariah. There's a spot in Edinburgh called the Elephant House. It's a restaurant. It's a short walk from the National Library, actually. They serve biscuits shaped like elephants. Here you'd call them cookies. Bit of a repository for elephant paraphernalia, actually. Over six hundred items, figurines, mainly. On Friday nights they have a lounge act, a chap who sings Frank Sinatra tunes."

Oh, God. Maybe he had Asperger's syndrome. How sad to be in another country and have no social skills. A person with Asperger's had little sense of private space. Once they began talking it was difficult to shut them up. "Is the singer any good?" she asked.

"Sadly, he is not."

Mariah leaned her elbows on the counter, aware that her grandmother was listening. Save me, she mouthed, but Gammy turned her head away. Dammit. "And this is important for me to know because?"

"Because were you and I in Edinburgh, which unfortunately we are not, I would ask you to accompany me there this evening. They make the best cup of coffee."

"Besides ours, right?"

"Certainly," he said. "That's it exactly. In addition, they happily provide instructions on how to make your own best Joe at home."

"If it's that good, why don't they guard the recipe with their lives?"

"I had a feeling you might see it that way, being in the café business."

"I'm just a waitress. I live on tips, not profit and loss statements."

"Is that so?"

She could hear the smile in his voice. God helps those who are willing to pick up a shovel and pitch in, Gammy would say. No free rides. "Thanks for the chat, Mr. Applecross, but I have the feeling you're trying to ask me out on a date and the thing is, I don't really date."

"Why ever not?"

She sighed. "For one thing, it's too complicated."

"Come along. A man, a woman, plates and silver, chatter, films. How can that be complicated?"

"It's extremely complicated. Dating convention largely insists you not tell the truth. When a man asks how you are, and you have tired feet or cystitis, he really means say you're fine. Then he'll ask you for a date and you won't reject him. I can show you statistics to support this. Men fear rejection more than anything else, including war. I'm sorry if that sounds blunt, but I don't like games. And dating is games. I don't have time for it."

"What a pity."

"Why is it a pity? Because I don't see it the way you do?"

"How do I see it?"

She bit her thumbnail. "Well, okay, maybe I don't know how you see it."

"Which is a good reason to have tea with me."

She frowned, and played with the toothpick dispenser. "Excising dating from my life has proved efficient. I never said you had to agree with it."

"I'm not asking for a date, or dinner, only for tea. What time shall I fetch you?"

"Mr. Applecross, thank you for your interest, but in addition to asking the wrong person you also have unfortunate timing. My mother's not well; I work long days that start at four AM, and I have a twelve-year-old daughter who's worried sick about her science project topic. Now do you see why I can't go out with you?"

"Not at all. Think about it for a second. The information

you've just given me only reinforces your need for time away. I'm not being selfish; many would agree. And meeting new people broadens one's view."

Mariah wanted to scream. Why now? Dateless for so many years, being hit on by a man even her grandmother found sexy. The opposable forces in her life refused to knit together. And a tiny part of her, maybe two or three atoms, wanted to go, even if it led nowhere. Did that make her a terrible daughter? "I really—"

"Damn," Fergus Applecross said, interrupting her. "Knew I should have sprung for tickets to The Elephant House. Would have been a long journey, though. Not sure I'd have been able to get you back in time for work tomorrow. And on my salary we'd have been forced to fly coach."

"Look, it's not that. I'm sure you're very good company, but we're having a family crisis just now. I'm not sure my mother's up to watching my daughter."

"I will hold while you check with her," he said. "I love that American term—'on hold.' Brings to mind barnacles on wharfs, handshakes and promises. In Dublin, you'll find the door of Reconciliation. Two men, their families longtime enemies, grew weary of the killing, so one chopped a hole in the door and put his hand through. He could very well have lost that hand, but they shook as gentlemen do, and in place of war there was peace."

Mariah set the phone on the counter, and turned to see Gammy standing right behind her. "Sean Connery," she whispered.

Gammy smiled. "I'm jealous, Mariah. Thought I'd hung up my dancing shoes but that man could put the jig back in my step."

Mariah whispered more urgently. "He wants to take me to tea. Help me get out of it."

"Say yes. I'll take Lindsay to bingo with me."

"Lindsay can watch herself. It's just that Mom needs us around her."

"That's fluffer-nutter and you know it. Alice can be sick by herself, or I can skip bingo. We'll be there if anything happens. Where's he taking you?"

"I have no idea because I don't intend to go."

"Well, hell's bells, Mariah. What's the harm in drinking a cup of tea and talking with someone of the opposite sex? You've spent your whole life with your nose in a book. Say yes or hand me that phone so I can make him take me instead."

Mariah picked up the receiver to hear Fergus Applecross laughing. "I apologize if you heard any of that. We're not your typical family."

"Whose family is?"

"Only one cup. My mother's not well. She needs her family."

"I understand. Shall I fetch you up around seven?'

"Fetch me what? Why not come over here? That way the tea won't cost us anything."

He laughed and laughed. "Forgive me. You're such a strange girl."

"Excuse me? How am I strange?"

"Strange in a refreshing way, believe me. I'll fetch you up around seven."

He hung up and she groaned. "Great. Now I'm getting fetched! Thanks, Gammy. What am I supposed to wear? My stinky work clothes? One of Allegra's hippie dresses?"

Simon came out of the kitchen. "Scarlett O'Hara's dress of draperies comes to mind."

"Very funny, eavesdropper."

"How can I not joke when every word that comes out of your mouth is so socially inept?"

"Thanks, Simon. This from the king of cool. The man who invented one-word sentences."

"Jealous," he said. "Losing your academic job may be your last chance for normalcy, Mariah. Write that dean a thank-you note. Send him one of Bess's fruitcakes."

"Don't you insult my fruitcake, Mister," Gammy said. "Mariah, you know I love you to pieces, but truthfully, honey, your hair could stand a perm. And have you ever heard of lipstick?"

"Gammy, give it up," Mariah said. "I am never getting a perm. I don't even have time to use conditioner, let alone lipstick."

"Which explains a lot," Simon said. "You could always—brace yourself for the shock—go shopping."

"Great idea, Simon. Except I have no money. The only shopping I can do is at the thrift store, and with my luck, I'd end up picking something I donated."

"Yes, and while that works for your mother," he said, "somehow I can't see it setting off your best feature, which, alas, is your mind."

Mariah gave him a withering look. "Isn't it time for you to go home and water your cymbidiums?"

"Why, so it is."

"Then go before I beat you to a pulp with my order pad."

"I pray for your soul, Simon," Gammy said.

"Now there's an exit line if ever I heard one."

He exited out the back door, and Mariah shook her head, trying to clear it enough to figure out how to undo this "date." Her mother had taken Khan for a walk, and Dr. Goodnough had gone along with her. Lindsay was upstairs researching topics like chaos theory and black holes. "Why does everyone around here know my personal business?" she asked her grandmother.

"Count your blessings," Gammy said. "I hate to think what things would be like if we left you to your own devices."

5
Lindsay

"YOU CAN SO STAND IT," Sally DeThomas said when Lindsay told her about Allegra's chemotherapy a week later, during yet another endless block of art. Mrs. Shiasaka, her homeroom teacher, had convinced Lindsay's mom to keep her in art class. "Just because you think, omigod, I am going to curl up and die when stuff gets bad, it doesn't mean a hundred percent that'll happen. Just cry for a while and then figure out a way to get through it. My dad croaked before I was even born. My mom's had one heart attack already, both she and my stepdad are in wheelchairs for life, and my aunt Ness is HIV positive. What is the common denominator?"

Lindsay thought hard. "Really bad luck?"

Sally waved her hand in Lindsay's face. "Hello? Me! I'm still here. And they're still here, too."

"I guess," Lindsay said, "except for your dad."

Sally shrugged like she didn't care, but Lindsay knew otherwise. Sally glued a feathery fin to her papier-mâché fish, which was edged in glitter and perfect. "Your grandma will be sick for a little while, but once she's on the right medicine, things will go back to normal."

Lindsay doubted it. Carl Sagan had not gotten better. He did everything right. He got his bone marrow transplant from someone in his own family, and he died anyway. If Allegra died, then what? Would Lindsay inherit Khan? Walk him every day to the cemetery to see Allegra's grave? Who would be left to protest for the underpaid hotel maids who wanted maternity leave? Who would take samples to the city council and make sure everyone knew just how much chlorine was in the drinking water?

"I know!" Sally said, setting her fish down, her beautiful purple-and-orange-spotted fish that looked like it had just been pulled up in a fisherman's net from a tropical island where happy people sang and ripe fruit fell into your hands. "Make her a card. Grandmothers go wackadoo over handmade cards. She'll be so happy she'll give you more money on your next birthday. When's your birthday? Mine's in November, only two months away. I can't wait to turn thirteen. God, I love the way the word sounds—thirteen—so French."

Lindsay looked down at her hopeless fish. This was the first assignment of the year that counted. She'd been working on it for two weeks and it was due at the end of this period. She'd given up on making it look realistic. Now it was a fish that had been in the back of the line when evolution was busy making all the other ocean creatures strangely beautiful and leaving him only strange. "I don't know how to make a stupid card," she said, throwing the fish-mess down onto the table. "I don't know how to make a stupid fish, either."

Sally took Lindsay's fish in her hands, turning it over and over. "This looks like that mongo weird fish at the Aquarium, doesn't it?"

"The ocean sunfish?"

"*Mola mola* in Latin," Sally said.

"Also translates to—"

"Millstone!" she and Sally said in unison, and several of the other girls looked up to see who was having more fun than they were.

"Actually, that's my favorite fish," Lindsay said.

"So maybe you made it subconsciously," Sally said. "That's what art is, you know. 'The conscious use of skill plus the surrender to the subconscious, blah-bitty-blah-blah.' I'm quoting my mom, and knowing her, she was probably quoting the dead aunt I'm named after. Sounds good, though, doesn't it? It's amazing how far bullshit can get you."

Lindsay had no idea what Sally meant. "Did you know that the sunfish has no caudal fin? In order to swim it has to work the dorsal fin really hard. That's why people sometimes mistake it for a shark. They bask in the sun. If you're out on a boat and conditions are right, you can see them lying flat right near the surface of the water."

"Cool. Have you seen one in the regular ocean?" Sally asked.

Lindsay pictured herself standing by Cousteau's great-grandson, charting the Monterey Coast, finding a new species of jellyfish and naming it *Allegras Oceanus,* after her grandmother so that when she died, a part of her would live on. "Not yet."

"Here's what you do to save your project," Sally said. "Paint him gray, but not just one gray, a bunch of different shades of gray. Especially on the ossicles. Do tone on tone, like Mr. Hiller is always saying. Do the body first. When it's dry, give it orange spots."

"But a sunfish doesn't have orange spots."

"So? You think Hiller will go over to the Aquarium and check? If he asks, say this one has a sand rash. Or it swam into a poison anemone, or ate a bad shrimp and lived to call the health department. Just make it weird enough and he'll be all happy you were creative and he'll give you an A."

"How do you know to *do* that?" Lindsay said, dipping the paintbrush into the white paint and making a pool of gray on her plastic tray.

"Duh. I live with artists. They mess up all the time. My mom says to just go for it when you do. She calls it having a 'happy accident.'"

Sally went to the supply cupboard and returned with an array of paper, colored, marbled, and the heavyweight water-color rag that Mr. Hiller got mad if you wasted.

"What's your grandma's style?" Sally asked. "Is she a get-her-nails-done-every-week grandma? Does she wear those expensive sweaters with dogs embroidered on them?"

"She wears long skirts and weird jewelry that my mother says is a leftover from the sixties counterculture."

Sally laughed. "Omigod! A hippie! Definitely we'll go with the marbled paper. It'll remind her of paisley, acid trips, and groovy happenings. I know all about that stuff from going through my aunt's scrapbooks. Man, grandmothers from then are so cool! Mine wears nurse's shoes and a girdle and she won't eat tacos. She says tacos are 'ethnic food.' Can you imagine life without Mexican food? It's my favorite. I probably get that from my dad. How do you spell your grandma's name?"

"Just like the allergy medicine," Lindsay said, and then dipped her brush into the main gray color. She painted carefully, afraid she'd ruin the fish with one badly placed brush-stroke. She was into shade of gray number two when Mr. Hiller came by to check on them.

"Will you look at this," he said, as if the two of them were inventing some miraculous new technique that would give the old masters a run for their money. "Lindsay, I think this just might be the breakthrough you have been waiting for. I'm adding ten points to your grade."

"Thanks," Lindsay said, shocked. The only difference between her failures and this mess was she hadn't given up.

Behind Hiller's back, Sally rolled her eyes. As soon as he was out of earshot, she said, "Ten points for trying! God, don't you ever wish they'd let us fail sometimes?"

Just the image of a C on her report card made Lindsay break out in gooseflesh. "No. Why?"

Sally was gluing what looked like comets to the card. "Because what if we're not really that smart? What if we're just average and getting accustomed to being called the best is going to wreck us in the long run?"

"How could that wreck us?"

Sally capped the glue stick. "In June we're done here. We either go to the public high school and are bored for four years, or get sent to a boarding school where the psycho girls cut themselves for fun when they aren't throwing up their dinner. I don't know about you, but I have a feeling the rest of the world doesn't lose sleep over my self-esteem. Of course, I'm trying *not* to go to high school at all. I already know everything I need to in order to become a famous writer, and writers answer to no one, except maybe their editors, but I plan on writing such amazing books that my editor will do whatever it takes to keep me happy."

"Like what, for example?" Lindsay asked, imagining Sally reclining on pillows while an editor made her taco after perfect taco while Sally's brain flitted from one brilliant idea to the next.

Sally squinted, as if she were envisioning her future life on a movie screen. "First of all, there has to be freshly made Kettle Korn, like they sell at the fair. And sharpened Mirado Black Warrior pencils, number two. Also, yellow lined legal pads. I'll sit at my desk in my Big Sur house and look out on the ocean all day long while I fill page after page in really cool handwriting that some university library will collect, and when I've been dead a hundred years scholars will look me up and write books about me. I'll hand my pages to my editor, and she will scan it into my computer in case they might want a change here and there."

"Your family has a house in Big Sur?"

"Not my family. Me! My dead uncle David willed it to me. I can't live there alone until I'm eighteen, though. Hey, maybe you could live there with me. We could set up a laboratory and you could do experiments while I write. But you have to like Kettle Korn."

Kettle Korn was high in fiber, but high in sugar, too. "I like it okay," Lindsay said, and squeezed out a worm of orange paint to decorate her resurrected *mola mola*.

At home that night, the doorbell rang while Lindsay was sitting on the couch looking at her grandmother's card, trying to figure out what she should write inside next to Sally's poem. She set it aside and opened the door to the pizza delivery guy.

"One thick-crust spinach and sun-dried tomato with extra garlic," he said. "That'll be fourteen ninety-nine."

"Mom!" she called out.

"There's money on the table," Mariah called from the bedroom. "Don't forget to give him a tip!"

Lindsay paid the guy exactly seventeen dollars and ninety-seven cents. He looked at her, shook his head, and pocketed the money. She carried the fragrant box to the kitchen and set it on the counter. Her favorite pizza on no special occasion? Not a good sign. She sat at the counter looking at the closed box until her mom came down.

"Hey," Mariah said. "Let's just eat it on paper towels, okay? I don't want to have to wash any dishes tonight." She pulled two paper towels off the roll and handed one to Lindsay. Then she got herself a Diet Coke, a slice of lemon, and poured Lindsay a glass of water.

Lindsay felt her antennae quiver. "How'd Allegra's treatment go today?"

Mariah looked at her. "Oh, you know, about the same as the last one. She rests while she gets the I.V., gets sick in the afternoon, and then she sleeps. Two weeks down and three to go. As soon as she gets back to work in the café she'll be happy."

"In time for Halloween?" Lindsay asked, poking at a fat garlic clove.

"Sure," her mother said.

Lindsay worried about Allegra's compromised immune system and contact with the general public. She would have liked to know what her latest leukocyte count was. The doctor had said she couldn't let Khan lick her face anymore, or sleep with him. Allegra loved Khan more than anything, even more than the original *Star Trek* series.

"So what do you want to talk to me about?" she said. "I figure it's something bad, since you got me the pizza I like even though you hate it."

Mariah sighed. "I can't hide anything from you, can I?"

"Why would you want to hide things from me?"

"It's just an expression, sweetie. I'd never hide anything from you. You know that." Her mother popped the top on her Diet Coke, poured it over ice, squeezed in the lemon, and took a long drink. "We're at a crossroads, Linds."

"What's a crossroads?"

"A dividing point. It means we have to make some changes."

"Didn't we already make a bunch of changes?"

"We need to make another one. Our finances dictate our path right now."

"Do I have to transfer to public school? Do I have to quit school and get a job, like Gammy Bess did when she was my age? Maybe I should start looking for a husband, too. That way I can get married before I have a baby!"

Her mother's lips compressed together in a tight line. "You don't have to do anything. And I don't much care for the attitude."

Lindsay felt a lump in her throat, but it was anger, not sadness. "Right."

"What does that mean?"

She set her pizza slice down on a paper towel and watched the grease leach out. "I know Allegra is really sick and I know you lost your job and you said we're barely making our bills, and I know how hard it is for Gammy to be on her feet all day. In science, Dr. Ritchie told us that the ozone layer is thinning out, that all drains lead to the ocean, and hardly anybody recycles. What I want to know is how come no one ever asks how

I am? How come I'm not supposed to ever get upset? What if Allegra's leukemia turns out to be genetic? What if you don't find another job? What if—" her eyes welled up. "What if the ocean gets so polluted that all the fish die? What happens then?"

Her mother ran a thumb down the condensation on her glass of Diet Coke, and then touched Lindsay's cheek with her chilly fingers. "Baby, there's no way to soften this. We need to let the condo go. It's a lot of money every month. I'd rather spend it on your tuition."

Lindsay hadn't even thought of that. The lump in her throat descended into her stomach. "Where will we live?"

"With Gammy and Allegra above the café. I already asked and they said yes."

Lindsay tried to imagine living above The Owl & Moon all the time. It was a fun place to spend the weekend. They let her do anything she wanted, including stay up late to watch scary movies. But to live there every day? The smells of food all the time, the early-morning noise when they started baking? On the bright side, she could go to the beach anytime she wanted. The library was really close, and the Aquarium was within walking distance. But it was a small apartment. It had three bedrooms, one of which used to be a kitchen. "Where would I put my computer?"

"Gammy's fixing up the attic just for you. She's having a phone jack installed, your very own DSL line. You can plug into that."

Lindsay picked up her lukewarm pizza slice. "When do we have to be out of here?"

"Actually," Mariah said, "by the end of this weekend."

The lump in her belly burned and she set the pizza down. "But that's the day after tomorrow! What are we going to do? Stay up all night and pack?"

Mariah smiled weakly. "I brought boxes home. They're in the back of the car. After you finish eating, go get them and we'll pack the living room. It won't take that long if we do it together."

"I don't want to move."

Her mother reached across the table and brushed Lindsay's hair behind her ears. "Change is never easy, kiddo. Especially at your age, with hormones surging through your body. I'm afraid there really isn't a choice. Not if you want to stay at Country Day."

Hormones. Like one would ever happen to her! Lindsay sat folding her clothes into the box marked "attic." She'd already filled one with books, and carefully rolled her posters inside mailing tubes. Her maps were trickier. *National Geographic* magazine could turn the simple act of folding a map into origami torture. She filled a trashbag with clothes that still fit her, but looked really babyish: pink shorts, ballet shoes, and assorted sweatshirts with stupid designs on them. She wanted to wear Gap clothes now, plain things, and all one solid color. She put her stuffed animals in the "donate" sack, too. Mostly they had taken up space and collected dust, but knowing she'd never see them again was hard. Lots of kids moved, sometimes really often, like if their parents were in the military or criminals or spies, even. But those people weren't moving to a house where other people already lived. And her mom wasn't starting some great new job. No matter how positive her mom tried being about it, this was a step backward.

"I forgot I owned this skirt," Mariah said from her bedroom when Lindsay lugged her boxes down the hall. "I found it squished between some other stuff, so it kind of ironed itself." She held it up, this pale blue denim thing that was way too short for a mom to wear. "I'm going to wear this to work tomorrow."

Lindsay pictured how sexy her mother would look in a short skirt and the white apron she wore when she waitressed. "Why? So Fergus Crabapple will ask you to marry him?"

Mariah laid the skirt down on her bed. She patted the mattress, indicating that Lindsay should join her, but Lindsay stayed where she was. "Do you have a problem with me having a man for a friend?"

Lindsay shrugged. "It's your life. You can have anybody you want for a friend."

"And so can you. Aren't you and this Sandy getting to be pals?"

"Her name's Sally, Mom. She's my science project partner. That's all. Somehow I doubt she might get me pregnant."

Her mother quickly looked away, and Lindsay could see her jaw trembling. She set her boxes down and went to her mom, not touching her but standing close. She knew she was being a brat about all this, but did everything have to change every single week? School started in August now. It took at least a month to get used to going to classes. Cancer, moving, her mother's job; couldn't one good thing happen instead? "I apologize, Mom."

"I know things are hard for you right now," her mother said. Lindsay cringed inwardly at the hurt in her voice. "It might take a while, but I'll find another teaching job. As soon as we're back on our feet, we'll move into our own place. Probably by summer."

Which was nine whole months away. "I really am sorry, Mom. Do you forgive me?"

"Of course," she said, and smiled, but Lindsay could see it wasn't her relaxed smile, and as a result, Lindsay's stomach continued hurting.

On Saturday morning, while her mother and Gammy Bess served customers, and Allegra took a nap, Lindsay began to decorate her attic room. She kind of liked the low ceiling painted a soft pink color, the single hanging light with the blue glass shade. The only place she could stand up straight was in the very center, where the two sides of the roof came to a peak. She angled her bed so there was room for her computer to sit on an orange crate. The Carl Sagan posters went up in chronological order, beginning with him in his orange windbreaker standing next to a satellite in the desert. Next came the promotion poster for his PBS show, *Cosmos,* followed by his author photo poster from when his first book was published. After that she had the ones she'd printed off the internet: Sagan and his wife, Ann, sitting in the woods and looking so in love with each other, and the last one, him bald and his skin yellowish because he was fighting his bone marrow disease and losing, but smiling for the camera.

She thumbtacked the map of the world directly over her bed. On it she had traced a pencil line connecting where Carl Sagan had lived and where he died. She wished she could see inside his house. Sit at his desk for just a few minutes. Maybe the Smithsonian would take all his stuff and build a replica room. Or maybe by now his wife had turned his office into a guest room. That was what people did when someone was never coming back. Gave away their clothes and erased all traces of them. Like her mother had with Lindsay's father.

Down the pull-up ladder stairs, she could hear Allegra being sick in the bathroom. Usually Gammy stayed with her, running a cool washcloth over her neck, but she couldn't serve customers and take care of Allegra at the same time. With only one full bathroom to share among them, Lindsay knew that sooner or later she'd have to pee and the smell of chemicals and barf would make her feel faint.

This room didn't even have a window. You only have to go up there to sleep, her mother said. But that wasn't true. Your room was everything. It was the place you went to cry, or pretend you lived alone, and it was where great Science Fair project ideas either came to you or didn't.

She picked up the card, put it in her pocket, and climbed carefully down the ladder. Taking Khan for a walk was her official chore now. Her feet hit the floor just as her grandmother emerged from the bathroom.

"I made this for you," Lindsay said, handing her the card Sally had designed.

When Allegra reached for the card, Lindsay saw that her hand was shaking. She opened the card and read out loud what it said inside: " 'Don't pay any attention to medical statistics / and when the doctor makes you feel like going ballistic / remember the really nice nana you are / at The Owl & Moon, you are the star.' "

Sally had written it. She really was a writer. Lindsay felt her cheeks stain with color while she waited for Allegra to respond.

"Oh, honey. This is the nicest thing anyone has—"

Lindsay watched her grandmother's face go pale as she braced herself against the wall and made her way to the bathroom again. In her wake, the card fluttered to the carpet. "Do you want me to stay with you?" Lindsay asked the closed door.

"No, I'm fine," she said, and vomited again.

Lindsay waited five whole minutes. Then she asked, "Allegra? Will you be okay by yourself if I take Khan for his walk?"

"Yes" came tiredly from behind the door.

Lindsay didn't wait for her to change her mind.

Downstairs, even though it was Saturday, the man from plaid was there again. Her mother had already had "tea" with him twice. Tonight they were going out for dinner. Lindsay figured her mom would come home late since Lindsay was safe here with her grandmothers. Probably they were already having sexual intercourse. All the books said a woman didn't reach her sexual peak until almost forty, which left her mother seven years. It made Lindsay sick to think of the two of them in some moldy motel. That was where adults went to have sex if they didn't have privacy in their own homes. It could take as long as an hour, or only a few minutes, and around Pacific Grove motels cost a lot, even in winter, so he had better be paying for it.

"Hey, there, pumpkin," Gammy Bess said, carrying two slices of apple pie to table six. "Grab me the cheese slicer, will you? I must be going senile to forget the cheddar. Pretty soon you're going to have to help me remember to put my shoes on the right feet."

Lindsay cut two equally sized hunks. "I'm going to take Khan for a walk, okay?"

Gammy nodded. Lindsay wasn't even sure she'd heard her. Well, it wasn't like anyone would miss her. Her mom was leaning over the counter talking to Scotland. She had her shirt unbuttoned lower than usual. The denim skirt—she'd worn it twice this week—was really cute and for some reason that made her angry. She harnessed up Khan and was headed out when the phone rang.

"Get that, will you, Linds?" her mother said.

Maybe before dinner they would go to his house and do it right then. How many times in a day could you have sexual intercourse before you got tired of it? Did you have to rest after? "Owl and Moon, may I help you?" she said.

"Hey, Lindsay! It's Sally. Do you work at the Owl and Moon? How come you didn't tell me?"

Lindsay paused, not wanting to lie or say too much. "I don't work here. My family owns it. I'm just— It's super busy and they asked me to get the phone."

"That's so cool! Do you get free snacks?"

"Sometimes," Lindsay said, thinking of how gross all the pastry looked at the end of the day. It would take being really starved to want to eat Danish for dinner.

"I got this great idea for our project. Can you come over?"

An invitation to Sally's house? Lindsay wanted to run across the highway right this second, not even look out for cars. "I don't think I could get anyone to drive me."

"No biggie. We'll come get you. Hey, you want to spend the night?"

Lindsay's world stopped. The words rang out like the Mayflower church pealing Sunday bells. She had a friend who liked her so much *she wanted her to spend the night*. "Let me ask." She took hold of her mother's arm. "Sally wants me to spend the night so we can work on our science project. You don't have to take me or anything. She's on the phone right now, so you can talk to her mother. Here." She handed her the phone.

The Scotsman grinned and she noticed his teeth weren't very straight. Or white. She hoped her mother was brushing her teeth after she kissed him because gingivitis could happen to anyone.

"How are you, Lindsay?" he asked.

"Fine," she answered.

"Are you having a good weekend?"

"So far."

He kept on smiling. "Your mum tells me that the school you attend has a rigorous curriculum. One hopes the weekends offer respite."

One hopes? Lindsay stared and said nothing.

"I hear you fancy science. Sounds like a crack idea, collaborating on a project with your friend."

"Sally's the smartest girl at Country Day," Lindsay said.

"Now, you see, that surprises me," Fergus said. "I would have bet my last shilling that honor would belong to you. Has anyone ever told you how like a Robert Burns poem your hair is?"

"I have to go," she said, and bent to untangle Khan's leash.

Mariah talked for a while. Lindsay waited, taking sly looks at the Scotsman. His nose was long. He had eye wrinkles. His name was stupid. Who could look down at their newborn baby and call it Fergus? Fergus the Freak. He could have been as old as Allegra or as young as her mother, but there was no way to tell without talking to him, which she did not intend to do, especially when he said dumb things like that about her hair. Try it on my mother, she wanted to say.

Mariah hung up the phone. "Don't forget your toothbrush, okay?"

Don't you forget that condoms are only ninety-seven percent effective, she wanted to tell her mother, but didn't. "I'll pack as soon as I get back."

"Check this out," Sally said as they made their way up the long winding driveway to DeThomas Farms, having been let out by the mailboxes to walk to the house. "Gregorio, he's the guy that drove us, is teaching me Spanish curse words so I can level Taylor. Want to hear some?"

Lindsay had initially been nervous climbing in the truck being driven by the Mexican guy who had to be at least twenty. Then Sally hung halfway out the window and waved, and suddenly it seemed like this might turn out to be the best day of her life. "Why say anything?" she asked. "Just ignore her."

"It's called psy-ops, Lindsay," Sally said, pulling a sprig from a rosemary bush and placing it under Lindsay's nose so she had to inhale the perfume. "She'll go nuts trying to figure it out."

Lindsay thought it was a bad idea. "What if you just go see Ms. Haverfield and tell her all the mean things Taylor's been doing?"

"She'll just assign us to mediation. Gregorio thinks the curses will shut her up. He's cute, isn't he?"

Lindsay pictured Sally leaning across the café counter flirting with Gregorio, saying *te amo* and *bésame mucho* while Ricky Martin music played in the background. She couldn't imagine wanting to be with a boy. It wasn't hormones that made her get mad these days; any hormone that wanted to come her way was more than welcome. She had no breasts and no hair down there and probably she would never start her period, which was economical but also worrisome. "I think English would be better considering how she keeps saying that stuff about your skin color."

"Good point," Sally said as they came into view of the sprawling farmhouse. "But from now on I'm collecting stuff like that. I'm writing it down in my notebook so I can use it later. That's what a writer does."

Lindsay heard the screech of a parrot, a barking dog, and someone yelling. Shortly thereafter, a brown-and-white rat terrier flew out the dog door, followed by a little girl so blond Lindsay wondered if she might have been dipped in bleach. "That's my cousin, Savannah. The biggest crybaby in the Western Hemisphere."

"Sally," she whimpered. "I can't find Uncle Andy and if I can't I lose at hide-and-seek and I don't want to lose."

"Jeeze Louise, Vanna," Sally said, lifting her cousin into her arms. "How many times do I have to tell you he always hides in the freaking barn? Where else can he go in his wheelchair?"

The little girl snuffled. "I'm scared of the barn. There are cats and owls in there. They might scratch me. Will you take me there?"

"Might as well or we'll never hear the end of it," Sally grumbled. The three girls continued down a flagstone path where Irish moss grew between the rocks, green dotted with tiny white buds.

"Those are fairy flowers," Savannah told Lindsay. "Don't step on them. The fairies only come out when you're asleep."

Lindsay tried to imagine what it would feel like to have a cousin. "I'd like to see a fairy. When do they show up?"

"At night," Savannah said, stepping carefully on the flagstone in her tiny sneakers.

"What time?"

"It depends."

Sally tickled Savannah and made her walk by herself the last few feet to the barn. "That's what we ought to do our project on, the nocturnal habits of fairies. Okay, Vanna, look. Do you see the stack of hay bales? Look carefully at the one on your right. What's that hunk of metal behind it? Here's a hint: It's round and big and someone can sit in it and even do wheelies."

"A wheelchair!" Savannah cried happily, and raced into the barn.

"Brilliant she's not," Sally said.

"How can you know? She's only six."

"All I know is that when I was six I could go in a barn without having a nervous breakdown. She's afraid of everything!"

Lindsay didn't want to admit that there had been a time in her own life when dark corners and animals larger than her invoked that same kind of fear. Even now she set up her bed so she could reach the cord for the light. Sometimes she lay awake in the dark wondering about the noises she heard, which weren't at all like the condo. In the past, whatever science couldn't explain, Allegra could vanquish. That was until the leukemia diagnosis, four weeks ago. It turned out that it wasn't the big things to be afraid of at all, it was the microscopic stuff that could cream you in broad daylight.

"Leave your backpack on the porch, okay? I want to show you the greenhouses."

Lindsay did not want to go into the greenhouse. Greenhouses were humid, which would make her sweat. Sweat gathered in her scalp and frizzed her hair out to freak-show level, which would cause Sally to call Gregorio to drive her back home.

"Wait. You have to meet my horse first." Next to the barn Savannah was terrified of were corrals with metal fences. Sally climbed up. "This is Soul Man," she said, hanging over the top rail and scratching the massive neck of a solid black horse. "Isn't he gorgeous? That's Penelope, my POA. That stands for Pony of the Americas. I let Savannah ride her, but she's mine. You can ride her if you want." She exhaled. "I'm already tired of this year, aren't you? I wish it were summer all year round. I could get on my horse in the morning and not get off until dinner. I'd ride bareback to the creek, and let Soul Man splash around, and omigod, you know what? We have three horses now counting our ancient gelding, Leroy. You can ride along with Vanna and me! Won't that be fun?"

Lindsay looked at the horse's nostrils, flexing and pumping in air. He was as tall as a Humvee, and his hooves looked like if he got mad he might use them to stomp a person to death. No way could she get on a horse. She had to confess. "Actually, I'm afraid of horses."

"Stop it! You are not. Horses are like big, friendly dogs. You could ride Leroy no sweat. He's a freaking antique. If you lit a bomb under him the most he'd do is yawn. If you know how to cue them they mind and you won't get hurt. Besides, I'll teach you everything. And don't forget the science project. It's going to be so much fun. Something we'll remember all our lives. I love that line, 'all our lives.' I'm trying to find where I could put it in my novel. When it's done, I'll let you read it first."

She jumped down off the fence and took Lindsay's hand. That was the moment Lindsay knew that no matter what happened to Allegra, she was going to survive it. Sally would be there. Her friend. She would show Lindsay how to paint or sculpt or whatever horrid thing they were required to do next in art class, and she'd force her to ride a horse. They'd be friends always. They would instant message each other when they couldn't be together and she would introduce Sally to the tree-of-life cypress and Sally wouldn't laugh. "What's it like, having a stepdad?"

"Andy? It's great," Sally said. "He'll play games with Vanna until Aunt Nance yells at him to stop. Part of it is because he can't have any kids himself, but it's hard to figure out why parents love kids, don't you think? I try to be nice and grateful and all, but sometimes I feel like I'm in a cage, you know? I just have to rattle the bars or else go mental."

Until recently Lindsay had never felt that way. Now there were mornings she woke up wanting to scream and **break** every rule and have nothing for breakfast, and when her **mom** pushed cereal she imagined cussing until she ran out of breath. What good did it do to admit feelings you could do nothing about? The pony dropped a steaming pile of hay-riddled poop, and Lindsay said, "We could do our project on how animal waste affects the water table."

"Give me a break," Sally said. "Isn't it torture enough to have to clean it up every day?"

"But it's a legitimate inquiry."

"Yeah, yeah, but it's too safe. We need a topic that borders on dangerous, and I've already thought of one."

"What do you mean, 'dangerous'?"

"You know," Sally said, weaving between rows of corn that held a few drying ears. "A hot topic. Something people like to argue about. And for sure something that leaves Taylor, Avril, and everybody else's projects in the dust."

"Well," Lindsay said, "I do have this one kind of radical idea."

"Me, too," Sally said. "But tell me yours first."

"Do you promise not to laugh?"

She held out her hand. "I pinky swear."

They linked little fingers. "Okay, you know how my grandmother has cancer?"

"Yeah. It's really sad, Linds."

"The chemotherapy makes her really sick, and she's worried that even with insurance she'll probably never pay off the bills completely. The insurance company already sent her a letter about her rates increasing. But the thing is," Lindsay said, "she doesn't want to eat. It's from the medicine. The doctor gives her pills, but they don't work. She's lost twelve pounds since they found out she had it and she was skinny to start with."

Sally pushed open the door to the greenhouse and Lindsay felt the damp heat loosen her pores. "So what are you saying? We investigate health insurance? Or chemotherapy's effects on middle-aged women?"

Lindsay shook her head. "According to the internet, the one thing that can really help cancer patients get over their nausea, well, it's marijuana."

Sally smiled. "I like it. Continue."

"A person has to practically be dead to get it medically. And you have to register with the state. Your name goes on a

government list, and Allegra says there's nothing more dangerous than the government having your name on a list. There're
growers all over California who sneak it into their crops and
sell it, not like pushers to get kids high, they sell it to people
with cancer. But if either one of them gets caught, it's a mis-
demeanor or a felony, depending on the amount."

"That's a completely stupid law, but it's not a science
project."

Lindsay cleared her throat. "But it could be."

"How?"

"There're so many ways. How do the illegal growers plan
their crops, farm them secretly, and what does that cost? Then
there are the medical effects. Chemically, what does cannabis
do to the human body when you have cancer? Is it dangerous
the way smoking is? If it's been proven to help cancer patients
or AIDS patients, why can't it be made legal and easy to get
from the private sector? Does insurance cover it, or do they try
to get out of it? Viagra had a shorter investigative study than
any other medicine besides Minoxidil and now Viagra's impli-
cated in blindness. The ethics part is that we could look into
the costs for drugs that don't work versus the complications
patients have to go through to get it. I know it's too broad a
topic. But if I could do it right, that would be my dangerous
project. The scientific and social issues of medical marijuana."

Sally began to dance in place. "Omigod, it's like we're
reading each other's minds. I can't wait until you hear my idea.
Well, I should just show you."

She pulled Lindsay by the arm through row after row of
hanging plants: fuchsias, geraniums, pothos, coleus, and more
Lindsay didn't know the names of. Then they came to the
taller plants: four-foot-tall ficus trees, false aralias, and dieffen-
bachia. In the second to last row, three-quarters of the way
down, she showed Lindsay some tall green plants. "Guess
what that is?"

Judging by the skunky smell, Lindsay had a pretty good
idea. "Where did you get it?"

"Gregorio grows it for his dad who has rheumatoid arthritis. It's the only thing that helps relieve his pain enough for him to walk. Think of it: Our project is right here, and it's already been started!"

Emboldened by the presence of the living, breathing thing she had been wondering about, Lindsay began to worry. "What if we don't have enough time? We'll need to analyze how long it takes to make it, and the purity of homegrown strains in contrast with government. How much time is there?"

"We have until the end of November, so relax. Gregorio keeps charts on everything. We can use his data as a head start," Sally said, cackling. "Isn't it wonderfully dangerous? For one thing, it's making something political out of something that has nothing to do with votes or hard drugs at all."

"That's the part that bothers me," Lindsay said. "Just for smoking something that helps my grandmother not lay on the bathroom floor all day. How can that be a crime?" Her underarms were damp from the humidity, and she'd forgotten about her hair. "You wouldn't believe how stupid some people are, Sally. They think you can catch cancer just by touching someone who has it. Which means we shouldn't use her real name or people wouldn't come to the café. I don't know. Maybe it's too complicated."

Sally got that look on her face like when she had gotten the better of Taylor. "You are abso-freaking-lutely right it's complicated! And if we do it together, we'll win first place and the scholarship. We don't have to base it all on your gramma. Shoot, my aunt Ness has been HIV positive since before I was born. Her husband died of it. She started this foundation thing in his name and I'm sure she knows some people with AIDS who use marijuana and might be able to give us enough testimony to make our claims unbiased. We'll just call them Subject one, two, and three. Anonymous."

Lindsay looked down at the pea-size gravel that lined the greenhouse floor, with its mossy cast, like lichen. "We could get arrested."

"Who cares?" Sally said. "We're twelve! Are they going to throw us in jail? Getting arrested would be great publicity. It could only help us. We have to do this as a team. That way we each take half the blame. Gregorio is always starting new crops. He showed me how he charts their progress. So there's a whole bunch of the work already done. We'll factor how much electricity and water it takes, and how much medicine one little plant makes. An individual crop for an individual patient. 'How much does it cost to feel better, not just get high,' that will be our thesis statement." She held out her hands as if they were standing in front of a billboard. "What do you think of that?"

"That's really good," Lindsay said.

"Good?" Sally said. "It's freaking great. People will go nuts. And the best part is your grandmother having cancer makes it relevant! We can like *dedicate* the project to her! The judges will freaking cry like babies! It's so far beyond an A it's off the charts. This alone will get us into Ivy League colleges."

"College?" Lindsay said. "We haven't even gone to high school."

"I already told you, there is no way I am going to high school," Sally said. "If I can't weasel out of it I'll condense it to two years. What a bore to have to sit around and wait for slowpokes to learn verb tenses and algebra theorems I already know. I was thinking I'd write my first novel instead of high school. Or sign up with Americorps to build schools in Mexico. What's high school anyway? Four years of cheesy classes, enforced school spirit, and feeling crappy because now not only will no girls like me but boys won't either? It's jail, Linds. It's social incarceration. A gulag. My aunt Beryl was in jail once. Prison, actually. She killed her husband. Now she's out and she has a regular life, and a husband who used to be a detective."

"You can do that?" Lindsay asked.

Sally nodded. "Of course! You can do whatever you want if you want it bad enough. Man, Lindsay. For someone so

damn smart you are too naïve for words! Taylor and the lemmings? The only reason they're at Country Day is their parents
have money. You and me, we're the ones with the future. You
gotta start believing in yourself or they'll walk all over you.
Believe me, you have more brains in your little finger than all
of Taylor's pack animals yoked together."

Lindsay tried to take it all in. Being friends with Sally was
like receiving all the presents on your wish list. Every part of
her insides was shaking.

"Separate, you and me, we're smart. Together, though?
We're brilliant," Sally said. "We are going to put together the
best damn science project on medical marijuana that old
Country Day will ever see. Not only that, we are going to
get our pictures in the paper, and probably make the news,
even, and I will totally lay down money that after this, Westinghouse will be begging us to take their stinkin' scholarships."

Sally laughed her winner's laugh, the joy-filled chortle of
someone who's figured out that the trick to getting out of a
maze is to simply follow the shrubbery on the left. If Sally
were on the periodic table of elements, she'd be mercury. She
had the ability to slip away from anything that tried to slow
her down. "Why?" Lindsay asked.

"Because!" Sally chortled. "It isn't just cancer and AIDS
patients, it helps old people with glaucoma. Man, am I glad I
stole those seeds from Gregorio's toolbox."

"You *stole* his marijuana seeds? I thought you said he let
you see his charts willingly."

"Well, what was he going to do? Rat on me to my mom,
'Hey, your kid swiped the pot I'm growing illegally on your
farm?' "

"I don't know," Lindsay said. "This sounds pretty risky."

"I *do* know," Sally said and stood up, brushing the dirt off
her jeans. She tilted her face up and smiled. "Do you smell
that?"

"Smell what?"

"Hamburgers cooking! I love it when it's Andy's turn to cook. I am so hungry I could eat a tree. Race you to the house!"

Sally shot out of the greenhouse like a rocket, but Lindsay lingered a moment, fingering the green marijuana leaf, imagining the smile on Allegra's face when she handed her the fruits of their project.

6
Allegra

ALLEGRA LAY ON THE COUCH, her head throbbing like a Jamaican steel drum. No matter how many acupuncture treatments she had, Krishna Dahvid, in his traditional white robes against a surfer's tan, always surprised her with something nice. Today, he'd brought along a portable Zen fountain, which beat the army of get-well cards—except for Lindsay's—propped up on the windowsill. Every morning he rose at dawn and headed out to surf. She imagined him stepping into the water, thinking the sound of the ocean, that's what Allegra needs. Imagining was her main source of amusement lately, thanks to chemo. While the fountain gurgled and the smell of burning moxa incense filled the air, he took her pulses. Allegra hoped the treatment he gave her today would drive away the headache and ease her nausea. With her mouth raw in places from throwing up, it was difficult to eat. "Best diet ever," she joked with the nurses. At least she still had her hair.

Allegra worried that the moxa incense didn't cover the weird, electric aroma emanating from her body. Probably the result of the chemo, it stayed in her nostrils twenty-four/seven-eleven, as Gammy would say.

"Remind me again why I'm allowing perfect strangers to pipe poison into my body?"

"Because you want to live."

"Oh, right." She shut her eyes, trying to relax, but they popped back open. "All these years I imagined myself the courageous person who'd throw her own 'death-day party,' gather my friends around while I took an overdose and listened to Jerry Garcia."

"And?" came his gentle voice.

"I'm four weeks into this mess and willing to eat mothballs if it means I get to stick around. And that's about how it's turned out, hasn't it?"

"Shh," he said. "Take a deep breath. Here comes a needle."

Dahvid was deft. Allegra felt only a momentary sting on the underside of her wrist. He did the other wrist, and then moved to her legs, running his finger up and down her shins, tracing meridians. He placed two needles in each leg, and then she felt him cover her torso with a flannel blanket. "Rest," he said.

But how could she when October was passing by without her? Her granddaughter stood poised on the lip of womanhood. Any minute now she'd break into blossom like that James Wright poem about the horses at the fence. Mariah had been shy about developing, and secretive. Mariah never wanted to talk. If only she would get that broom out of her butt and bed that handsome Scotsman. They could have this grand love affair, something Mariah could tell stories about when she was an old lady, Allegra imagined. Her stomach gurgled.

"Did you eat today?" Krishna whispered.

Allegra couldn't recognize hunger pangs anymore. "Why put anything in when it's just going to come back up?"

"You need to eat."

"My gut thinks otherwise."

"Allegra." He paused a moment. "I know where you stand on street drugs, but a little weed might help you get started. I know an organic grower, a safe connection."

"No."

"Will you think about it? It could give you a little peace."

She didn't answer. There would be no peace so long as she held on to the secret that Mariah's father was here, living among them. Allegra played dumb at every checkup when Doc asked questions.

It must have been challenging, raising Mariah without a father.

Not really. I had Mama.

I wish you'd met my mother, Allegra. I swear, the way Mariah holds her chin up, she reminds me of her.

Mariah has the kind of face that reminds everyone of someone else.

That daughter of yours—where did she get all the determination and drive? I bet she could do anything she set her mind to—even med school.

It's the yo-yo effect, lazy mother, diligent daughter.

Carrying the secret was like allowing a harpy to fly around loose in the apartment. A harpy with Mariah's scowling face. She squawked out the same question she always did. Who's my father? Why won't you tell me? I just want his name, not his kidneys!

Allegra took a cleansing breath, and blew it out. Then another. She willed her meridians to loosen the clogged-up chi. Her head throbbed. Too weak to walk among the living, she needed something more substantial than daytime television, and it was shocking how tired her arms could get from the effort of holding up a book. And being kept from Khan was absolute torment.

"You know, it's a week since I've seen a single customer. I don't know how Kiki's divorce is going. I can't remember if I told Mariah to buy nutmeg."

"Be here, Allegra. Be still and listen."

"I'm trying."

When pressed for news, Mariah said everything was the same as yesterday, customers in a hurry who left pitiful tips.

Which meant her tableside manner had not improved. How *had* Mariah turned out all brain and prissiness? Even Gammy was less of a hard-ass. Long ago Allegra had stopped trying to find answers to those questions. Doc was Mariah's father. How would she react when she learned her mother was keeping that secret from her because she was too afraid to tell him?

"Allegra, you're not relaxing."

"I can't. I have so much on my mind."

Krishna Dahvid sighed. "What's your favorite time of year?"

"Summer."

"Okay. Imagine a warm summer wind outside your window. Feel it enter your lungs, carrying goodness to every cell. Exhale your worries."

"What if I'm not worried? What if I'm downright pissed off at cancer?"

He rubbed her arm. "Anger is bad for your heart chakra. Anger gets stuck in places like the liver. Let it go. Your liver needs to breathe."

"My liver must be royally pissed off," Allegra said. "There is nothing happening here other than my head pounding and my angry liver being angry. Do you have any Tylenol?"

He put his hands on his hips. "How can I help you unless you're willing to participate in the process?"

"I'm trying now. I promise."

Her ear itched. She scratched it, dislodging a needle. Krishna Dahvid reinserted the needle. Allegra shut her eyes and immediately a harpy with Mariah's face swooped through her mind. More came with it, a flock large enough to make her wish she had a flyswatter, but she tried to watch them without feeling. The portable fountain swished and Krishna Dahvid removed the needles, dabbing the insertion points with Tiger Balm. He rang his bell to indicate the session had ended. Allegra tried to sit up, but the room spun.

"Lie still for a bit," Krishna Dahvid said.

She watched him pack up his bamboo doctor's bag. Having others do for her had never sat well with Allegra. She was the one everyone came to for nursing or soothing.

Krishna Dahvid took her hand in his. "Come on now, time to say our affirmations."

"I don't feel up to it today. Can't I just think them privately?"

"'Allegra Moon,'" he started.

"All right, all right. Allegra Moon," she said, "this is a brand-new day, no matter what time you start it. Chemo is temporary. You're nearly through your scheduled treatments. You will heal yourself more quickly if you meditate. You are in control of your faculties and environment. Remember to . . ."

She glanced at him, and his lips moved along with hers. "Breathe."

"Good. Now try to get some sleep."

She could hear him cleaning up. But the problem with Mariah was that nothing was ever enough. She self-sabotaged. Bought a beautiful new car—but oh, the payments! An "Excellent" on Lindsay's anatomy test was terrific news—but was all this early success going to push her into a nervous break-down? Ohs and buts tempered every facet of her daughter's life. Yes, she was an adult, but somehow Allegra had failed to convince her daughter that life was to be lived, relished, to greet every new day like the miracle it was and to wring every single drop of enjoyment out of it.

"Do you need refills on your herbal supplements?" Krishna asked.

"No."

"Why not? By my reckoning you should be out."

"Doc won't let me take them."

"How about your wheatgrass?"

She barely suppressed a gag. "Please, not another word unless you want to mop barf off your robes."

Mariah wouldn't even try wheatgrass shots. She had no time to meditate, recycle, or gather signatures for a meaningful protest. Vitamins? A waste of money. Pop-Tarts and Diet

Coke? Breakfast of champions. Allegra shut her eyes and placed her hands over them. Her headache had moved in permanently, she feared. She felt Dahvid's warm hands on the balls of her feet, where the skin used to be tough from dancing. Now it felt paper thin.

"How's your head? Better?"

"Still hurts," she managed.

"I'll do the pressure points in your feet. That often helps."

"Thank you."

"Allegra, a lot of wonderful things have happened to you this year. Picture yourself in one of those places."

The beach. She thought of a day at the beach with Mariah and Lindsay. Khan was there, his little paws damp with sand.

"Re-create the scene, leaf by twig. Place every grain of sand, every piece of driftwood, each gull's cry."

She felt the pinch of a needle and the electric shock of her chi and gasped. She pictured herself in the café kitchen, breathing in steamy bergamot tea, and reaching for the feverfew capsules. Doc insisted no herbal medicine; it could muddy up her test results. Remember good things, she reminded herself. Her Meals on Wheels days, which were now covered by another volunteer. The women's shelter. She hadn't popped in for ages. Dancing at her favorite club. Sex with a partner who just wanted to have fun. Sex, period. But days at the beach ended, sunsets were brief, and she didn't want to listen to the radio because when a favorite song ended, so did the dance. There was no lasting passion in sex with someone you didn't love. Nada. Not since Doc.

Doc had resurfaced at the worst possible time. She was almost fifty, dried up like an old walnut. Her life would play out like a World War II movie, a romance that might have been; only in her case, instead of Nazis, goose-stepping leukocytes. Doc would do his valiant best, but eventually those cells would beat him down. All that would be left of them was Mariah. Hurricane Mariah.

The February day when Mariah was born had been rainy

and gloomy. Business was slow. Allegra labored right upstairs from The Owl & Moon in her own bed, with a midwife in attendance. Mariah was stubborn, even then. Twenty hours of labor, she fought to stay where she was.

Gammy patted Allegra's face with a washcloth drenched in warm water and herbs. Chamomile to calm her, vervain for energy, and essence of roses because after pushing for three hours straight a girl needed to smell roses. When Allegra could push no more and dissolved in tears, the mother of all contractions stabbed her, so of course that was the moment Mariah decided to be born, when her mother was drained dry and out of tears and screaming.

"Relax," Krishna Dahvid said.

Relax, the midwife had said, too.

And then out shot Mariah, the angriest little baby in the world, eyes wide, shocked that from here on in, she had to breathe on her own, mad at the world.

Allegra had never felt so tired, so used up, so done in until that moment, but this illness trumped it. She'd named her daughter Mariah for the wind, but Mariah was fire. No before yes. Mariah was a rag-shaking terrier, who had only to hear the word *rat* to start digging. The harpies circled.

Who's my father? Who's my father? Who's my father?

He's John Muir, Mariah. Abe Lincoln. Mahatma Gandhi. He's the man in the moon.

Allegra felt herself drift into sleep, and dimly noted the sounds of Krishna Dahvid's steps, the click of the door opening, then shutting. He wasn't gone more than thirty minutes before her stomach rumblings returned full force. She groaned and sat up, and as she pushed the hair away from her face, a whole chunk of hair came out in her hand. She stared at it, roots and all, trying to believe what had just happened. The nurses had warned her, but Allegra vainly believed that that side effect would slide by her. The first time Doc touched her hair, he'd put his whole face into it, breathing. Black satin, he called it. Before the tears could take hold, Allegra uncapped her antinausea medication, tapped two pills into her palm, and then swallowed them dry. They didn't do much, other than to lodge her between almost sleep and actual sleep. In a half-hour she knew she'd feel the buzz that hitched a ride along with the medicine, and that was enough.

Thirty-three years ago, everyone wanted to feel like Allegra did now. They'd do anything to get high—drop acid, smoke hash, chant Hare Krishna for hours on end, drink horrid cheap wine, and dance themselves into dehydration. Allegra managed to convey the illusion she was doing drugs, but truthfully, she was a member of the drink-dance-a-little-pot-when-it-was-available crowd. Only in the right circumstances, though. Pot made her hungry, and when you were hitchhiking around the state and had no money, you did not want to feel hungry. She liked to take one or two puffs, just enough to take the edge off the world.

No matter how many lectures she heard on the Tim Leary/Aldous Huxley mind-expanding qualities of LSD, she was too scared to try it. When Art Linkletter's kid took a dive off a hotel balcony, Allegra decided drugs were poison. They didn't matter. The sixties and seventies were all about love.

The Beatles had gotten that part wrong. Love wasn't all a person needed. No matter how beautifully Joni Mitchell sang the lyrics, for a lasting bond, you needed that piece of paper from City Hall.

Allegra blamed her own hair for much of her unhappiness. Hers hung down to her waist. She enjoyed girls' jealous stares. She used her hair to draw close whichever boy she wanted, and she had wanted Doc. Him in that buckskin jacket with fringe and beads, his hair down to his shoulders, and a beard that somehow made the whole package irresistible. She decided then and there, Doc would be her first lover.

They'd met hitchhiking in Mendocino. He'd come home from Vietnam, where he'd been a medic, just six months before. They introduced themselves—Alvin, like the chipmunk. Alice, as in Wonderland, laughed, and decided to use only road names from that moment forward. To have a summer adventure. Not to hold each other accountable for the past or the future, but to be here now. This was Doc's last free summer before entering medical school. He told her right off that he was as good as engaged to the daughter of his family's best friends. He showed Allegra a picture of a horse-faced girl named Ruth.

"Do you love her?" Allegra asked, because Alice wouldn't have been so bold.

Doc said, "We've known each other since we were babies."

"But do you love her?"

"I like her all right. She's smart and everything, but no, I can't honestly say I love her."

"So why on earth are you planning to marry her?" Allegra asked as they rolled out their sleeping bags on a bluff overlooking the ocean. The sun was going down in one of those goldfish bowl sunsets Dylan Thomas had written about, and Allegra desperately wished it would linger.

"Med school costs, you know? My parents will pay for it, but there's always a string attached."

"A string? Sounds to me like it's a rope with a big noose on the end."

He sighed. "It's family. Hers, ours—business, social crap—I don't want to talk about it because it will bum me out."

"Marriage is a life sentence," Allegra said, "and I don't mean that in a good way. Hey, don't you qualify for benefits being a veteran? There are always student loans. No matter what it costs, it'll be cheaper in the long run if you pay for it yourself."

Then the sun set, he kissed her under redwood trees so ancient they predated Christ, and the fact that someday Doc would be wearing a white coat seemed distant and dreamlike. The ocean roared, birds settled in their nests, and all across the sky stars winked at them while they lay in their sleeping bags, each waiting for the other to make the first move. Allegra knew it wouldn't be just "sex." She also knew that Doc wasn't sleeping any more than she was. When he whispered in her ear "Alice?" she put her finger to his mouth and shushed him. "Call me Allegra, remember," she said, and he kissed her finger, and that was how it had begun.

Allegra woke, her headache was gone; the buzz of the pills had vamoosed. She picked up the bedside phone, winced at the effort, and dialed the café.

"Owl and Moon," Gammy said. "Bess speaking."

"Hi, Mama. It's me."

"It's about time! I was starting to worry you weren't ever going to wake up. I came up there once, but that hippie pin fiend chased me away. Feeling better?"

"A little. How's business?"

"Let me hold the phone out so you can listen. Everyone, say get well to my daughter."

The roar in Allegra's ear made her eyes fill with tears. She wanted to be schlepping plates and making the Springerle cookies using the custom owl and moon stamp. "Thanks, Mama," she said when Gammy was back on the line.

"Hang on a second."

She heard her mother ringing up customers, Simon furiously hammering at the bell for her to pick up orders. He never did that when Allegra was there. She heard her mother say, "Can you just wait a cotton pickin' minute?" and assumed that was directed at Simon.

"It's crazy around here, Alice. I have to go. You want me to send up a tray?"

"Just a cup of miso soup. I don't know how much my stomach can take."

She hung up the phone and picked up the handful of hair that had come out, studying it. Before leukemia, Gammy had told her if she wanted to keep wearing it long she had better start braiding it. Women get to an age, she said, helmet hair makes sense. You don't want to look like a witch.

Had that been the sum of her? A loose broad with excellent hair?

When Allegra next woke up it was dusky out, a little after five PM. At this time of day she was usually sweeping the floor, emptying trash, the smell of garbage giving the alley a fruity tang, and oily rainbows from the delivery trucks' tires glinting on the cobblestone. Somebody's dog was barking. Khan joined in. Five o'clock meant his handful of kibble and a walk to the park, where he could huff and growl and make believe the deer were afraid of him, and then take the teeniest little poop, so small that it was hardly worth picking up, but Allegra did anyway. She missed her little man as fiercely as she missed Pacific Grove. Her town was precious, just as valuable as the butterfly grove, the twisted cypress and coastal pine, Fisherman's Wharf and Cannery Row that Steinbeck made famous. So much history had happened there. A few hours north, even more history was made, most of it musical.

Country Joe and the Fish. Janis Joplin. Those old blues players, Mance Lipscomb, Blind Lemon Jefferson, Bessie Smith. Hare Krishnas handing out free sticks of incense. Flower children in bloom. Gays kissing each other in broad daylight. Native Americans story talking. Allegra Moon, age fifteen, sitting on the stone bench in Golden Gate Park, weaving a macramé belt she planned to give to her friend Doc. After that first night, they'd run naked into the freezing cold ocean to baptize themselves forever as lovers in the summer of love. It felt like time speeded up, that it was running out of the hourglass a hundred miles an hour. When Doc came loping up to the bench, shouting her name, she dropped the weaving in the grass. He picked her up and twirled her around. "I got us tickets!" he said. "Right up front. Can you believe it?" Allegra couldn't remember what concert it was, only that the way his voice went squeaky at the end made her realize she wasn't the only one so happy.

They danced around the campfire on Stinson Beach. Swam naked in Lake Tahoe. Did they climb the rocks to Bridal Veil Falls in Yosemite, or was that a future plan? She remembered peeking into the box marked "free puppies" as they walked down Telegraph Avenue in Berkeley. "I'm taking the runt," she said, and in her hands Lieutenant Uhuru made little grunting noises because she missed her mother. With a lump in her throat, Allegra did, too, and wished she were in her mother's apartment, eating popcorn or trail mix or nothing at all. Doc told Allegra, "If you tuck that puppy in your shirt, you can keep her warm and she can feel your heartbeat at the same time."

From then on, she slept between them.

The sex was so powerful that Allegra got scared. The facts of sex, she knew. You could get venereal disease or pregnant. But in her head the theme from *Dr. Zhivago* drowned out everything else. Doc was slow and gentle. That first time, when he slid all the way inside, she gasped, and he placed his hand on the small of her back, waiting for her to catch up. He knew where to pet her. How to cup her breasts and kiss her nipples, and to look down at her as if to say all this was special. Afterward, he held her in his arms. When Lieutenant Uhuru bit him on the leg, they laughed so hard that the puppy growled. Doc gave the dog a tiny piece of beef jerky.

Sometimes they did it all night, and slept late. Other times they were lazy. Once they were alone in the forest, and things just happened. In the middle of a dusty trail lined with ferns, they had opened their eyes to see a curious jay staring at this strange, noisy human mess blocking the path.

Free love, bah! When you spent twenty-four hours a day with a man, when you told each other your secrets, when Spam heated over a campfire became a gourmet repast, you were in love. She had spent that summer suspended between fear and bliss. They never said the words, but she knew he felt the same way. Only one problem loomed in their future: He was heading off to medical school, and already engaged to this equine Ruth. What did Allegra have to compete with all that?

Her heart was her only wealth, so she gave it entirely.

"Anybody home?" she heard a man call out, and there was Fergus Applecross, standing in her bedroom and her looking a fright. She pulled the afghan up to her neck. "What are you doing here?"

"I brought your tray," he said.

Allegra tried to cover her bald spot. "Where's Mariah?"

He set the tray on the end table. "Down the stairs, making a wedding cake."

"Who's getting married?"

"I'm afraid I dunno. Mariah's good at cakes, is she?"

Allegra settled back against the pillows that allowed her to sit upright. The dizziness passed, and she sighed, tucking her fallen hair beneath her covers. "Did she tell you she was a college professor? It was stinky of them to let her go after so many years."

"I'm afraid the academic world has its own set of rules. Do you need help with your tray?"

"I'm fine." Allegra took little sips from her spoon. "This doesn't taste like miso soup."

He frowned. "I didn't watch it being made, so I can't attest to it being what you asked for."

She took another spoonful.

"Any better?"

"Oh, everything tastes like some kind of fluid you'd find in a car engine. But I'll get it down." She finished a quarter of the bowl before her stomach decided she was pressing her luck. "I feel like a prisoner of war."

"I suppose, in a sense, you are. But you mustn't give up, Allegra. Your family, your customers—every day when I have my breakfast they're asking after you. 'Tis not small talk, either. They admire you. I must say, I do, too. I heard a rumor that you were instrumental in starting the homeless shelter."

She felt tears gather in her eyes. "Back when I was in fighting form I had energy to burn. I did a lot of things."

"What a lovely effort. Too many people have problems these days. A good hot meal can be a blessing. It can send a bloke on to better things."

She wanted to get onto the subject of Mariah, but her mouth hurt, and it was time for *Star Trek* reruns. "I don't mean to be rude," she said, "but . . ."

"Say no more," he said, rising to collect the tray and her napkin. "A pleasure to visit with you. Keep fighting, Allegra. You'll beat this thing. Tirrah."

When he was gone, she picked up the clicker and found Captain Kirk in an embrace with a beautiful woman who would turn out to be an alien. It was a rerun she'd seen a hundred times over, but this was the first time she identified so completely with the alien.

II

Serve soup. Believe it is chocolate.

—STÉPHANE GRAPPELLI,
gypsy violinist

7
Mariah

THE THIRD WEEK IN OCTOBER the weather was wet and foggy, impossible to distinguish from the week before. Mariah, out late with Fergus, had overslept, so when she dropped the heavy dough hook mixer attachment on her foot, she could only blame herself. She pulled off her shoe and examined the bruise already rising. Because there was nobody else to decorate twelve dozen pumpkin cookies, she stuffed her throbbing foot back into her tennis shoe, washed her hands, and spread orange buttercream onto the cooled cookies. Next, she filled the frosting sleeve with black, and lined the cookies with happy grins.

"Did you notice the puddle under the dishwasher?" Simon asked as he hung up his jacket.

Mariah shrugged. "Maybe something spilled?"

"Something spilled, all right," Simon said, bending down to look at the dishwasher. "The thing's incontinent." He opened the dishwasher door and a mildewlike odor filled the room. "Rocking bad news, Mariah. The dishes inside it are still dirty."

Mariah couldn't look. Allegra was ill, Gammy had lost at bingo, and Lindsay was obsessed with her science project to the point that she was getting stomachaches on a daily basis. Fergus, the fabulous kisser, had informed her he was headed home to Scotland in May. "I don't care how you do it," Mariah said. "Fix it with duct tape if you have to."

"I may be many things, Mariah, but a magician is not one of them," Simon answered, using a screwdriver to expose the machine's guts. "If I were, I would have sent Bess to another galaxy ages ago."

"Please," Mariah said. "I can't take one more thing going wrong today. I know this is terrible, but I can't stop wishing Mr. Cashin's grandkids would park him in a home. Any home, so long as it isn't mine."

Simon laughed. "Get some coffee. As soon as I get the soups started, I'll wash the dishes, but you're going to have to dry them."

Mariah filled a mug and stood by the window, watching the sunrise. One of the many deer from the cemetery was nibbling greenery. How come things worked out just fine for some people and others could spend their whole lives trying to grab a shred of that? Was the easy life random? Had leukemia hit her mother utterly by chance? Was it the same kind of chance that made Lindsay's father take off? She wished she knew where Ephraim was now, because she could sure use the child support to pay Lindsay's tuition, not to mention Allegra's hospital bills. The insurance people were the Antichrist. They made a game out of denying every claim, and then required notes from Dr. Goodnough. It didn't matter what he said. In the end they'd pay only half, or a quarter of the bill submitted. The debt continued to mount, and bills began to arrive stamped overdue, which made Mariah want to go directly to the insurance company and ask them "What if your mother got cancer? What if some doughnut-eating insurance bimbo like you was doing this to your mother?" Whenever she called them the line was busy.

The deer continued browsing.

Health insurance was the perfect example of society's

decline. Based on a hierarchy of rich old white men driving Jaguars and playing golf in Hawaii, the industry depended on the working class to keep things running. This meant the more claims the employees denied, the richer and happier the golfers became. Eventually the employees noticed they weren't getting anywhere near a Jaguar. Something had to give. This explained their predilection for denying claims. Maybe, if they denied the most that month, they got a nickel raise. When they declined to pay for the added dose of methotrexate her mother needed, all Mariah felt was rage. Who were these deniers? Her peers. Her fellow working-class citizens, who were no doubt busy planning office potlucks or playing Free Cell on their computers, or choosing which Krispy Kreme doughnut to have at break time.

Why couldn't her family catch a goddamn break?

Just then she heard the familiar whirr and whoosh of the dishwasher. "I could kiss you!" Mariah yelled to Simon.

"Please," he answered, "restrain yourself."

The café was so busy all day that Mariah didn't have time to count her tips. Judging from the bulge in her apron, she figured they were substantial. She seated a party of four in the yellow booth and handed them menus. "What can I bring you for drinks?" she asked.

"Coffee for me," said the mousy-haired mom. Her daughter asked please, could she have a Coke. Her son said please, too. The husband/dad in his sky blue cardigan looked like he worked a steady job with normal hours and health benefits the insurer paid right away whenever he filed a claim. All day long the customers rolled right off Mariah, but this family, enjoying one another's company, gave her that "I've wasted my life and shortchanged Lindsay" feeling.

"I don't suppose you serve macchiato?" the father asked. "We're celebrating my promotion."

"Congratulations," Mariah said, writing their order. "I'm

afraid you have to go to Starbucks for that kind of thing, but I can add a shot of vanilla."

"Great," he said.

"Our specials today," Mariah said, pasting her server's smile on her face, "are pumpkin soup with roasted red peppers, and Hungarian mushroom with tarragon. I'll be back shortly with your drinks."

Maybe if she'd stayed home with Lindsay for five years instead of toughing it out in college that could have been her family. Were she still teaching, she'd be knee-deep in student portfolios. Her grad students' fieldwork reports would be coming due, and every office hour she had would be filled with a waiting list. Instead, she poured Cokes, located the dusty bottle of vanilla syrup, and doctored coffee. Then it was back to the kitchen, pick up their orders, wash her hands again—it was cold season—and move on to the next table.

October featured Pacific Grove's Tomato Festival. Silly people dressed up like the plump red globes for old-fashioned, corny fun that warmed residents up for the crown jewel, November's Butterfly Festival. There was a parade and a butterfly queen, but the magic was in the monarchs themselves. During "clustering season," a tree trunk could turn black and orange, covered with hundreds of wings. The Grove Path was deliberately unmarked. Only a few visitors were allowed each day. The sight of a thousand butterflies was humbling. Scientists could calculate their life cycles, but they hadn't a clue as to why they returned to Pacific Grove instead of someplace else.

So it made sense for Pacific Grove to claim the butterflies like a trademark. Were she in class, teaching, Mariah would tell her students about societal façade, a community's longing for gemeinschaft, a concept defined in the early 1900s by the German sociologist Ferdinand Tonnies. A community that had worked together to better themselves didn't want to forget their roots. The time she used to spend throwing five-syllable words around, babying students with personal crises, or arguing in faculty meetings seemed wasted now. At night she picked up one of her mother's romance novels, and after mocking the many euphemisms for sex, she studied this strange concept of romantic love like a high school freshman. Of course, the star-crossed lovers would find their happy ending, but it felt great to stop dissecting human behavior. What made people tick wasn't automobiles or money or even one's zip code. It was the human heart, plain and simple, craving its other half. Mariah's had softened, thanks to Fergus's stories of peat bogs and castles, and all that good kissing. Simply put, he activated long-dormant hormones.

In her old life, all she and Lindsay did was rush from here to there. Now Mariah set the alarm for four AM, got up and baked like her mother had before she got sick. Those dark hours in the kitchen gave her plenty of time to think. Lindsay's science project kept her occupied. Gammy's bingo buddies alleviated her bickering with Simon. Mariah tried to sit with Allegra, not just when she was throwing up her guts, but the truth was, she couldn't stand to look at the sallow skin and thinning hair. Only a few more weeks of chemo remained, but what if all her mother's efforts turned out to be for nothing in the end?

She rang up three customers and boxed the last of the rosemary-garlic Cheese Pennies she'd made from her mother's recipe. Nibbling a broken one, she could no longer tell the difference between hers and Allegra's. She turned the page on her order pad for the last customer of the day. In two hours, Fergus would be by, taking her to dinner again. It was a doomed relationship, but it got her out of the café, and she relished those breaks the way a plant turned to sunlight. Mariah turned on the neon sign, and then went to wait on the elderly couple at the window table.

"Sorry," they said, rising to leave. "Didn't realize the time. All we wanted was soup. Could we get it to go?"

Mariah hesitated. If Allegra had been in her place, she would have let the couple stay, and cleaned up while they ate, chatting to them. But Mariah was tired, and she needed a shower. "Of course," she said. "Let me get the containers."

In the kitchen, Simon was loading the dishwasher. He looked up from the powdered detergent. "Don't even breathe on this thing or it will fall apart."

Mariah capped the soup containers and put two plastic spoons in her apron pocket. She threw in a couple packets of crackers, and then hesitated at the doorway. "I'll put up an electric fence. Simon, all your help—" she felt a lump rise in her throat and commanded it to retreat. "Thank you."

"Are we having a wee bout of PMS?"

"Gammy's right," Mariah said. "You are evil."

"Oh, please," he said. "I'm the only person around here who tells the truth."

She didn't take the bait, instead, she watched as he turned a screw on the dishwasher and pushed the "on" button. When there was neither a horrible grinding noise nor flood, she returned to her customers.

"I don't suppose you have those small bottles of wine?" the elderly man of the couple asked as Mariah rang them up.

If they did, Mariah would have been on her second. "Sorry. We have tea, coffee, bottled water, and soft drinks, though."

"We'll take two coffees," the woman said.

Mariah gave them the flavored creamer packets, napkins, and threw in two butterscotch squares to make up for hurrying them along.

After they left, Mariah sat at the counter separating the day's take into the till for the next day and what went into the deposit. She tossed junk mail and unfolded bills. Three from the hospital today, gray numbers spit out by a computer assigned to little boxes marked thirty, forty-five, and sixty days overdue. Two rejected claims from the half-baked health insurance. Apparently even when you're sick with leukemia two sets of blood tests in one week were "above and beyond necessary care." The final envelope contained a notice of a rate hike come the New Year. Mariah wondered what kind of penalty there was for dipping into her teacher's retirement. The hard times, just like Gammy predicted, had arrived.

"Guess what?" Allegra said when Mariah opened the door into the apartment. "Doc called, and I get to skip a whole week of chemo!"

The twin spots of red on her mother's cheeks were new, Mariah noted. Health or fever? "Is that good news or bad?"

"Who cares?" Allegra said, hugging a throw pillow to her breasts. "I don't have to go sit in that apricot-colored room and watch *Days of Our Lives* with sick people."

When she turned back to her talk show, Mariah saw the bald patches the bandanna didn't hide. Mariah pulled off her apron and kicked off her shoes. Then she saw the untouched tray on the coffee table. "Mom, did you eat anything today?"

"I'll eat when I feel hungry. Any cute guys today? Competition for the Scotsman?"

Mariah felt her hackles rise. The carefully prepared tray of not too spicy, not too bland wholesome foods intended to build her strength would go into the trash, wasted. "I wasn't really paying attention, Mom. I was too busy working."

"Come on," Allegra said. "You can multitask. Not even a hottie too young for both of us?"

Mariah had her thumbs in her belt loops, ready to shuck her jeans right there before she went to shower. Could she make Dr. Goodnough put in a feeding tube? If her mother wanted to stop eating, wasn't that her right? "If there was a hottie present I'm afraid I missed him. I'm going to take my shower now. Fergus is picking me up in an hour, and I have to wash the onion stink off me."

"Be sure to wear cute underwear. You never know."

The rise and fall of audience laughter from the talk show was almost more irritating than hearing her mother's sexual innuendo, but it was the innuendo that tipped her over. "Look. If you were seeing Fergus, I'm sure cute underwear would be a high priority. It's not for me, okay? Eat something off that tray. I mean it, Mom."

Allegra muted the television. "What's that supposed to mean?"

"I'm just letting you know underwear's not an issue for me. You eating is."

Allegra kneaded the pillow fringe between her fingers. "Bullshit. You're trying to make me feel bad for still having a healthy libido when I have cancer and I'm supposed to be all over that."

"That's not what I said."

"Mariah, it's what you say every time you look at me. I wish you'd freaking get over it once and for all. Your mother has sex! Sex is fun! Lots of women over fifty do it. Over sixty, even. Except your grandmother."

Mariah looked at the floor. The rug needed vacuuming and there were dirty glasses that needed picking up. Would it kill Allegra to use the same glass all day? "I'm aware of the statistics. I'm also aware that if you limit sex to one partner, it often leads to that strange concept called intimacy. You know? It's right next to commitment on the supermarket shelf." Mariah immediately thought of her own track record and wished she could take the words back. With Lindsay's father, there was commitment; only it had all been on her side. "Mom, I'm sorry . . ."

Allegra had her mad face on, all thin lips and looking away. "Thanks for reminding me what a slut I am. What's your problem, anyway? It's not like I can go barhopping in my condition. Are you worried Fergus might find me attractive? I don't understand how you can take one measly comment and read so much into it. What difference does it make if I've slept with one man or fifty? So what if I have boyfriends younger than me, so what if I try to make myself happy. Is that a crime?"

Mariah zipped her dirty jeans back up. "Sex is easier for you than it is for me. If that's all you want out of a relationship, if both parties agree, fine. But sex has consequences or I wouldn't be here, would I?"

"The same can be said of Lindsay."

Mariah's face flamed. "At least she knows who her father is! Why can't I? All I ever wanted was a picture. A face to look at. I'm nearly thirty-four! Whoever he is doesn't matter. He certainly can't make my childhood up to me. Or is that a secret you plan to take to your grave?"

"My grave?" Allegra tried to throw the pillow at her, but her lack of strength landed it on the table. "How did you get to be so cruel? I don't even know you." She got up, braced herself against the wall, and closed the bedroom door behind her.

Mariah stood there. God, her mouth was out of control. Where had that business about her father come from? She should apologize. Picking up the tray, she noticed yesterday's lunch behind the couch. Screw it. Leukemia or no leukemia, she was calling Dr. Goodnough and asking for the feeding tube. Her mother wasn't only after sex. Plenty of times she'd caught Allegra standing out in the alley, arms folded across her breasts, staring at the ocean, two blocks away. She knew Allegra was thinking about true love. In the café, she sang along with the radio's love songs. She didn't mop the floor so much as dance it clean. Love, love, love; she ran around town leaving cheerfulness in her wake like goddamn wedding confetti. But no one besides Mariah heard the click as Allegra shut the door on her daughter's questions. No one else lived with that simmering stomach longing for just this one truth, except maybe Lindsay. Did that mean she should pack her daughter up, drive around the country until she found Ephraim? Of course not. She'd find Lindsay a picture somehow. A picture and a name—that was sufficient.

She dialed the doctor's number, but he was gone for the day. "Tell him Mariah Moon called," she said. "Tell him Allegra hasn't eaten any solid food in two days. Actually, four days. Ask him what it would take to get a feeding tube installed. Thank you." She hung up and cleared the untouched trays.

She showered, shaved her legs, and rinsed her hair with the expensive conditioner she'd bought because she thought it might add body to her hopelessly straight brown locks. It cost a lot, but she deserved good conditioner. She deserved a date, too. Dinner someone else fixed. She turned the water off and thought of the way Fergus tilted his head as he kissed her, and shivered while she towel-dried her hair.

Mariah had planned her outfit based on observations of the women her age who came to the café. She would wear the DKNY blue jeans found at the thrift store while shopping for Lindsay's Halloween costume. Carl Sagan being too wide a reach, she'd decided to go as Einstein. Mariah's white Gap blouse freshly ironed with Gammy's spray starch would make her winter skin look rosy. Her high-heeled boots, also a thrift store find, weren't very comfortable, but everyone seemed to be wearing them and no one could tell she'd glued the heel back on. At the last minute she went to the closet and took out her mother's suede jacket with the beaded fringe and slipped it on. She looked in the mirror and tried to imagine Allegra wearing it, chanting "Give Peace a Chance" and dancing to bands that were now called classic rock. Why shouldn't she wear it? Retro was in.

"Er," Fergus said as they got out of his car—a gray Mini Cooper—and Lindsay's favorite model, "what have you done with your hair?"

"Nothing," Mariah said. "Why?"

"It smells like, I don't know what exactly. Chewing gum?"

She looked at him, stunned. "If you find my hair offensive you can take me home."

He looked back, silent for a moment. "Well, my goodness. Somebody is having a bloody awful day. Mariah, you remind me of *Mimosa pudica*."

"Here we go," Mariah said, thinking the term had to be sexual. "Say hello to Mr. Get in Your Pants." She put her hand on the door handle. Fergus reached over and put his hand on hers. "I had a feeling—"

"Keep your knickers on, girl. It's a plant. They call *Mimosa pudica* the 'sensitive' plant because if one touches it, the leaves close in on themselves. My admin assistant has one on her desk."

Mariah forced herself to meet his eyes in order to show him she didn't give a rat's ass if they finished this date or not, but inside, she could feel cliffs crumbling. "The conditioner was supposed to— Oh, pull over at the corner and I'll walk home."

"Why ever would you want to do that?"

The trees were lit with fairy lights. They made everything soft and romantic, even in the fog. They had been on two "tea" dates and a couple of dinners and still she struggled to find conversation material. Probably that was her fault, mulling over gender roles and courtship rituals instead of responding spontaneously. She couldn't help it, which was why she was studying the romance novels so closely, but they seemed to be of help only if you ran into a handsome man in a horse stables, or a swarthy gardener gave you a steamy look.

"I'm not fit company tonight."

Fergus touched her arm. "I disagree. I didn't mean to insult you about your hair. I rather like it, actually. It's, well, it's certainly refreshing." He stared at her soberly, and then there was just the tiniest twitch to his mouth, and he flared his nostrils.

They both started laughing at the same time. "I smell like a cough drop, don't I?" Mariah asked.

"Oh, I dunno. Myself, I've always favored Altoids lozenges. Opens the sinuses. Refreshes one's view. Quite invigorating." He leaned in and kissed her right there, in front of the Italian restaurant where they had reservations at the table next to the fireplace, and the bad day fell away. The jolt Mariah felt from that kiss went straight to her center. When they broke apart, she heard her own shallow breath and his. If Allegra could see them now, she'd be laughing her ass off.

"Still want to go home?" he asked.

Then, like the woman her mother had been before leukemia tied a knot in her tail, Mariah pulled Fergus to her and kissed him back.

"I'll take that as a no," he said, and they got out of the car.

Raffaello's, in downtown Carmel, off Mission and Ocean at Seventh Street, was famous for its northern Italian cuisine, and expensive. Mariah looked over the menu, having to read everything twice, she was so unsettled by those two kisses, and the lingering bad feelings about the words she'd had with Allegra didn't help. The flickering candlelight, soft classical music, and nice paintings on the walls helped soften her edges, but she planned to excuse herself as soon as they ordered, call Gammy, and have her convey her apologies to Allegra.

There was no view other than the fireplace. That pretty much left the face of your dining partner. Some diabolical architect's formula for romance, Mariah thought. Well, it's working. I'm the same person I was before he kissed me—a woman who could terrify a classroom full of graduate students—only now I'm the one feeling terror.

She sneaked glances at Fergus. His ruddy skin had its share of pox scars and frown lines. His brow jutted out harshly, in a Neanderthal way. She liked the way his strong chin offset the nose that bordered on hawklike, and the sum of the parts made her feel certain that, just like it had with Ephraim, whatever birth control she'd try would fail her. Having loved Lindsay when she was just a raspberry of clustered cells, she knew she couldn't get rid of a baby. She wondered, if they ever got around to sex, whether Fergus would agree to wear not one condom, but two.

He touched the top of her menu and pulled it down to the table. "Are you avoiding me?"

"I'm sitting right here. How can I be avoiding you?"

The waiter appeared, and both sat back while he filled their tumblers with ice water and set down a basket of sliced bread, which, Mariah noted, had uneven cells—the result of not enough kneading, and inadequate rise time. "Have you decided?" he asked. "Or shall I go over the specials one more time?"

Mariah said, "I'll have a glass of iced tea, and the shrimp salad appetizer."

"And for your main course?"

"No main course. Just the appetizer."

"An affordable date, this one," Fergus said.

"I'm paying for my dinner," Mariah said, "and that's all I want." Or can afford, she held back. "If you haven't learned by now, American women are eternally on diets."

"And quite unnecessarily."

"Sir?" the waiter prompted.

"Stout. Bring a mug for me and one for my lovely friend, to whom I plan to introduce the finer points of such beverages. So long as it isn't the Manhattan variety, I'll begin with your chowder. Then I'd like the rack of lamb, rare, with mashed spuds, cream and butter. Also, if you could bring us some more of this lovely bread, that would be great. Oh, and bring an extra plate for my dieting friend in case she decides to nibble."

"You have a large appetite," Mariah remarked as their drinks and the second basket of bread arrived, as Fergus had gone through most of the first. He broke a piece in half and prepared to butter it.

"I live on a boat, remember?" he said. "The galley's not much. A microwave oven. When I eat, I eat. I utterly despise cooking for myself."

Mariah wanted to ask if his socks were damp when he put them on. How awful that would be on a daily basis. And going to Laundromats, even worse. "I could live on candy and soda."

"Because you're cooking every day at the café instead of teaching sociology?"

"Who told you I taught that?"

"Your daughter."

"Lindsay?" Mariah sipped her tea, which was way too sugary. "When?"

"I ran into her in the public library the other afternoon. She was looking up books on growing herbs. Has her interest in science focused onto horticulture?"

Mariah reached for a slice of bread. "It may have something to do with her science project. It's very top secret, so I only have scanty details, but she's been lugging books home every day. Was your exchange . . ."

"Pleasant?" Fergus set his stout down and licked away the mustache it had left above his upper lip. "She no longer looks at me as though she wants to drive a stake through my heart, which I consider something to build upon."

Mariah wondered why Lindsay didn't tell her, especially lately, when she so vehemently reminded her mother of the circumstances of her origin. "Lindsay's slow to make friends," she said.

"How's that tea?"

"Not so great."

"Care to try a pint of stout?"

She took the glass he offered. "You probably wonder why I didn't order very much. I snack all day, so by dinnertime I'm not all that hungry. As soon as I find a teaching gig, I'll revert to my old habits."

"Have you made applications locally?"

"I really can't until my mother's well enough to return to work." If ever, Mariah thought, this notion causing her heart to sink. How could you tell a person battling to save her life to hurry up? "I have a question related to your job."

He leaned in close enough that Mariah could smell his spicy soap. "Fire away."

"Why does a full professor take a leave from a prestigious teaching post in Glasgow for a one-year slot at a community college halfway around the world?"

"Adventure?"

"Aren't you afraid someone will steal your job out from

under you? That's basically what happened to me. Of course, it's my own fault for not finishing my thesis. Not that I had the time."

Fergus set the bread down on the plate and appeared to study the foil butter wrapper. "What a funny packaging. In Scotland, butter comes in a roll, not bits like this."

"What are you saying? American butter sucks?"

He laughed. "Your infrequent descents into the vernacular captivate me, Mariah."

"All I know of you is that you live on a boat and like your lamb rare. I have to ask questions."

"I suppose I'm like any bloke who sees the big four-oh looming, and wants to scarper off. I certainly don't intend to live the remainder of my life the way I did the first half."

She swallowed a gulp of the stout and coughed. "God, it's like drinking yeast."

"That's what makes it so wonderful."

She grimaced. "Are you going to tell me about the first thirty-nine years over dinner? If so, when will you have time to eat all that food?"

"Excellent points, all. Being of like mind—academic mind—I'll go straightaway to the essentials. I feel I must confess something to you."

"Confess what?"

"About the love of my life, Theodora."

Mariah felt her heart pull back like the worn-out rubber band that it apparently was. Jesus Christ Almighty. This wasn't a budding relationship clunking along until it found its way. Fergus wanted a quick bout of athletic sex with the American waitress, and figured two "teas" and a couple of dinners were payment enough. Men and their waitress fantasies! Why was sex so uncomplicated for them? She took hold of her purse strap, ready to bolt. "Theodora," she said. "By all means, tell me. I can't wait to hear about her."

Fergus smiled, retrieved his wallet from his jacket and flipped it open to where most men kept photos of their wife and children. He took a long, loving look at the picture before he turned it to Mariah. "Look at that face and tell me she isn't the most beautiful girl on the planet."

Mariah steeled herself and looked. Inside the plastic sleeve was a photograph of a brownish-gray dog with a shaggy coat and whiskers. Mariah reined in the embarrassment of being duped as best she could. "She's breathtaking," she said. "How long have you two been together?"

"Six months now."

"Any kids?"

Fergus chuckled. "I wish you could see your face. Priceless."

Mariah went hot. "You ought to know I don't like being made fun of."

"Come along! Did I really upset you?"

"Take a good look, Mr. Applecross. You won't fool me again."

"I might."

"I don't think so."

"Now you've gone and done it. Thrown down the gauntlet. I'm compelled to defend the clan plaid. Fifty quid says I can fool you again. Quite possibly tonight." He picked up the bread again, and then set it down. "You see, Mariah, you're—"

He was unable to finish his sentence because at that moment the waiter showed up with his dinner—a huge, steaming portion that would take him at least an hour to eat. Mariah stared at her small salad. Fergus held up his Guinness. "To forging a lifelong friendship?"

She raised her own glass. "To shaggy dog stories."

"Theodora'd have a fit if she heard you say that. She's a purebred Scottish deerhound, the breed of choice for the Picts, the Earls, and the likes of me, a bit of a fool for history and tradition."

Mariah rolled her eyes.

"She's a rescue animal. Everyone should have a soul mate, don't you think?"

Mariah agreed. But if you could find a soul mate in a large dog that needed a home, wouldn't the world be thick with dogs already? Oh, this night was just one awkward moment after another. How could you not admire a man who rescued a dog? Allegra was right: Fergus was more her type than Mariah's. Maybe after he drank another stout he would loosen up, tell her she was pretty, or comely, or whatever the hell the Scottish slang was for that. She'd put herself in this situation, even when she knew better. It was going to be a big, drawn-out, messy, emotional entanglement that would end badly. "Can I meet your dog?" she said.

"Of course."

After taking the Carmel Gate onto Seventeen Mile Drive, they rounded the Spanish Bay golf course, and Fergus exited at the Lighthouse Gate, turning toward the wharf. Mariah wondered if after introducing her to Theodora, Fergus would try to put the moves on her. Seemed like by the second date everyone had sex. Allegra's voice rang in her ears: Wear cute underwear! Mariah was horrified to realize she was wearing a pair of Lindsay's panties because she'd put off doing the wash. Maybe if she didn't let him grope her, he wouldn't want to see her anymore. They lived in a world of computers and think tanks, but did communication between men and women get any easier? All those internet dating services, personal ads, and blind dates doomed attempts to fill yet another chasmlike gap. Sociologically—oh, shut up, she told herself.

Fergus opened her door, then walked her down the pier, unlocking a gate, and headed toward a sailboat with the name *Ellen Cole II* painted on the side. "Who's Ellen? Another greyhound?"

"Deerhound," he corrected. "There's quite a difference. Ellen was my mother, rest her soul."

"I'm sorry. That was thoughtless of me."

"Not to worry. Let me just switch on the lights, and find

Theodora's leash. You cannot let a deerhound off-leash," he said. "Their brains revert in a matter of seconds. By the time you shout 'come back' they're two kilometers down the lane, chasing imaginary lure."

Mariah's dog experience had been strictly limited to Allegra's Chihuahuas. They were spoiled rotten things, especially Khan, who only liked a select few people. But this dog coming on deck from the cabin below was elegant. Quiet and somber despite the shaggy coat, only her thumping tail gave away her delight at seeing Fergus. Mariah held out her hand. Theodora sniffed her fingers, then the suede jacket. Then she moved away until she was beside Fergus, her head coming to rest under his palm.

"I should have brought her something from the restaurant."

"There are three things to remember about deerhounds," Fergus said. "First, they're an ancient breed, once only available to those with the rank of Earl, or above. Second, they have an insatiable desire for human companionship, and generally bond with only one person. Third, Sir Walter Scott got it crack-on when he called the deerhound 'the most perfect creature of heaven.'"

Mariah listened to the burrs in his accent. Drinking the stout—Fergus insisted she finish the glass—made his accent even more intriguing. He switched on the cabin lights, as well as the fairy lights twining up the mast like electrified ivy, and she realized that this was the boat she'd noticed when driving by the arena the night Allegra was told she had leukemia. A small beacon, beckoning. All the ropes were tightly coiled. Fergus wasn't a neat freak, but clearly he liked order. He'd never find that in Mariah's life.

"I'm plugging the kettle in," he said. "Fancy a cup of tea?"

"What kinds do you have?"

"Chinese powder keg, blackberry, some herbal crap I've never tried. And, of course, Red Rose, which I drink by the bucketful. Don't think for a moment that I buy it for the little ceramic creatures that come with it."

He pointed to the ledge above the tiny sink, which had a good start on Noah's ark. Mariah picked up a pastel blue rhino, felt its horn, and set it back in place. Fergus sat down, and Theodora walked sure-footed toward Mariah, resting her head on Mariah's knee. She stroked the dog's ears, and her eyes closed in bliss. I'm still not sleeping with him, Mariah thought. Not even if he wears three condoms.

"So do you own a kilt?" she asked. "Do you play bagpipes, or the pennywhistle? Do you have haggis down there in that tiny refrigerator? Clotted cream for your tea?"

"Every Scotsman worth a sod has a kilt. I've messed about with the pipes. I thought you might notice that I've been having my tea at The Owl and Moon. I like the food, as well as the company."

Mariah was grateful for the low light, so he couldn't see her face burning. "Tell me about your job in Scotland," she said. "Did you love it?"

He looked out to the water, where a seal was splashing around before settling on one of the buoys for the night. "I did indeed love it. But when the chance to do this came about, I jumped at it. Offered the position of academic dean, I thought, here's a way to see if I fit in with that sort of thing. If that's a direction I care to pursue."

"I envy you having options," Mariah said. "Instead of being let go, I was hoping for a tenure track offer." She looked out onto the black water, tried to laugh and failed. "My life's just one slippery slope after the other these days."

Fergus reached across and handed her a cup of tea. "Don't think I haven't noticed how hard you work, and the pressure you're under."

"Thanks."

"My pleasure. If you let me kiss you I'll pull strings at the college when you put in your application."

"There's a deal I can't turn down."

Five minutes into the "snogging," his word for it, Mariah was out of breath, all beating heart and racing pulse. Their previous dates had consisted of tea at Bookworks on Lighthouse, and listening to the Puss Pinebluff Trio practice for their evening gig at a dimly lit nightclub filled with people who appeared to have a close relationship with the bartender. Fergus wouldn't care about the panties. Maybe Allegra was onto something, using sex for fun. But when the silence stretched and she could have asked for it, she found she couldn't.

Oh, try to sleep after a night like that, Mariah thought, as she tossed and turned in her bed, a room that had in a previous life been a kitchen. Feeling desire like this again almost made her sick. There was scientific proof that infatuation did crazy things to a person. Anytime the body was focused on one feeling, fixed with hormones and neuropeptides and yearning, good sense sailed right out the window. PEA—phenylethylamine— the in-love hormone, acted like crack cocaine, speeding the body up, causing one to stay up all hours talking, kissing, anticipating the inevitable fast-and-furious sex, like she had with Ephraim, once in his office, even, while students walked by outside, oblivious.

He'd offered her five hundred dollars when she told him she was pregnant.

"What for?" she said, shocked that such a shabby dresser had that much money in his wallet.

"An abortion."

"You want me to flush our child down the toilet? Are you insane?"

"You're the one with the pro-choice bumper sticker," he'd said. "I sure as hell don't want to raise another kid at this stage of my life."

Ephraim had been through a nasty divorce, lost custody of his son, and now he wanted the sex life of an adolescent boy. He was Mariah's first. She could hardly sleep for thinking of seeing him again.

Just as quickly as phenylethylamine spiked, so could it crash. When the depression set in—just remembering his words—Mariah would have sold her soul to have that happy-crazy state back again.

With tears rolling down her face, she'd told Gammy she was pregnant with Lindsay. "I'm sorry. I know how much you were counting on me to do better," she said. "I wanted to be the person you hoped I would be, smart, with a good job, maybe someday married, having kids when it's respectable instead of like this. I guess I'm just like my mother after all."

Her grandmother held her in her arms, patting her back. "I won't say I'm thrilled. I wish you'd waited. But remember, Mariah, Jesus loved the little children most of all."

Mariah had sniffled and said, "Jesus didn't get pregnant and humiliate his family."

"He did call a little attention to himself, though." A wistful smile crossed her grandmother 's face. "Mariah, let me tell you a story. The year is 1960-something. I'm working as usual, stocking the same old shirts and belts that haven't sold in two years and won't in two more. A men's haberdashery—what the devil was I thinking? I'd come to a crossroads, and I had to make a decision. Bess, I told myself, maybe it's time to sell this property, buy a little house in some small town, and live simple. Maybe work for somebody else, manage their accounts payable. I've always been good with money. In walked your mother, pregnant, penniless, holes poked in every one of her dreams. I wasn't surprised. From the day she was born Alice was as stubborn as a two-headed goat. She was carrying on just the way you are now, like it was the end of the world. Honey, the thing with spilled milk is you have to wipe it up and rinse out the dishcloth or things start to smell awful. Your mom had the pioneer gene. She made great bread and cookies, so I thought, why not have a fire sale with these old shirts and try a little bakery? It'll take her mind off turning up pregnant, barely sixteen years old. The Owl and Moon was a goofy name in my opinion. I asked her, Alice, what do you think people will think we serve when they see that name? She had her heart dead set. With all of us here, your baby will have three times the love."

Six years ago, Mariah had started the secret trip fund. At seven, Lindsay had adored the James Herriot books. Because Mariah hadn't time, Allegra had read them to her. Mariah thought, I could save enough to take her to his fictional stomping grounds. By the end of next quarter, she would've had the price of two coach tickets. The plan was to sublet the condo and fly to England for the summer. Rent a tiny cottage with a thatch roof. Bluebells in bloom. By the fireplace she'd write her first book. Not a textbook, a novel. Everyone had one novel in them, didn't they? The love story they wished for that hadn't happened? She and Lindsay would take day trips to the standing stones, shoot rolls of film, and collect rocks. It would be their first real vacation.

All her life Mariah had worked. She wasn't much older than Lindsay was now when she'd begun waitressing at the café. At first she raced home from school, excited about earning tips. Even before losing her job there were days Mariah thought about quitting teaching. Should the student's paper that lay on the cusp of an A, get the A? She knew firsthand that it was possible to break a student's spirit with a B. C's were no longer acceptable.

Lying there in the dark, Mariah thought of Fergus's dog. She was as tall as your average fence. People made fun of Chihuahuas, but no matter how many jokes they told about hairy little rats and froufrou purse puppies, Mariah knew a big dog would chase a squirrel right out into traffic and get creamed while a small dog would deliver you an expression that said, "Surely you don't expect me to prove my worth by chasing a rodent?"

There was no point to any of this. She had to get up in four hours. Turning onto her side, she heard her mother cough in the other room. Dr. Goodnough had called to say he'd stopped Allegra's chemo because her blood counts were dangerously low. Keep her away from anyone with a cold or the flu, he said. Mariah knew Gammy was listening with the same peeled ear on her side of the wall. Then another cough came, and the sound of Allegra hurrying to the bathroom, getting sick.

Mariah waited to hear the toilet flush, and her mother head back to bed. When that didn't happen, she got up and put on her robe, opening her bedroom door nearly into Gammy, who apparently had the same idea. They looked at each other in the narrow hall, listening to Allegra retching. Gammy said, "Surely it'll stop soon."

But it didn't stop. After a while, it seemed like Allegra couldn't stop. "I'm calling the doctor," Mariah said, handing Gammy the nausea first-aid kit: a Seven-Up, ginger candy, and clean towels from the closet. "You go sit with her while I'll find out what he wants us to do."

"Okay, honey," Gammy said. "You tell him I said to step on it."

8
Lindsay

LINDSAY STOOD AT THE end of her grandmother's hospital bed unable to say a word. This person connected to tubes and monitors didn't look like the Allegra who baked cookies and told dirty jokes and watched really old *Star Trek* reruns. She looked as if a secret killer was slowly poisoning her with arsenic. Lindsay's stomach clenched. She felt a hand on her shoulder and looked up to see Dr. Goodnough looking down at her. "Don't be frightened," he said. "She's responding nicely to the antibiotics. When she eats three meals a day, I'll let her go home."

If that was the catch, Allegra could be in the hospital forever.

Even though it was Sunday, Lindsay's mother was at the café, baking. She'd dropped Lindsay and Gammy off at the hospital, and then gone back to work because if she didn't make cookies today there wouldn't be enough to sell tomorrow. Gammy sat next to the bed like she had every day since Allegra was admitted for pneumonia and anemia. She held Allegra's hand and prayed out loud, which would have made Lindsay's mom crabby anyway, religion being a topic they didn't agree on, so it was better she was at the café.

"Allegra doesn't look better to me," Lindsay said to the doctor who had asked her to call him "Dr. G." "How can you be sure?"

"See that I.V.?" he said. "When a person feels too ill to drink water, they dehydrate. Without water, the body can spike a fever. That creates a playing field for lots of stuff to go wrong. She needs to drink more fluids, eat more, too."

"But what if it hurts to eat and drink? Allegra has mouth sores."

"That's why we have her drinking out of a straw. Simple things like that can help. As soon as she's had enough fluids, she'll get hungry. The human body is simple that way."

Lindsay frowned. "It seems like the medicine you've given her is what's making her sick. I think she might die."

Dr. G squatted down so they were face-to-face. "Fighting cancer is hard work. Sometimes we have to make patients sicker before they get well. Allegra's tough. She managed almost six weeks of chemo. And she is getting better."

"Then why couldn't she stop throwing up?" Lindsay asked.

"The side effects of her medication—"

"I'm tired of hearing about that!" Lindsay said. "Why don't you just prescribe Marinol?"

Dr. G looked at her, surprised. "Where did you learn about that?"

Lindsay squared her shoulders and looked directly into his eyes the way Sally did when she stood up to Taylor and the clones. "Researching my science project. It's on palliative care with controversial medicine. Marinol has side effects, like headaches, but it helps some people want to eat again. Why don't you give her that? Or medical marijuana?"

"I'll bet you get straight A's in science. Early on, I offered. She didn't want any part of anything remotely connected with marijuana."

"But ProCon.org says there are no adverse effects of marijuana components in the use of chemotherapy patients with unremitting nausea. And Marinol is *synthetic,* not marijuana like dope dealers sell. Everyone has the endocannibinoid system pathway in them. Marinol might even help boost the immune system. One-third of patients experienced significant improvement in chemo-induced weight loss. You have to talk her into it, Dr. G."

He pushed his glasses up his nose and stood there, quiet. Lindsay worried he'd go straight to her mother and say she had better look into this so-called science project. Maybe he'd call the cops. Sally was going to kill her. Why had she opened her mouth in the first place?

"Don't believe everything you read on the internet," Dr. G said. "How about we go to my office, where I can give you some substantiated information on the subject?"

Lindsay looked away. "I don't get in cars with people I don't know. Besides, I don't want to leave my nana."

"You're misunderstanding me, Lindsay. As chief of hematology and oncology, I have a small office here at the hospital, too. Go tell Bess and then we'll go see it."

Lindsay weighed her options. Allegra's hospital room made her stomach hurt. She could only glance at the tubes, and she might throw up. Gammy was busy praying, and prayer was like watching the same humans who had invented space travel revert to crawling. "Only if I can see your literature on palliative care, specifically regarding medical marijuana."

"Deal."

"My science project has several aspects," Lindsay added quickly. "Maybe I could also interview you?"

"Sure," he said. Dr. Goodnough interrupted Gammy's Hail Mary's to let them know where they were going. "We'll be back before you reach the Apostles' Creed," he said.

"Some churchgoer you are," Gammy said, waving him away. "That's the prayer that begins the rosary." She went back to her beads. Allegra smiled faintly, but she didn't open her eyes.

They rode the elevator. CHOMP was pretty nice as far as hospitals went. There were plants near the elevators, paintings on the walls, sculptures up on pedestals, and an aromatic coffee cart somewhere near, because Lindsay could smell it.

At the office door Lindsay studied the shiny brass sign: Chief of Staff: Hematology/Oncology: Alvin P. Goodnough, M.D. "What does the P stand for?" she asked.

"Percival," he said. "Name-wise, you can see I was doomed at birth."

Lindsay smiled. Some words were scary. Oncology, for instance, sounded as awful as cancer. According to the internet, oncology was a relatively new field, only about thirty years old. Before then, people with cancer either had surgery or got radiation therapy. Dr. G slid his key into the lock.

"This is a really small office," Lindsay said when he opened the door. "Why did you come to our house when my mom called and why are you here on a Sunday?"

He smiled. His teeth, she noticed, were very straight and white, and they looked real. "For comprehensive care, I see patients in my private office. Your grandmother's an old friend. For friends you make exceptions."

Lindsay wondered if they had been more than friends. If Allegra hadn't been a hippie, free-spirited and all that, maybe they might have gotten married. She pictured Dr. G standing at the bathroom sink, whistling as he patted on spicy aftershave instead of how he looked when he'd carried Allegra down to his car. Lindsay would hand him the newspaper first, so he could read the sports page before he went to work.

His office had cushy chenille chairs. Built into one wall was an aquarium filled with neon tetras. "Characins!" Lindsay said. "Dr. G, did you know their Latin name is *Paracheirodon innesi*?"

He tapped the glass and they all swarmed to that spot, their blue backs and white pectorals shimmering like mica. "I did, but I didn't expect anyone else to."

"It's good you have the sides and bottom of the tank backed with dark paper," she said. "They think they're back in the Amazon jungle."

"That's why I have the floating plants," he said. "The canopy makes a good place for them to hide. Your Latin's impressive, kiddo. How come you know so much about tropical fish?"

Lindsay tracked the shimmering fish. "Except for Khan, I don't get to have pets, so I research the ones I like until I know everything about them. That way, if I had a pet, I could take the best care of it possible."

"I see. What other pets have you imagined?"

She held up her hand and counted off her fingers. "A hedgehog, a llama, an angora rabbit, and a cat. Just a regular cat, not Siamese or anything. An orange cat would be the best."

"Want to feed my fish?"

"Sure," she said, taking the container of fish flakes from him. "How much?"

"About the size of a quarter."

"Why does everyone use coins as comparison?"

"Probably because they're so universally recognizable."

Lindsay sprinkled the flakes and together they watched the fish dive-bomb through the water, chasing one another and gobbling until all the food disappeared, which happened practically instantly. Most of the fish remained at the surface, still looking for food. "They'll try to fake you out every time," he said. "A bunch of good-for-nothing greedy guts, I call them."

Dr. G tried to look tough, but Lindsay could tell he secretly loved his fish. "Why did you choose neon tetras? Why not cardinals or goldfish or saltwater fish?"

He capped the food and returned it to the shelf. "Saltwater tanks are difficult to maintain. One chemical out of balance and I come to work to find my seventy-dollar beauty belly-up. Goldfish belong in a pond. Also they poop a hell of a lot. Cardinal tetras are pricey. I like neons. They're flashy, like Corvettes."

Lindsay imagined cars driving around the pirate chest bubble feature. "They remind me of commuters in San Francisco, getting off BART, heading to work or shopping."

Dr. G laughed. "We think alike, Lindsay, don't we?"

"Because we're scientists?"

"That must be it."

"Is this where you perform bone marrow biopsies?"

"Nope. Only paperwork here. Procedures I do in my private practice."

"Do they hurt?"

"Bone marrow biopsies sound a lot scarier than they are. The needle looks huge, but I anesthetize the area beforehand." He opened another door. "Here's my desk."

Lindsay walked around the glass-topped desk that swooped in a semicircle. His bookcase was filled with medical texts. She ran a finger down the spine of the *Merck Manual*. "These must have cost a lot."

"True. But when you keep them over a lifetime, it's a good investment."

She picked up a loose stack of photographs sitting on his desk. The top one showed a bearded guy wearing beads and a headband and flashing the peace sign. "Was this a Halloween party costume?" she asked.

He laughed. "God, no. That's back in the days when I knew your grandmother. Actually, Allegra took the picture. We were camping. I found them while unpacking and thought Allegra might get a kick out of seeing them. There's a picture of George Harrison in there somewhere. You know, the Beatle."

Lindsay looked at him blankly. "Were lots of people camping with you? Did you sleep on cots? Did you have one big tent or lots of pup tents?"

"Just us two. No tent. It was summer. We slept in sleeping bags under the stars." For a moment, he got that faraway look in his eyes like she'd seen Allegra do when she talked about "the good old days." "Lindsay, you have no idea what a brave girl she was. She'd march on the City Hall steps and hand out flowers to policemen. Not one thing scared her. I'm not surprised she decided to have a child all by herself. She had an independent streak in her a mile wide."

"When was this picture taken?"

"Nineteen sixty-seven. You can see the redwoods there behind me, though they're a little out of focus. Not long after that I went to med school."

"Can I look at it a while longer?"

"No problem." He opened a cabinet and took out some files.

Lindsay sat down in one of the chairs facing his desk, the picture in her hand. If you took the year 1967 and added thirty-three years to that, the sum was this very year. In February, her mom would turn thirty-four.

"Sit in my chair," Dr. G said. "Imagine how it feels to be a doctor facing his patient."

Lindsay took the swivel chair. She imagined Allegra and Gammy sitting in the two chairs facing the desk. I have very good news, she'd tell them. Under the Compassionate Investigational New Drug treaty, you are allowed to keep six mature cannabis plants, and/or a half-pound of marijuana. However, if you move to Sonoma, you can keep ninety-nine plants.

But that drug's addictive! Gammy would gasp. It's one step from pot to mainlining heroin! Lindsay would interrupt her. Don't be afraid, ma'am. That's why we have Marinol. It will help Allegra feel better. Not only does it ease nausea, but also you will look forward to meals. Allegra, you will feel so good you'll even want to dance again. I am a doctor. I can make this promise.

Then they would cry from relief, and Gammy would call her a godsend. Allegra would start out on Simon's kreplach soup, and in no time be eating pasta and apples and bread dipped in olive oil, everything she used to love. They would make cookies. Tell jokes. Throw a Halloween party and dress up like witches.

Dr. G set papers on the desk blotter. "Here's a fact you

should make certain gets into your project. Before the 1937 ban, marijuana was used to treat over a hundred different medical conditions."

"I'm starting our interview now," Lindsay said. "Dr. G, which of your patients use medical marijuana, and how does it work for them?"

"I'm afraid the Hippocratic oath means I can't talk about my patients personally," he said. "But I can tell you that on the average, I'd say about ten to fifteen percent of them use Marinol or medical marijuana."

"Why do they use it?"

"It's unfortunate, but for some of them we just don't have comparable antinausea meds."

"So Marinol works on everyone?"

"It can be quite effective, but not for everyone."

"Why not?"

"Every drug has side effects. Some patients find a combination of the drug and the herb do the best to combat nausea, but less is more when it comes to marijuana. The issue is to treat it like a prescription drug, not an excuse to smoke yourself stupid. There's a page in there on Proposition Two-fifteen you might find interesting. A lot of doctors were involved in getting that on the ballot."

Lindsay leafed through the pages, scanning for new material. She and Sally were swimming in Internet downloads. They'd interviewed Gregorio's dad, who mostly spoke Spanish, so Gregorio had to translate. They didn't get much because he was one part embarrassed about it and one part worried he was corrupting them and the last part sure they were cops. "Can I keep these?"

"Sure. You want a sheet on hospice care? Morphine pump use? I have a lot more."

Lindsay set the pictures down. For a moment, she felt blinded, as if someone was shining a flashlight into her eyes from really close. She couldn't answer Dr. G because in order for her mother to be born in 1968, Allegra had to be pregnant in June 1967. People who camped together, even if it was in separate sleeping bags, could still get out of those sleeping bags and have sex. She wanted to ask Dr. G right out, but what if he didn't know? If Carl Sagan were in this predicament, he wouldn't blurt out a conclusion without examining all the evidence. What he'd do was ask a question. "Dr. G," Lindsay said. "If Allegra gets worse and she's going to die, promise me you'll tell me ahead of time."

"Honestly, that's not going to happen."

"Gammy would be fine, because she can talk to God, but I should know before my mom does so I can prepare her."

"Why?"

Lindsay hesitated. This man could be her grandfather. She wanted to chart his every feature. She wanted a swab of his cheek cells to look at under her microscope, and DNA testing, which they probably did right here in this hospital. Private labs did testing, too. She wondered how much it cost. "My mom and Allegra are always arguing, but if Allegra dies, my mom'll be the one who, you know, loses it."

"That puts a lot of pressure on you, doesn't it?"

"It's okay. I'm used to it."

"Will you promise to call me if it gets to be too much? I can be a good listener. And scientist to scientist, we already have rapport."

Rapport, Lindsay thought. *An emotional bond based on mutual trust.* "Yes."

He scribbled on a business card and handed it to her. "That's my pager. You call it anytime if you need to talk about anything."

She slid the expensive bond next to the photograph and thought how what he said was like what a grandfather would say. Was this like long-lost twins finding each other? Allegra could have had sex with other men. The sixties, she knew from her mother's lectures, which she often practiced at home back when she had a teaching job, were the sexual revolution. But it felt like their DNA was talking to each other. Carl Sagan's voice came into her head. Look closely. Inspect the corners. Don't hurry.

Which was easy for him to say.

They stopped by the fish tank on the way out, and again Lindsay studied the tetras. It wasn't a jungle, but they had a good life here. The plants were real and the tank was clean and no predators lurked in the shadows. Lindsay imagined Carl Sagan being Dr. G's patient, sitting in the comfy chair feeling sick, and watching the fish swim by, flashing their colors. He would have had something to say about those fish. Something only Carl Sagan would think to say. Dr. Goodnough might have even saved his life.

A week later, Lindsay sat at the teak conference room table someone's dad had donated to Country Day when he remodeled his office. She was trying to concentrate on Mrs. Shiasaka's questions, but Allegra was still in the hospital, Dr. Goodnough could be her grandfather, and now there was the upcoming Halloween party. She didn't want to go, but not only was the whole eighth-grade class invited, the party was at DeThomas Farms, Sally's house. Sally was her best friend, and if she didn't go, Sally's feelings would be hurt, and then she wouldn't have a friend anymore. The invitation was printed on orange paper in black lettering:

> Come to DeThomas Farms for an old-fashioned, fun-filled Halloween! Under careful supervision your child will bob for apples, play pin the coccyx on the skeleton, and take a tour of our famous Haunted Greenhouse!
>
> DeThomas Farms, your one-stop shopping spot for:
>
> Unique gifts
> Fresh flowers
> Imported Christmas ornaments

The DeThomas strain poinsettias (only available
here)
Custom Easter baskets
Parties
Weddings/receptions

There was nothing safe about a party if Taylor Foster was
there.

"Lindsay Moon, I asked you a question," Mrs. Shiasaka
said. "Are you woolgathering?"

Lindsay startled and dropped her pencil. "No, ma'am, I'm
listening. Could you please repeat the question?"

"Certainly. Can you think of an example of human kindness that goes above and beyond normal, everyday manners?"

"My grandmother's doctor made a house call."

"A house call. That is unusual in this day and age, isn't it,
girls? Why did he do that?"

"Because she has cancer?"

Behind her she heard Taylor Foster snort, and Cheyenne
Goldenblatt snicker. How was cancer funny? Without turning
her head to look, she could sense Sally, two chairs down from
her, getting mad, or madder, since this morning they'd made
fun of Sally's Vera Bradley backpack, even though it was hot
pink and lime green, and those were the popular colors.

"Belva?" Mrs. Shiasaka said, zeroing in on the only girl who
was quieter than Lindsay. "We haven't heard a peep from you
all morning. Surely you have a valuable contribution to group
discussion."

Belva Satterly was president of the grammar club and allergic to wheat. She was one of those girls who got B's but was
okay with it. Lindsay tuned her out and tried to imagine various responses to the awful comments that would come her
own way at lunchtime. Cancer! It's catching! It'll eat her up in
no time! This year all her classes were like art. Paintings,
essays, Science Fair, hair style, backpack, it all had to be perfect, even if your mom was a waitress even though she hated

it, and since you were the one who balanced her checkbook, you knew how little money there was to live on.

In her backpack, Lindsay carried a jumbo-size bottle of Pepcid bought with the fifteen dollars Gammy had slipped her so she could take Sally to the movies to make up for Lindsay practically living at DeThomas Farms. Tums didn't work anymore. The Pepcid directions read: *Do not take for more than fourteen days in a row without consulting a physician.* Every thirteenth day, Lindsay skipped one.

"Girls, attention please," Mrs. Shiasaka said over the chatter. "If you could choose any person, living or dead, to have dinner with, whom would you select, and why? You have ten minutes to create your brainstorming cluster. That way we'll have time for all to share before nutrition break. You may begin as soon as I put on our creativity enhancement."

That meant playing a CD during class. Music supposedly assisted the linear thinking part of the brain to release creative answers. Lindsay Moon knew Country Day's CDs by heart. The adagio that made Avril cry, the album that had Pachelbel's Canon played every which way there was, and R. Carlos Nakai's CD of flute music. Why couldn't they play Vivaldi's *Four Seasons* so she could hear "Winter"? Allegra had it. Maybe she could burn a copy, but wait, wasn't that stealing? If everyone in the world took one thing like that the economy would suffer and eventually collapse and then where would humanity be?

She tapped her pencil against her fingers. When she'd signed up for this course—"an interdisciplinary approach to human ethics and alternative evolutions in decision-making"—it sounded useful. Who wouldn't want a chance to learn something that might help a geek like her prepare for whatever fresh hell came her way in high school? But so far, "Life Paths, Life Questions" was pretty much like every other class at Country Day—another "circle of learning," as Country Day did not believe in desks in rows.

The facts were this: Allegra had been pregnant in 1967. In

most cases, a person became pregnant by having sex with someone, someone they knew, unless they were on LSD or worse, "taken advantage of," which was Gammy's way of saying raped. Sometimes you could tell when people were having sex, like if they couldn't keep their hands off each other or made a lot of eye contact. Sometimes, though, you had to snoop around your mother's cosmetics, looking for birth control pills. When you didn't find any, then you had to consider the possibility of condoms, which the man was supposed to always carry, and that pretty much made it impossible to draw a conclusive conclusion about your mom having sex. Allegra had either skipped the birth control or had something like condom failure, which, according to statistics, was a three percent chance.

Then, as if he had been hanging around in her head all this time listening, and just now decided to speak, Lindsay heard Carl Sagan's voice. It seems you have a grandfather paradox of your own, Lindsay.

The Pachelbel Canon burst forth from the speaker, cello, this time, and Mrs. Shiasaka said, "You may begin."

Mechanical pencils clicked, but not Lindsay's. She waited for Carl Sagan to say something else. But three whole minutes went by, and nothing. All kinds of clustering thoughts arrived, Occam's Razor, for one. But first Lindsay had to fill in the center with Carl Sagan's name, and she was embarrassed and no way was she going to open herself up like that when other girls made jokes about her liking him already. The thing was, Mrs. Shiasaka knew when you weren't "passionate" about your subject. "Well, that is a good start, is what that is," she would say. "However, I think if you try again," she'd continue, patting a shoulder, smiling right down at you so you saw that her top teeth were perfect and white, but the bottom ones, like the true portrait of Dorian Gray, were all yellow and crooked, "I think you'll uncover gold."

Gold. Au on the periodic table of the elements. Gold had made people go crazy all the way to Alaska. Gold was the most precious metal. You could save a tooth with a gold crown. Gold was popular for wedding rings. It came in white, yellow, and rose. She wondered what a ring might look like on her mother's finger, if she married Fergus the Freak. They'd move to Scotland. Lindsay hoped she didn't marry that weirdo. No way did she want to live where people talked funny and never went to the dentist. Lots of times, rings were passed down in families. Gammy claimed not to remember where hers was, and neither Allegra nor her mom had ever married, so there went that possibility.

CARL SAGAN, she printed. Things to ask him:

1. At Cornell University, did you get a special office for being so brilliant and famous? How many windows did it have?
2. What was it like working for NASA, inventing the Pioneer Space Probes 10 and 11, and then Voyager I and II? Did you worry about accidents like what had happened to the *Challenger*?
3. What do you mean, I have a "Grandfather Paradox" of my own? A paradox is a statement that contradicts itself, but might be true. Isn't Dr. G the opposite of that? Or were you speaking "figuratively"?

She would take him to dinner at Tillie Gort's because anyone who cared about their health ate mostly vegetarian, and he would like their salads as much as she did. When it came time for important questions, she would open her mouth, and out would come only the stupid things that made her want to cry and didn't matter at all when you compared them to scientific theories.

4. Why are people so mean to each other?
5. Why do they lie, and judge each other on stupid things like your backpack?

6. Why does anybody spend even one second
being mean when there is cancer in the world
just waiting to get you?
7. If I ask Allegra about Dr. G, will she tell me the
truth?

Mrs. Shiasaka sat in her armchair opening her mail. At the window, a tree limb brushed the glass. On the counter below, Geico the iguana ran up and down the dead branches inside his cage. Lindsay worried that Geico was lonely. Six of the ten girls in this class belonged to Taylor Foster's clique: Cheyennes one and two, Avril, Siouxie, and Hannah, but Hannah was absent today. That left Frankie Post and Madison Kerrigan, who always wore black nail polish and gothic crosses under their uniform blouses. During lunch, those two huddled beneath the cypress trees reading tattoo magazines. Last year, when Taylor called them vampires for refusing to play volley-ball in the sun, they'd answered, *We're Wiccans, bitch. If you know what's good for you, you'll keep your distance.*

"Time's up," Mrs. Shiasaka said. "Finish what you were writing and turn your paper facedown on the table. Who would like to be our initial presenter?"

No matter what, it was bad to go first. If you did, then who-ever came after you had the chance to give a better answer. Taylor's hand flew up. "I chose Britney Spears," she said.

After pausing one terrible moment, Mrs. Shiasaka said, "That's an interesting choice. Share with us the reasons that led you to your selection, Taylor."

"Um," Taylor said, as if sensing Mrs. Shiasaka was not on board, "first, we could have our dinner at Kobe Sushi because sushi isn't fattening, and Britney needs to stay in perfect shape, which I do, too, since I have similar ambitions. I'd ask her about when she was my age, thirteen—"

"You are *so* not thirteen," Sally said.

"I am *almost* thirteen," Taylor fired back. She took a ragged breath, and Lindsay could feel the whole room collapsing inward, like a vacuum was sucking the air out of it. "Because when you're a celebrity you have so much wealth that it's easy to help poor people or make a Make-a-Wish dream come true for a child with a fatal illness."

"And then win humanitarian of the year," Sally said.

Mrs. Shiasaka shot Sally her "first warning" look and Sally handed it right back to her. "What? I was just verbalizing a potential chain of events."

As soon as Mrs. Shiasaka turned her head, Sally rolled her eyes. "Watch me sink Taylor's boat," she whispered, and raised her hand. "Mrs. Shiasaka?" she said.

"What is it, Sally?"

"May I ask a question?"

"That all depends. If it is a respectful inquiry of the subject at hand, certainly."

"Well, it's more like a thought than a question."

"Is it an unbiased observation that will lead to deeper discussion?"

"I'm pretty sure of that," Sally said.

"Do you promise not to curse?"

Sally nodded vigorously. "I am completely done with cursing, honest."

Lindsay's stomach burned, and she pictured her Pepcid bottle in her plain old Target backpack, a faithful dog waiting for his master.

"So, Taylor," Sally said. "There's lots of stuff you can ask a pop tart, I mean star, but why not someone who made a contribution to the world?"

"Her music is a contribution."

"Yeah, but will it be around in two hundred years?"

"It could be."

"I don't know," Sally said. "It could be just me, but if I could have dinner with anyone in the world living or dead, I sure wouldn't pick a bottle-blond Madonna wanna-be. I'd have dinner with Bill Gates, or maybe Secretariat, or if I had to pick a dead guy, Mozart, or Jim Henson, because Kermit the Frog has persisted all these years, a puppet some guy made that people listen to like he's a philosopher. I'd damn sure pick somebody who did something *significant,* for God's sake."

"Sally," Mrs. Shiasaka said wearily, "once again you have not delivered a respectful inquiry and once again you have chosen to use swear words when so many others are available to you."

Taylor stuck out her tongue, hot pink from Gummi worms.

"How mature," Sally said in return.

"Girls, enough!" Mrs. Shiasaka said. "Did anyone else notice that Sally's choices were all of the male gender?"

"So what?" Sally said hotly.

Taylor leaned close to Avril Corrigan. "That's because she's a lesbian. A dyke lesbian giant!"

Everyone laughed. Lindsay put her head in her hands. Where was Carl Sagan when you needed him? She longed for Mrs. Shiasaka to put the "kibosh" on it, as Gammy would say. But Country Day had shared governance. If the disagreeing parties couldn't work things out themselves, they had to go to Mediation.

"Taylor," Mrs. Shiasaka said, "apologize to Sally or you can go to Ms. Haverfield's office."

"I'm sorry," Taylor said.

"Sally, accept Taylor's apology."

"I accept," she said, but everyone except Mrs. Shiasaka knew better.

Mrs. Shiasaka nodded. "Good. Now let's hear your choice, Sally. Then perhaps Taylor will have a few questions for you."

Without hesitation, Sally said, "Eve. She probably had wolves for pets and rode wild mustangs and caught her own food and figured out fire before guys did, plus taught herself to build the wheel."

Taylor burst out laughing. "Omigod, *Eve!* Everyone, can't you just see Sally sitting around a campfire grunting and biting raw flesh off squirrels for dinner? She'd fit right in. She even has the right skin color."

Except for Madison and Frankie, who looked bored, and Sally, whose face was flaming, there was a collective gasp.

"Taylor Foster!" Mrs. Shiasaka said. "I am deeply disappointed in you for referring to skin color as a polemic for any argument. Go to Ms. Haverfield's office immediately. Leave your backpack in the cloakroom and your paper with me. Go."

Taylor started crying. "Why am I in trouble? She made fun of my pick and she hates me. Ask anyone! She's always teasing me on the quad."

Sally had her head tipped back so far it looked like her neck was broken, but Lindsay could tell she was trying to stave off tears. "Sally," Mrs. Shiasaka said, "go to the lavatory and get hold of yourself. You will stay in from nutrition break. Geico needs his cage attended. The rest of you are excused."

Pachelbel came on, played by horns. Sally nearly toppled her chair running out. The room emptied.

Lindsay couldn't help herself. "Mrs. Shiasaka? It's not totally Sally's fault."

Mrs. Shiasaka looked at her the way she always did—distracted, taking a moment to remember who she was. "Lindsay, I know you mean well, but Sally has had problems in the past that contributed to this outburst."

"It's Taylor who's been going after Sally."

Mrs. Shiasaka began collecting their papers.

Lindsay stamped her foot. "God, will you just listen a second, please?"

Mrs. Shiasaka folded her arms across her chest. "I always listen to my girls."

"They made fun of her teeth. How tall she grew. And her skin being darker this year. This isn't the first time."

When Mrs. Shiasaka touched the jade necklace that she always wore Lindsay wondered if she was praying to Buddha the way Gammy touching her cross meant she was talking to saints. "This is valuable information, Lindsay. I'd very much like it if you'd agree to sit in on Mediation."

Lindsay's stomach flip-flopped again. If she did that, they'd go after her next. "Why can't you just punish us like regular schools do? All you have to do is say 'no' really loud and make us write I won't be mean to girls of other races six hundred times. Why can't you act like teachers instead of friends!"

Mrs. Shiasaka remained silent long enough for Lindsay to realize she'd done a bad thing. "Please, join Sally in the lavatory, Lindsay. Frankly, I'm speechless at the moment. I'll be speaking to your mother. Go compose yourself."

The last thing Lindsay's mom needed was more bad news. Gammy Bess would be so disappointed she might have a "spell." But worst of all it might cause Allegra to have a setback. "This is just like the Salem witch trials," Lindsay mumbled as she ran from the classroom, hoping to make it to the lavatory before she threw up.

After she flushed the toilet and washed her mouth out three times, she saw Sally sitting on the floor crying into the paper towel she'd pulled from the wall dispenser above her head. It had a motion sensor. All Sally had to do was lift her hand and roll out more paper towel to cry into. Lindsay took a tissue from her pocket and offered it to her. "This is softer."

Sally took it. "Gum?"

Lindsay took two pieces. "Thanks."

"You shouldn't hang around me anymore," Sally said, wiping her eyes. "You'll catch cooties that'll follow you to Carmel High."

"I don't mind cooties. You're my science project partner. We're going to win the prize, remember? You and me and Charlie and her clones. Though we should have named her Charlene."

Sally laughed, and Lindsay snorted. It was true. Every marijuana plant was a clone of the mother. That was how you got the best strains. The plants with the biggest crop were like photocopies. In three and a half weeks, Gregorio's plants had grown two feet tall. They thrived on bat guano, which Gregorio insisted was like giving the plants top-of-the-line vitamins: Centrum-stinky.

Since Sally's punishment was staying in at nutrition and cleaning Geico's cage, Lindsay stayed in to help. The girls moved Geico from his cage to the fish tank where he stayed while his cage was cleaned. "You gave up nutrition for iguana dookey," Sally said, scrubbing. "I guess that makes you a masochist."

Lindsay sprayed cleaner onto the cage bars. "I'd rather clean iguana poop every day of the week than get tortured outside for a half hour."

"Ew, dead crickets," Sally said. "Can you fish them out? We don't want our class mascot, a reptile—how fitting—to get sick from eating rotten insects."

Lindsay looked down the counter to the aquarium, where Geico was trying to climb the glass wall without success. "Do crickets have a shelf date?"

"They're crickets. How could you tell?"

"That's why I'm asking."

"I have a question, too. Lindsay, why do you love Carl Sagan?"

"He had really good ideas. He made astronomy accessible to—"

"Omigod, speaking of good ideas! Let's put these dead crickets in Taylor's backpack. On second thought, the live ones, too. Put 'em in here."

"Sally, we're already in enough trouble."

Sally held out a plastic sandwich bag. "Lindsay, we have to do this to show her we're the law in Room Thirty-two! What we say goes."

While Sally located Taylor's pack and unzipped the top enough to shove the crickets in, Lindsay worried. Could crickets have heart attacks? Was a rudimentary central nervous system enough for an insect to feel terror? Taylor screaming in their cricket ears would be like getting caught in acid rain. She heard the sound of the zipper closing.

"Come on," Sally said. "Let's put Geico back. We better haul ass."

"We?" Lindsay said. "All I did was stand here and watch."

"Wake up, Sleeping Beauty. You scooped. That makes you an accomplice."

After lunch—"Life Paths, Life Questions" class was four dreadfully long modular segments—one by one, students were interrogated about their pretend dinner guests. Avril picked Meg Ryan as a good role model because her movies were never gratuitous. Frankie and Madison picked Romania's Blood Countess, but didn't get a chance to explain why before Mrs. Shiasaka looked at the clock.

"I think we've broadened our minds enough for one day," she said. "Your homework assignment is to write a dialogue with your chosen dinner companion each and every day from now until Thanksgiving."

"But what am I supposed to write about?" Avril asked.

"Avril," Mrs. Shiasaka said. "If you can't think of anything to write to Meg Ryan, think of someone else. Or ask yourself where you'll be five years from now. Ten. Fifteen. A grown-up."

Avril sighed and set her pen down. "Then all I need to write is the same line over and over, because until I'm eighteen, I'll be wherever my dad is, with his latest girlfriend."

Lindsay was thrilled they hadn't time to get to hers.

There were no bells at Country Day. Instead, over the loudspeaker they played the music of a different artist every week. Today it was Wagner. Sturm und Drang, Lindsay thought. We need Zeus to be our principal. Somebody who can throw lightning bolts. Girls began putting things in their backpacks.

"Handwritten, not typed," Mrs. Shiasaka called out. "And at least a page long, no skipping lines, and no entries written entirely in capital letters. Before I dismiss you today, I'd just like to say, girls, I am feeling extremely disheartened about today's class. I tried to give you a mature assignment and trusted you to respond honestly and respectfully, and what happens? Fighting? Racism?"

She looked away, and right then, Lindsay felt as if she were inside Mrs. Shiasaka's skin.

"As someone whose family was interred at Manzanar, I sincerely hope that the next time we meet you will all have developed more tolerance. Otherwise, well, I just don't know if there's hope for the world. Sally and Lindsay, I will be in touch with each of your mothers. Taylor, your parents are waiting in Ms. Haverfield's office."

All the way down the hall and outside Lindsay's legs shook. If she could do this day over, she'd cut school, spend the day in the library, look up Manzanar, and come to class ready to work. Her mom was going to cry, she was sure of it. If there was a silver pocket in today's dark cloud, like Gammy always said there was, she wouldn't be allowed to go to the Halloween party, and that would take care of one problem. "What do you think Mrs. Shiasaka's going to say to your mom?" she asked Sally as they walked toward the bus.

"Probably that I need a therapist."

"Why? You don't have anything wrong with you, Taylor does."

Sally looked out across the quad to the street, where the afternoon traffic was growing thick. "Maybe I do. Kids as smart as us are ten times as likely to off ourselves even without the Taylor Fosters of the world. Check the statistics. Did this day suck or what?"

"It sucked."

"It sucked dead donkey!" Sally yelled. "Green dead donkey dong!"

Lindsay laughed. Soon Sally would board the bus, and she would head down the block toward the café. "Manzanar," she said. "Don't you feel bad for Mrs. Shiasaka?"

"Listen," Sally said, smiling, "if I feel sorry for anybody, it's the crickets whose last moments on earth before they die of fright will be smelling Taylor's stinking breath when she screams her lungs out the minute she opens her backpack."

The bus driver honked, and Sally ran. "See ya! Email me later and tell me what Mrs. S. said to your mom, 'K?"

The bus belched exhaust and Lindsay covered her nose. She and Sally had the exact same grades. Sally rode horses, and she'd had her picture in the paper three times, and while Lindsay had never been on a horse, her picture had been in *The Blue Jay,* once, her holding Khan dressed up as a bunny for Easter Sunday. Sally's photos were because she won horse shows, and a two-page feature on her mom's flower farm. The article referred to the story of Sally's dad's death, which everyone from Pacific Grove to San Celina knew about already. A man on his way to marry the love of his life dies in a chain-reaction car accident leaving wheelchair-bound fiancée alone and pregnant. The photo showed Sally at her computer, writing—a budding novelist, the article said.

All the time the teachers told them they were super intelligent. In language arts, Mrs. Potter would say, right out loud in class, "Girls, Sally DeThomas is reading at a college freshman level. Lindsay Moon has earned the highest grade on a vocabulary exam ever recorded in the history of Country Day Academy for Girls." Taylor's group made kissing noises. Mrs. Potter was hard of hearing.

Country Day students came from mostly wealthy, forward-thinking families. Taylor Foster made sure everyone knew her dentist dad had built that new hotel in Marina that was brown stucco and everyone called the fifteen-story wart. During Choose a Career month, Taylor said, "It doesn't matter what you do, what matters is that you make enough money for a comfortable life."

Lindsay's mom worked ten times as hard as Dr. Foster, but her life was far from comfortable. And look at Allegra. It wasn't her fault that chemo made her hair fall out and that she sometimes had to use a wheelchair. Sally's mom was in a wheelchair full time. But instead of seeing a woman trying to save her own life, and a woman succeeding despite her handicap, the Taylors of the world saw only freaks. Gammy said everybody had an Achilles' heel. Sally had three. One was her chipped front teeth, and being called Roger Rabbit. Two was the subject of her Mexican father, who had died before she was born. Three was the fact that both her parents, mother and stepfather, were confined to wheelchairs.

Lindsay hated her curly hair, but that was nothing compared to being short. She wished she could stop thinking about everything. She knew she wasn't clinically depressed—she took the internet test but didn't have enough of the symptoms. But the pressure of conforming to the loose, interdisciplinary structure of teaching was so much worse than following hard-and-fast rules over time. She ached for tests with right and wrong answers, subjects so hard she'd have to resort to using acronyms in order to memorize difficult terms. And to top it off, how about some kind of P.E. that made sense? Some people were just no good at hatha yoga. She knew where the Louvre was, that the political climate in Chile was unstable, and that Billy Collins was the poet laureate of the United States though some people didn't think it was fair because his poems were too easy to understand.

Mrs. Shiasaka was right to give them the imaginary dialogue assignment. You could have an imaginary conversation with someone and see things differently. Maybe Carl Sagan would talk to her again. A lot of pretending and listening to Carl Sagan—that was what it'd take to get through this last year of Country Day.

As she entered the café she looked up at the owl. He wasn't great art, but he was always there, his talons gently curved over the moon, not poking. His beak had chipped. Someone should climb up and paint it. When she saw Dr. G sitting at the counter, she said, "Is Allegra going to die?"

"Of course not, Lindsay. I'm sorry I alarmed you."

"Then why are you here?"

"Picking up some soup for dinner. Apparently hospital food isn't organic enough for your grandmother."

"Can I visit her?"

"It's a school night, isn't it? Why don't you call her? She needs to rest. Tomorrow or the next day I'll probably release her. How was school?"

Lindsay set her backpack behind the counter. "You really want to know?"

"I wouldn't have asked if I didn't mean it."

She sighed. "I got in trouble and my teacher's going to call my mom and I'll probably get a mark on my permanent record. School sucked. Big time," she said instead of "donkey dong," like she wanted to. Her face flushed. "Sorry about saying 'sucked.'"

"Don't apologize. It sounds as if it did indeed suck." He patted the stool next to him. Gammy was waiting on customers and her mother wasn't anywhere to be seen. "I'd be happy to listen if you want to talk about it."

"It's complicated."

"I've got time."

"Some girls at my school are kind of mean to this one person. I stood up for her, and my teacher got mad."

"Sounds to me like you did a good thing. What's this teacher's name?"

"Mrs. Shiasaka. I have her for homeroom and 'Life Paths, Life Questions.'"

"Sounds like an interesting class. I don't understand why you would get in trouble for standing up for a friend."

"Probably because I might have . . ." she hesitated, trying to swallow the lump in her throat. "Been kind of emotional."

"There's nothing wrong with showing emotion," he said. Dr. G took his cell phone from his jacket pocket. "What's your school's telephone number?"

"You don't need to call them," Lindsay said. "It's my mess."

"Oh, but you see I have to, Lindsay. I took an oath to heal others, and this teacher sounds mentally ill."

Lindsay laughed. "She's not, honestly. Most of the time she's pretty nice. We kids drive her crazy."

"What's the number?"

Lindsay repeated it, and Dr. G pressed all the numbers.

"Sure, I can hold," he said, and winked at Lindsay.

Her mother came out from the kitchen. "Hi, Linds," she said. "How was your day? Did you do anything—"

Dr. G held up a finger like the call was important, and she shushed. Then he walked outside onto the sidewalk and began talking. What was he saying? Was she going to get into more trouble because of it? "My day was pretty much the usual," Lindsay said, which was the truth. "How was yours?"

Her mom looked around the café like it was a jail cell. "Same here. Hungry?"

"Not really."

"How about some cocoa?"

"I have a lot of homework."

Dr. G came back in. "I love it when problems can be so easily resolved. Now, if your grandmother would follow my instructions, the two of us would be going out to dinner and a movie instead of back to the hospital. There's my soup. Thank you, Mariah."

"You're welcome, Dr. Goodnough."

"I wish you'd call me Al."

While she waited for her mother to say "Sure, I will," Lindsay scrutinized Dr. G's strong chin that jutted out just like her mom's when she was making a point. His eyes were big like her mom's and the exact same color. A grandfather paradox, or a grandfather of her own? What if he was her mom's dad, and this was only the very first time he'd come to her rescue? Wasn't a good scientist supposed to say something? Or would the truth reveal itself over time? How did a person decide what to do?

"I'll try," Mariah said, but to Lindsay it didn't sound like she meant it.

Lindsay didn't want him to leave just yet. She wanted to examine him, gather more evidence. "Dr. G, what is your opinion on the Human Genome Project?"

He thought a moment. "Lindsay, it's so controversial I couldn't really sum it up in one sentence. How about we take a walk and talk it over?"

Lindsay looked at her mother. "Can I?"

"Fine with me. Take Khan, why don't you? I'm sure he'd appreciate some fresh air. I'll put the soup back in the fridge. When you're ready to go, you can find it there."

9

Allegra

"THE DAY HAS ARRIVED," Allegra said to Lindsay the morning after she was released from Hell Central, aka the hospital. Her darling granddaughter had brought her toast, tea, and a tiny cup of berries in yogurt for breakfast, and sat there while she ate what she could. Bless her heart. If anyone understood how touchy eating could be to a person who wasn't hungry, it was Lindsay. "I'm finally ready to do the deed."

Lindsay grinned. "Good for you, Allegra! Lots of people do it. It's not just men anymore. If we lived in Europe no one would even notice."

"Brace yourself, babe. People are going to notice. Gammy, for one. Fetch the clippers. They're in the hall closet, behind the towels."

Allegra watched her granddaughter with delight. Her last night in the hospital, Al had stayed long after visiting hours. She laughed when he related Lindsay's "getting in trouble" at school story, and at how he'd taken care of it with a phone call. How dare you inflate normal schoolgirl tiffs when Lindsay is under such tremendous stress, he'd said, and that was the end of that. Allegra thanked him for stepping in to fight the battle when she was too weak to do it. Which of course was exactly the right time to tell him he was Mariah's father. But she'd held back, and she knew why. She didn't want to invoke Hurricane Mariah.

Where Mariah would have grounded Lindsay for talking back to a teacher, Allegra thought the child deserved a reward. Lindsay was standing up for her beliefs—Allegra had filled her with examples: Martin Luther King Jr. speaking for the black man, the scores of kids protesting the Vietnam War, Cesar Chavez organizing migrant workers—here was proof that her investment in the future was paying off. A future that despite Doc's insistence, she wondered if she'd live to see.

She'd thanked him again, and cried a little. He'd taken her in his arms and patted her back. *Allegra, you'll be there for her graduation,* he said. *Her first child, too, maybe even her midlife crisis, if you take good care of yourself.* Taking care was the key. These days her heart felt as tender as a rosebud. Any more sadness heaped on it would cause it to wither before it could bloom.

"I found them, Allegra," Lindsay said, holding up the clippers.

"Thanks. I think the number-two blade will work best. Spread some newspaper around my chair. We don't want to make a mess, especially since our vacuum is temperamental."

At the sound of the word *vacuum,* Khan barked.

"Yes, Khan, we know the vacuum's your mortal enemy," Allegra said. "Now go back to sleep."

"Want me to cut it short before we start?"

"Just shave it as close as you can. The nurse at chemo told me that sometimes a wig can be made from it."

"No offense," Lindsay said. "But wigs look fake. I think you should just go bald."

"Let's see how it turns out."

Allegra heard the fateful click and the buzzing began. At the pinch on the sensitive hairs at the base of her neck, she closed her eyes, dropped her head toward her chest, and felt the clippers take their first row, and then the next. With every pass, she felt cool air touch her scalp and a weight lift. When the buzzing stopped, she opened her eyes and saw Lindsay arranging handfuls of hair evenly alongside one another at the edge of the newspaper. Mariah was downstairs baking. Gammy was at the store. Allegra had planned the haircut so neither of them would be able to talk her out of it.

"Ready to look in the mirror?" Lindsay asked.

"As ready as I'll ever be."

Lindsay held up the glass, and Allegra ran her hands over her pale scalp, feeling the bumps and slight depressions. Her scalp felt like Al's cleanly shaven jaw. Lindsay handed her a ponytail of her former hair. She held it against her cheek, but it no longer looked like it belonged to her.

"Allegra, please don't cry."

She sniffled. Step one of her plan was now ticked off the list. "I'm fine, sweetie. Just a moment of barber's remorse." She hugged her granddaughter to her, then spoke into the wavy strawberry blond hair so full of health it had a will of its own. "Now be a good girl and find me the prettiest scarf in the drawer."

Step two, a few days later, required alone time with Al, but halfway through the movie Johnny Depp was doing such a good job of holding in his grief that Allegra lost control of hers. At first it was only hot tears welling in her eyes, the kind of sorrow she felt watching the Pedigree commercial "We're for Dogs." Sappy, the last shreds of her idealism waving in the wind like tattered prayer flags, proof her tired old heart could be had for a jingle. But the tears evolved to sniffling, followed by snuffling, and finally she had to hold the popcorn napkins over her mouth to muffle the noise of struggling not to sob.

While the credits ran, Allegra balled up the evidence,

stuffed it in her shoulder bag, and walked out of the theater into the balmy October evening on the arm of the man she had never stopped loving.

"I told you we should have gone to the kung fu movie," he said for the third time when they were seated at a table in Fifi's, more of a restaurant than The Owl & Moon would ever be. Fifi's may have had a larger variety of pastries, but Allegra felt sure The Owl & Moon's were superior. "It's better to laugh than cry any day of the week."

She looked up at Al, this growing-old version of the happy hitchhiker, Grateful Dead Head, granola-for-breakfast Vietnam vet. "You're right," she said, regretting having lobbied so hard for what was described as the feel-good chick flick of the year. Lying bastard reporters having their fun. "Why do love stories have to be so doggone tragic? Can't anyone write a happy ending anymore?"

He unfolded his napkin. "Beats me. In the online *Chronicle,* the critics said this movie was a sure bet for an Academy Award. If all it takes is crying, they should come to the E.R. Plenty of sad stories there."

Allegra squinted at her menu. Could they make the print any smaller? "When did you turn into that kind of person, Al? Checking reviews before choosing."

"Now don't you dare pick a fight with me. I took you out tonight so we could have some fun."

"What's that supposed to mean?"

He reached across the table and took hold of her hands. "Woman, we're grown-ups with jobs and responsibilities and illnesses and children and this wonderfully rare connection. I find you sexy as hell and I was hoping if we had an old-fashioned date you might let me kiss you someplace other than your cheek. I'm sorry I researched the movie. Next time we'll throw the I Ching."

How did she tell him about Mariah? Her plan that a love story would soften him up had failed. Just as she was about to speak, Al cleared his throat.

"I guess this is as good a time as any for me to lay my cards on the table, Allegra. Do I have a chance with you? If not, let me down right now. My old heart can't take leaping up if it's going to be swatted down like some catnip mouse."

"Al! Is that the way you think I treat you?"

"Not yet, but the possibility exists."

She sipped her water, hoping that the right thing to say would come to her. She wanted to be brave, to tell the truth, but which truth did you start with? Buying time, she said, "You can't find me sexy. I have no hair. I'm a scrawny old hen and my boobs have disappeared. You feel sorry for me because my life didn't turn out very well and yours did. You're worried that I'm going to die. That's not love."

"Horseshit."

People were looking. "Al, there's no need to raise your voice like that."

"Why not? You seem to have no trouble saying blunt things and judging me. Seems to me I'm allowed to say anything I want if you are. I love you, Allegra." He turned to the other diners. "Everybody got that? I love this woman."

Allegra was shocked. This was her type of behavior, not his. "Al, let's go. We'll finish this in the car."

He balled up his napkin and threw it down on the table. "No. I don't want to finish anything. I want to start something. I love you, Allegra. Now look me in the eyes and tell me you don't love me back."

She was three days out of the hospital, pneumonia free, hematocrit rising. Instead of resuming the chemo, Doc had decided to put her on the wonder drug, imatinib mesylate, a name that sounded like pig latin. The pills cost three grand a month, and the insurance company was holding some kind of summit meeting to decide if they'd pay for them. What would happen if they said no? With her kind of leukemia, if you stopped the pills, the disease was more than happy to come back and finish what it had begun. The waiter came to the table and lit the votive candle in the glass holder.

Before he could rattle off the specials, Allegra said, "Can you give us a few more minutes?"

"Of course. How about I bring you sourdough bread just out of the oven, and some oil and balsamic vinegar, unless you'd rather have butter."

"Plain bread and butter," she said.

Allegra looked into Al's eyes. "Of course I love you. I never stopped loving you. That's the truth. I've spent years being a party girl, trying way too hard to have fun because I thought it would numb my feelings about you."

He grinned. "Then for God's sake, marry me! Let's go do it tonight and spend the rest of our lives together. No more lost time. Not one single breath apart."

Allegra bit her lower lip. "First I have to tell you something, and I'm scared."

"Scared of what?"

"That it might change how you feel about me."

"Allegra, there's nothing you could say that will do that. Tell me already."

"I'm trying to. Give me a minute. I want to say it right."

The bread arrived. Al picked up a piece and began to rip it into pieces. "Are you planning to tell me anytime in the next hour?"

"First I need to use the restroom." Allegra excused herself and headed for the door marked women. Inside, she braced herself on the vanity and looked in the mirror at the paper-thin copy of who she was at this time last year. She splashed water on her face, patted it dry with a scratchy towel, dislodging one of her press-on eyebrows. She fixed it, then she turned to the door, and opened it. He was still there, the man who had more hair than she did, her hopeful Doc, sitting and waiting, a tattered pile of bread on his plate that looked like something to feed to ducks.

Back at the table, she folded her hands, and looked up at him. "The Sufi poet Rumi once said that 'Lovers don't meet, somewhere along the way, they are in each other all along.'"

"Always with the poetry," he said.

"Al, I'm trying—"

"Okay. I'm good with the poetry. Go on."

She sipped her water. "It's taken me thirty-three years to understand what Rumi meant. I was barely sixteen when I met you. Nobody thinks anyone that young is capable of loving somebody forever. Gammy sure didn't."

"Ancient history, Allegra. You're an adult with a grown daughter and a grandchild. You can speak for yourself without checking in with the bingo queen."

She tugged at the edges of her cloche hat, feeling the ribbon rose on the left side. "I know that now. I wish I'd fought for it all those years ago. Al, Mariah's going to turn thirty-four this February. She's your daughter. And Lindsay's your grandchild."

When she devised her plan back in the hospital, the pneumonia sat on her lungs like bricks. Between sips of breath, she bargained with Gammy's God. More time, please. Let me do this one thing right to make up for all the times I got things wrong. She'd imagined Al hoisting her in the air and whooping with excitement; Al buying a round of drinks for the restaurant; Al yelling at her for keeping a secret but instantly forgiving her because he was so happy; the two of them throwing money down on the table and rushing to find Mariah and Lindsay for a family—a *family!*—hug. Instead, the man who had just proposed to her sat there, the expression on his face unreadable. "If you'll excuse me for a moment," he said, standing up, his napkin falling to the floor.

"Al, come back," she said, but he turned and walked out the entrance of the restaurant.

Allegra retrieved his napkin and folded it, setting it next to the plate of ruined bread. How had her plan gone so wrong? Fuck poets anyway. Flowery language was one thing, but real life? Altogether different. She picked up the remaining slice of bread and checked out the cell walls. Really nice for sourdough. Her own starter, begun when Mariah was in kindergarten, had made so many rolls and loaves she couldn't count that high. She hadn't used it since she became ill. By now it was probably black with mold. She would give up her hair forever if it meant she could knead dough again.

Ten minutes later, she told the hovering waiter, "I'll have the soup."

When it arrived, she sat there staring at it, wondering if she could manage a few tablespoons. What if Al didn't come back? He could turn her case over to a colleague. She could just hear Gammy: You made your own bed up with those slippery satin sheets and now you're crying because you keep falling out of it. Well, all I can say is lie still and try not to sneeze. She set the spoon down and looked out the window.

October was unpredictable. Some days it was heat wave hot; other days felt like winter had settled in. Nights, it was damp and cold. Halloween, one of her favorite holidays, didn't have much appeal this year. Lindsay was going to a party, not trick-or-treating with her scary-looking grandmother who didn't need makeup to look like a zombie. Mariah had a date with Fergus. Allegra hoped that meant sex. Long ago Gammy had quit making popcorn balls for neighborhood kids due to urban legends about razor blades. Now she avoided the whole mess by playing cards with her friends out in the valley and the café stayed dark.

What was left for a bald, skinny broad in a fragile remission? She didn't want to watch another made-for-television movie, or read a phony-baloney romance novel, or even listen to music, considering the majority of songs were all about love. The whole idea was to escape from reality, not have it slap you in the face. She'd gotten along without Alvin Goodnough all these years. She could do it again. Maybe she'd take a taxi down to Pier Two and spy on Mariah. Serve her right, for being so secretive.

She bent to retrieve her bag from the floor, and as she came up, a large bouquet of carnations appeared under her nose. Behind them was Doc, the flowers in one hand, and chocolates in the other. "Okay, poetry fan," he said. "I wrote you a poem. Let me read it to you."

Several more dinner parties had arrived. Allegra felt her cheeks redden. "That's okay. I'll read it to myself."

"Oh, no you won't. Every time we're together you're quoting this poet or that one. You're all about the poems. I wrote this poem and I'm by God reading it." He cleared his throat. " 'Thirty-four years ago Allegra Moon stole my heart. If I'd been smart, I would've run after her.' " His voice broke, and Allegra reached for his hand, but he waved her away, and cleared his throat. " 'Back then we were both pretty wild, but I didn't know that we'd have a child. Now that I do, it's all up to you. Allegra Moon, please don't be a donkey. Say you'll marry this old honky.' "

Tears rolled down her cheeks. "That's a terrible poem."

He nodded. "I'm clumsy at matters of the heart, and my last wife left me for a guy with a stainless-steel speculum. But shouldn't it count in my favor that if the situation warranted it, I could perform rudimentary heart surgery? Doesn't that prove I'm not a total doofus with the organ?"

Allegra could feel every restaurant customer waiting for her "yes" so they could toast them, send over champagne, and feel reassured in their own relationships. But all she could do was look into her flowers, dip her nose into the peppery scent of carnations, and try not to feel sick. "Sit down and let's talk."

"No. Damn it, Allegra, I spent thirty minutes writing this poem in that florist's shop. I'm serious. I want to marry you. Right now."

"But Al, we don't even know if I'll be here a year from now."

Doc hung his head. When he looked up, he said, "You see, that's where you're wrong. I do know you'll be here. It's you that doesn't know it. For Christ's sake, Allegra. You used to believe world peace was possible, so why can't you believe you are?"

The display having no happy ending, the patrons had gone

back to their meals and conversations. She reached into her purse and touched the crumpled up movie napkins, ready to use them if the tears came. "Do you still want dinner?"

"I'd go without ten dinners if it meant you'd take me seriously. Twenty."

She tried to laugh, but all she could see was Johnny Depp's face at the funeral. "Can you wait for me to believe I will be around?"

He reached across the table and took her hand. "I'll give you three days."

"Al—"

"Enough, Allegra. This is fate. It was back then, and we were so young we blew it. Who are we to spit in the face of finding each other again? Now that's choosing dying over living."

She was crying again. "Okay. If I'm still here in six months, I'll marry you."

Al had a first-paper-route, adopted-mutt, ten-speed-bike-for-Christmas smile. A person could get slammed going around like that, but it was his choice. "Excellent. But why do we have to wait six months?"

The man at the table next to them tipped his chair back. "Listen, pal, I don't want to be a buttinsky, but don't press your luck," he said, and several people were laughing, and then they started clapping.

Al flagged the waiter down and handed him a credit card to pay for the soup and the torn up bread.

The waiter handed it back. "The manager said to tell you the soup's on the house. This is the most fun we've had since Jane Smiley stopped by for cannoli. May we suggest you have your wedding reception here?"

Allegra held up her hand. "If I get married it will be on the beach with sun in my face and the wind in my hair. When it grows back."

"My God, will you just look at her," Doc said, spreading his arms to include everyone in the room. "Everybody, isn't that the face of an angel?"

And Allegra thought, of course, to become an angel, all you have to do is die.

"Mama?" Allegra said into the telephone at Al's "beach house," a four-thousand-square-foot palace that she told him was as far from a beach house as Camp David was a Y camp. "I'm not coming home tonight. I just wanted to let—"

"You're not coming home?" Gammy said. "Alice, are you going back in the hospital?"

"No, Mama. I'm fine. I'm spending the night with Al."

"Have you lost your mind?"

Allegra sighed, while Al kissed the back of her neck. "Mama, Al asked me to marry him tonight. I said yes. I'm staying at his place. I called so you wouldn't worry when I didn't come home. Mama? Are you still there?"

Bess gave a heavy sigh. "Alice, the minute you turned fifteen you were as wild as duckweed. You nagged me for hip-hugger bell-bottom pants and money to hear rock bands. You sneaked cigarettes whenever you got a chance. I let you go to one concert in San Francisco and boom, suddenly you're on the road like that Jeff Kerouac. I probably should have called the cops, reported you a runaway, but how could I when it was my own fault for not chaining you to your bed? I did the only other thing I could, which was turn it over to our Lord. Then you come home, pregnant with Mariah. I bit my tongue and helped you raise her. She turned out to be such a good girl, but she didn't escape the Moon family curse."

"Mariah's a grown woman, Mama. When are you going to stop judging us on getting pregnant outside of marriage?"

"Be that as it may, now you're calling to tell me you're spending the night just because the man said he wants to marry you. I'm sorry. I don't care if you're fifteen or fifty, Alice, marriage is a holy sacrament. The fun stuff comes after you get the ring. Now you call a taxi and come on home."

Allegra could hear Lindsay squealing in the background.

Did she say engaged? Is it to Doc? "Mama, be serious. I've just been through chemo. We are not having sex. Even if we were, it's not like I'm going to get pregnant. If my ovaries had any eggs left I'm sure they got fried."

"Alice, your words are arrows in my heart. How are you going to explain this at the pearly gates? Good gravy, Lindsay, will you hold on a second?"

Next, Allegra heard some muffled conversation, while Al nibbled her ear. Oh, it felt good to be with someone who wasn't afraid you were going to give him cancer. Whenever she felt well enough to run the café register, people set the money on the counter and it hurt her to think they saw her as infectious.

Don't listen to Gammy, Lindsay was saying. A person should take a chance to be happy no matter what.

"You hear that?" Gammy said.

"Hear what?"

"Me holding the phone to my creaky knees attached to my legs with the varicose veins that could burst any minute. I'm kneeling down for your immortal soul, Alice. I'm willing to make the sacrifice even if you're not."

Allegra could hear Lindsay in the background, saying don't listen to her, Allegra. Dr. G will make a good husband.

And Mariah was out with Fergus. Allegra hadn't planned having to postpone the third part of her plan, which was to tell Mariah and Lindsay face-to-face. Chemo hadn't dulled all her nerve endings, for Doc had now moved on to her collar-bone, and things were humming. Al wanted a wife. What did she want? Him to stitch her family together? Was it sexist, thinking that a man could do all that simply because of a shared pool of genes in the offspring you loved? She cleared her throat. "I'll see you tomorrow, Mama. Give Lindsay a goodnight kiss for me." She hung up and turned to face the man who was getting her all stirred up. "That didn't go well."

"Who cares? Put on this jacket and let's walk on the beach."

To Allegra "the beach" meant walking three blocks, crossing

three lanes of traffic and sharing the sand with whoever else happened to be there. The beach in front of Al's house was empty. Not a single person besides them was there. There was no fast-food litter, no radios blaring, no stink of suntan lotion, just the gentle roar of the surf and strewn kelp. Standing there by the moonlit water, the Pacific Ocean once again became Allegra's faithful and trustworthy companion. If she and Al married, they could start every morning naming the shorebirds over coffee. What a complete cop-out to live simple all these years only to discover you wanted the big ticket items after all?

Behind her, Al spread out a blanket. "Come sit," he said.

She lowered herself to the blanket and ran her fingers through the sand, sifting the cool, dry grains through her fingers. Al put his arm around her and they kissed like longtime married couples, all lips, no tongue. "Thirty-four years is a long time," she said. "Wanna mess around?"

"I'm afraid we can't."

"Why not?"

"Allegra, even if I did have a condom, which I don't, it's not a good idea." He slid his hand across her leg. "Baby, you're radioactive."

"Ha ha, Doc. Very funny. Maybe I used to be, but not anymore."

"I'm serious. Most physicians will tell you that chemo transferring from patient to partner is a myth. I'm conservative. Chemo is present in exchanged fluids, probably too small to hurt anyone, but why take the chance? In addition, whatever cold or virus I've got brewing would love to latch on to you. Doctor's orders: No fun stuff until you're stronger. Look at it this way. We're about to become experts in the field of hugging and kissing."

"For how long?"

"Only eight or nine months."

"Are you kidding me?"

He laughed. "Yes. Come on, let's go to bed and try snuggling."

Snuggle. Allegra rolled the word around in her mind as they settled into this chasm of a bed Al insisted was only king-size, but felt bigger. Allegra was wearing one of his T-shirts. Al slept nude, though he kind of backed into bed so she couldn't see his penis, which she found silly but also kind of adorable. The second he was asleep she planned to lift the covers and look. For now she nestled into the nook of his shoulder and sighed at his tenseness. If he were bread dough, she'd give him some thorough kneading, a slap or two, and he'd become flexible to her hand, waiting for her to shape him. She ran her hand down the inside of his arm, feeling the difference between muscle and soft skin. She leaned in and kissed him in the fold of his elbow, where the skin was smoothest, careful to keep her lips closed. "We can have sex if we use a rubber, can't we?"

"Please," he said. "Don't start. I'm having enough trouble keeping my hands off you."

"So don't keep your hands off me."

"Will you please just accept that this can't go anywhere right now?"

Allegra continued stroking his arm, feeling his skin and her own buzz from touching him. Sex makes the body act like an anemone, she thought. So sensitive that the slightest touch makes it pull inward. "Sleepy yet?" she asked a few minutes later.

"Of course not."

"I know you said I'm radioactive, but isn't there something we can do?"

He sighed. "Do I have to log onto the internet and show you studies?"

"Can't I just touch you?"

"It depends on how you plan to touch me."

"I was thinking like this." She moved her hand to the furry space below his bellybutton, though her true destination lay a few inches south.

He closed his fingers around her hand. "Stop it," he said.

"We're not in a hurry anymore. Let's get up and eat cereal. We never had dinner and I'm hungry."

"I'm not hungry."

"Allegra, what are you afraid of?"

"That the chemo took it away."

"What could it possibly take away except your cancer?"

"Me wanting sex. I feel about as attractive as a spayed cat."

He breathed into her neck. "You're a knockout because of your soul, not your body. It'll come back and you'll rock this old man, I promise. Your body's been working hard to get well. Give it time to grow stronger."

"That is a promise I'm holding you to," she said.

As they began to settle into sleep, Doc said, "Must we really wait six months to get married?"

"Tell you what. We can get married the minute we can have sex."

In bed that morning, Allegra startled awake at the scent of coffee. She could hear someone bustling in the kitchen, but Al was right here beside her. She shook his shoulder. "Al, wake up. I think someone's broken into your house."

He roused and propped himself on one elbow. "It's only Cricket."

"Who the hell is Cricket?"

"My housekeeper."

She looked around the spartan bedroom: a platform bed, a chair and ottoman in the corner, a pile of books beside it. The only other item was a large abstract painting that looked to her like so much weathered wood with an orange paint spill on it that she wanted to touch it. His closet was one of those walk-in types, bigger than any of the bedrooms above The Owl & Moon. And tidy. Last night she'd watched him put his clothes into the hamper. There was nothing to clean. "What do you need a housekeeper for?"

He rubbed his eyes. "It's a big house. I don't have time to

dust or keep the mildew at bay. She cleans up and—" he yawned and stretched his arms, falling back on the pillow. "Makes my dinner, does the laundry. Stuff like that. Don't worry, I pay her a lot, and I give her a Christmas bonus and a paid vacation. Nobody's getting exploited."

Allegra turned and looked out the window. There it was, a daylight view of an empty beach, curlews and sandpipers at the water line, poking their beaks into the sand in search of sand crabs. "I have to get to work," she said.

"No, you don't. It's Saturday."

"Saturday is one of our biggest days at the café. I know I can't do the baking, but I can run the register. Besides, Gammy needs to be able to yell at me for being a wanton sinner or she'll be mean to customers all day."

Al traced a finger down her spine. Doc, her fellow stargazer. The man who could make Spam and Swiss Miss cocoa haute cuisine. She could still hear the sound of his whoop when Damnation Creek Trail ended with the ocean view they'd hiked hours to see. Sex with someone you loved was different. There was youth and risk and adventure to measure up to. What if after all these years, she wasn't any good? "I need to shower," she said, getting up from the bed, standing there in the T-shirt, afraid to let him see her naked.

Al turned over and whistled. "Nice legs. Come back to bed."

"I can't. I have to get changed and call a cab unless you're willing to drive me."

"Then take my car."

"But how will you get around?"

He gave her a sheepish smile. "Actually, I have two cars."

"Two cars? Why on earth do you need two cars?"

"The Porsche I drive to work. Sometimes I use the Land Rover on the weekends. I still like getting into the woods, hiking. Oh, God. I'm going to have to sell them, aren't I? Stop looking at me like I enjoy wasting fossil fuels. Until you said you'd marry me all I had for fun was my cars. As soon as Mercedes comes out with a hybrid, I'm there."

She looked at his sleepy face. "We're so different. What makes you so sure we can do this?"

"Hey, I know Pascal wasn't a poet, but he did say 'the heart has its reasons.' Dammit, Allegra. I'll sell everything and deed this place to the Nature Conservancy if that's what it takes for you to have faith in me. In us."

She decided he meant it. "You don't have to sell anything. For now."

He tossed his pillow in the air and caught it. "Thank you. Come back when you're done working. We can have all night and tomorrow together."

"I'll try. It depends on how things go with Gammy and the girls."

"Let me come with you. We'll tell them together."

"Thanks, but I think I have to do this alone."

Allegra parked on the street at a meter she'd have to feed quarters to all day, but at least she could keep an eye on the ritzy car. She slid her key into the front-door lock, pausing first to look up at the sign. All these years it had been her touchstone. Then Al came back. She wanted to believe that their finding one another was as magic to him as it was to her, that maybe it had drawn him here, but she knew the true reason was her illness. The moment she entered the café she heard Gammy in the kitchen, speaking to Mariah. "Four in the morning, Mariah?"

Her daughter countered, "But you said you'd babysit Lindsay, and she sleeps late on Saturday. I didn't realize you wanted me home early."

"I suppose four AM is normal for some folks, like milkmen or newspaper delivery boys."

"I'm sorry. If I'd known it was going to upset you . . ."

Allegra tried to send Mariah a mental message: Don't cave in! If she'd learned anything over the years, it was don't give Gammy ammunition and don't ever apologize.

"That's not the point," Gammy continued, and Allegra could see Mariah's stricken face through the cutout for the order counter. Whatever brief joy a late night with Fergus had given her, it was gone now. "Dating is good for you. God wants us to find mates, but premarital sex, that's a big N-O."

"We didn't have sex."

"Not this time."

"I said I was sorry, Gammy."

"That isn't the point."

"Then, well, what other point is there?"

That tremble in Mariah's voice meant she was going to cry. Her tough cookie of a daughter, finally taking a chance on love. Allegra set her keys down on the counter and picked up Khan for a quick snuggle. She kissed him all over, and inhaled his doggy smell, which was earthy and funky and better than perfume.

"Mariah, that old saying about why buy the cow when you can milk it through the fence is as true now as it was when people still owned cows. I'm going to tell you something not even your mother knows. I was starry-eyed myself, once. Then I had an argument with my beau over something so silly I can't even remember what it was. Along comes Myron Moon, the heir to a lumber company, and every girl's idea of a happy ending. He poured me a drink while I boo-hooed my troubles to a boy I thought was a good listener. Turned out he listened so well I let him lift my dress. Thirty days later I have to say good-bye to the boy I could have been happy with to marry the one who made me pregnant. You think that was any way to start a marriage? Let me tell you, Sister Sue, it was not. I was a conquest, that's all. He got tired of me when I was there every day. When he was killed his family couldn't wait two days to ship me off. This building we're standing in? It was my go-away-and-forget-you-ever-knew-us present."

Allegra was stunned.

Mariah said, "That's not fair. You should have told me

when I got pregnant with Lindsay. You should have told Mom a long time ago."

"I was ashamed. Some things are personal. Premarital sex is a sin. Why else does the Church advise against it? Come on, now. Don't make me lose faith in you. Think of the example you're setting for Lindsay."

That did it. Allegra put Khan in his basket, but he'd already started trembling. He'd always sensed her moods. "Mama," Allegra said, pushing her way into the kitchen through the louvered saloon doors. "You shut your mouth this instant."

"Here comes another one who thinks it's acceptable to stay out all hours with a man," Gammy said. "Is anybody going to work today?"

Allegra took down from the wall the oversized ladle someone had given to her one year as a joke present. She lifted it up, and then brought it down as hard as she could, enough to leave a dent on the metal counter. "That's enough out of you! Don't you dare talk to my daughter that way."

"Why not? I raised her."

"Gammy!" Mariah said. "You take that back. Allegra may not have been the best mother, but she loves me and Lindsay with all her heart."

Allegra blinked away tears on what should have been the happiest day of her life. "Honey, you go start folding napkin bundles. I need to talk to Gammy alone."

Mariah fled. Gammy squared off, the ailing dishwasher at her back. Allegra composed herself as much as she could, but every nerve was bristling. "I know life didn't turn out the way you wanted it to, Mama. I know raising me by yourself wasn't easy. But I can't think of one reason why you'd keep your pregnancy story from me all these years except to punish me. I have to wonder what your God thinks about that, Mama. I just have to wonder."

Gammy sniffled. "You think the world stopped in its tracks when I made a mistake? It did not. I didn't tell you because I was trying my darndest to keep it from happening to you. And look what happened. It did. I failed."

Allegra took hold of her mother's hand. "You didn't fail, you were human. But do you have any idea how much easier it would have been for Mariah if she'd known you got pregnant accidentally, too? Here I lived my whole life feeling sorry for you losing Myron so early, and his family rejecting us when it turns out you didn't even want to be there." She hung the ladle up. "Where Mariah's concerned I admit I screwed up a lot of the time. But she's an adult, and if she wants to spend the night with Charlie Manson, that's her decision. Are your legs bothering you? Why don't you go back upstairs? We can handle things down here without you."

Gammy snorted. "You have no more flesh on you than a scarecrow. I'd like to see you try to get through this day without me."

"Then take a seat at the counter."

Gammy took hold of her cross and looked away. Allegra, fire in her belly, went into the café and found Mariah standing at table four, crying. She put her arms around her from behind, and for once, Mariah allowed it. "Imagine that. Us loose broads having something in common with Gammy! Who'd of thunk it?" She pressed her face into Mariah's hair, which smelled of a man's soap. Allegra patted her daughter's shoulder. "We'll cope, honey. Gammy doesn't mean to be so harsh. It's her legs. Sooner or later we are going to have to get Al to give us a Mickey to slip into her food. Then we'll rush her to the hospital and have the varicose vein surgery done. Maybe when she isn't in pain all the time, she'll act human again. And for what it's worth? Good for you, staying out late. I bet you had fun."

The way Mariah smiled, Allegra knew she was right. "Simon will be here any minute, and I have croissants to bake."

"Yes," Allegra said. "And I seem to have lost one of my eyebrows. Thank God they come in packs of three."

Gammy stayed upstairs all day. Lindsay came down around ten, and surprised Allegra by putting on an apron and taking up an order pad. "Can I wait on tables? I need to earn some money for supplies for my science project."

For once Allegra thought before she answered. "Go ask your mother."

Allegra watched the way Mariah placed her hand on Lindsay's shoulder. That restrained gesture said it all. She was a better mother than Allegra had been to her. Lindsay smiled broadly and began taking charge of her tables. Timing, she told herself, was everything. Part three of her plan—telling Mariah and Lindsay—could wait a little while.

10
Mariah, Lindsay

"I FAIL TO SEE HOW shopping counts as a date," Fergus complained on the Wednesday afternoon of Halloween as Mariah dragged him into the used bookstore near the Monterey Bay Aquarium. "If it's secondhand books you're after, Hay-on-Wye's the place to go."

"Where's that, I'm afraid to ask," Mariah said, running her finger along the spines of the science books, trying to find the *S* authors. Interesting organizational skills were at work here—there was a *B* in the middle of the *R*'s, and that was followed by an *M,* for crying out loud.

"Wales."

Of course it was. Fergus thrived on telling her how everything "across the pond" was superior to America, to Northern California in particular, to which she always replied, then why do you live here? "Next time we're in Wales, I'll make a special point to check out the bookstores. Just give me a few minutes, okay? I've been looking for this book for months."

"Why?"

"Because Lindsay loves this author."

"Allow me to help you."

She felt his lips graze the back of her neck. "That's not helping. As soon as I find the book, we can go have our conventional date. Dammit all, they told me they had it when I called. I can't believe someone else in Pacific Grove would be on the hunt for *Communications with Extraterrestrial Intelligence*. I'm going to ask the guy at the desk. If he sold it to someone else I'm going to be very mad."

"If I was that bloke," Fergus said, "I'd run hell-bent for leather."

Mariah stuck her tongue out at Fergus, then marched up to the elderly gentleman behind the counter who apparently didn't hear very well. Finally she wrote the title down on a business card and pointed. "It's by Carl Sagan. You know, 'billions and billions'? That guy."

"Never heard of him."

"But I called here this morning. Whoever answered the phone said you had it." She glanced at her watch. "That was only a few hours ago."

He began counting out his till. "Sorry. We're closing now. Come back another time."

"You're dreaming if you think I'll come back after this lousy service."

Fergus took Mariah by the arm and dragged her through the doorway.

"Why did you do that? I wasn't finished telling him what a terrible shopkeeper he was."

"Precisely why I removed you. Into the car with you. Theodora's waiting."

Mariah rode along in silence to Noah's Bark, the doggie day-care center where Fergus left Theodora on workdays. Her feet hurt, and she had a burn on her wrist from not paying attention to the oven door this morning. This book would have made the perfect Christmas present. Mariah had imagined the look on Lindsay's face. She'd immediately stick her nose into the pages and inhale like some people did with coffee beans.

"Cheer up, lass," Fergus said. "You'll find it yet. Of that I have no doubt. You're as stubborn as you are pretty."

"You don't have to butter me up," she said. "I was planning to have sex with you tonight anyway."

Fergus braked so hard for the red light that they both had to brace themselves against the dashboard. He cleared his throat. "I must know. Was it retail frustration that prompted this decision? If so, we must shop more often."

She looked out the window at the fog rolling in, bringing salt air through the air vents. "Now you're talking like a sociologist trying to find some weird logical thread. It wasn't that. We've established you're a good kisser. Continual sexual frustration isn't healthy. We end every evening with our hearts pounding and so breathless we sound like we have asthma." She opened a stick of gum and peeled off the wrapper. "Even though the plague of AIDS looms over the world, safe sex can be had for minimal effort."

"You're dead romantic, aren't you?"

She grinned. "Maybe I just want to see what's under the hood."

He continued to look at her while the light cycled its way to green again. "I have no idea what that means, but it sounds terribly racy. My da warned me about you American girls. So forward."

"Fine, I won't sleep with you. The light's green."

He accelerated. "I take that back. But seriously, Mariah, we'll go to bed only if you're ready."

She had been ready since day one, but it had taken her eight weeks, two "teas," one dinner out, one at the café, and one on his boat to make her brave enough to act on it. "I appreciate that about you, Fergus. You let me say whatever I want. You might be the only man I've ever met who's done that for me." She kissed his mouth, and then leaned back in the seat, trying to forget she'd missed finding that book.

He raised his eyebrows. "Don't think I'm not grateful. Or won't be more so in an hour."

"You have a filthy mind for a college administrator."

"Pot calling the kettle black, missy."

"Stop that."

"Stop what?"

"Saying things Gammy would say. I'm still mad at her and I don't want to think about that."

"Your gran's of a different era, Mariah. She wants the best for you, and in her estimation, the rules are the same as they were when she was your age."

"You don't know the whole story."

"Well, I do know that life's brief enough. I say forgive her and move along. Yet why do I feel certain that isn't the course you'll choose?"

She was touched that her life dilemmas actually caused him to frown. "Admit you like the stubborn in me."

He downshifted. "I've always appreciated pushy women. My mum was one. Fought her way to everything, until the bitter end."

"What happened to her?"

"Dreadful disease. Ovarian cancer. I held her hand while she died."

"I'm so sorry." Mariah thought of Allegra, and tried to imagine her allowing such a thing as company on her deathbed. It would never happen. Allegra would run off like a sick dog and die somewhere hidden, it never crossing her mind that maybe those who loved her would like to say good-bye. Your mother's going to be fine, Dr. G said, but he didn't hand out guarantees. "Sounds like you did everything a good son should."

"I tried. I do miss her. I've named every boat I've ever owned after her."

"You have other boats?"

"Had. Sold them when I needed cash, or grew tired of the maintenance. 'Tis bad luck to change a boat's name."

"I'd heard that." She patted his leg, and looked out the window toward the ocean until he took a left that headed them off in the direction of the valley. Gammy's card-playing friends lived there. One of the "biddies" had a ramshackle farm and raised ladybugs that she sent through the mail to organic gardeners. Another tatted lace tablecloths that took her years to finish. Gammy was of a different era. Her legs needed a surgeon. With her mind so sharp and her draft horse work ethic it was easy to forget she would soon turn sixty-nine.

)

"We love having Theo with us," the girl behind the counter at Noah's Bark said. "She's so patient with everyone, even the shy dogs. We call her the canine Gandhi. I wish all our clients were like her."

"Thanks. We love her, too," Fergus said. "Do I owe you any money?"

The woman checked the computer. "Nope. You still have a hundred dollars credit on your account."

Mariah watched Fergus greet his dog, taking note of the routine: First they shook paws, and then butted foreheads. Theodora's long pink tongue darted forth to sneak in a kiss, and then Fergus scratched behind her ears, and her immense tail thumped the floor. The deerhound trembled with pleasure when he hooked the leash onto her harness. Fergus told Mariah he never missed a day, even if it was raining, even if he had a cold. On the weekends she got two walks a day, three if he was feeling ambitious. She wondered what Theo would make of two bodies thrashing on the bed she slept next to. Would she be offended? Try to intervene? Just then, Mariah missed her overly expensive condo. So many places to stretch out, and the whole time she'd lived there she'd never once had a man over, unless she counted Simon, who asked her why there were no paintings on the walls, and Mariah realized it was the first time she'd noticed.

The three of them piled into the Mini Cooper, Mariah wedged in the back so Theodora could stick her head out the passenger-side window.

"If you want to have a girlfriend, you should get a bigger car," she said.

"I didn't have a girlfriend when I leased the automobile. I plan to turn it in come December, just before I fly home for the holidays. Get one of those wagon things for the remainder of my year lease. Plenty of room for comfortable snogging."

In May he'd leave for good. And he wasn't spending Christmas here. She wanted to ask when he was coming back, and to hear him say it was only a week, but that was pushing the limits of the relationship, controlling, and also assuming the relationship was at that level, which was something normal women her age would know. "For Christmas you could give me a gift certificate to a chiropractor."

"Mariah, what is this preoccupation with the holidays? It's only All Hallows' Eve. Fifty-five more days until Father Christmas arrives."

"Fifty-five days will be gone before you know it, and I stopped counting on Father Christmas as soon as I could walk. I have to shop when Lindsay's not around. She's had that book on her wish list for years. This year's been so difficult for her that I really want to find it."

"You're a fine mother."

"Thank you for saying that."

"Did I mention how beautiful you are?"

Mariah dodged Theodora's tail. "You should save some of that for the bedroom. Don't want to run out of compliments at a crucial moment."

Fergus tsked. "The things you say, Mariah. Shocking."

At the Pier Two parking lot, Fergus extricated Mariah from the backseat. "This is going to be the fastest dog walk ever recorded," he said. "Come along, then, both of you. Let's jog."

Behind them, the sun set. Little children dressed in costumes ran across the path, followed by parents with flashlights. When Lindsay was little, Mariah had let Allegra take her trick-or-treating. Allegra dressed up as a witch, and served meals all day in that get-up. That she looked so authentic was enough reason for Mariah to shy away. Back then she'd been embarrassed by her mother. Now she looked at the emaciated, bald person bussing tables and saw only courage. The way she'd stood up for her with Gammy—that was rare. Gammy's secret, who would have thought the old girl had it in her? Please let Lindsay escape the Moon women's curse, she prayed. Wouldn't Gammy rail and pound her chest if she knew her mean comments were what made Mariah finally decide to sleep with Fergus? How far had being "good" gotten her? Why not try "bad" for a while and see what happened?

Mariah stopped to rest at a picnic table, winded. "Go on without me," she said. "My feet are killing me. If you want me awake for sex, I had better go mainline some coffee."

"You're certain?"

She waved him on and walked back to Pier Two. Lindsay was at Sally's tonight. DeThomas Farms' Halloween bash went all out—a haunted greenhouse, refreshments, and games. Lindsay was spending the night there. Sometimes Mariah lost track of where her daughter was, but odds were she was at Sally's.

Every November Mariah drove Gammy over there to buy Christmas ornaments, but in picking Lindsay up so often Mariah had learned that out of season DeThomas Farms was a serious working establishment, with employees tending rows of plants and a steady flow of flower customers. Sally's mother looked so tiny and frail in her wheelchair until Mariah saw her heft up a clay sculpture out of the garden and place it in her lap. Then she rolled away to the hobbitlike outbuilding, let herself in, and closed the door behind her.

Mariah was thrilled Lindsay had a friend, but Sally wasn't your run-of-the-mill eighth grader. Some nights she overheard Lindsay on the phone, seriously discussing some boy named Charlie. Incipient adolescence, she told herself. Puberty doesn't care that she isn't five feet tall yet.

Just as she poked her key into the pier gate, here came Fergus. He feinted one way and then another, and Theodora followed, their body postures presenting a universal "play pose"

observed in people the world over. Cultural anthropologists believed these gestures and signals—the semaphoric code of homo sapiens—were stored in the body as memory. Imagining the body having a mind of its own was freeing enough that maybe they could skip dinner. Just go straight to his small berth and stay there all night while all around them the town teemed with spooks and aliens who could be bought for a handful of M&M's. Earlier she had made sure she was wearing her underwear, not Lindsay's.

DeThomas Farms was lit with strand upon strand of fairy lights, and from the barn a speaker emitted moans, shrieking, and clanking chains. Lindsay stood on the back deck surveying the fake spider webs and dry ice smoking from a pseudocauldron. She was almost thirteen—too old to feel this shivery, as if decorations really could create magic. Since Allegra got sick, she'd learned to telescope the world down to her attic room, a small enough place where she could control things. Suddenly Sally let out a string of cuss words and Savannah started crying.

"Sorry!" Sally yelled, from high up in the tree where she was tying a hangman's noose so it would dangle over the already set tables. "I lost my footing and thought I was going to fall on the freaking table."

"Sarah Juanita DeThomas!" Sally's mother called from the kitchen. "Do you want to miss your own party and spend the night sitting in your bedroom without access to your computer?"

"I *said* I was sorry!"

"One more outburst and that's where you're headed. Apologize to your cousin."

"But I wasn't swearing *at* the worm, I was just swearing generally!"

"Do not call her a worm. Savannah is sensitive and you know it. Your foul language upsets her. Apologize or go to your room."

Sally climbed down the tree to where Savannah stood, dressed up like a sobbing green bug with gold antennae. Sally knelt down so she could look into Savannah's eyes, and said, "I'm sorry I called you a worm. I should have said butterfly-in-progress. Please forgive me so we can have the best damn Halloween party ever, okay?"

"Will you take me trick-or-treating?"

"You betcha, if you tell my mom you accept my apology."

"Auntie Phoebe, I accept."

"See?" Sally yelled to her mother, who was probably in the kitchen listening anyway. "All's well that ends well. A quote attributed to William Shakespeare but probably a woman said it!"

"I'll bet she wasn't a mother," Sally's mom yelled back.

"Come on," Sally said, waving Lindsay over. "Let's go get the rest of the game prizes so we'll have time to check on Charlie and friends. Savannah, come on."

Charlie. Just the name sent Lindsay's stomach tumbling. She was growing so tall. They had to pinch off buds so she wouldn't lose her mother-plant abilities. Her army of clones was growing right on schedule. According to Gregorio, September through November were the flowering months, especially if you grew marijuana outdoors. The equal daylight/night cycles stimulated the plant to flower, and for as long as it continued, the flowers increased in number and in size. Gregorio impressed upon them the care taken with light cycles. "Think of a photographer's darkroom," he said, and Sally said, "Why? Nobody uses them anymore. When my dad wants to print a picture, he downloads his camera onto the computer."

But Lindsay knew what he meant. Light leaks could leach the pigment out of photographs, and apparently things like a flashlight left on could do the same to *Cannabis sativa*. Finding out that in these cycles the plants could also experience stress-related sexual problems, like hermaphroditism, was interesting. Premature flowering caused the plant to think, oh, no, I haven't got a chance at reproduction, so I had better self-pollinate. And there went the entire science project, future scholarships, everything. Lindsay would end up waitressing at The Owl & Moon and having to be nice to Mr. Cashin for his grimy old quarters.

In the kitchen, they loaded party favors into shiny black lunch-size bags that each party attendee got to take home. Inside were licorice witches, chocolate fraidy cats, a light stick—*chemiluminescence,* a word Lindsay loved to say—and seed packets for plants that liked to grow in the dark, along with a brochure on planning a night-blooming garden. In addition to all that were stretchy beaded bracelets with silver charms, candy corn–flavored lip-gloss, and a CD of scary sound effects.

"Who are you supposed to be?" Savannah asked Lindsay.

"Um, Einstein."

"Who's that?"

Sally slapped witch stickers on the front of the bags and DeThomas Farm stickers on the back. "Omigod, Vanna, he only invented the theory of relativity! Go on my computer and Google him right now. You have to know who he was if you want to get anywhere at Country Day!"

"He was only one great scientist," Lindsay said. "There were lots of others. Einstein was the only one who got made into a poster."

"Probably because of his hair," Sally added.

"His hair looked like Lindsay's hair?" Savannah asked.

Lindsay immediately lost her appetite for the chocolate cats. "I told you this was a bad idea."

"Jeeze Louise, will you relax? It's a costume party! You're supposed to look funny."

But Lindsay couldn't relax. She knew that Savannah was only pointing out what Taylor and her army would jump on first thing. Look at Lindsay Moon! How sad that she tried to fix up her hair nice for the party and that's the best she could manage. "I think I want to go lie down," she said. "Maybe I should call my mom."

Sally reached into the cardboard box full of treats and

handed Lindsay a chocolate cat. "You can't. Your mom's out with the Scotsman tonight."

"Do you think they'll have sex?"

"How should I know? Eat some chocolate. Not only does it contain antioxidants, but it also stimulates endorphins."

"I know that," Lindsay said. "I still don't want any."

"Then go make a Pepcid sandwich or take some aspirin, but you are not leaving this party. Please? It won't be great without you."

"What's sex?" Savannah asked, her mouth smeared with chocolate.

"Savannah," Lindsay said. "Your antennae are really cool. Jiggle them for me."

"I've got mer-lot for my baby, and biscuits for my hound," Fergus sang as he nudged on the boom box and fed Theodora her dinner. "What do you think, Mariah? Have I a chance at a singing career?"

Andrea Bocelli he wasn't. "I'd hold on to the day job," Mariah said, sitting on the bed contemplating the mother of all relationship tests—sex: Will it go well or not? There's only one way to find out. "Fergus?"

"Yes?"

"I don't feel like red wine. What else do you have in the way of alcohol?"

"Well, let me see."

The sun had set. Mariah wondered if Lindsay was having a good time at the party. She looked out toward the horizon and thought of how all over the world there were couples going to bed together for the first time. They fussed with condoms and diaphragms, sniffed their breath, worried they'd applied too much cologne, or not enough deodorant. Fergus handed her a glass with amber liquid. "What's this?"

"Properly aged Scots whiskey."

"But there's no ice in it."

"Egad, what a thought. Drink it slowly, love. It's precious."

Precious in Scot-speak meant expensive. Scarper meant to run off. Fatal meant beautiful. The confusion his dialect caused forced her to take his word for lots of things. A seal barked, and another one joined in. "Four o'clock Fergus," Gammy had nicknamed him, forgiving *him* for keeping Mariah out late but unwilling to let her forget it. Allegra was probably with Dr. G again, having dinner she wouldn't eat. Why was it so hard for her mother to muster appetite? Every time he visited, Dr. G came bearing gifts: flowers for Gammy, candy for her, and books for Lindsay. Mariah had to award him points for that, though she found herself wanting to yell at him for not forcing Allegra to eat. But something prevented her from liking him. The academic in her considered the Jungian concept of "the shadow self." It was possible she recognized her own troublesome qualities in this man who was apparently going to be in their lives forever. She sipped the whiskey and tried not to think about it.

"Back shortly," Fergus said, taking Theo ashore to "do her business."

Mariah quickly took off everything except her bra and panties and got under the covers, only bumping her head once on the low ceiling. She sniffed the sheets and smiled. Instead of salt and damp, she smelled detergent and softener. He'd washed them just for her.

Taylor Foster and Cheyenne Goldenblatt were dressed like *Melrose Place* girls. Loaded with rhinestone jewelry and pink marabou, they entered the party carrying metallic silver purses that held little stuffed dogs, and they didn't stop giggling long enough to say hello. Lindsay checked out their platinum blond wigs enviously. Why couldn't she have thought of that instead of Einstein? When her mom had two minutes to spare, they dug through the thrift store's costume bin where they found the wig. "God, I hope this doesn't have lice," Mariah had muttered under her breath as she dug a dollar out of her pocket to pay for it. Lindsay had sprayed the inside with Lysol just to be safe, and now it kind of itched.

"Welcome to the party, girls," Sally's aunt Nance said. She was prettier than Paris or Nicole would ever be, and her straight blond hair wasn't a wig. "Come on in and get your-selves a glass of goblin punch," she said, and Lindsay cringed at the are-you-kidding-me look Taylor and Cheyenne sent her.

"Hi, Lindsay," Taylor said. "Great costume."

Determined to stand up for herself like Sally did, Lindsay said, "Thanks."

"How's your science project going?"

"It's going all right. How's yours?"

Taylor batted inky fake eyelashes. "Perfect. It's too bad you won't win the award, since your family is so poor they have to work in the service industry."

Lindsay's cheeks blazed. She tried to think of a comeback, like wasn't everyone a service worker in some way if you broke life down into the smallest components? "They do work really hard, but as my great-grandmother always says, 'To enjoy the lemonade, you have to break a sweat.' "

"That's such a homey old saying, but it's not exactly fac-tual, is it? Hard work has killed lots of people, such as miners, or farmers, or anyone of the blue-collar class, which includes cooks and servants. That's why everyone goes to the best col-lege they can. If they can afford it."

Belva Satterly arrived, carrying a sack of her own food, since you never knew what might have wheat in it. "Lots of great people didn't go to college," Lindsay said.

"Name one."

Lindsay didn't want to say Edison; everyone knew he was self-taught and had 1,093 patents to his name. "Guglielmo Marconi."

"Really?" Taylor said. "What did he invent? SpaghettiOs?"

"The radio. And no matter what college I end up at, I'll still make straight A's."

But Taylor was no longer paying attention, having found someone else to torment. There was glitter on her cheeks, and her shoulders, too. Even if she didn't win the scholarship she'd never have trouble making her hair look good or finding a boyfriend. As Lindsay stood there in her lab coat and baggy pants, she wished she were serving the punch like she poured coffee at The Owl & Moon. Even though waiting tables made you invisible, at least you ended up with a pocketful of tips.

Sally came up behind her and said, "Can't wait for the Haunted House this year. There's going to be some surprises, let me tell you."

"What kind of surprises?"

Sally turned up the collar on her black satin cape, so only her eyes showed. "The kind where you stick your hand into what's supposed to be brains, and it turns out it isn't spaghetti, but something else."

"Sally, what did you do?" Lindsay asked, her heart pounding. "If you did something to Taylor, you'll get in trouble. Please, whatever it is, take it back."

Sally didn't blink. "Linds, relax! It's Halloween. Pranks are expected. Hey, Taylor, come over here for a second."

Taylor took her time, allowing the other girls ample time to tell her how cute her costume was. "What are you supposed to be? A cape?"

"This is only half my costume," Sally said. "You'll see the rest when it's time. What happened to your Juicy backpack? I haven't seen you carry it lately. Did you lose it or what?"

"You freak! I know you put the crickets in my backpack."

"Ah, but can you prove it?"

"I told Mrs. Shiasaka."

"Mrs. Shiasaka is a half-full glass kind of teacher," Sally said. "She tries to believe the good in people. And crickets do like to hide in dark places, like your soul."

"First chance I get I'm going to tell."

"Go ahead. I never said I did it."

"You asked about my backpack. That proves—"

"Exactly nothing," Lindsay said. "Move over. I want to get out of here."

Taylor focused her hate ray on Sally. "I hate you, Sally. I can't believe I was ever stupid enough to think we were friends. This party sucks and so do you." Taylor turned to stomp off toward her friends, who were all dressed like glam queens.

Sally pulled Taylor back by the strap of her purse and the toy dog teetered precariously. "Right down there past the fields is Bad Girl Creek," Sally said. "Our old ranch foreman's daughter drowned in it when she was little. She haunts the place. I double-dog-dare you to go down there and put your hand in the water, Taylor."

"Please," Taylor said. "Like there's such a thing as ghosts."

Sally pointed toward the greenhouses, where a flickering light moved around the rows of plants. "Then what do you call that?"

Taylor squinted. "Maybe your mom didn't have enough money to pay the light bill."

"I triple-dog-dare you."

"Don't talk to her anymore," Lindsay said. "Let's go help Savannah bob for apples."

Sally shook her head no, pulled her cape higher—she was the headless horseman—and stalked off toward the stables, where the entrance to the haunted house was attracting a line of giggling girls. "When can we go in?" they asked.

"When it's time," Sally said, disappearing into the barn.

"Lindsay?" Sally's mother asked from her wheelchair, which she'd decorated with cellophane to look like Professor Xavier's in *X-Men,* the movie. "Don't you want something to eat?"

"No, thanks," Lindsay said. "I'm not really hungry."

Mrs. DeThomas-Callahan rolled forward. "I've noticed that you don't eat much. Sally's aunt Nance used to be like that. Are you afraid you'll gain weight? You shouldn't be. Girls your age burn calories right and left."

"I just don't like eating," Lindsay said.

"Not even hamburgers?"

Lindsay shuddered. "Especially hamburgers."

"Why's that?"

"The rain forest depletion due to grazing cattle, fat clogging arteries, and I like cows."

"What do you like to eat?"

No one had ever really asked her to make a list. "Salad, artichokes, broccoli, pasta, nuts and fruit, especially pears. I like whole-grain crackers and sun-dried tomatoes and olives with the pits still in them."

"Come on along with me into the kitchen," Mrs. DeThomas-Callahan said. "Let's find you something in the fridge."

"What have we here?" Fergus said, sliding into bed, effectively pushing Mariah toward the wall with the porthole, and leaving no escape route. "Not a trick, I hope." He peeked under the sheets. "No, that's definitely a treat."

Mariah felt a little woozy from the whiskey, the lack of headroom, and the nerves jangling through her like static electricity. She let herself be kissed, felt all her muscles surrender and turn limp. She even attempted kissing back, taking herself back over a decade and then some, aiming for simply feeling good and praying not to worry about it, but the memories pressed on her all the same. She opened her eyes and watched this man tear off his clothes, fight with them, really, until he was sitting there in his briefs, his hair a mess, and out of breath—all because of her. She grinned, but tears lurked right behind her smile, and she prayed they did not show.

"What?" he said. "Do I look a fright?"

"No," she said. "You look like a man in a hurry. Come over here."

Lying alongside him, she ran her hands across skin formerly covered with clothing, felt each individual hair push forth from its root. He did the same to her. She got the plain old-fashioned shivers, and closed her eyes, hoping to prolong the sensation. Fergus pulled her bra strap aside and Mariah felt the chill of air on her breast. She wasn't going to think about whether they were big enough or perky enough. She lay back against the pillow, letting Fergus explore. He cradled her small breast in his hand, kissed it, and then bumped his head on the low ceiling. "Ouch," he said. "That smarted."

She snickered.

"Find that amusing, do you?" he said, and began to tickle her. She laughed and tried to scoot away, and when Theodora barked, he stopped. "Theo, fear not. You'll always be my true love. You've nothing to fear from this wench in my bed. 'Tis purely carnal love I have for her. Ours is chaste and above all that fleshy nonsense."

Mariah gave him a little slap. "That cuts both ways, buddy," she said, climbing over so she was on the side away from the wall. She kissed his chest, raked her fingers down his skin, and slid her hands down to the underwear elastic. Fergus drew in a breath. "What?" she said. "Don't tell me you're the one having second thoughts, because that will break my heart. I swear, I'm serious."

He stilled her hand with his own. "God, no. It's just, well, wouldn't all this . . . first time business . . . be easier in the dark?"

She looked into his eyes, trying to ferret out what was behind this attack of shyness. "It is dark. Outside anyway." She reached up and turned off the light near the bed, so that there was only the glimmer of the night-light in the boat's head. "Is that better?"

"Somewhat," he said, but she could tell they were going to have to start all over to get back to where they were.

"Oh, my God. You're shy. Listen, Fergus. I haven't had sex in nearly thirteen years. I don't even remember what a penis looks like. If you're worried about performance, don't be, because I won't know the difference. Since my grandmother has already branded me a hussy, we're not in any hurry. Lindsay's got a sleepover. I can stay all night."

He popped the latch of the porthole. Cool air and the sound of lapping water seeped in. "Well, I've told you I was married."

"And that you were too young, it was the wrong woman, and that you're gun-shy when it comes to marriage. It's okay. I'm not expecting anything else."

He turned onto his back and touched her cheek. "That's the rub of it, Mariah. I am. Us making love. I expect it will be wonderful, how could it not, but I don't know how to say this. I'm afraid I'll expect you to be somehow more mine than before."

She thought it over, then kissed him five or six times. "Every time I think you've said the nicest thing anyone's ever said to me, you say something to top it."

She tucked her thumb back into the elastic of his briefs.

He slid the other bra strap down her shoulder.

The skin there, where his leg met the fold of skin, was ridiculously soft.

His mouth on her neck was waking up nerves she'd forgotten existed.

She felt him stirring, and began to remember what a penis looked like.

Then, everything stopped. "Mariah?"

"Yes?"

"I have a large family. A few of them are a bit strange."

Determined not to lose her stride, she pulled at his underwear and waited for him to awkwardly wriggle out of them before answering. "How could yours be any worse than mine?"

"Well, my brother, for one."

"Do we really need to talk about this right now?"

"I suppose not."

"Then we'll talk—" she began, and then Fergus pressed his body against hers and she swore her panties melted. They were simply there one minute and not there the next. "Later," she managed to say, though words seemed half-baked things, unable to communicate. She looked into his eyes, startled by the deep blue of his iris. Whenever one of them made a noise, Theo whined. Fergus shushed her, but Mariah laughed, and said, "She has a right to her opinion." Deep inside her it felt as if someone had blown on embers that had been covered for years in ash. Blown sweet and steadily, and here came this small blaze. She had missed this. No, she had forgotten this. And in remembering this, she forgot to worry about Allegra's not eating, Gammy's hellfire and brimstone, and whether Lindsay could handle a party without her mother's fretting. In fact, she was so grateful to remember the simple ways bodies could fit together that she wrapped her legs around him as if she would never let him go.

Most of the snacks were gone by the time the lights went down. Lindsay recognized Sally's uncle James, dressed up like Bigfoot, as the one operating the sound effects. It was time for the Haunted House to open, and here came Sally riding on Soul Man, her cape flying out behind her, the thudding of horse hooves hitting the dirt. She had her cape up on top of her head, and held a pumpkin under one arm. Saying nothing, she used her free arm to gesture to the barn.

Her uncle James's voice rang out. "The Haunted House is now open . . . for those brave enough to dare."

Sally rode off in the direction of the creek, and Lindsay wondered again if the prank she hinted at would end badly. "I'll go first," she said, figuring maybe she could get there first and defuse the bomb.

Lindsay didn't see the owls that lived in the rafters. All this noise would interrupt their hunting. She pushed aside a curtain and heard a squeak. Then something brushed her foot, and she jumped out of the way.

"Watch out for rats," Uncle James intoned.

Next a spider jumped out of the dark, trailing against Lindsay's face. She brushed it away, and saw on a table three bowls labeled "eyes of newt," "human brains," and simply "guts." Behind them dry ice emitted smoke. Lindsay heard the screams of other girls as they fell for the rat trick, too.

"Will you dare to touch the guts?" Uncle James said breathlessly, "or will you take the easy way out?"

"I'm not afraid," Lindsay said, and plunged her hands into what felt like Jell-O. The brains were spaghetti, and the eyes of newt felt like gumdrops, so maybe Sally had changed her mind, and undone the prank. Lindsay wiped her hands on the towel offered by a skeleton wearing a pirate hat. Only a little more to the haunted stuff and she'd be back outside at the party. She forged ahead, determined to check out every item in order to keep Sally from getting in trouble. The witch on a broomstick cackled. The sound of chains clanking was punctuated by a horrible laugh that turned to a cough and then a groan.

"Can you help me find my brain?" Sally said, standing at the barn exit, holding a pumpkin in her arms. "Reach into the pumpkin for me. I know it's there somewhere. Find it and you'll win a treat."

But when Lindsay tried to reach in, Sally turned away. "Out of the barn—I mean house—before I take your brain for my own!"

So the prank had to be in the pumpkin. Lindsay figured it was pumpkin guts, which did feel gross, but you could always wash that off. She exited the barn and waited for everyone else to come out. Belva Satterly came after her. She was dressed like a nurse, and Lindsay felt sorry for her. Her hand was covered in the spaghetti. Lindsay handed her the towel that hung over the corral railing. "Here, Belva."

Belva took the towel and wiped her hand thoroughly. "That wasn't very scary."

"I agree," Lindsay said. "But it might be for younger kids."

"How's your science project going? The Thanksgiving deadline is only twenty-seven days and thirteen hours away."

"We have more research to do. Our paper's not very good."

"With Sally as your partner you'll win first place," Belva said.

"I don't know," Lindsay said, as three more girls screeched and reached for the towel. "There's lots of competition. What's yours about?"

Belva inched backward until she felt the corral rail against her back. "Fast food and nutrition."

Lindsay felt sorry for her. What was new or pertinent about fast food when Belva couldn't eat it anyway? Wheat being in practically everything.

Then they heard a scream that was above and beyond pumpkin guts. "Out of my way," they heard Taylor Foster yell. "Sally DeThomas, you are dead meat!"

Taylor emerged from behind the barn with her hand covered in brown goo, which Lindsay worried was probably dog poop. Taylor was gagging in between yelling, and Sally's aunt came running. "Whatever is the matter?" she said. "Did you fall down and hurt yourself?"

"No, your bitch of a niece made me stick my hand in dog shit!"

Sally's aunt lifted the gooey hand and sniffed. "Sugar, that's peanut butter! It'll wash right off. Come on, we'll get you cleaned up. You look adorable in that dress. Are y'all supposed to be Barbie?"

When everyone had been through the barn Sally came back, leading her horse, then taking off his bridle and penning him in the corral. "Way mega fun," she said, her smile wide. "The only thing that would have been better would have been if it had been actual dookey. It was bad luck the gardener picked up Cal's poop today. Oh well, there's always next year."

Lindsay gasped. "Are you serious? You're lucky everything turned out the way it did." She rubbed her chest. "Now I know what it feels like to have a heart attack."

But Sally was already on to something else. "Come on, let's go eat cupcakes before Taylor licks off all the frosting. We still have to trick or treat with Savannah."

Orgasm could be defined in several ways. First was clinical: sexual stimulation, engorgement, then the orgasm proper, consisting of muscle spasms that allowed pleasurable waves to move through various parts of the body. Mariah lay there dazed, thinking of the others. Metaphorically, the earth moved. Euphemistically, the squirrel got his nut. Colloquially, you were "coming," or if you were from Scotland, you were "going," she learned, as the words issued forth from Fergus's mouth. What the hell. Everyone was happy, including Theodora, who had finally settled down on her cushion and tucked her head under the blanket.

So it felt great, but why did it make her want to say "I love you"? She remembered blurting out those words to Ephraim all those years ago, at a moment exactly like this. He'd inched away from her on the excuse that he needed a drink of water. This time she held her tongue. Fergus, on the other hand, couldn't stop smiling, and complimenting her in a more and more pronounced brogue. Mariah touched his face, the whiskers having had all day to grow. He wasn't handsome, he was rugged. His eyes were movie star quality, but the rest of him had been shaped by genetics and environment. Fergus Applecross was his own particular invention, and he was here with her, basking in the afterglow like a plant turning to the sun.

"Mariah Moon," he said.

"Yes?"

"Thank you for the most memorable Halloween a lad can hope for."

"You're welcome."

She turned in his arms until her left hand connected with his shoulder. Likewise, her left leg eased over his, and last she nuzzled his chest, a mass of wiry hair that tickled her nose. "Think your dog will forgive us by morning?"

"Most decidedly. Empty stomach trumps betrayal every time."

Oh, God. I love him, she told herself. How is it possible that a person I misunderstand half the time can touch my flesh and give me an orgasm and my brain flies out the porthole? I've studied this stuff. I know what sex does to people. A decent sociologist would say that poor girl, she cannot separate sex from love. Say that's true. Say we have a dozen orgasms, or fifty, and I still feel like I love him.

So long as I keep it to myself, what's the harm?

11
Lindsay

"Is this disgusting or what?" Sally said as she peeled crushed candy corn from the patio flagstone Thursday morning after the Halloween party. Then she stepped in gum, lost her footing, and stubbed her toe. She yelled the F-word, and Lindsay waited for Sally's mom to render her latest punishment.

When there was no reply from the house, Lindsay said, "You're lucky your mom didn't hear you. You can't get in any kind of trouble until our project's done."

Sally rubbed her toe. "So? Neither can you."

"I don't get in trouble because I don't swear."

"Shut up."

"You shut up."

"Crikey, Lindsay, who cares? If either one of us gets into trouble, we're both screwed."

Lindsay had a headache from not enough sleep due to eating a giant Hershey bar, which kept her awake most of the night. Savannah had made them trick or treat practically every house in Carmel-by-the-Sea and then carry home her loot. "Let's just finish."

The sooner they were done, the sooner they could get to

Charlie and company. It was time to harvest the first plants, and Gregorio had told them how cutting and drying the plants correctly was essential to producing a crop. Every time they went to the greenhouse, Lindsay's stomach hurt so badly she could barely breathe. She knew they were going to get caught. It was only a matter of time. It might even be today.

"Finally!" Sally said, throwing the last smashed cupcake into the trash can. "I should get paid for this," she told her mother, who had wheeled out to serve them breakfast, which was juice, toast, and tofu scramble.

"It's you who ought to be paying me," she said. "Particularly after that peanut butter stunt. Mrs. Foster-Lewis gave me an earful this morning. She didn't back down until I offered to pay for Taylor's therapy."

"Mom," Sally said, grabbing her around the shoulders. "You rock! But where's the bacon? The real eggs?"

"Still inside the chicken and the pig. Your friend doesn't like meat, and since she's our guest, we should pay a little attention to what she likes. It won't kill you to eat tofu once in a while. Bring your dishes inside when you're finished." She wheeled herself across the deck into the house.

"Eat fast," Sally said. "We have work to do. Your mom's going to be here pretty soon."

From the cloying smell in the greenhouse, Lindsay could tell it was time to change the activated charcoal filter. She kept note of the scent variations in her lab book. During the first weeks of the growing experiment, the plants had a newly cut grass smell. As they grew, they took on a skunky odor, reminding her of rare summer nights when there was no wind. Now the thick resiny odor coated everything, including their gloves and hair. For this reason, she and Sally had changed into overalls and rain boots, and tucked their hair into shower caps.

"I can't believe how stupid I look in this shower cap," Sally said as they checked each numbered plant against their log-book.

"Try thinking how you'd look in a prison jumpsuit," Lindsay reminded her.

"Omigod," Sally said. "I'm so nervous. What do we do first? Cut the leaves off, or hang the plant upside down on the fishing line?"

"What we do is we go over the list again," Lindsay said. "This is our one chance at harvest if we're going to be ready for Science Fair. We can't make a single mistake."

Sally grimaced. "My gut is killing me! What did my mom put in that tofu, Ex-lax? Please tell me you brought your Pepcid with you."

Lindsay put her hand in her pocket and fished around. "Sorry. It's in your room in my backpack. Where's the list?"

Gregorio printed so neatly Lindsay wished she could copy his style:

1. Have the fan leaves turned yellow?
2. Has the smell reached its peak?
3. Has the plant stopped producing resin and crystals?
4. Has the bud mass stopped increasing?

The answer to all the questions was yes on seven of the fifteen plants. They unfolded the canvas and set it on the gravel floor so they'd be able to lay the cut plants on top and not lose anything. The project could win them a scholarship. The evidence could get them expelled. Lindsay handed Sally the tree saw.

"Here goes," Sally said, and began to hack at the first woody trunk.

The leaves trembled, and Lindsay wondered if plants felt pain. If so, how depressing to be a dandelion. She reminded herself this was all for Allegra. She wanted to put her gloved hands out to catch anything that might fall so they wouldn't lose even one leaf that could be made into organic medicine to help Allegra feel better enough to eat. After they finished, they'd transfer the canvas to the shelf made of wooden slats and begin the pruning. To see which method yielded the strongest crop, they planned a wet manicure as well as a dry one.

A wet manicure involved immediate cutting, trimming away the fan leaves—the outer leaves—which you kept. The advantages were less resin to deal with, but careless cuts could harm the bud. With the dry manicure, you only trimmed the fan leaves, and then did the remainder of the cuts when the plant was dry. The harvested plants needed to hang upside down in a dark utility cupboard until curing.

"We should get a lock for the drying cupboard," Lindsay said.

"Why?"

"So no one can get in."

"This cupboard looks like nine million other cabinets in all the greenhouses," Sally said. "The floor's gravel, which means my mom won't come in here. It'd wreck her wheelchair."

"Never mind. Forget I said anything." Lindsay studied the first plant. Useful parts went into one pile. Throwaway stuff would be carted down to the compost heap. The last time she had begged Gregorio to do the cutting, he refused. *You can do it, chica,* he said. They'd used Lindsay's tip money to buy new manicure scissors, eighteen bucks, which seemed like a lot until they found a pair designed for harvesting pot on the internet that cost $500. They had sterile glass canning jars with rubber washers and pull-down lids. Curing was essential for chlorophyll breakdown, which had magnesium in it. Magnesium was responsible for the harsh taste of smoke, so you wanted that out of there as much as possible. A gallon of rubbing alcohol would be enough to cut the accumulating resin, which really did stick to everything, Lindsay discovered as she scratched her nose and felt some sticky goo. There were so many ways to be found out.

Lindsay had completed one wet manicure and Sally was

still cutting the second when they heard the horn honk, and someone call out her name.

"Damn!" Sally said. "The one time your mom's early!"

"Sorry," Lindsay said, and hurried out of her overalls and back into her sweats, which she'd stowed in a plastic bag. She had just toed her feet into her untied tennis shoes when the door to the greenhouse swung open. Her back was to the door, and she felt her heart stop while she waited for the worst. But it wasn't her mother who came in, it was Taylor Foster.

"I left my stuffed dog at your stupid party—" she started to say, but stopped when she saw what Sally was doing. "Did I tell you my cousin's a cop?"

In the background, Lindsay heard her mother's voice calling. She really was here early. "Sally," she whispered. "What do we do?"

"Just go," Sally said, dropping the plant and whispering in her ear. "Act like you don't know anything. I'll take care of Taylor. Now run."

Lindsay slid by Taylor and raced down the gravel path until she came to the corral where her mother stood petting Soul Man. "Hi there," she said, smiling. "Isn't this a beautiful horse?"

"I guess," Lindsay said, panting. Her mom had never mentioned liking horses before. "Sally wins ribbons riding him."

Her mother was smiling like she'd gotten her teaching job back. She pulled her car keys from her pocket and twirled them around. "Hey, I saw your other friend run down to meet you. What's her name?"

"Taylor."

"She's cute. Linds, I'm so glad you're making friends. Did you have fun at the party?"

Lindsay found it gross that her mother couldn't stop smiling. "It was all right."

"Great." She kissed her on the top of her head. "Hey, you smell funky. What have you two been up to?"

"Making a compost heap," Lindsay said. It wasn't a total lie.

After this morning, all their hard work just might end up there. She wished they could throw Taylor Foster into it. Just bury her in coffee grounds and eggshells and let the worms work her over.

At the café, everybody seemed to be in a good mood except Gammy. She was dressed in her navy blue slacks and the red sweater with the sailboat on it. For accessories, she wore her silver bangle bracelets. Each time she poured a coffee refill, the rattling made Lindsay think of prison bars clanking shut. They put kids in jail now. Tried them like adults.

Just like every day, people were impatient and crowded the counter, but Gammy's responses were stern and clipped. She'd put up the Thanksgiving decorations—the cornucopia and the pumpkins in the window—by herself. Had Sally's mom called and told Gammy about the pot? Ogodogodogod, she prayed. If I have to get busted, please let it be Allegra who finds out. She'll talk my mom out of sending me to Wilderness Camp. Lindsay thought about calling Dr. G, but there were so many customers waiting for orders it was out of the question.

After the lunch rush, Gammy went upstairs to lie down. Lindsay waited tables for an hour, trying to concentrate, but she worried about what was going on at Sally's so much she was sick to her stomach.

"Hey, you," Mr. Cashin said as Lindsay made a pass with the coffeepot. "How about a smile with your service, girlie?"

Lindsay stretched her lips over her teeth. "How's that?"

"Better," he said. "How about a refill while you're at it?"

She knew it was mean to fill his cup all the way to the brim, that when he lifted it he'd spill a little, but the fifty-cent tip he'd leave just wasn't enough to make up for his bossing her around. When she served her last order, Lindsay went into the restroom to throw up. On her knees, she tried to time barfing with the flush of the toilet so no one would hear. This time, besides the tofu, there was black stuff. Little grains and some clumps. It looked like pepper, or coffee grounds, but she didn't drink coffee. Then it hit her. Omigod, was it resin? Had the cannabis resin gone into her nose and traveled down to her stomach? Who could she ask besides Sally? She heard Carl Sagan say, Occam's Razor. Begin there, and work outward.

"Mom, where's Allegra?" Lindsay asked when it was almost closing time.

"I don't know. If you're done bussing tables, Simon could use a hand."

"All right." Lindsay walked into the kitchen only to find Simon holding a screwdriver above the dishwasher.

"It's official," he said. "Time of death, four-oh-five PM."

"What happened?"

"I'm pretty sure your great-grandmother scared it to death."

Lindsay's hands felt small inside the yellow rubber gloves. She scrubbed and rinsed and Simon dried.

Suddenly it was all too much—Carl Sagan's voice in her head, her mom singing songs, Gammy angry, having to buy an expensive dishwasher, her black throw up, Sally back there in the greenhouse alone with Taylor Foster, not to mention Allegra and the insurance company and how much her pills cost. Lindsay would have given *Dragons of Eden* to the thrift store if it meant she could undo the events of this day. Oh, God, what if this was what it meant to be a grown-up? That life became harder and harder and eventually you were so weighted down with worry you never smiled anymore. It sure explained all the antacid commercials on television.

"I'd better go walk Khan," she said, handing Simon the last pot. "See you tomorrow, Simon."

He waved, and Lindsay fetched an orange-and-blue argyle from Khan's wardrobe. He hadn't worn that sweater in a long time.

"Your friend Sally called," Mariah said as Lindsay took over mopping so her mother could cash out the register. "Something about your science project?"

"I'd better go call her."

"You can finish the mopping first. And where in the hell is Allegra?" Mariah said, tucking money into the deposit bag. "The bank's going to close in a few minutes."

"So use the night deposit," Lindsay said.

Her mother sighed. "I had plans that didn't include stopping by the night deposit."

"Are you going out with Mr. Crabapple again?"

"Very funny. Just for dinner. Then I'll be home. We can spend some time together. Won't that be nice?"

Nothing sounded worse. "I know one place Allegra could be."

"Where's that?"

"Out buying a diamond engagement ring."

"What are you talking about?"

Lindsay dipped the mop and squeezed out the water. "Dr. G asked her to get married and she said yes and spent the night at his house which was why Gammy got all angry, even before you stayed out all night. Maybe you didn't hear about it because you hardly ever come home at night anymore."

Her mother blushed. "No one told me anything about any engagement. Are you sure you didn't misunderstand?"

"She called Gammy and I heard everything. Ask her yourself if you don't believe me."

Her mother looked toward the stairs. "Gammy's legs hurt. You know how she gets. She could have been exaggerating."

Nice try, Lindsay thought.

"Allegra better not forget about the café during this so-called romance of hers. What's she thinking, agreeing to marry a doctor? They aren't fiscally equal, and statistics prove relationships like that don't last. I may be younger than her, but I can't run this place all by myself, and as soon as I get a teaching job, things are going to change, you just watch . . ."

Maybe happiness didn't last that long after all.

)

"I don't get it," Lindsay said into the telephone. "Why do you have to pretend you hate me?"

"Because," Sally hissed, "otherwise Taylor's going to tell on us about Charlie."

"What if she's lying? What if she tells anyway?"

"I don't have much time," Sally said. "She's in the bathroom and she'll be out any second. All you need to know is that I promised her I'd stop being friends with you and go back to hanging out with her so I have to pretend to hate you. I swore to God, even. But only until the project's done. After that, Taylor can go haunt houses for all I care. Omigod, she's coming! I gotta go!"

The phone clicked off and Lindsay set the receiver down in its cradle. No matter what Taylor promised, it didn't make sense to trust her. But Sally knew her better, so maybe it did. Sally didn't *really* hate her. At this point, what else could they do? It wasn't that big a change, really. All Lindsay had to do was go back three months and step into the life she lived before Sally was her friend. Go back to having the "tree of life" for her lunch partner.

)

While her mother was out to dinner with FTF, aka Fergus the Freak, Lindsay logged on to the internet to check her e-mail. The first message was from an African prince who needed help with his inheritance. Two others were offers for credit cards. Nothing from Sally.

She deleted it all, flopped back on her bed and stared at the world map she had tacked to the rafters. America wasn't so big. She looked at all the places she wanted to visit, starting with Auschwitz, because people who didn't examine history usually ended up repeating it. Then there was Antarctica, because what with global warming, it might not be there in another generation. She glanced at the British Isles, which interested her because of the standing stones and museums and as babyish as it sounded, she wanted to see Yorkshire. There was Scotland, lumpy as a rotten cauliflower, infecting England.

Ever since Mrs. Shiasaka told them about Manzanar, and how during World War II nobody thought anything about interment was wrong, Lindsay began to look at countries differently. Scotland's history was all about war, too. Scotland was full of really great writers. Maybe Sally would live there one day, when her books were all bestsellers and she couldn't walk down the street without fans asking for her autograph. Of course they'd be friends again by that time. Taylor wasn't that powerful.

"Get your buns out of that bed and put on a dress," Gammy said Sunday morning, when she poked her head into the attic space where Lindsay was lying in bed, reading *Lives of a Cell*. "We're going to church."

Lindsay set the book down. "I don't own a dress," she lied. "And I'm pretty sure my mom wouldn't like me going anywhere without checking with her first."

"Is that so?" Gammy said. "Well, do you see your mother anywhere around here?"

"No. But I haven't looked in her room. Or the café."

"You'll find the kitchen empty and the bed made," Gammy said. "That's because she didn't come home last night. Again."

"Well, what about Allegra? I bet she told her where she was going."

"You know the old saying, Lindsay, 'Like mother, like daughter'?"

"No," Lindsay said, though she did.

"Doesn't matter. You take a cat-bath and change your panties. We've got a date with ten o'clock Mass."

She started back down the stairs. Using a yellow sticky, Lindsay marked her place in Lewis Thomas.

"It's up to us to save their souls, Lindsay," Gammy yelled. "You have five minutes to find a dress or I will make you wear one of mine. And don't forget your hat. The good Lord is waiting."

Why couldn't religion happen at home? Lindsay wondered as she pulled the hideous green dress Gammy had bought for her last Christmas over her head. Even worse, it was partnered with a red sweater with candy canes on it. No way was she wearing that. She kicked her one and only hat—a straw boater with a red gingham ribbon—to the back of the closet and covered it with a beach towel.

The Carmel Mission had thick adobe walls and history. The Mayflower Church held pancake breakfasts and quilt shows. Gammy's church was a plain old Catholic church with hard bench pews and stained-glass windows and statues of the holy family that made them look resigned to the horrible fate that had been their lives. Lindsay tried not to look at the statue of Mary. Between being surprised by poor doomed Jesus' birth to watching him die to stepping on snakes, Mary never stood a chance.

Lindsay pictured her own mother's smiling face the night before as she got into Fergus's Mini Cooper, imported from the UK. She couldn't wait to get away. FTF made her happier than her own family. That was why she didn't come home. They were having so much fun they stayed up all night and went out to breakfast and maybe straight to the Aquarium after that. She could do the baking for Monday later. It didn't have to be on Sunday morning.

A woven wall hanging that was probably once considered

modern now hung limply behind the crucifix on the altar. The scent of mildew wafted through the air. Gammy laid her sterling silver rosary across her fingers, as she talked to "the man upstairs." Lindsay watched Gammy pray, wishing she could believe in miracles and sacraments. It was evolution's fault that she couldn't. Lindsay pictured Sally and Taylor sitting in Sally's room watching videos, eating Halloween candy all day. Tomorrow, on the school grounds, Sally would look at her like she was lower than dirt. They had to make it look real.

Gammy finished, sat back in the pew, and waited for the church to fill and Mass to begin. She reached over and smoothed Lindsay's hair out of her face. "You look like you have the weight of two worlds on your shoulders. What's cooking?"

"I'm fine," Lindsay said. "Just tired."

"Maybe you're getting the curse," Gammy whispered, her eyes turning merry for no good reason Lindsay could think of other than to embarrass her.

"Gammy," Lindsay said, "in case you haven't noticed, my secondary sexual characteristics are running late."

"Lindsay!" Gammy said. "Don't talk like that in church."

Lindsay knew better than to ask why not. Gammy's rules had her own special logic, which you could only learn by making mistakes.

"You'll have the curse soon enough, honey. It's every woman's fate. A blessing and a curse. Just remember, if you're having problems, I'm all ears."

Every woman's fate? Every woman except freaks like her. She studied Gammy's face, soft and sagging a little bit in the cheeks and under her neck, where the wrinkle cream wasn't doing its job. There was enough wrong in their family already without her adding marijuana to it, not that Gammy would understand. She'd only have to hear the word *marijuana* and be on the phone to We Tip. She'd donate whatever reward money they gave her to the church. "I'm fine, Gammy. Just tired from homework."

"You read too much."

"I like to read."

"There're other things in life besides reading. Things you need to do to maintain your spiritual self. Why your mother wouldn't let you attend catechism, I'll never understand."

Lindsay wondered if you could just save God the trouble by turning your soul in early. Even the Buddha said all life was suffering. Why pretend it was going to get any better if it really wasn't?

"I have an idea," Gammy said, smiling. "How about after Mass we go to Marie Callender's for the Early Bird Special? You can have that salad you like."

Food on top of everything else? "I guess," Lindsay said.

They scooted over in their pew so other people could file in. Old-time Catholic women, the same as Gammy, wore scarves over their hair. Lindsay thought that was a good idea, at least when it came to her own messy hair. Because she'd "forgotten" the hat, Gammy had bobby-pinned a Kleenex to her hair. At least it was a clean one.

"Two for lunch," Gammy said as they walked into the restaurant. "I get the senior discount," she told the hostess who led them to a booth. "That means I get the free slice of pie, too."

"Yes, ma'am," the girl said, while Lindsay withered.

"Just the thought of Banberry pie makes my mouth water," Gammy said when they were seated. "How about you, honey?"

"I might not be hungry enough for pie."

"You can have ice cream if you'd rather."

"Maybe." Something cold on her stomach sounded good. The restaurant was barely half filled. Across the way in another booth, they could hear girls laughing.

"Must be somebody's birthday," Gammy said. "Good Lord and little fishes, Lindsay. What's all over your hands?"

Lindsay looked down. "Printer toner. It brushes right off."

"You don't want that stuff in your pores. Believe me, your pores are going to matter in the long run. Go wash up."

"Okay." Lindsay walked by several booths until she came to the one the laughter was coming from. Sitting there was Taylor and two of her clones, and with them was Sally. Lindsay stopped in the aisle and looked at them until they noticed her. "Hi," she said tentatively.

"Look, it's the gherkin," Cheyenne Goldenblatt said. "Are you here for the child's plate?"

Everyone laughed.

Lindsay looked directly at Sally. Sally was doing her fake laugh, and when Avril picked up a pickle from her plate and threw it at Lindsay, Sally fake laughed even harder. Lindsay walked away.

She ate all the hardboiled egg whites out of her salad, and the chunks of cheese. The bacon, tomatoes, olives, and lettuce, she put into her napkin when Gammy wasn't looking.

"Looks to me like somebody was hungrier than she thought," Gammy said. "Now how about dessert?"

Mariah was in the kitchen when they got home. The Hobart mixer was running and the smell of cinnamon filled the air. Gammy tucked the church newsletter under a wooden spoon that lay on the counter. Mariah punched down bread dough and shook her head. "Where did you get that awful dress?" she asked Lindsay, and Lindsay, her day in ruins, ran upstairs.

Monday morning, before the bell rang, Lindsay searched fruitlessly for Sally in all the usual places. She wasn't in homeroom. When it was time for Dr. Ritchie's class, Lindsay entered the classroom without her, taking her regular seat. Sally came in late, tardy slip in hand. She carried a hot pink Kate Spade backpack. On her wrist were two yellow Livestrong bracelets. She briefly flicked her eyes over Lindsay and then sighed dramatically, taking the seat between Taylor and Avril. Dr. Ritchie huffed at her for interrupting her deadlines on the upcoming Science Project Presentation night, then droned on about some movie they were going to see, but Lindsay didn't listen. She knew it was pretense, Sally sitting with Taylor, them making faces at her, but it hurt. Even Belva was giving her the oh-poor-you look. On Wednesday Lindsay had been Sally's friend, and by Monday she was nothing. Sally had to act like their friendship had been nothing more than a blip in her life before she went back to Taylor and the clones. The trouble was, to Lindsay, it really did feel that way.

She put her head in her hands and rubbed her temples. If this was what it felt like to lose a friend, then maybe it wasn't worth having one. What if Taylor decided to tell after all? What would happen to the science project? There was time to do something else if she did it quickly, but nothing as great as what they'd planned. Nothing that said, "Wow, these girls deserve the scholarship; or, ladies and gentlemen, the future of the world will soon lie in these girls' hands." Maybe Sally didn't care about grades since she wasn't planning to go to high school, but Lindsay didn't want an F anywhere near her. She compared Belva Satterly getting a B for her fast-food investigation with all the planting, growing, feeding, and harvesting that went into the cannabis project. All that work, Gammy might say, would fly right out the window. Lindsay pictured little hand-rolled cigarettes winging their way to freedom.

Then she pictured Allegra's funeral.

What if the blackmail never ended? What if Taylor Foster—she was rich enough—invited Sally on a European vacation? Lindsay couldn't compete with that. She raised her hand. "Dr. Ritchie?"

"What is it, Lindsay?" she asked, clearly irritated at the interruption.

"I need to go to the nurse."

"It can't wait?"

"No."

"Very well, then. Go. But remember, your rough drafts for science projects are due tomorrow."

"I know." The paper was already done. It "discussed" the growing of marijuana, but didn't exactly admit they'd grown it. Subject A, Subject B; they could have been in a hospital laboratory where it was legal to grow pot. She would e-mail the paper to Blackboard the second she got Sally's okay. It was weird that it hadn't arrived yet. Lindsay hefted her backpack and headed for the door. As she passed by, Taylor stuck her foot out and Lindsay tripped, but caught herself before she went down. Dr. Ritchie, as smart as she was, didn't even hear the giggles that followed, a sound that hurt Lindsay a lot more than her stubbed toes.

The next day, around dinnertime, Lindsay said she didn't want any, and stayed upstairs, too upset to eat. She heard Dr. G talking to her mother and Allegra. They were worried, because on Monday Lindsay had made her mother come and get her before school even started and now it was Tuesday and she didn't feel any better and Lindsay never missed school. Sally had not e-mailed, or called, so Lindsay had sent the paper on to Blackboard and ever since this weight in her heart was more than she could bear. Why not miss school? Why not get a B? It didn't matter all that much. Her stomach was its usual dull achy self, and plenty of people skipped school. She even felt a little dizzy. Emotions took a lot out of a person. As did crying, which she managed to put off until she had her face in her pillow. Crying made a person tired. That was because of ACTH, the stress hormone. Onion tears were about irritants. Emotional tears were higher in protein, hormones, and neurotransmitters. Dr. William Frey's theory was that emotional crying was like sweating, exhaling, or even taking a dump: a way to rid the body of wastes, but that didn't mean it had to feel good.

Dr. G poked his head up into the attic space. "Hi there. I heard you weren't feeling a hundred percent. That's a shame, because I was hoping to take all of you to dinner to celebrate the engagement."

He looked so happy she had to smile at him. "Sorry I can't go."

"Your mom says you've been resting all day. Sure you don't feel well enough to have some dinner?"

Lindsay shook her head no.

"Mind if I come up?"

She rolled over on her bed. "The ceiling's pretty low. Don't bump your head."

Dr. G looked around her room and smiled. "Aw, this is nothing. In Vietnam, I had to crawl through much tighter spaces than this."

"You were in Vietnam?"

"Yep. I crawled around in tunnels and put bandages on guys. Then I came home and went to med school and learned how to put on bigger bandages. It's a toss-up to say which place taught me the most. Okay if I stay a minute?"

"I guess."

He sat on the end of her bed. "Here's how we did it in Nam. Symptom review. Fever?"

"I don't think so."

He felt her forehead. "That's a negative. Belly ache?"

"Yes."

"You're supposed to say 'affirmative.' Get them a lot?"

She shrugged.

"Unknown. They run in my family, too, Lindsay. All of us, our tension goes right to the gut."

"I'm the only one in my family who gets them."

"Okay if I prod your tummy a little?"

She put her hands over her stomach. "No. Really, I'm okay. It's better than it was."

"Private refuses examination. Disregard. Are you a junk-food junkie?"

"I don't even like Coke."

"Soldier, that's excellent. Resist the Doritos as long as you can. Your cholesterol will thank you for it. Did you have a rough day at school yesterday?"

She sat up and crossed her legs. "Affirmative."

"This have anything to do with the science project you've been working so hard to finish?"

Lindsay pushed a thumbtack that was about to fall out back into her Carl Sagan poster and bit her lip. She had to lie to Dr. G to make things sound authentic, and she didn't like to lie at all. "The paper is finished. All that's left is the lab work. But my project partner, well, she went back to her old friends, the ones she had before me."

He made his eyes wide, and lifted his eyebrows. "Is this person, by any chance, insane?"

Lindsay smiled. "No, she's the smartest girl in the whole entire school."

"Except for you, of course."

"Maybe in some subjects, but definitely not all of them."

"So what's the worst that can happen?"

Lindsay picked at her jeans. "If she doesn't finish it with me I'm afraid I'll get an F."

Dr. G rubbed his chin. "The way I see it, you have three options. You can do nothing and you'll get at least a C. After all, you did complete the paper. You can try to convince her to act like a professional and finish what you started, or you can take the project away from her and finish it yourself."

"I'd do the last option if it wasn't for our long-term experiments. They're all at her house. I don't have the right set-up to finish it here."

"Guess that only leaves option number two." He gave her shoulder a pat. "Lindsay, I look at you and you know what I see?"

"A crybaby?"

"Just the opposite. I see someone highly intelligent, like her mother. I see someone who cares passionately about the world, just like Allegra. Don't really know if there's any Gammy in there, but I suspect you have her common sense. Don't let that flame of yours be doused by anyone, particularly someone who clearly doesn't realize what she's losing by excluding you from her group."

Lindsay felt a tear sneak down her cheek and swiped it away. If only he knew he was her grandfather, she could have hugged him. She put her hand out, and Dr. G shook it, holding on for an extra minute. "Thank you for talking to me, Dr. G. I hope you and Allegra have a special dinner. I'm extra happy you're engaged."

"Why is that?"

"Because I never had a dad, and getting a grandfather kind of makes up for it."

"Now you're going to make me cry," he said. "Feel better, kiddo. We'll have dinner another time."

12
Allegra

WHEN ALLEGRA WAS SIXTEEN and bursting with ideals, she scoffed at diamonds, branding De Beers a thief for profiting from what should have been Botswana's good fortune. Thirty-three years later the buzz about "conflict diamonds" was even worse news. If terrorist groups sold diamonds in order to finance their bombings, how could anyone deliberately buy one? So when Al said it was time to shop for rings, she imagined a plain gold band, or maybe a piece of turquoise, which not only opened the heart chakra, but also facilitated communication and promoted healing—all of which she could certainly use.

Yet they weren't in Gaspar's Jewelers two minutes before she looked into a case of estate jewelry, brooches and pins, and saw her ring. Circa 1850, the card beside it read. Never before had her heart leaped up like that at something man-made. Set in platinum filigree, the stone was small but it caught the light. The clerk working that section was a woman about her age, but that was the extent of their common ground. Allegra was dressed in elderly jeans, a T-shirt, and her decades-old suede jacket. The clerk's silk blouse, dressy slacks, and hundred-dollar haircut were the correct outfit for picking out engagement rings. Not that she needed more jewelry, as she wore diamonds at every pulse point. It took Allegra a few minutes of pretend looking to drum up the courage to ask, "May I try on that ring, please?"

Al walked over from the case where he'd been examining loose diamonds by the carat weight. "Don't you want something new?" he asked. "Something bigger than a freckle?"

She turned to him, showing him how perfectly the ring fit. "Nope. Besides, all diamonds are the same age, really. I like this one."

The clerk produced a jeweler's loupe and Allegra reluctantly handed her the ring. She peered at it for a minute, and then said, "It's got a rather significant flaw."

"Don't we all?" Allegra said, and Al laughed.

When the clerk started to put the ring back in the case, Allegra gave a little shriek. "But that's the one I want. It spoke to me."

The clerk held the ring out and Allegra took it. For the first time, she looked at the price tag and gasped. "I could buy the café a new dishwasher for this price."

"You didn't tell me that your dishwasher was broken."

"Well, it is. Where are the plain gold bands?"

Al put his hand on her arm. "No way are we walking away from a talking ring. What did it say to you?"

Allegra touched the rounded stone, and peered inside the band to read the worn engraving. There were two sets of initials, but she couldn't make them out. "That the woman who wore it had a happy marriage. That there were more good times than bad, and that whoever wore it next would have splendid luck."

Al looked at the clerk, who had already begun filling out the invoice. "Can you find us a talking band to match?"

She laughed. "Those kinds of settings aren't done anymore, but we have a craftsman who can make you one. I'll need the ring back to make an impression."

Allegra blanched. "No, I have to wear it immediately. Believe me, there's no time to waste, and so much time to make up for."

"I understand. I can make a wax impression now and you can take the ring with you."

Allegra exhaled. "Thank you! Oh, Al. I just love it. It's perfect, even if I'm not. Are you sure it's not too much money?"

"Not for a diamond fortune cookie," he said. "If that's what you want, we'll get it. Now help me find one, too."

She followed him to the men's rings, all the while watching the clerk polish her ring. She couldn't help it. This was a second chance ring for second chance lovers, or would be, when she was no longer radioactive. So far, November was sunny. The monarchs were returning a few at a time. Dylan Thomas could have turned those facts into words that dripped off the tongue, but this occasion called for the sheer stubbornness of Rilke, who admitted that returning again and again to the landscape of love was as formidable as it was compelling.

"I like that one," Allegra said, pointing at a gold band incised with an Art Deco design.

Al tried it on, as well as several others, but returned to the one she'd first pointed out. "Guess I'll go the antique route, too," he said. "What the hell, I'm practically one myself."

They kissed, he wrote a check, and outside on the street Allegra had to sit down on the edge of the store's brick planter if she wasn't going to faint. She pretended to be captivated by the autumn-colored mums. "Look at these precious little flowers," she said.

Al put his hand on her shoulder. "You're not fooling me."

She could tell he was looking at her like a doctor, assessing symptoms, weaving them together to make a diagnosis. "I was only dizzy for maybe one second, and that was due to overexcitement."

"Excitement has nothing to do with it," he said. "You're still dizzy."

"I feel better now." She stood up and took his hand, willing herself to balance. "See?"

He shook his head. "What am I going to do with you?"

Love me for as long as I'm here, she wanted to say. She looked away so he wouldn't see the tears in her eyes. They walked along, passing shops and bed-and-breakfasts, and realtors' offices hawking ten-million-dollar properties. Would the real estate boom ever stop? How could a young couple make it, let alone anyone her age?

"Chilly?" Al said, as they reached the car.

"The breeze feels good."

"Then why are you shivering?"

"I'm trembling with happiness."

"Allegra—"

She stopped. "Are my white cells running with the rough crowd again?"

"Your white cells are behaving just fine, thanks to the Gleevec."

Which has a copay of three hundred dollars, she wanted to say, but didn't. It was her bill and she was going to find a way to pay it. "I'm sorry. That was rude of me. What were you going to say?"

"While I understand that our plans didn't work out the way we wanted them to—telling Mariah and Lindsay and your mother about everything all at once—now I think we ought to tell Mariah alone. Give her some time to process things before we talk to the others."

Allegra frowned. "But I pictured all of us sitting around the table, with a glass of champagne in hand. Over flickering candlelight, we tell everyone the good news and toast the future."

"That's romantic as all get-out," he said, "but has it occurred to you that Mariah might be angry when she hears I'm her father? After all, I've been in your lives a while now."

"Since the day I got sick."

"Yes, and Mariah's going to wonder why we waited so long to tell her."

Allegra looked up. "You mean me. She's going to be pissed off at me."

"I didn't say that specifically."

He didn't have to. Hurricane Mariah would stamp her feet and call her mother names, and probably take Lindsay and drive off in her Subaru and not come home for days. "But she'll adjust, don't you think? Mariah's so intelligent," Allegra said, thinking it could turn out that way, that a happy ending was still possible after a firestorm. "She gets that from you."

"And you. I just think we need to plan for other possible outcomes," he said.

They stopped in front of a Mexican restaurant, and the smells wafted out, turning Allegra's stomach sour. Chemo was done, but the pills she took—Al's thirty-thousand-dollar-a-year wonder drug—upset her stomach, too. She tried to breathe through her mouth while Al bent down to tie his shoe. "Mariah'll be fine. I'll tell her myself."

"Are you sure? Mariah seems to have a fair amount of the Goodnough gene pool in her, the 'my way or the highway' attitude. She reminds me of my great-aunt Clara, who suffered no fools."

"How about we wait until Thanksgiving?" Allegra said. "From noon until five we serve dinner at the homeless shelter, but we could plan a late supper, make it a special occasion, one we'll always remember."

He reached into his pocket for his car keys. "I promised my son I'd drive to the city, spend the weekend with him, but I'll see if I can come home earlier. And by the way, you're not going to be serving anywhere unless you turn into Wonder Woman and gain twenty pounds. Do we really have to wait until Thanksgiving? That's a long time to wait."

"It's nothing compared to thirty-three years."

"Exactly! Doggone it, Allegra, I want Mariah to know who I am. I want a chance to hug my granddaughter. To spoil both of them rotten. You've had them all these years."

She leaned in close enough to kiss his neck. "But you know they're yours. Isn't that enough?"

"What the hell is good about knowing without the hugs?"

"What good is marriage without sex?"

"Always with the sex."

"I want it."

"And you'll have it, soon. We both know I'm not exactly Mariah's favorite person. I say we talk to her tonight."

"She's out with Fergus," she said. "Will you look at that sunset?"

"Beautiful," Al replied.

Allegra turned to him and smiled. "Yep, it's beautiful. But not as beautiful as my ring!" Out came her booming laugh and her yip-yip-yip war cry, and Al shook his head.

"How did you manage to stay the exact same person you were all those years ago?"

"I refused to grow up. Won't that be fun when we're married? I'll add a little spice to your world, and you'll bring some leavening to mine. Not too much, though. I hope you can live with that, Doc. I want to rattle the rafters until I'm eighty if I can."

"Rattle away. Let's drive over to that Italian place. There's probably plenty of tables this early."

Just steps from the car, a wave of nausea overcame her. Imagining marinara sauce and antipasto and overdressed salad was too much. She had to swallow hard twice before she could answer. "Maybe not Italian."

He put his arm around her waist. "Allegra, you have to try the Marinol or you're not going to gain weight. Ounce by ounce isn't going to get you back to the life you love."

"I've already taken more drugs than most people do in a lifetime," she said. "There has to be another way. Something else."

"Compazine put you to sleep, and Reglan was a dismal failure. There isn't anything else except for Mary Jane, and I know how you feel about that." He opened the passenger door and helped her into the car. "Let's swing by my office and I'll pick you up some samples. We'll start you out with two and a half milligrams. If you tolerate that, we'll add a second dose."

She touched her diamond. "Okay."

After her falling out with Sally, Lindsay had holed up in the attic. Gammy wasn't overly worried. Mariah said it would blow over. Allegra, however, watched her granddaughter walk out the door with a sober face every morning and return in the afternoon looking exactly the same way. Lindsay climbed upstairs to her room and worked on her computer until dinner, and sometimes Allegra ate more than she did. That fancy girls' school put too much pressure on kids. So what if their I.Q.'s were higher than Allegra could count? Twelve-year-olds needed to play with dolls, not memorize Plato. And this Science Fair business had gotten way out of control. Lindsay just wasn't herself since that snotty Sally had kicked her to the curb. What could a skinny bald nana do about that? Hire a hit man?

It was three in the afternoon. Allegra lay on the couch, the pills in her hand. A bright yellow-orange, they looked like the penny gumballs she used to chew when she was a kid. Khan snored away in her lap. He was wearing his tie-dyed T-shirt today. Printed all across the front were Grateful Dead dancing bears.

"Allegra?" Lindsay said, rousing her from her reverie, "can you drive me to Sally's house?"

Allegra tipped the pills back into the bottle. "I'm so glad you two patched things up! Every girl needs a best girlfriend to tell secrets to."

"Actually," Lindsay said, "I just need to collect the laboratory stuff part of our project. I called Sally's mom and Sally isn't there so this is the perfect time. Do you think you can drive me?"

Allegra hadn't driven since she'd gotten sick, but she felt good today, or better. It wasn't that long of a trip, and it would give her time alone with Lindsay to talk. They could zip over and back and Gammy and Mariah wouldn't even notice. "Sure," she said, sitting up slowly, giving herself time to adjust. Khan waddled to his bed. "Let's go see if Cronkite wants to turn over. He can be pretty crotchety when he hasn't been driven in a while."

It felt good to be behind the wheel of her ancient beast plastered with bumper stickers proclaiming all her causes, and no chemo in the near future. Someday a courageous president would decide Leonard Peltier had done enough time and let him hold his grandchildren without bars between them. Not this president, but maybe the next one. As soon as they crossed the highway, the smell of the Valley—eucalyptus and grapevines—replaced the beach damp. Streets turned to country lanes. Every car passed the VW bus, but Allegra didn't mind. Looking at the lush green hills—California's winter was everybody else's spring—she could have driven twenty miles per hour all day.

"Turn there," Lindsay said, pointing to a cluster of mailboxes and a winding driveway.

Allegra drove up to the house and stopped.

"It'll only take a minute," Lindsay said, hopping out and jogging down the pathway between the greenhouses and the acres of planted fields. Allegra could just make out rows of poinsettia plants behind the glass in the nearest greenhouse. Some had already turned red. She'd never been fond of the plant. Thanksgiving centerpieces were supposed to be cornucopias filled with corn and nuts, real edible food. They set up an artificial tree at Christmas so no firs had to give their lives to hang ornaments, but that was as far as she'd go in the fake versus real arena.

Al told her that Cronkite's bumper stickers alone would fetch good money on eBay, but Allegra told him no way was she driving some gas-guzzling SUV or that midlife-crisis

Porsche of his. "Will you at least allow me to put in a new engine?" he said.

"Maybe, if you agree to sell both your ritzy cars and buy a hybrid," she'd countered. But get rid of Cronkite? Never. He was a fixture at protests. Her van was vintage. He reminded her of the old days, when she was strong enough to organize a sit-in, and camp out for days. Maybe she'd organize a protest against the cost of her prescription. Should it be held in San Francisco? Or did it need to happen on the steps of the Capitol? It would be such a great arrest to add to her record: CANCER PATIENT STAGES RALLY TO PROTEST DRUG COMPANY'S OUTRAGEOUS COST: How much is a life worth these days?

A good headline was everything.

Sally's mother opened the back door and rolled herself out. Allegra waved. "Hi there," she said. "Hope we didn't disturb you. Lindsay needed to fetch something to do with the science project."

The petite woman rolled her wheelchair to Allegra's car door. "Yes, she and I spoke earlier. I wish those two would make up. I miss her. She was such a good influence on Sally."

Allegra nodded. Gammy would say Lindsay and Sally were thick as thieves, double trouble, but what she meant was best friends. Mariah would say they were "age appropriate peers exploring common ground while heading into puberty." But Allegra knew that those two girls had the rarest kind of love for one another. Mended now, theirs was a friendship that could last forever. Once dismissed, however, they would never be able to recapture it. Hormones and boys and a life made up of high school dances, grade point averages, summer jobs, and college would intrude. "I wish there was something we could do, but I think we have to let them fight their own battles."

Sally's mother nodded. "I agree, but if you think of anything we can try to hurry that along, please phone me."

"You bet."

"Lindsay said you were through with chemo. How are you feeling these days?"

"Good," Allegra said, smiling. "I may look like a bag of bones, but I'm on the road to recovery. And so lucky. Did Lindsay tell you about my engagement?"

"She did. Congratulations. That's my cue to turn into a shill, I guess. If you haven't picked out a place for the ceremony yet, please think about having it here. I'll give you our special friends' discount. We can take care of all the details, catering, photography, justice of the peace, rabbi, shaman, whatever you need."

"Thanks," Allegra said, "but I've got my heart set on a beach wedding."

"Sounds wonderful. Take care, and have a lovely Thanksgiving." She wheeled back inside the house.

Thanksgiving, Allegra thought. Wasn't it yesterday she'd sat in the chemo clinic with the bag of Kool-Aid-colored medicine dripping into her veins, her legs trembling with fear? Once she'd sneaked Khan in, tucked him into her tote bag. She had her reasons ready should she get caught, but no one noticed, and so whenever she felt particularly scared, she reached down to pet him.

Lindsay set a large brown paper sack with the top folded over onto Cronkite's floor. "We can go now."

"You've got everything?" Allegra asked, curious about what was in the bag.

"Yes."

Lindsay looked away, and Allegra could tell her little heart was cracking in two. They executed a hair-raising left turn onto the highway. "Doesn't anybody give a driver a break in traffic anymore?" Allegra said when the horns had stopped and they were safely traveling.

"Did they ever?" Lindsay asked.

"Once upon a time in the sixties, they did. People were a lot nicer."

"Then I wish we could go live there," Lindsay said.

Lindsay was such a stoic. Unless you knew the signs you'd miss how upset she was. She wasn't much of a crier, either. "Omigod!" Allegra said. "You know what we should do?"

Lindsay shook her head no.

"Go to the Aquarium!"

Lindsay's face brightened. "Really? Won't you get tired?"

Allegra thought of the Marinol. The hell with Mariah. She'd take one tonight. Just to try it. If it made her high, she'd eat meals in her room. "Maintain!" they used to shout back in the sixties when a cop pulled your car over. "Due to the Americans with Disabilities Act you know the Aquarium's got to have wheelchairs," she said. "If I need a nap, you can park me in front of the jellyfish exhibit. Come on, let's go, just for an hour. We might as well use our passes since they need to be renewed at the first of the year."

)

A diver in the outer bay exhibit was taking photographs. Allegra sat in her wheelchair, thinking of Sally's mother. It was a different world when you looked people in the waist instead of their faces. She imagined this was Lindsay's view, too, being so short, and tried to see the exhibit through the handprints on the glass. Giant bluefin tuna swam by, and silvery barracuda, those hobgoblins of the water world. The yellowfin tuna swam in a school, making tight turns in unison, shining, to borrow Gerard Manley Hopkins's turn of phrase, "like shook foil." The wise old faces of the sea turtles reminded her of Al. The hammerhead sharks looked scary, but their mouths were only large enough for small fish, squid, and crustaceans. According to the sign, this fifty-four-foot-long by fifteen-foot-tall tank was "the largest window in the world," and held a million gallons of seawater kept fresh by a state-of-the-art filtering system. Sitting here was like being inside the ocean, still and peaceful, the room dim and quiet. Allegra wished she'd thought to come here months ago, because no pill in the world could take her mind off her illness like watching Lindsay watching the fish. Her granddaughter would have happily waited hours to see the lumpy old sunfish. They were the underdogs of the sea, and Lindsay was their lone cheerleader.

"Look, Allegra," she said, when one finally swam into view. "There goes my favorite fish in the world."

"He's a lucky fellow," Allegra said. "We should bring Al here. He's so busy I'll bet he's never been. You could give him a tour."

"Dr. G's nice," Lindsay said. "We talk about science a lot. He helped me with the project. And let me sit in his office chair."

"I'm glad. Oh, God! Look at the time. We better get our butts in gear. Gammy will flip her lid and your mother will give birth to a cow."

"No way," Lindsay said, pushing the wheelchair toward the exit. "My mom's probably already out to dinner with Scotland Weird."

"Why don't you like Fergus?" Allegra said.

"I don't hate him," Lindsay answered. "I just miss how things used to be."

"Me, too," Allegra said. "But good stuff rarely happens without painful changes. Look at me, Doc wanting to marry me. Who would've thought?"

Lindsay smiled. "It's like you're a princess. It's just that . . ."

Allegra saw the waver in her granddaughter's jaw. "What, honey?"

"Sometimes I wish the good part would hurry up and happen for me."

"It will, sweetie. Any minute now. I promise."

The second week of November, Doc flew to New York for a convention. Every night he called to catch up on news at home.

"I just want to call her up and tell her," he said, referring to Mariah and the paternity issue.

"Let's wait until you're home. How's the Big Apple?"

"Dreary."

"So take a walk through Central Park."

"And get mugged?"

"Take a cab ride." Allegra suddenly remembered the poet Diane Wakoski, who had written "The Ten-dollar Cab Ride" for Beat poet Robert Duncan. Duncan was thinking about suicide, and gave his last ten dollars to a cabdriver, saying take me ten dollars' worth of anywhere. Golden Gate Park, with its beauty, saved him. Surely Central Park had similar powers.

"New York's fun," Al said, "but not by myself. I wish you were here with me. I'd take you shopping on Fifth Avenue."

She laughed. "I wouldn't let you buy me anything."

"Then we'd spend it on our girls."

She liked the way that sounded. "Hurry home, Doc. Fly safe. I love you."

A week and a half later, Al was busy at work, and Allegra felt up to working the register for a few hours each day. Her old customers chatted with her, and she got an update on Kiki's divorce-in-progress. Mr. Cooper was having a change of heart. He wanted a second chance. Kiki fully intended to give it to him. "But I want him to sweat bullets before I say so," she told Allegra.

"Love's precious," Allegra said. "I wish you the best of luck."

Kiki ordered butter cookies. Her card game mates had come to expect an Owl & Moon treat. Mariah made them smaller than Allegra did, but they were good cookies, crisp on the edges, soft in the center. When Lindsay returned home from school, she washed dishes. As soon as she got a moment, Allegra popped in to say hi. "School go okay today, honey?"

Lindsay nodded.

"Project all ready for the Science Fair?"

Another nod.

Allegra looked at Simon, who shrugged and continued drying dishes. Back out in the café proper, Allegra watched Mariah breeze through orders and deliveries and smile while she was doing it. Her daughter was happy. The new boyfriend had melted the glacier that had grown around Mariah's heart from the minute she learned she was pregnant with Lindsay, and the stinking father took a powder.

Al was wrong. Mariah wasn't going to be upset. She'd be ecstatic to learn that not only did she have a father, but also that he was joining the family. But maybe she should tell her alone. Wouldn't a good mother take her aside, give her a chance to get used to it before she brought Al into the room? Right now, there were butterflies winging past the window, and in came Fergus. When Mariah saw him, she beamed like a woman in love. No hurry on the father stuff. Allegra would tell her another day.

The next morning, as if elves had been at work all night, the day's baking was done. It wasn't yet seven AM so Allegra figured that Mariah must have returned from her date with Fergus feeling anything but sleepy, and put that energy to good use, because there were dozens of cookies shaped like Thanksgiving turkeys, braided loaves of egg bread, Russian teacakes—a cookie Allegra had stopped making because besides being labor-intensive, all that powdered sugar made a mess—and fudge, pounds of it, on all the available counter space.

A testament to the power of good sex, Allegra thought. She began arranging and wrapping cookies, checking orders off against the list. She sliced a wedge of fudge, admired its sheen, and set it on a marble slab. She folded napkin bundles. There was nothing left to do but replace the flowers in the bud vases. The café phone rang, and though they didn't open for another hour, Allegra picked up. "Owl & Moon, Allegra speaking."

"I overslept," Mariah said into the receiver in lieu of hello. "I'll be down in just a minute."

"Take your time," Allegra told her. "Sometime today I'd like to talk to you in private." She could hear Mariah yawn.

"About anything special?"

Allegra thought a minute. Mariah was a step away from having her questions answered. "Yes," she said. "It's actually very special."

"Okay. See you in a few minutes."

Allegra hung up the phone and looked around her café. The Christmas cactus had buds. She'd upped their prices for holiday cookies and cakes by a few dollars, and so far nobody'd complained. For every extra dollar she took in, maybe a quarter of that could go toward paying her medical bills.

Simon blew in the back door, the wind behind him. "Morning, Allegra," he said as he hung up his jacket. His T-shirt read: *Rainbows are gay*.

"Don't let Gammy see your shirt."

"But that's the reason I bought it." He tied on his apron. "How's love?"

"Love is great."

"Happiness," he said. "How utterly cloying."

Allegra smiled. "You're jealous. This is going to be a terrific Thanksgiving. Come to the shelter and help serve."

"I'd rather have dinner with Pat Robertson." He began seeding roasted peppers for his Santa Fe tomato soup.

Allegra turned. Mariah was in the doorway.

This was it. The moment of truth. "Let's go sit in booth four, where we can talk privately."

"This sounds juicy," Simon said. "Can I come, too?"

"Go peel your peppers," Allegra told him.

She followed Mariah to the table, where carnation buds lay wrapped in florist's cellophane. With every step, her warm feeling shrank and her cold feeling grew.

Mariah sat down and began clipping carnations. "Am I not

smiling enough at the customers? Did I mess up the till? I know Gammy's mad about me sleeping with Fergus, but I never thought you'd be."

"You're doing great at the café and I for one am thrilled you finally got a sex life. I know this will sound odd for us, this year, anyway, but it's happy news." She placed her hand over Mariah's, stopping the carnation clipping. "It's Al, babe. He's not going to be your stepfather."

"Why not?" Mariah asked. "Did he break things off? Well, doesn't that just take the cake! Does he have affairs with all of his patients? That's got to be against the Hippocratic oath, or at least malpractice—"

"Hush," Allegra said. "The wedding's still on, and I'm counting on you to be my best woman. What I meant to say is that Al can't be your stepfather, because he's already your father."

Mariah paled. She looked out the window. She exhaled, shook her head, and looked at her mother with tears in her eyes.

"Honey, say something," Allegra pressed.

Mariah picked apart a flower bud. "Are you smoking pot again?"

Allegra sat back. "I resent that! You know darn good and well that I haven't smoked pot for twenty years. I promised you I'd never do it again. I stuck to my promise. You apologize for that right now."

She watched her daughter fold her arms across her chest and close up as neat as any lock. "As soon as you apologize for keeping my father from me for thirty-three years."

"I will not. I'm your mother; it's my prerogative to decide when to tell my child things and when to hold them back. Apparently it runs in the family. Ask Gammy about that."

Hurricane Mariah blew. "Damn it, Mother! You had so many opportunities to tell me but you chose not to. Did you get some kind of kick out of torturing me? Was he in on it? A freaking sadist for a father. Isn't that just my luck? Dammit!"

Allegra focused on the old Perrier bottles they used as vases. "I should have known you'd see it this way. Turn my wonderful news into a weapon against you."

"Forget about me," Mariah said, "what did you think this would do to Lindsay?"

"Lindsay and I are very close. She'll understand. You have every right to be angry. I'm sorry I didn't sit down and tell you before. But I had to work up the courage, Mariah."

"The courage for what?"

Allegra slid a red flower into the green bottle. "I had to tell Al first. He never even knew I was pregnant."

"So it was some one-night stand?"

"It wasn't like that. I loved him. He was headed—"

Mariah stood up. "Don't talk to me right now. Just leave me alone."

She walked into the kitchen and Allegra watched her go. She snipped stems and filled vases, poured water into each one, and added a spring of baby's tears. Eventually, she got up and placed one on each table. Suddenly she was exhausted, and decided to go back to bed.

"What crawled up Mariah's behind?" Gammy asked when she passed Allegra on the stairs.

"Who knows?" Allegra said. "Maybe she has menstrual cramps."

Gammy sighed in relief. "Thank the Lord for small miracles. At least she's not pregnant."

Allegra picked up Khan and shut herself in her room so she could cry in peace. She popped a Marinol before she lay down and prayed for good side effects. Seven AM was a great time to get royally plowed.

Thanksgiving morning, she was still waiting for Mariah to say she was forgiven. Worse, she'd kept the news from Al, and what kind of soon-to-be wife did that? Tomorrow she'd put up the Advent calendars, the one with chocolates for Lindsay, and the one with recipes for the café. She'd ask Simon to hang the fairy lights in the windows, and break out the reindeer mold for cookies. But her heart wouldn't be in the holiday spirit.

Mariah came into the café and set the case of juice boxes meant for the shelter on the counter. "We specifically asked for cranberry and they sent us orange juice."

"People won't mind," Allegra said. She looked at the clock. "We have to hustle. Take the box to the car and we can worry about flavors later." She walked past her daughter and as she did, their shoulders brushed. "Sorry," Allegra said.

"Sorry," Mariah said at the exact same moment.

"This is ridiculous," Allegra said. "We live in the same house. How long can we go on not talking?"

"How long did you keep the truth from me?" Mariah said, and walked in the other direction.

"Happy effing Thanksgiving," Allegra muttered to herself. In the kitchen, she tore foil from the roll and covered the trays of green beans and sweet potatoes. She thought of Al, driving to San Francisco to see his son, and hoped traffic wouldn't be dreadful. She tried to imagine what Doug might look like— did he have his father's beaky nose, or did he resemble the clearly stupid wife who ran away with her gynecologist? She had been looking forward to meeting him, to the blending of their families, but maybe they should stay on separate sides of the fence.

Mariah came into the kitchen, kicked the river rock doorstop out of the way and closed the door behind her. This happened so rarely that Allegra looked up. "Are you still worried about the juice? Don't be, it's—"

"No." Mariah crossed her arms over her breasts. "I've made a decision."

"Obviously you want to tell me about it."

"I do. Please do not stress Lindsay out when she's having a hard enough time with that science project. Keep this information about Dr. Goodnough quiet until I consult a psychologist. It's difficult to get an appointment this close to Christmas, but I'll find someone if it kills me. Then, depending on what the professional has to say, we'll sit down together and explain all this to Lindsay. I don't really care if that sounds amenable to you because that is the way we are going to play it."

Allegra finished crimping the foil around the sixth pan of mashed potatoes before she spoke. "I'm sorry, Mariah. I automatically assumed you'd be as happy as me. I wanted to tell the world. I have a big mouth."

"I'm not finished yet. Regarding Dr. Goodnough."

"He doesn't expect you to call him Dad," Allegra said, and saw at once from the look on Mariah's face that that was not the best comment to make. "Or Father."

"It would be best," Mariah said, keeping her voice low, "to downplay the father/grandfather aspect of this and instead focus on the idea that he will be your husband, and therefore an extended part of the family. This will allow Lindsay time to get used to him before we place too much emphasis on biological ties. How does that sound to you?"

Asinine, Allegra thought, feeling faint again, but it wasn't from her anemia, or inability to eat enough to make Al happy. The crushing blow that she had so gravely misjudged her daughter's reaction was the culprit. "Whatever you want."

"You will talk to Dr. Goodnough about it, and get him to agree."

"I'll talk to Al, but I'm not promising anything." Allegra expected that would be that, the day would pass quickly because they'd be too busy to interact, but Mariah wasn't finished.

"Mother, I know you have a generous heart, and that you'd just as soon give the shirt off your back to a stranger as your own family, but there is a problem with airing our dirty laundry with customers. I'd appreciate it if you don't mention this to any of them, either."

"Dirty laundry? You think that wonderful man who is your father and who's going to be my husband is dirty laundry?

Mariah Janis Joplin Moon, I should wash your mouth out with soap."

Mariah gave her the glacier face. "I'd hoped to avoid arguing. I'm not the one who needs punishing. You knew all these years. And then he shows up. Why didn't you tell me the day I took you to your first doctor appointment? I have to ask. Are you certain he's my father?"

"Stop it, Mariah! He was the only man I slept with."

"Ever? Or just that month?"

Allegra took a deep breath and exhaled. "I'm going to let that slide because I know you didn't mean it. Al was my first time! I loved him. Then, all these years, and now, more than ever. I've made foolish choices between now and then, but I never once stopped loving him."

Mariah's stony face broke Allegra's heart.

Allegra looked down at the foil-wrapped trays. "When you were little, you loved to draw pictures on the foil. Nothing made Gammy angrier than finding a drawing of a sun on her potato salad, especially if the foil tore. I stood up for you, Mariah. I defended your right to call whatever you saw as a canvas. I hoped by now you might understand me better. I'll be leaving here soon enough to move in with your father. You can deny it all you want, but that's what he is. I hope my leaving will make life easier for you. Now if you'll excuse me, I have hungry people to feed."

She picked up a tray and walked past Mariah, headed out the back door, and loaded it into Cronkite in the same way she had last year and the year before that. Tired already, she stopped to take a breath. She needed to go back for the next one, but she didn't have the energy. Her lungs ached. The streets were dead quiet. Every shop from Lighthouse to Central Avenue was closed, and the only living things on the beach were sand crabs and obsessed joggers. If only she were a runner, someone who could make the bad feelings go away by moving fast through the fog, peeling off miles. She knew exactly where she would run to—Hawk Tower at Tor

House, the stone marvel Robinson Jeffers had built for his wife. The spiral staircase was narrow, but she'd climb it anyway, and when she reached the top, she'd stand there and look at the Pacific, that steely blue ocean full of secrets, and try to figure out how to make her daughter not hate her so much.

But instead she would drop these trays off at the shelter. Since Mariah could toddle upright she'd helped, folding napkins. Allegra secured the tray, and then turned to go back for the next one, and nearly had a head-on crash with Mariah, who was carrying pies.

"When I met him, he had just come home from the war," Allegra said. "Vietnam."

Mariah continued loading pies. "Is that supposed to excuse you?"

Allegra touched her fingers to her racing heart. "Boys went off to war and came home men, quite a few of them in boxes. They left believing they were doing right by their country, but came home to jeers and protests and being called baby killers. It's easy to pass judgment when you haven't walked a mile in the other person's moccasins, Mariah."

Mariah didn't respond.

"I didn't even know his last name, let alone think I'd ever see him again. It wasn't until he'd been gone two months that I even knew I was pregnant." She stopped herself, feeling the tears threaten to spill down her cheeks.

Mariah slammed the Subaru's hatchback and Allegra could imagine the fault lines cracking across the pies' surfaces. When the hatchback shut, Allegra could see the café's back door again. Lindsay stood in the doorway, holding the box of napkins.

"Why are you guys fighting?"

"We're not fighting."

"Yes, you are. Is it because of me? Because if it is that would be dumb. I figured out Dr. G was my grandfather a long time ago. He showed me pictures, I asked a few questions, and then I applied Occam's Razor. If the simplest solution is the truth, go with it. Maybe I *want* a grandfather, did you guys ever think of that?"

The three of them stood in Gardner's Alley, not knowing what to say.

Then Lindsay held up a brown card with a stylized turkey on it. "I thought we could put them on the tables for decorations. Should I print more?"

"That's a lovely idea," Allegra said. "Go do that, and then find Gammy. We have to leave right away."

"Okay." Lindsay jogged back into the café.

"This is all wrong," Mariah said the minute Lindsay was out of hearing range. She knuckled away a tear. "I used to fantasize about my father showing up one day. I suppose I can blame our Disney culture and fairy tales for that. Does he have children?"

"He has a grown son. He had a daughter who died."

"So it's not just us? There are half brothers to deal with? Cousins, too, I suppose?"

Allegra gave her a half-smile. "Geronimo said, 'May your tribes increase.' Why can't you look at it like a blessing?"

"Because I can't! He wasn't here for the hard stuff. It's not like I can take it all in and rejoice. You have to give me some time. Make sure you tell him that. I don't want him calling me and expecting hugs or anything."

Allegra reined in her disappointment. "I will."

Soon Lindsay came running back with her cards, and behind her came Gammy, limping a little, and Allegra could tell this day was already hard on her. They got in the van and buckled up.

"Half-pint just filled me in regarding the grandfather thing. Good gravy, Alice, why didn't you tell me?"

Allegra said nothing. She was no Edna St. Vincent Millay, not even smarmy Rod McKuen; she was just a crappy mother. "Mama?" she said. "Why is it that on *All My Children* things like this are ordinary?"

"Soaps are fiction, honey. Too bad we can't stay young and forgiving like Lindsay."

Lindsay climbed into the van. "Mom said she wants to drive over there by herself."

Four hours later, Gammy was taking the first of the turkeys out of the oven. "Alice," she said. "You'd come in dead last in a tanning contest even if the only other contestant was Casper the friendly ghost. Sit down and take a rest. I can't believe Al said it was okay for you to work today."

Al hadn't. Allegra promised him that she would spend the day resting, letting everyone else do for her. The more she imagined herself lying on the couch watching the Macy's Day Parade, the less appealing it sounded. She'd work for a little while and then rest. Then Al would be back, and they could have their family meeting and sort all this weirdness out.

Gammy snapped a foil tent over turkey number one to let it cool before carving. Then she disappeared down the hallway, barking orders. "I need six pair of hands. Who wants to earn a Brownie point with the Lord?"

Allegra's tiredness wasn't an age thing, not when Gammy was running circles around her. The only culprits she could blame were the pills making her well and her own tendency to overestimate her energy. All her joyous feelings of Thanksgiving, her gratefulness for remission, turned to crap.

"Don't worry, Allegra," Lindsay said, giving her a hug as she passed by with a load of trash. "Mom will get over it. She likes to think she's in control of stuff."

Allegra forced a smile. How humbling to hear your words parroted back to you. "Lindsay," she whispered, "I think you're going to love having Doc as your grandfather."

Lindsay grinned and whispered back, "I already do."

Allegra felt tears well up in her eyes. "You're growing up so fast. I hope you'll come visit me after I move out."

"Allegra, stop worrying," she said, tying the twist-tie on the trash bag. "Every summer I'll come home from college and work at The Owl and Moon. After college, I'll live in Pacific Grove. I like being near the beach and I love you. I'll come back."

Then she went on her way, and Allegra decided a nap on an empty cot made perfect sense.

III

To make an apple pie from scratch,
you must first invent the universe.

—Carl Sagan

13
Mariah

MARIAH SPENT THANKSGIVING morning unpacking food, heating vegetables, and making meals for people she didn't know. She accomplished all this with the energy that came from being wholly annoyed at her mother, humiliated that even her twelve-year-old daughter had figured out and dealt with Dr. Goodnough being Mariah's father while Mariah had to be *told,* and told *two months* after the man had arrived on the scene and begun treating Allegra. When she tired of that subject, she reviewed her early-morning conversation with Fergus and wished it hadn't gone like this:

Mariah: Hey, handsome. Are you awake?

Fergus: I am now.

Mariah: Last night was incredible.

God, what a stupid thing to say. It made her sound fifteen, not closing in on thirty-four.

Fergus: Huh? Oh, yeah. Listen, I'm knackered, Mariah. I have to get some rest.

Mariah: You can go back to sleep in a minute. I called because I need to talk to someone.

Fergus: Er, what is it?

Then after waking him up and annoying him, what did she say? Nothing. Like a total coward, she went for surface stuff, because what if her family complications turned him off? I'll miss you today. Can I invite myself over later for dessert?

Then came the horrible silence, the empty stretch of phone line that lasted probably ten seconds but to her was endless, until he said, Actually, I have plans. Can I take a rain hat?

She knew he meant "rain check." She could not, however, imagine what it was that was keeping him busy all Thanksgiving Day and night that he couldn't tell her. The fact that she was basically throwing herself at him and he was making excuses caused the unpleasant feeling in her temples to ramp up to a migraine.

Of course, she said, and hung up before things could go any worse.

"I need that burner," Gammy said, jolting Mariah out of her daydream. "We got a twenty-pound bag of yams someone forgot needed cooking. Mariah, dump those green beans into a tray and light a Sterno can underneath."

Mariah moved through each task woodenly, trying not to engage anyone in conversation, especially her mother. She'd always had the ability to compartmentalize, to keep family in one place and work in another, but now they were one and the same. When Fergus left for Scotland in May, she was going to have to find something all-encompassing to fill the void. Maybe she'd take up rock climbing. Or learn Navajo. Then Portuguese.

Her peace lasted only a half hour, when one of the volunteers borrowed Gammy's sweater and took it into the room with the cots. Since it was Gammy's lucky sweater, the one with card faces embroidered on it, and the one she wore to bridge parties and bingo, Mariah had to see what could possibly make her give it up. On one of the cots the homeless claimed each night, her mother lay curled up nearly fetal, and Mariah stood there watching the way her every breath moved the sweater the tiniest bit. Her skin was so pale. She'd developed a facial rash from the medication. Though her beautiful black hair was growing back in, it was only about an inch long, and so very thin that bald patches showed under her red bandanna.

Mariah lingered. She knew somebody would pick up her slack because holidays brought out American guilt. Only one generation ago, the poorest age group in America was the elderly. Social Security taking the current administration's political hits could send them back there in no time, but today the bulk of the poor were children, twenty percent of people under the age of eighteen. Oh, a million theories as to why this happened were spelled out in her textbooks: the welfare system, overpopulation, drug use, illegal immigration, the loss of jobs in America when manufacturing moved overseas, a frozen and completely unrealistic minimum wage, but none of that mattered when a person looked out into a room of cots that would be full up by nightfall, and turning still others away.

The only reason her mother was here in the first place was because she wanted to offer comfort the best way she knew how: through food.

Fergus adored Allegra. He laughed at her jokes. He didn't flinch when she wore thin T-shirts that showed her nipples, though Mariah did. Fergus visited her when she was feeling too ill to come downstairs. Probably elders were more respected in Scotland. Thanksgiving wasn't a holiday they celebrated in his family. Mariah wished she were in Fergus's bed on the sailboat, feeling anything other than guilt over her mother and the fear that she might be losing him. Maybe Gammy was right about sex, though it was a little late now. She left her mother still asleep, and returned to the kitchen, now steamy with cooking food and too many well-meaning people trying to help.

The savory aromas of turkey, sage, and pumpkin forced her to take stock. Allegra gladly gave up her holidays to serve meals to strangers. When the United Way Campaign sent out

requests for donations at school, Mariah threw them away,
pissed off that the university had the nerve to ask teachers to
volunteer for one more thing that took away from her time
with Lindsay. Allegra was raunchy, but she spoke from the
heart. Mariah was too afraid of rejection to finish her doctoral
thesis, let alone pen the novel she kept saying she wanted to
write. When Allegra's hair started falling out, she shaved her
head. Granted, Mariah didn't think her hair was anything special, but if she lost it, she'd go into hiding. So what was it she
couldn't stand about her mother? Her ability to bounce back
up when one of life's bowling balls rolled over her?

Recalling sins, Mariah knew, was an avoidance tactic
hauled out to keep her from thinking about Dr. Goodnough;
Alvin, like the chipmunk. Unless she demanded lab tests, she
had to take on faith that he was her biological father. Being
kept in the dark hurt. Selfish, stupid, yes, but she couldn't get
beyond the pain and embarrassment.

Volunteers came and went. Green beans were spilled on
the floor. A mop was commandeered. Messes got cleaned up
to make way for the next mess. There was a time Mariah
wished so badly for a father she would have asked any old
bum on the street to fill the role. Forget birthdays and holidays; if only she'd had a father to teach her about men. What
she missed wasn't having someone to show off on Parents'
Night, it was his part in shaping the person she became: A
woman who chose the right boyfriends, and who would be
so well adjusted that she'd be married by now, own her own
house or at least a condo. A grandfather-rock for Lindsay to
turn to, not just now, but there from day one.

Gammy would have a tweaked cliché for that, but feelings
weren't clichés, and learning Al was her father had set in
motion a grieving for everything she'd missed. Grief was
unavoidable. If you tried not to feel it, you turned into a
cranky, odd person who took things out on innocent
bystanders and ended up in a place like this, depending on
the kindness of strangers, just like Blanche Dubois.

"Mom?" Lindsay said, tugging at her sleeve. "Allegra's still asleep."

"I know, babe. She needs to rest, so let's not disturb her." She could feel Lindsay standing there, waiting. "What?"

Lindsay stared at her openly. "Nothing."

Mariah knew her daughter was in shock at seeing her mother's zeal with the kitchen duties. "Hey, even Gandhi had to start somewhere."

Lindsay smiled. "Admit you like helping out."

"Don't smile at me like that," Mariah said. "This is *one* day out of the year."

On a bathroom break, Mariah stepped outside just in time to see a gull fly by. Did gulls have nests? She could give an off-the-cuff serious discussion of Marxism, but she did not know where seagulls raised their babies. Every Christmas Allegra saved the ribbons from presents. In the spring, she and Lindsay took them out to woodsy areas in the Valley and threw them into the wind so that, theoretically, birds could use them for nests. They had yet to see a decorated nest, but that didn't stop them from believing in the possibility.

Gammy whistled from the shelter doorway. "You with the deep thoughts. Get your buns back inside, pronto. There's turkey to carve and prayers to say. Word is the musical entertainment will be up shortly."

"Can't miss that," Mariah said, though the idea of someone singing off-key hymns was no balm for her headache. How did Allegra do this and stay sane? The answer had to be marijuana.

The last of the turkeys was carved and laid out in the heated trays. Mariah still didn't know what to say to her father. She had tried out the proper words and each felt wrong. Dad. Al. Doc. Sorry I hated you until I knew you were my dad, but I need a little more time to hate you because I'm incredibly self-ish and can't get over embarrassment? A shot of Fergus's whiskey would help, but she couldn't exactly serve meals at the shelter with alcohol on her breath.

Lindsay tugged on her arm. "We need to get in line or the order will fall apart. You're at station three."

Mariah looked at her daughter, hair up in a net, an apron doubled up so she wouldn't trip over it. "Did I ever allow you to be a little girl?"

"What's that supposed to mean?" Lindsay asked.

"Never mind," Mariah said, and slipped into the serving line, dreading Brother Fowler's sermon. She looked for her mother, didn't see her, and then spotted Gammy on the left side of the room, wearing her white apron that did nothing for her shape, and her silver beads that did little for the apron. When she noticed Mariah, she shot her a stern look.

What? Mariah mouthed. Her grandmother's response was to incline her head to the left. She did the head-cocking thing three times in a row. Mariah didn't get it. Was she having a bout of wry neck? The usual faces had turned out to help. Everyone except Mariah was over sixty, silver-haired and well intentioned, except for the man standing in front of the turkeys. What in the heck was he dressed in? A kilt? She'd have to tell Fergus there was another Scotsman in Pacific Grove. The shelter attracted all kinds. In winter, fog seeped into your bones. You wore what you had to keep warm.

Here came her mother to the microphone, looking frail, walking slowly. Allegra tapped the microphone with her finger and smiled. "Every year we have Brother Fowler from Valley Baptist to give us his good words, but this year he's taken a trip to be with his family, bless his heart. We have a newcomer today, Reverend Diane Smith, from First Unitarian. Reverend Diane, welcome."

As the tall blond woman came forward, the first thing Mariah noticed was that she couldn't be out of her twenties.

Her smile appeared genuine, but she could have gotten her braces off last week.

"Thank you for having me here to share on this holiday of uncertain history. By that I mean to say that Thanksgiving is less about the issue of pilgrims seeking religious freedom than it is about sharing our bounty. Now, don't nod off into your turkey until you hear me out. Some of us are here today because we're struggling. We can't find the bounty in our lives. We're scraping by. We've lost track of the hope that is every citizen's birthright, but it doesn't have to be like that. Look around you. Others are here because of a deep desire to share what they do have. To help those who are struggling to find their way back to having a home, a job, self-respect, a pair of shoes, a warm jacket, a place to sleep, a toy for a child's Christmas. . . ."

Platitudes versus action, Mariah thought as she stared at kilt man some more. His face was hidden because of the hat and the collar on his jacket, but something about him was familiar. She wondered if he'd come into the café, and whether Fergus knew him, if there was some kind of Scots support group, a community of his fellow countrymen who gathered to eat blood pudding or haggis. Reverend Diane wrapped it up quickly. Her sermon was a nice break from the metaphor of loaves and fishes, but when would someone come up with a practical solution to hunger instead of prattling on about hope?

"I know you're all waiting to eat," the minister said, "so I'm keeping things short this year. I do however ask you to be patient just a few minutes longer. We have among us a gentleman who has kindly offered the gift of his music."

Mariah couldn't help it—a small laugh escaped when she saw the man striding toward the microphone, bagpipes in hand, was indeed Fergus. When he'd asked, she'd told him she found bagpipe music schmaltzy and loud and just plain irritating. If he'd agreed to play in public, he must be pretty accomplished. When he reached the front of the room, he muttered " 'Highland Cathedral' " into the microphone, cast a quick glance her way, and her spirits perked right up. As he played, her heart filled with thistles. Becoming lovers so recently meant the images in her mind were too new to call memories, but calling them miracles might not be far off. When she was in his arms, the rest of the world went on without her. This displaced foreigner asked only for her company. She came and went from the boat, but her heart stayed on board. As she listened, she thought of his country's complicated history, the bardic tradition, steins of dark ale as common as water, and tough old women like Gammy tending bar. Allegra would fit right in there. She would have the regulars coming back for more. When that song ended, he finished up with "Amazing Grace." Not an eye in the room was dry.

Allegra returned to the microphone and after the applause ended, said, "Thank you, Mr. Applecross. Now, everybody, let's eat," and Mariah got busy ladling potatoes and gravy. Every so often she had to rush into the kitchen for a new tray. A few stations away from her, Fergus was serving stuffing and cranberry sauce. She caught his eye, and smiled. He raised his eyebrows back at her and she wondered if he'd enjoyed teasing her about his "previous commitment" that meant they'd be apart on the holiday.

"God bless," she heard Gammy say, over and over again.

There were perks to giving up your family holiday. Serving at the shelter meant that you didn't have to wash dishes or mop floors. At the end of the meal, some servers took their own plates of food, sat down at the empty tables, stripped of linen and flatware, and ate a meal that tasted better because they'd waited so long to eat it. Others, like Mariah's family, packed up leftovers to enjoy at home. Mariah looked around for Fergus, and spotted him by the exit, slipping into his jacket. "So," she said. "Now that I've found out your previous engagement, can we get together later?"

He frowned. "Honestly, I've a previous commitment I cannot break. Really, Mariah. It's an urgent matter."

"Sure," she said, "I understand."

He placed his hands on her shoulders and leaned in to kiss her cheek. "This is a significant matter. Please forgive me."

"Will you call me later?"

"There's no telling how late this could go. Tomorrow or the next day, possibly."

He held the door for one of Gammy's bingo buddies, then took up his instrument bag and went out the exit himself. Not that she could go, with the day after Thanksgiving being the biggest sales day of the year, but why hadn't he invited her along?

"So," Gammy said. "Four o'clock Fergus can play the pipes. Makes you wonder when he finds the time to practice."

"There's a lot I don't know about him," Mariah said.

Her grandmother put her arm around her. "Which is why the mattress tango is a bad idea. He could turn out to be a serial killer, like that Ted Bandy character."

"Bundy, Gammy, and Fergus is not a serial killer." Mariah rubbed her temples, where her headache was gathering force. "What did you think of the new minister?"

"She's all wet behind the ears. Give her a year tending to this weary world and she'll be turning the pages of the Old Testament and talking a different story."

"Is there anything you're grateful for?" Mariah asked.

"Darn tootin' there is. I'm grateful that there's still a chance for you to curb in your hormones and catch a husband. That man knew you worked at the shelter on holidays. He got up in front of strangers and played the pipes. I think he's falling in love with you. Which is why you need to back away from the hootchie-coo. There's a reason they call it holy matrimony, Mariah."

Mariah wanted to remind her the reason marriage was

invented was to secure property deals. Those bonds originally had nothing to do with commitment and desire; they were about ownership of land, plain and simple. But there had been enough arguing for one day. "I have to get Lindsay home," she said.

"Suit yourself," Gammy told her. "I'll catch a ride with your mother. But I tell you what, nobody had better cut into that pie until I get there."

14
Lindsay

NOW THAT THE NEWS of Dr. G's biology was out, Lindsay couldn't understand why her mother was so unhappy. Except for Dr. G, this was like any other Thanksgiving. They made up plates of leftovers and Gammy got out her sherry wine to pour everyone except Lindsay a glass. They ate, drank, told stories, and went to bed. Tonight her mother wouldn't sit still for two seconds. First her excuse was she needed to stretch her legs, but on her way to stretch them, she poured a glass of wine and drank it. Now it was the can of almonds down in her car. She had to have the almonds—she was craving them, but she filled up her wine again before she hurried downstairs.

"Mariah'll get over this in two shakes of a lamb's tail," Gammy said, as she unwrapped turkey and vegetables. "That Al's a good egg. Although you could have broken the news more gently, Alice."

Allegra held pills in one hand and bottled water in the other. "I *was* gentle! I took her aside and gave her time to think it over. What else was I supposed to do? Line Mariah's world with down pillows?"

Gammy shook her head at the container of cranberry relish. "No wonder nobody ate this," she said. "It looks like a dog's dinner. Next year we're going back to the jelly kind."

Khan barked at the word *dinner.* Allegra swallowed her pills. Lindsay and Gammy pulled the oval coffee table to the center of the room so they could lay out the leftovers like they always did, and pick at what they wanted. Khan circled their feet, hopeful.

"My legs are killing me," Gammy said as she sat down in her recliner.

"You should have them operated on," Lindsay told her. "Maybe Dr. G can get you a discount."

Allegra laughed.

"I don't see what's so funny about me going under the knife," Gammy said. "These legs will get me to the pearly gates just fine." She tried to give Khan a turkey wing, but Lindsay stopped her.

"Gammy, don't give that to him, you know it makes him fart."

"Say 'pass gas,' sweetie," Gammy said. "It sounds so much nicer."

"Actually, flatulence is the correct term," Lindsay said. "But that sounds worse than fart."

Allegra laughed again. "Lindsay, you have my permission to say fart."

Gammy sighed. "Alice."

"Alice what? I'm her grandmother. I'm supposed to indulge her. It's a holiday. Relax."

"I will if you have some turkey."

"I will in a minute."

"Alice, you have to eat something."

"Mama, get off my back."

Her words hung in the air and Lindsay wondered where her mother was. It didn't take that long to go downstairs and come back up. The turkey looked dried out. With the statistics on food poisoning, no way was Lindsay having any stuffing. All she wanted was a sliver of pumpkin pie. She was about to top it with whipped cream when Allegra stood up and opened the door to the bathroom. It was a quirk of the upstairs apartment that one could not open the bathroom door and the entry door at the same time without them crashing into each other. They did just that, causing Mariah to drop the can of almonds, which of course spilled everywhere. Khan seized the opportunity to eat himself sick, and Mariah dove to the floor to keep him from eating them.

Lindsay handed Khan to Gammy and began picking up the nuts and putting them back into the can.

"Don't eat any of those," Gammy said. "I don't need anybody sick during the Christmas season."

Lindsay watched her mother get up and brush her front clean. Then Allegra came out of the bathroom. "Fergus's music was great," she said. "Where did he disappear to in such a hurry? I was hoping he'd join us tonight."

Oh, boy. Lindsay braced herself for her mother's response.

"I guess he had someplace he needed to be," Mariah said crisply.

Lindsay knew that tone. It meant a grad student had plagiarized or the car battery was dead or she'd had her fill of picky customers and needed to take a break before she threw their orders at them.

"I'm sure he'll call you later," Gammy said. "Such a nice thing to do, playing for everyone for free. I hope we can count on him for the Christmas dinner."

The wine bottle was empty now. Ignoring the sherry, Mariah retrieved a second bottle from the fridge and popped the cork. "He's going to Scotland for Christmas."

"Who's going to watch his dog?" Lindsay asked. "Can I do it? I'll be on winter break and I could use the money."

"For what?" her mother asked.

"Excuse me;" Allegra said. "Did you just open the bottle of Korbel I was saving?"

"He takes Theo to Noah's Bark," Mariah said, holding her hand out to refuse when Gammy tried to hand her a plate.

"I'm not sure if they board dogs. The champagne was in the fridge so I figured it was fair game."

"You know we always have cream sherry at Thanksgiving," Gammy said. "I don't see the need to open a bottle of wine when only one person's planning to drink it."

"I was saving it," Allegra said. "For when Al gets here."

Mariah's eyes flashed fire. "Oh, let's get a head start before *Dad* arrives. His daughter deserves champagne on such a memorable occasion, doesn't she?"

Mariah drank one glass and poured another. Again, Lindsay watched her drain it dry like it was water and fill it a third time. The more she drank, the more the disapproving silence grew. Lindsay imagined her family ramming into each other like bumper cars. It was funny, and then it wasn't.

"Great champagne," Mariah said. "Tastes expensive."

"I am so sorry for all this," Allegra said for the jillionth time that day. "I wish there was something I could do to make things better."

"Look at me," Mariah said, "I'm so fine that I'm smiling."

"I'll tell you what won't make things better," Gammy said as she speared turkey and dropped it on her plate. "That's splashing alcohol on facts that can't be changed. What in Hades do you think you're going to accomplish by getting drunk, Mariah?"

Lindsay watched her mom stare into her glass and then drain it. "I'm not drunk."

"Yet," Gammy huffed. "For the love of God, you two! What's done is done. Alice can't take it back. Mariah, you make peace with your mother this instant and let's move forward into the holiday season grateful for our blessings. Today's news is tomorrow's birdcage liner. If you ask me, your mother and Al making things legal is the best thing to happen in years, not to mention a good example." She wagged her fork at Allegra. "I have only one request. Alice, please don't wear white to the wedding."

Lindsay fed Khan her pie.

"Mama," Allegra said, "give me a break! Last time I checked, Miss Manners didn't live in Pacific Grove."

Lindsay sipped ice water. Tension zapped through the small room like tiny bolts of lightning, and her stomach lining sizzled as if someone had branded her insides the way cowboys did cattle.

"You're right, Alice. I take it back. Wear leopard skin if you want. And a purple tutu." Gammy looked out the window.

Lindsay set Khan down.

There was a knock at the door, and Allegra called out, "Al, sweetheart, come on in," and then there he was, standing in the doorway dripping wet, Lindsay's grandfather, her mom's father, Gammy's soon-to-be son-in-law, and Allegra's future husband.

"Hello, all," he said. "Happy Thanksgiving."

Allegra took his coat. "How was the city? Traffic beastly? I heard the fog was terrible along the coast. I'm so glad you made it back in one piece. Do you want coffee or tea? I have decaf. There's sherry, too. And maybe, if you're lucky, there's a little champagne left." She looked at Mariah, who was studying the bubbles in her glass.

"Dr. G? Did you know that carbonation occurs when carbon dioxide gas is added to a water-based liquid?" Lindsay said. "It's true. Most 'champagne' is actually sparkling wine. Real champagne only comes from this one town in France. It gets its bubbles from sugar and yeast and a second fermentation."

"Absolutely right," Dr. G said. "The sugar gives it its sparkle. Way back in the 1690s, a monk named Dom Pérignon said that drinking champagne was like 'drinking the stars.' So how is it, Mariah?" he asked, and sat down next to her.

"It gets the job done."

Lindsay watched her mother deliberately move away a few inches, something Taylor Foster would do.

Dr. G took the glass Gammy offered and filled it with the last of the champagne. "I'm glad we're all together," he said. "Allegra and I have some news."

"Don't waste your breath," Mariah said. "The alley cat, as my grandmother would say, is out of the bag."

Dr. G smiled. "Good. We waited too long to tell you, but Allegra assured me this was the best way. There's so much I want to ask you, Mariah. So much to make up for. I want to help in any way I can, be it Lindsay's tuition, a college fund; tell me what you need and I'll do my best."

Lindsay could tell by the tight look on her mother's face that it didn't matter what Doc said. This was because Fergus the Freak wasn't here. If he were, her mom and Allegra would have men between them like shields. They could talk to each other a lot better that way. Lindsay tried to think of all the reasons why FTF wasn't here, but all she could come up with was that maybe he had another girlfriend.

"By all means," Mariah said, her words beginning to slur. "Fix everything with cash. Lots and lots of cash. Pay off my car. Buy a house. Send Lindsay to MIT so she can escape waitressing and the damn café."

"Mariah, you put that glass down right now," Gammy said, getting up. "I'm going to make some high-test coffee and you're going to drink it."

"No," Mariah said. "I'm sticking with fermented sugar. And bubbles."

Allegra looked like she might cry. Khan was trembling.

"Listen," Dr. G said. "I know all this is new to you, and I don't expect us to become family overnight. Now, how about we have that long overdue toast to our engagement?"

Allegra handed Dr. G a plate. "Mariah gets in snits," she said. "Give her time."

"I am not in a snit," Mariah said.

"Yes, you are," Allegra said. "You're miffed at the way I delivered the news. All I can say is have fun in your corner and let us know when you come out of it. Al, would you like pumpkin pie or pecan?"

"Some of each. But first, the toast."

Lindsay dutifully lifted her glass of water. Everyone lifted a glass, including her mother. Gammy tinked hers with Al's. "Welcome to the family, son. We've been waiting on you for thirty-odd years. And I do mean odd!"

Soon everyone was talking, telling stories, but nothing melted the ice around her mother. Lindsay imagined Thanksgiving at DeThomas Farms. There would be so many people around that table there must have been two turkeys at least. Calpurnia, the rat terrier, no doubt laid under the table waiting for spilled food. Savannah would cry at least twice. Sally would sneak sips of champagne and then ride her horse bareback because everyone else was preoccupied with talking or eating or something that made them forget Sally's tendency to run wild. It had to be more fun than sitting around waiting for your mom to blow a gasket. She wished the pretending game was finally over, but there was still a week to go.

Dr. G finished his plate, wiped his mouth with his napkin and reached a hand out to Mariah. "Maybe we can start as friends. Sound acceptable to you?"

Mariah smirked at him. "Sure! Why not?"

"Mom," Lindsay said. "This is so dumb! You share DNA. Big deal. At least Dr. G didn't pick up and move when he found out Allegra was pregnant like my father did. You're already grown up, so what is the big problem? If you ask me, you're lucky."

"Lindsay!" Mariah said. "Apologize."

"What do you want me to apologize for? Telling the truth?"

Gammy chuckled. "Out of the mouths of babes . . ."

"Mariah," Allegra said when she saw her daughter reach for the sherry, "I think you've had enough—"

"Don't tell me how much I can drink. You of all people! All the times you came home slaphappy, Christ, I can't even count that high."

"Do not," Gammy said, rising to clear dishes, "take the Lord's name in vain like that, especially on a holiday."

Dr. G interrupted her. "It's all right, Bess. Mariah has every right to be upset. It's a shock."

"That doesn't excuse cursing."

Mariah looked down at her hands. "I just can't see where in my life you're supposed to function. What your responsibility is. What I am to you. What you are to me. I mean, the hard part is already over. You weren't there for any of the things I needed you for. I learned to ride a bike by myself. I flunked algebra, and probably you could have helped me pass it, but no, you were raising another family when I needed fatherly advice. It's too late for you to matter."

Allegra started crying.

Dr. G stayed quiet a while. "It makes me sick that I wasn't there. Had I known Allegra was pregnant, things would have been different. I know you think you're angry at me and your mother, but I wonder if it's yourself you can't forgive."

"Excuse me?" Mariah spluttered. "I am perfectly *fine* with who I am and where I come from."

"Good," he'd said. "I want my daughter and granddaughter happy and living productive lives."

Everyone flinched when Mariah set her glass down so hard that Khan barked. "Is that crack supposed to make me feel bad because I lost my job?"

Gammy wadded napkins and placed them in the wastebasket. "Mariah, it's been four months. Get over the job loss already. Waitressing is honest work. Your mother's done it for thirty-five years and so have I. Are you ashamed of us?"

Lindsay watched her mom start to cry. She knew exactly what she was feeling. That she didn't have her job or a friend or even Fergus the Freak. All she had was this weird family that didn't follow the rules, and she wanted the other kind so badly it was breaking her heart. Lindsay wanted to tell her how nobody at Country Day had a family like that, that maybe happy families were an urban myth, like the story of the businessman waking up in a tub of ice because his kidneys had been removed and the note telling him to call 911.

But then her mom said, "You've got this prestigious job. My mom will be your charming but eccentric wife. You'll move her into your house and we'll be left with what? This so-called restaurant?"

Gammy slammed dishes down. "I won't listen to one more minute of this, Mariah. I have about broken my back holding this ragtag family together all these years. I give you advice you won't listen to. I pray for your soul. The least you can do is be civil on holidays. If you can't manage that, then, then— go to your room!"

Then Dr. G got mad. He did it in such a quiet way that Lindsay could tell he was really good at winning arguments. "Please don't malign the business your mother and grand-mother built from scratch. Lifework is precious no matter what field. They did it for you. If it weren't for them, you could be scrambling to pay for child care, or on welfare."

Everyone got quiet. Allegra sniffled into a tissue. Gammy had her pursed lips on. Lindsay watched her mother for any small clue that she realized she was out of line, that this awful night was ending, but it was as if nobody knew what to say. Then Allegra cleared her throat. "I've spent the last thirty-four years letting all of you with the exception of Lindsay pass judgment on me, and frankly, I'm tired of it. Mariah, clearly you have no use for the love and support your father's offer-ing, and I'm going to be his wife. I'll go pack a few things and get out of your way so you don't have to feel all this hate and resentment. Mother, Lindsay, I'm sorry I ruined your Thanks-giving."

"Alice, don't go," Gammy begged. "Once Mariah sobers up we'll work this out."

But Allegra didn't sit back down. She steadied herself by holding the back of the couch, and Dr. G stood up and took her arm. When she wobbled a second time, he picked her up in his arms, just like in a black-and-white movie, Lindsay thought. Lindsay hurried to get Khan and his leash, and put him into her grandmother's arms. "I love you, Nana," she said, using the only word Allegra would allow because "grand-mother" made her sound too old.

Allegra touched her cheek. "I love you, too. Call me any-time."

Dr. G opened the door, and they went downstairs. Lindsay heard the unmistakable sound of Dr. G's Porsche revving up. Gammy said, "She didn't pack her clothes. What about her medicine? And what will happen to the café?"

Mariah went to the window and yanked it open. "Happy fucking engagement!" she yelled, and then she went into her room and shut the door.

Gammy was already on her knees, praying her most pow-erful prayer, the "Hail, Holy Queen." Lindsay listened until Gammy got to the part about the "mourning and weeping val-ley, the vale of tears." She climbed the ladder to her loft, and lay down in her bed, trying to imagine how their lives would ever be the same after this. Allegra leaving hurt almost as much as having to pretend Sally wasn't her friend, but that was temporary. This felt permanent.

"I saw some butterflies out back in the alley," Lindsay told Simon the morning after the worst Thanksgiving Day in the history of man.

"Well, whoop-de-freaking-do," Simon answered. "Ask them to come in and wash dishes, why don't you?"

Lindsay recognized that was a rhetorical question, so she went out front to bus more tables. The counter was crowded with people eager to get in their holiday orders. Her mother was serving tables, Gammy was at the register, and every ten seconds Simon smacked his order-up bell. The booths were full as well as the tables, even the rickety one that had a matchbook under one leg to steady it. People waiting to eat stood in a line that went out the door. Lindsay wanted to say, don't you notice the monarchs gathering on those trees, their wings trembling like autumn leaves come to life? Are your stomachs all you care about? A break in the rain, one bite of Thanksgiving turkey, and the alarm sounded. Shop! Find the perfect present. Maybe Christmas was fun for families who liked one another.

Simon's bell slammed in her ear, so she picked up the plates just so he'd relax. Other girls Lindsay's age were at the malls, getting a chocolate at Godiva and trying on perfumes. They'd tell their parents they were Christmas shopping, but really all they did was run around and have fun. Maybe they were just waking up from sleepovers, and the mother of who-ever's house the sleepover was at was bringing them orange juice and blueberry pancakes. Once Lindsay had made the mistake of asking if they could have pancakes for Sunday breakfast, and Gammy said, "The cobbler's children always go barefoot," which really meant nuke a frozen waffle instead.

Lindsay needed to earn Christmas money, since all of her earnings had gone into Charlie and company. She would bus tables, wash dishes, walk Theodora if that's what it took. The new dishwasher was back-ordered, due to arrive in January. Lindsay, who made it a regular practice to check out the bills, wondered where they'd found the three thousand, one hundred, and thirty-nine dollars plus shipping to pay for it. Maybe Dr. G had lent the money to Allegra, or bought it for her as a Christmas present. Present buying was easy. All it took was one trip to Bookworks on Lighthouse. Gammy liked true crime. For her mother, Lindsay usually bought travel books on the British Isles, but this year that wasn't such a great idea, considering Fergie the Freak was going home to Scotland for good in the spring, so maybe she'd get her a gift certificate. Khan was happy with a squeaky toy. For Simon, a bag of special potting soil. She'd buy Sally a calendar of famous writers' quotes, make Dr. G a card on her computer, but what rhymed with grand-father besides bother? Allegra's present was the surprise. She had a feeling she would be taking it to Dr. G's house.

Lindsay served, took bills to the register, and then carried another tray of dishes to the kitchen, where Simon was busy washing pots. "When will these miserable people have enough to eat?" he whined.

"When they're full, I guess."

He raised his head and asked the ceiling, "Can this day get any worse?"

"Don't talk to me about bad days," Lindsay said. "You should have been here last night. My mom got drunk and made an ass of herself."

"Do tell," he said. "Was it a big cat fight? Any other secrets besides the prodigal father? That's a story you could sell to Lifetime."

"Simon, it wasn't funny. My mom got drunk, Dr. G got mad, Allegra moved out and took Khan with her, and Gammy's still praying about it."

"All this and Christmas coming?" he said. "Deck the halls."

"I hate Christmas," Lindsay said. "I'd rather live in a gulag."

"A gulag," Simon said. "Now there's looking on the bright side. So where'd Allegra spend the night? Is the wedding off?"

Lindsay just wasn't up to explaining. "Where do you want these dirty dishes?" she asked.

"Just stack the bastards over here with the other unfortunates. I mean it about you coming back when it slows down to help me or, screw the environment, we're going to have to start using paper plates!"

But it didn't slow down. The butterflies that had begun showing up early that month, just a few here and there, today were everywhere, which meant if the bed-and-breakfasts weren't full yesterday, they would be by tonight. The galleries switched out their art so butterfly sculptures and paintings faced the street traffic.

The butterfly people reminded Lindsay of pictures she'd seen of Venice Beach. The self-proclaimed butterfly princess folded back her net wings to sit in a booth. A natty old man who dressed in a yellow suit, sneakers, and derby, came into the café, pointed at what he wanted, and paid without ever speaking. Lindsay wondered if she might run into him in the library, which was where she spent a lot of her time these days. She'd seen FTF there one time. She had three books on cultivating marijuana ready to check out, and she was sure he'd seen the titles. If Santa existed, Lindsay's Christmas wish was to please keep Scotland Weird from mentioning the book titles to her mom.

Days later, Allegra still hadn't come home. Since Khan was with her, there was no dog to walk. Lindsay's mother was downstairs standing in front of the café television but not watching it. Fergie the Freak had not called. Gammy was either at bingo or bridge or church. Lindsay had finished her regular homework for class on Monday, so she stayed up in her attic room with her journal. Writing in longhand sucked, but she wanted an A, so she took her time and tried to give all the letters the equal amount of space so Mrs. Shiasaka wouldn't think she was just trying to fill up pages.

Dear Professor Carl Sagan,

Helicobacter pylori is something twenty percent of all people have, but not everyone who has it gets an ulcer. Gammy says Dr. G could have been arrested for "taking advantage" of Allegra all those years ago. My mother says she is "perfectly fine," which means she is sad about FTF not calling, but she can't admit it, so she has to stay mad at Allegra. Allegra is either out shopping for Christmas presents with Dr. G or maybe ordering things from a catalog and charging them to his credit cards with his permission, of course. It's lonely without Khan here. I wouldn't even mind if he pooped on the rug. I'd clean it up and not say anything. I'd even walk him two times a day. All it takes is one time around the block and he's happy.

Here is my research so far of reasons a person my age could have recurrent stomachaches:

Anxiety in living situations—true
Fibromyalgia and/or chronic fatigue—I don't have
    enough symptoms
Lactose intolerance—not true—I like milk
Constipation—gross—I don't have it
Helicobacter pylori infection—unproven, but
    possible
Stress—see anxiety above
Overuse of painkillers—does Tylenol count?
Overuse of antacids—true
Cancer—doubtful, given someone my age, but now
    that Allegra is sick a potential family link exists

A person can lie to herself a whole lot easier than
tell an outright lie. Gammy puts lies in categories
because she is Catholic. Little white ones don't need
confessing, but big hairy ones, like my science
project, can send you to hell. Professor Sagan, you
smoked marijuana even before you had cancer. You
wrote a book about it under a fake name. Why?
Would the other scientists have made fun of you? Isn't
a scientist supposed to spend all his life building
rockets or finding stars or theorizing what life was
like before the universe began? More than anything,
including having Sally be able to publicly like me
again, I wish Allegra would smoke some marijuana. I
miss her and Khan. My mom got so many orders
wrong today that Simon had to wait tables while she
pulled herself together, which took fourteen minutes,
and you would be surprised how many customers
can get mad in that amount of time and think nothing
of yelling at a kid my age.
    Tonight nobody said anything about dinner, so I
ate six olives, two almonds, and the raspberries that
were meant for the scones. They looked sweet but
tasted sour. Also, I drank a whole glass of the café's

milk, which I know I shouldn't because it costs so much, but my stomach hurt and I thought it would help. It didn't.

Suppose my living situation is causing me both anxiety and stress. What can I do? Allegra has cancer, which I can't change. She is engaged to her old friend who is also my grandfather, which makes me excited, which is not the same thing as anxious. Thirty-three years ago she had sex with him, which resulted in my mom, and without her, I wouldn't be here, so how can Gammy talk about people having sex outside of marriage being a sin? I do take a lot of antacids, way more than I should, but if I don't, my stomach hurts. At least I stopped throwing up that black stuff.

Professor Sagan, are you glad to be out of this world? I bet you are. AIDS, overpopulation, homelessness, heart disease, cancer, Ebola virus, killer bees, mad cow disease, the Norwalk virus, anthrax— the list never ends. I bet you are glad you don't have to think about that stuff anymore. I would be glad not to think of it. Are you stardust? Allegra says that's what our spirits become. Gammy says heaven is whatever you want it to be, but God is there and he'll want to chat with you about things you did while you were alive, which sounds to me an awful lot like the principal's office. Buddhists believe your soul passes from one place to another, mostly to a person, according to your "karma," which is like points on a scale. If you did enough bad things, you could come back as a fire ant. If you did good, you could be a redwood tree in a National Park protected from logging. Personally, I think the best thing to come back as would be a drop of water. People always need water. Just imagine how much a cactus would love you.

Why do you talk to me, and how do you decide

when to do it? You are a dead scientist who believed in searching for extraterrestrials, smoking marijuana, and protesting for causes, just like my grandmother. Maybe that is why I love you. You'd fit right in here at The Owl & Moon. I'd call you "Dr. Sagan," but that makes me think of Dr. Goodnough, who is my new grandfather I can't be happy about because he is what's making my mom cry right this second while she's pretending to watch TV, which is not helping my stomachache, which is not from eating too many holiday leftovers, but is from not getting invited to Sally's birthday party yesterday. Professor Sagan, this whole thing started out as pretend, but she doesn't e-mail me anymore. No phone calls, either. I don't have a lot of experience with friendship. How someone can go from being friends one minute to not the next, because that is exactly what happened in my case. What if Sally realizes she wants to stay friends with Taylor for real?

This is the stupidest letter/journal ever. I'm going to get my first B, I just know it.

I have to go to bed now, so goodnight, Professor Sagan. I hope your heaven is just what you wanted.

Your friend,
Lindsay Moon

)

Mrs. Shiasaka had gone home sick, so they had Dr. Ritchie for both science and "Life Paths, Life Questions." Lindsay got chills when she asked for final progress reports before Science Project Judging and Parents' Reception, which was only a couple of days away. Lindsay looked over at Sally, and Sally looked back. She wasn't smiling, but she also wasn't making her usual mean face. What did that mean?

"Sally DeThomas and Lindsay Moon?" Dr. Ritchie said, looking up from her clipboard.

The girls stood on opposite sides of the table. Lindsay spoke first. "I posted the finished draft of our essay on Blackboard."

"How about your models and visuals for Presentation and Judging?"

Sally took over. "We'll set them up as soon as we get access to the classroom. By the way, will there be security? I don't want anyone kyping our ideas."

Dr. Ritchie looked at her. "The door is locked at night, and only Ms. Haverfield and the janitor have keys."

"Is the janitor bonded?"

Dr. Ritchie gave her a hard look. "Sally, sit down. Belva Satterly?"

Belva launched into her research on the insidious way fast food leaves its mark on cells, droning on in such a monotone that Lindsay wondered what medications she was on for her many allergies. "That's sufficient, Belva," Dr. Ritchie said, interrupting her, and everyone sighed in relief.

Then Sally did a strange thing. She not only fake-laughed, she blurted out, "Omigod, Belva, that project is so last year! Don't you, like, have any other interests besides animal fats and extruded chicken? How about nuclear waste or smart bombs? Or don't they have those on your planet?"

The posse laughed hysterically, but Lindsay knew that that was over the top, even for Sally. Belva looked like she might cry.

Dr. Ritchie said, "Sally, when Mrs. Shiasaka told me about your outbursts I thought she was exaggerating. No recess for you. Instead, you can stay in and clean the rabbit's hutch."

"That should be a breeze," Sally said, "since I have previous experience with the iguana."

Dr. Ritchie ignored her. "Now that we've finished our science project reports," she said, "let's return to your 'Life Paths, Life Questions' journal projects." She read down a list. "Lindsay Moon, it seems we haven't heard from you yet. How about you read us a passage?"

"How about I don't?"

"*Excuse* me?"

Lindsay could feel all eyes riveted on her. "Can't I just turn it in and have you look at it instead?"

The posse snickered, and even Belva gave her a snotty look.

"Lindsay, did you complete your journal?"

Lindsay picked at the edge of the notebook. "I completed it. It's just kind of personal."

"Well, pardon me, but isn't that the idea of creating this journal? To dialogue with one significant person from another walk of life? How painful can it be for you to share with your classroom community when they are here to support you?"

Lindsay watched the posse collapse in laughter. She swallowed hard. There were a lot of things she could have said, but she was sick of words. She would rather bus tables. At least you got money for it, even if it was only a quarter. Mrs. Shiasaka would have let her off the hook, but Dr. Ritchie was like the salesman who came into The Owl & Moon, pressing pamphlets in your face. He wouldn't take no for an answer until Gammy got down the giant ladle and threatened to smack him.

"Lindsay," Dr. Ritchie said, "the class is very interested in your choice, as am I."

Lindsay looked around the room, wishing right then that a California earthquake would strike and they'd all have to brace themselves in doorways to feel safe. "I chose the one person who made science live and breathe for me."

"Live and breathe!" Cheyenne Goldenblatt whispered. The posse snickered.

"Carl Sagan."

"Carl Sagan, the scientist?" Dr. Ritchie said, smiling.

The posse's giggles exponentially increased until Avril shrieked, "But he's a dead man!"

Lindsay's face heated up. Her stomach followed suit. "So what? Do only live people matter? Carl Sagan talks to me sometimes."

"Lindsay's gone mental," Siouxie said.

"Probably from you guys torturing her," Belva said. "I'm going to ask my mom to transfer me to public school."

Sally pinched Siouxie. "Shut up for a second, will you?"

It was like Dr. Ritchie heard none of it. "Carl Sagan talks to me, too," she said. "In his books. Which one's your favorite?"

"Why do I have to pick one when all of them matter?" Lindsay said. "When Carl Sagan died, the world kind of forgot about him, but I didn't. It's sad when anyone dies, but it's tragic that no one will know the ideas that he didn't live long enough to explore. He wasn't a soldier who died in battle, or a pop singer or a movie star, he was just a man who died from stupid old cancer, which can kill whoever it wants to."

She began to cry before the last syllable was out of her mouth. The one thing you could never do at school was cry. The only thing worse was peeing your pants. The rest of December was guaranteed to be ten times worse than how she felt right this moment. "Lately," she said, hiccupping extra syllables as her sobs wound down, "I think about how Carl Sagan got sick, how it all started with the diagnosis that was really only a warning, not even the real disease, which is mostly manageable with certain medications that are very expensive like the ones my grandmother is on where they make you pay twenty percent up front even if you do have insurance. So he had a bone marrow transplant, which is also common these days, according to Netdoc, who says the success rate for bone marrow transplants is seventy-nine percent, which sounds really good until you think about the twenty-one percent that he fell into. So then I had to research that, to see if any progress has been made since Professor Sagan died, if they were any closer to a cure."

"And?"

"They aren't. People care more about backpack brands than they do cancer." She stopped there, exhausted. "Can I sit down now?"

"Certainly." Dr. Ritchie calmly walked over and handed her

a tissue. "Girls, that's what I mean by passion. Lindsay Moon, A plus for you today."

Sally held up her hand. "Can I ask one question?"

"No, Sally. You may not. Your question quota was reached long ago. You'll have to wait until after the New Year."

She threw up her arms. "Fine! Censor me. Forget the First Amendment already."

The chorus began before they were halfway out the door for lunch and recess. "Humanity! Humanity!"

"Lindsay Moon loves a dead guy!"

"The only kind of boyfriend she can get is a zombie!"

Then she felt a hand grasp her arm. She turned, and saw it was Sally. "Don't listen to the freakazoids," she said. "They'll turn anything into an insult, because that's a whole lot easier than trying to understand it." Then she twisted Lindsay's arm just a little so the others saw, and Lindsay cried out. "In about ten seconds," Sally whispered, "Taylor will be around the corner. Sneak back in, okay? We have to talk."

Lindsay rubbed her arm. "How was your birthday party?"

"Oh, mega-fun!" Sally said. "It rained, Savannah had to win all the games or she'd cry, and my presents were freaking useless."

Lindsay had planned to buy Sally a Moleskine blank writing book before they had their fake falling out. "You didn't get even one good present?"

"Taylor got me ten flavors of lip gloss. Buy me some saddle soap, I told her. That I can use. Or a gift certificate to the bookstore. Gah! I don't think Taylor ever reads, unless it's her mother's *Star*."

"We haven't done our project presentation yet, so why are you talking to me?" Lindsay said. "You never answer my emails."

Sally pulled her into the classroom, toward the rabbit cage, which stunk, even though herbivores generally had nonsmelly excrement. Rabbit urine was another matter. "When I said I was being blackmailed I meant totally blackmailed. Taylor made me tell her my password! She checked my outgoing mail every day."

"I don't believe you."

"Why would I lie? She is on me like stink. This is the first time I could get alone long enough to tell you."

Lindsay shrugged. Sally was a writer. If someone snapped their fingers, she could make up a story on the spot. "Why should I believe you?"

"Because I'm your friend, that's why!" Sally flipped open the rabbit hutch and let the rabbit onto the floor, where it immediately peed, then hopped away. "Come on, Linds! Why would I make up such a stupid idea? You know I'm smarter than that. You're my best friend."

"Really? You're not mine. Not anymore."

She stood there while Sally tried not to cry. It was some-how a relief to watch Sally wad up newspaper, clean the cage without help, and replace the rabbit's dishes, clean and filled with food and water while tears tracked down her face. When Sally went to the cloakroom, Lindsay followed, watching her rifle through backpacks until she found carrots and celery, which she then put in the rabbit's cage as well, because she was spoiled rotten and saw nothing wrong with helping her-self to whatever she wanted. "Help me catch that idiot rabbit," Sally said. "Honestly, this animal belongs in grade three, not eight."

"No."

"What?"

Lindsay hated the fact that her heart was beating so quickly, urging her to take the hard words back, but some-thing inside her had torn loose, and the bad scene at Thanks-giving had started it. She watched Sally wash her hands, looked out the window where the posse had gathered under Lindsay's "tree of life," and were picking off bits of bark and throwing them at each other.

"We're almost there," Sally said. "All we have to do is pretend we hate each other until after Science Fair."

"I don't have to pretend."

Sally didn't try to stop the tears now. "Come *on,* Lindsay!" she begged. "We can't let Taylor tell on us this close to Science Fair. We have to win the prizes. Our future depends on it."

"What future?" Lindsay said. "Even if I win the money that's no guarantee I'll get into college. People like me, we can work our hardest and still end up in crappy jobs. Screw the project. I don't care anymore."

She walked out the classroom door, down the hallway to the nurse's office because her stomach hurt and she was out of antacids, and that big bottle of Tums sounded better than birthday cake or rabbit stew or chocolate anything.

"I need to telephone my grandfather," Lindsay told the nurse, who was watching a talk show on the office TV.

"Are you sure?" the nurse asked. "Wouldn't you rather talk to your mother?"

In Lindsay's hand, the business card Dr. G had given her was growing damp from her clutching fingers. "No, ma'am. He's also my doctor, and he's concerned about my stomachaches."

"I'm glad to hear somebody is. You certainly have enough of them." She handed Lindsay the receiver. "Don't forget to dial nine and wait for the dial tone. I'll leave you alone so you can make your call in private. Then I'll need to speak to him to get you released."

Lindsay punched in the numbers of the pager, and then when prompted, pressed in the school telephone number, and the suffix, 9-1-1*. Dr. G had told her it was code for I really need to talk right this minute. She hung up, and sat down on her favorite cot, which had a red plaid flannel comforter. She thought of all the days she spent there, waiting for her gut to calm down. Little bits of her DNA were here in this office, all over the place. Lindsay knew she had ulcers, and she knew it was time to tell someone about it, and that it had to be the right someone to tell to make it better.

The nurse's phone rang. Lindsay pressed the button for speakerphone before she answered. "Country Day, nurse's office."

"This is Dr. Alvin Goodnough. I received a page from this number."

"It's me, Dr. G," Lindsay said, picking up the receiver so only she could hear him. "You told me to call if I needed to talk. Well, I do. It's important."

"Lindsay, I'm with a patient right now, but she's my last one today. How about I come pick you up and we spend the afternoon together?"

"I want to, but I'm afraid to ask my mom."

"Why don't you leave that to me? Just be ready in a half hour."

"Um, Dr. G. There's one more thing."

"What's that, kiddo?"

"I, well, I told the nurse you're my grandfather."

He was silent for a few moments, and then he said, "Well, I am, aren't I? Now put whoever I need to convince to spring you on the horn."

15
Allegra

"GOOD MORNING, SOON-TO-BE Mrs. G," Cricket said when Allegra walked into the kitchen. "I fix your little doggie breakfast and he eat it all up so good."

Allegra hesitated, uncertain how to speak to Al's housekeeper, a tiny Korean woman who could have been anywhere from sixty to one hundred years old. There were no hints on her smooth face, and her hair, thick and lush, was still mostly black, with a pretty gray ribbon beginning at her widow's peak. She multitasked like a dynamo, washing clothes and cleaning blinds while cooking up dinners, but taking over Khan's diet? "That's so thoughtful of you," Allegra said, keeping her voice soft and kind, "but don't go to the trouble. I brought his kibble. It's on top of the washer in the laundry room."

"Trouble?" Cricket said, and fetched the food, which came in a plain brown bag supposedly one hundred percent biodegradable. "You ever look at ingredient in this stuff?"

"It says 'all natural' on the label," Allegra said, bristling. "What's wrong with it?"

Cricket rattled off five-syllable chemical-sounding words,

and then damned them with a "bah!" as she emptied the bag into the garbage disposal and turned it on. Over the racket, she yelled, "This handsome fellow need good food just like you do. I fix him little egg yolk, some chicken liver, and the wheat germs. That what I fed my Chihuahua, Ming. She live to be twenty-four years old. Never sick. Took her for acupuncture last ten years of her life to help arthritis. Die in sleep. Good dog. I miss her every day, but now this little man come to live at Dr. G house, my heart happy again." She patted Khan's back and he licked her fingers as if they were covered in bacon.

Traitor, Allegra thought. Who knew you could be bought for the price of organ meat and half an egg? "Thanks, Cricket, but honestly, I don't like him having people food. I have to brush his teeth as it is. And believe me, he lets me know he doesn't like it."

"Oh, let me try new diet. You see, Mrs. soon-to-be Dr. G. I never brush Ming's tooth a day in her life. Strong white teeth until day she die, bless her spirit. Just let me try new diet. You see."

Allegra watched Khan sniff his way across the kitchen floor—a warm gold and gray textured slate—and thought about breakfast. Maybe she'd try yogurt again. Sometimes she could get a few spoonfuls down. She opened the fridge and stared at the containers of yogurt, lined up so perfectly, labels facing front. She closed the door, and opened a cupboard to look for crackers.

"What you looking for?" Cricket said, her hands in a sinkful of steamy, bubbling dishwater. She scrubbed each plate, rinsed it in scalding water, after which she loaded the dishes into the dishwasher, which was set on Sani-cycle. "You want coffee?" Cricket asked. "Only take minute in fancy-schmancy coffee machine."

"Thanks," Allegra said, "but I drink tea. I can nuke a cup of water in the microwave."

Cricket stripped off her dishwashing gloves and laid them

down on the counter. "That not way to make proper tea! You, go sit down, watch, I teach you how to make tea. Green tea or black? You pick."

"I usually drink Lipton in the morning, just to wake up."

"Lip-ton!" Cricket said. "I make you a black tea so good you forget about Lip-ton. You watch, Mrs. soon-to-be Dr. G."

"Please, call me Allegra," she said, and sat down at the kitchen table, feeling cheered when Khan trotted over and begged to be picked up. She held him so his front paws rested on the windowsill, and he could look out. When birds raced across the sand, his little heart thumped beneath her hand.

Cricket handed Allegra a glass of juice. "Pear," she said. "Easy on stomach." Then she held out her palm, inside which rested two bright orange pills. Marinol. "Dr. G say make sure you take this first thing. He insist."

Allegra swallowed them down with a gulp of juice. She wasn't going anywhere today. If she felt stoned, she could zone out on television. She looked around Al's kitchen, a modern, hard-edged room with the latest appliances and a pot rack filled with copper skillets. She'd always wanted a copper skillet, a Mauviel professional ten-inch skillet from the *Sur La Table* catalog, but they started at one hundred fifty, and that was for the small ones. And here was the entire set. Allegra wondered if she could ever take one in her hands and call it hers. The six-burner cook stove had two ovens. The fridge was the size of the bathroom at The Owl & Moon, the same Owl & Moon that was now operating without her.

Cricket banged pots around and unrolled a bamboo place mat on the table in front of Allegra. On it, she placed five white teacups without handles. "Tea set called *ch'a-gi*. Cups called *ch'at-chan*."

"Why do you need five cups if there's only the two of us?"

"Stranger might come by. Ancestor might visit in spirit. Only use bottle water. Tap water turn tea bitter."

Allegra nodded as each bit of information was delivered. When the teapot was warmed, Cricket measured a scoop of black tea into the pot, added the boiling water and let it steep. She placed saucers under each cup, and when Allegra reached for one, Cricket pulled it back. "Not yet. Wait until ready. Only tea maker serve cups. Pass *by saucer* to person. Hold cup in both hands like this. Five steps to drinking tea, Mrs. Allegra. First, look at it so pretty in cup. Second, breathe in comforting smell, nice, huh? Third, sip and taste in mouth. Fourth," Cricket said, and tipped her head back, "taste in throat. Tea have six tastes, sweet, salt, tart, two kind pepper, and bitter."

"What's the fifth step?" Allegra asked.

"Fifth step, remember family."

After her tea lesson, Allegra took a shower, using all five of the showerheads. She washed her hair, which was definitely an inch long now. Khan lay on the thick, loopy bath rug waiting for her. Unwrapping herself from the obscenely thick bath towel, Allegra surveyed her paltry body in the full-length mirror, wondering if she could eat lunch. The Marinol had given her a bit of a buzz, but it also made her feel sick to her stomach. Maybe fresh air would help.

On the beach Allegra watched Khan race around the sand. The salt air revived her spirit. She watched the waves crash. She picked up a broken clamshell, rubbing her fingers over the grooved surface. So far as the future went, how could any sane person go back to an overcrowded apartment after this and not feel depressed? Hermit crabs changed their shells all the time.

Remission. In love with her one true love. Planning a wedding. Yet Allegra had never felt lonelier. Until now, her days had been filled with trying to keep Gammy from arguing with Simon, waiting until just after lunch to stand on a chair and tell her daily joke. She didn't have the strength to anymore. All this opulence felt sinful, but dang it all, why shouldn't it happen to her? She pondered going back inside to read a book, take a nap, or to ask Cricket to teach her to do the laundry ceremony. She could lie in bed all day, or drive whichever fancy car was in the garage, but what she wanted most was to sit here, listening to the waves.

Khan jumped into her lap and began to lick her hands. She kissed the dome top of his furry head. The only thing to do was to face Mariah, stand there and let her say all the terrible things she'd apparently been keeping bottled up over the years. Life was too short. Hadn't she learned one thing from her illness? Allegra got to her feet, felt the rush of blood, the Marinol and not eating causing her world to shimmy. That was okay. Sometimes the world needed to be out of focus.

When the phone rang, Allegra was half asleep on the living room chaise. Cricket nudged her shoulder and handed her the phone. "Mr. Dr. G," she said.

Allegra roused herself, and Khan, who'd been snuggled up near her belly, growled at having his slumber disturbed. "You be quiet," she said, and then into the receiver, "Hello, handsome."

"Why do I have to be quiet?" Al said. "Are you holding a séance?"

She laughed. "I was talking to the dog. You, my love, can talk as loud as you want."

"I know we planned the afternoon together, but something's come up. You should go on and have dinner without me."

Allegra wanted to ask if that was supposed to be a joke, since her dinners were mainly cups of vegetable broth and Jell-O. Not enough calories to keep a lab rat alive, Al said. "That's all right," she said. "Unless . . . did you want to talk about it?"

"Actually, I do, but not just now. Later on, definitely. I shouldn't be too late. Maybe seven-ish."

"I love you," she said into the phone, still thrilled at saying the words, feeling their tingle and newness.

"I love you right back, doll. Did you try your new dosage?"

"I did."

"And?"

"Al, it made me sick to my stomach. I'll eat more, I promise."

"We'll find something else."

"Try not to worry."

After a pause, he said, "I've got someone waiting. See you later. Eat what you can. If you get a craving, call the market. I have an account and they deliver."

"Sure," Allegra said, knowing she'd never do it. She had schlepped her own groceries for as long as she could remember and planned to continue. She held on to the phone long after Al hung up, thinking about calling Mariah, but no, it needed to be face-to-face.

When Cricket finished her intense dusting and thorough vacuuming on this gray December day and packed up to go home, it was five, and the sky was a dusky blue, the fog already rolling in. Allegra moved to the couch near the fireplace, a black granite monolith Khan had barked at the first time he saw it. Cricket had laid a fire, which crackled and sputtered in the grate. Allegra looked into the flames and felt herself stuck in that half-dozing, half-waking state where memories surfaced and bobbed against the present. Her eyelids grew heavy, and part of it was the Marinol, because this was what it had been like smoking pot, time spooling away from you, feeling sleepy, in no hurry to go to bed. These days she needed ten hours of sleep, and she wanted to be fully aware for the remaining fourteen. She smiled, remembering how once she'd stayed up for three days straight, for the one and only 1967 Monterey Pop Festival.

"Three days, thirty-two acts, a lifetime of memories," the concert promoters described it. Allegra remembered being fifteen minutes from home, but not even bothering to call. After all, this was her "summer of love." She knew Gammy would take one look at her dirty feet and tell her, "Get outside and take a scrub brush to those terrible things!" She wasn't up for that; she was up for three days of incredible music, and Doc at her side.

Monterey was the first time she saw Janis Joplin, who had sung her heart out, screaming into the microphone, stamping her feet like she couldn't wring enough emotion out of mere words. She hadn't been on stage five minutes before she brought Allegra to tears with "Down on Me." That was why, when February rolled around, and she gave birth to Mariah, two middle names went on the birth certificate—Janis Joplin.

Allegra had hopes that Mariah would belt out whatever song her life handed to her. She supposed that for Mariah that had been teaching college. She'd never seen her teach. All she knew of the university was that Mariah lugged around a heavy briefcase and was continually rushing from one meeting to another, and then the bastards had yanked her job away after eight years of work. It scared her to think she might never hear her daughter hold forth on her passions.

While Otis Redding sang "Sittin' on the Dock of the Bay," Doc had whispered to Allegra, "When I was in line for the can I heard someone say this is his first time in front of a nearly all-white audience. Look at him, the poor guy. He's so nervous he's shaking."

Otis Redding "brought down the house," the *Chronicle* would later write, but so did Jimi Hendrix, setting his guitar on fire, and Hugh Masekela, the African trumpet player who later worked hard for the antiapartheid movement Allegra sent money to. Sometime in the late eighties, his song "Bring Him Back Home" had become Nelson Mandela's anthem. Now *there* was a life well lived. And Buffalo Springfield debuted— the band that came about because of a Los Angeles freeway traffic jam: Stephen Stills happened to be in the car behind Neil Young's. Tired of waiting, they got out of their cars and started talking to each other, found out they were both musicians, and that chance meeting had laid the groundwork for musical genius. The Mamas and Papas were still intact. Simon still had Garfunkel. Herb Caen's column always had something funny to say. R. Crumb comic books were affordable, and Allegra was young enough to feel immortal.

These days a good concert ticket could go as high as five hundred bucks. Bands like the Stones continued to tour year-round. MTV videos had choreographers, directors, and could cost as much as making a movie. At the Monterey Pop, though, every act played for free. "Let's not be sad about anything this summer," she told Doc. California had its Monterey Pop; New York had its Woodstock. Nothing that happened afterward could compare. The best part about it, being a part of the history of a generation of incredible music, was simply being there. And even then Mariah might have been inside her, growing into the daughter she loved but could never please.

At six, Allegra got up and inspected the tray Cricket had left her. A bowl of soup covered with an inverted second bowl, a few almonds, and peaches sliced so thin she could see through them. The meal was arranged like a still life, too pretty to disturb. She picked up a peach slice and let it sit on her tongue a long time before she swallowed and strained to keep it down.

On the floor basking in front of the fireplace was where Al found her when he walked in at seven PM, with Lindsay in tow. She had found *Sgt. Pepper's Lonely Hearts Club Band,* successfully negotiated the stereo system, and was listening to it for the third time.

"Will you look at this, Lindsay," he said. "Time stops for no one, except your nana. To her, it's 1967 all the time."

"That's okay with me," Lindsay said. "I'm ready to give this year to the thrift store."

"Aw, you don't mean that," Al said. "Lots of great events took place this year. Hey, you got a grandpa out of it."

Allegra tried to get to her feet without invoking the wrath of Khan, who'd made a nest in her shirt. But if Lindsay was here instead of home with Mariah, something was wrong. "Hi, honey," she said. "Your mom have a date tonight? Is that why we have the pleasure of your company?"

Lindsay frowned. "Scotland Weird kind of stopped calling."

"Uh oh."

"Let's talk about all that later," Al said. "Right now let's go make ice cream sundaes or root beer floats."

Lindsay squatted down to pet Khan, who wagged his back end so much he had to adjust his front legs so he wouldn't fall over. "I don't like sweets," Lindsay said.

"That's because you've never had a Goodnough sundae," Al said. "This is my one culinary skill. My daughter Kaylie loved them. Come on in the kitchen." He looked back at Allegra, and she saw what mentioning his dead daughter's name had cost him, and further, she understood why he'd done it. He was fitting Lindsay into the space in his heart that had once held his daughter. "Coming?" he asked.

"Always," Allegra said.

They sat at the kitchen table, talking. Lindsay had a lot to say, and Allegra listened, hoping to build a bridge to Mariah and Gammy with this beautiful child's inability to lie.

"On Thanksgiving," she began, dipping her spoon into the root beer float, "something kind of broke, I think, and I don't know how to fix it. Mom is so mad. But she's not really mad at you, Allegra. She's mad at losing her job, having to move, and really mad at herself for liking Fergus the Freak, because what if he dumps her, and him going to Scotland for Christmas is like step one in that happening."

"Those are all good reasons to be angry," Allegra said. "If she needs to take it out on me, so what? I won't stop loving her."

"You don't get it, Nana. I'm not saying it right." She put her face in her hands and Allegra looked at Doc.

"Let's review," he said. "Your mom doesn't like waitressing.

She was a college professor. That world's apples and the café is oranges. But Allegra's too sick to work full time, so Mariah in effect is pulling double shifts, which if they're anything like I had to do in med school, can make a person ferociously cranky. She sticks with it because she wants to pay your tuition. That doesn't give her much time to look for another teaching job. And she blames me."

"But you haven't done anything except show up," Allegra said.

"Allegra, you heard her. I wasn't there when she needed me."

"But that couldn't be helped. You're here, now."

Lindsay took another spoonful of her float. "It's my fault, too. Next year I go to high school. That means in four years I'll go to college, which will cost even more if I don't win the science scholarship."

In the guest room, Allegra sat on the bed, running her fingers over the blue and white quilt. Slate floors ran all through the house, but every bedroom had a kilim rug. Lindsay opened the bathroom cabinets and said, "Allegra, look. There are towels and toothbrushes and really good lotion. Look at all these fancy soaps. Dr. G's house is like staying in a hotel."

"On the surface it might seem that way," Allegra answered. "But your grandfather is human, just like everyone else."

"The bathtub has Jacuzzi jets! Can I take a bath?"

It was ten PM, but Allegra had already decided she was keeping Lindsay home from school tomorrow. She needed a day to herself worse than any of them. "Just be sure you fill it up to cover the jets before you turn them on," Allegra said. In case Lindsay was shy about her body, Allegra left her alone to take her bath.

Al came to the bedroom door. "How's it going?"

"Good," Allegra said back, and they smiled as they heard the Jacuzzi jets turn on. "I'm going to wash her clothes. Anything you need washed?"

He looked at her blankly. "The thing is—"

"Cricket takes care of that, right? It won't kill her if I do a little laundry now and then. I'll go check your hamper."

"Thanks, doll."

"For what?"

"For not hating me for being able to afford all this. This sure isn't the same world as the one we fell in love in, is it?"

"Everyone our age says that. Just don't think you're going to make a golfer out of me."

She washed Lindsay's clothes and rested on the couch until they were ready for the dryer. Al sat beside her, opening his mail. "Nothing important," he said, and set the envelopes aside and took Allegra's hand. "It's great having Lindsay here."

"It's always great having Lindsay around. Are you ready to tell me what happened today? How you ended up with her staying here on a school night? What did you do, knock Mariah unconscious?"

He laughed. "Actually, our conversation was fairly civil. I told her Lindsay asked to spend the night, and how nice it would be if she could have some alone time with you. Then I listened to the maternal rulebook, no TV after eight, no internet after eight, and check the homework."

"Which you have no intention of following," Allegra said.

"Hey, we're the grandparents. It's in the contract we have to spoil them."

)

Sliding Doc's T-shirt over Lindsay's head, Allegra caught a glimpse of her granddaughter's body and realized just how much she'd grown since summer. Not so much in height, but as if from the inside out. She carried herself like a woman aware. Her face had thinned out, and her smile had widened. Her little calves had turned shapely, probably from riding horses with her pal Sally, whose neck Allegra wanted to wring for breaking off their friendship. This year of changes has been hard on her, Allegra thought while Lindsay arranged her pillows, yet the sad stuff had given her mettle. All she needed was someone to show her how to use it, and Allegra figured that task fell perfectly to a hippie grandmother.

The spare bedroom had a waterfront view, so Allegra left the curtains open. Lindsay slipped into bed and pulled the quilt to her chin. "This sure is a big house, Allegra."

Allegra nodded. "It's humongous. Sometimes I'm afraid I'll get lost looking for the bathroom. So, do you want me to tell you a story, or sit and talk for a while?"

"I'm too old for stories."

"Oh, honey. We never get too old for stories."

"Can I touch your new hair?"

"Sure." Allegra pulled off her baseball cap. "Look how curly it's coming in. I wonder if it will stay that way."

Lindsay touched it. "I hate my curly hair. If I had chemo and lost my hair, I'd pray that it would come in straight." Lindsay stopped smiling. "Dr. G told me the Marinol made you sick. What are you going to take now?"

"I don't know if there is anything else to take."

"But you have to gain weight. Statistics show that people who have a BMI of nineteen or lower are predisposed to bone loss, nutrient deficiency, heart irregularities, depression—"

Allegra placed her hand over Lindsay's mouth. "Why are we worrying about me when Al tells me you have some health stuff of your own going on? What's all this about stomachaches? You know if you have tummy troubles you can take papaya extract, and drink chamomile tea." She saw tears glitter in Lindsay's eyes and reached for her and pressed her sad face against her own. "What is it, honey?"

"I think I have generalized anxiety disorder."

Allegra sighed. "That damned internet! I wish the world would go back to chalk and slate!"

"You can't fight the internet, Allegra. It's here to stay, and once libraries get books on line, it won't matter where people live, they will have access to all kinds of books. The reason I called Dr. G instead of Mom or you is I knew he would listen and know what to do and wouldn't make a big fuss about it that would upset everyone again when they aren't even finished being upset about the last couple of things that went wrong."

"Lindsay, my God, take a breath!"

"He wants me to have some medical tests done to see if I have an ulcer."

"I bet I know why you didn't tell anyone you felt ill," Allegra said. "You were afraid of taking the attention off me, weren't you? Oh, Linds. This year has been no fun, but I'm getting better. And guess what? Your grandpa has a volleyball net. When it gets warm we'll set it up and play."

"I suck at sports."

Allegra brushed the wavy hair from her granddaughter's face. "So we'll play without the net."

"Can Khan sleep with me?"

"Sure. I'll go find him."

When she did, he was sleeping in front of the fireplace, having dragged a corner of the afghan from the couch to make his nest. Of course he growled when Allegra touched him. "Now you listen here, Mr. Smart," she told him. "Tonight you have a very important job to do. You, little man, have to make Lindsay feel safe and loved. Are you up to it?"

He yipped. Allegra took him to Lindsay's room, and found her already in dreamland. She tucked Khan in beside her and told him to stay.

As Allegra lay down next to Al, who was already in bed, reading a medical journal, she turned on her side and touched his whiskery face. "Time to spill the family secrets," she said. "I want to hear every detail."

He set the magazine down. "She called me to come get her from school. I asked what was bothering her, you know, why me and not Mariah, and she told me she thinks she's got an ulcer. Apparently she's been having stomachaches for months."

"And then what?"

"We walked on the beach, got a veggie burger of which she only ate a few bites. We spent some time in the bookstore, and I bought her a book on clouds. Then we came home."

"That's not telling me anything," Allegra complained. "Where are the details? What did she say?"

Al set the journal aside. "You see this right here is why there're so many divorces in America. The genders aren't taught how to communicate properly. If you'd told me that information, I would be satisfied enough to go to sleep. But you want a woman's point of view coming from the man who loves you. Ordinarily, this is a task any man would fail, but being a clever lad, I memorized a few details I think will satisfy you."

"Why do I feel like I'm in bed with a self-help book?"

"Don't laugh," Al said. "Might do us all good to carry a manual. Okay, here are the details. Lindsay keeps her distance from tide pools because she doesn't want to disturb any creatures. She shakes the sand from her shoes without being asked. She can't pass a window box without smelling each flower, and if you ask her their names, she'll tell you the Latin as well as the common names. At dinner she said thank you to the server, folded her napkin, started to stack our empty plates and would have cleared the table if I hadn't stopped her. She pushed her chair back in toward the table before we left. And we sat in the car for a long time while she talked about her gut. Was that satisfying?"

Allegra lay against his chest. "That's pretty good for a first-timer."

"Good? It's fucking great. And one more thing. She told me she thought Mariah's beau should go see an American dentist before he goes back to Scotland."

They laughed. Al returned to his journal and Allegra to her book of poems. She read a little every day, and tonight it was

Mary Oliver, who understood nature the same way Allegra did. But as graceful as the poems were, and as much as Allegra wanted to stay with them and linger, something kept nagging at her. She got out of bed and sat cross-legged on the carpet and began to do her yoga stretches.

Doc looked down. "If you're that limber all the time I guess I'm a lucky man as soon as the chemo clears your system."

"What a dirty mind you have."

He laughed. "Am I supposed to not say how good you look? How much I want you?"

After only a few poses, Allegra grew tired. She got back in bed and lay there, thinking. "Al?"

"The answer is yes," he said over his journal.

"But you don't even know what I was going to ask."

"The answer is still yes."

"What I was going to say is maybe I should sign my half of The Owl and Moon over to Mariah. Let her run it as is, change it to something fancy, or hire someone else to run it if that's what she wants."

He set the journal down. "See? The answer was yes."

"You really think so?"

"I do."

"This in no way assures you that you're getting a good old-fashioned housewife for your bride, you know. I like to garden, yes, but I also like circulating petitions and I'm willing to get arrested for the right cause."

He gave her a quick kiss. "I only wanted you for sex, anyway. But I warn you, Allegra, you will have to dress up once in a while, and accompany me to those mandatory doctor events. I can't wait to have you there on my arm, my shining bride. I am sick with how much I love you."

"Me, too, you," she said, and shut off the light.

16
Mariah

A WATERY WINTER SUN was just rising as Mariah punched down her nine-grain bread dough and left it to rest for five minutes before shaping. She unlocked the café's front door and stood in the center of the mariner's compass, her feet on true north as she peeled bits of dough off her fingers. Above her, the café sign creaked on its chain. As if he'd lost a fight to a larger bird, the owl's beak was snapped off at the very tip.

"You better get that fixed, toots," Mr. Cashin had told her yesterday. "Your mother never let things like that slide. She ran a class establishment."

"It's on the list," she'd assured him, keeping her voice even. Customers had been telling her that for a week, and did she care? No.

Her grandmother was asleep upstairs. Her mother was shacked up with Dr. Goodnough—at some point Mariah was going to have to figure out what to call her father—and her daughter had spent the night in the enemy camp. Since Thanksgiving Fergus had been busy at work, a little remote and twice had broken dates at the last minute, claiming budget meetings. When Dr. Goodnough called and asked if Lindsay could sleep over, Mariah said yes for purely selfish reasons. Once the café closed and the mop was squeezed clean, she got in her car and drove straight to the marina. Though Fergus had a pile of papers on his bed he was working on, she refused to take no for an answer. Half in their clothes, they made a kind of breathless love, Fergus because he needed to get the papers done before morning, and Mariah because in less than two weeks, he was leaving for Scotland.

"I've heaps of work to do," he'd say when she called for a little phone fooling around.

"It's not a simple matter of lifting a rope and motoring out," he'd responded when she asked him to take the boat out in the harbor.

The street sweeper drove by, and a few early commuters followed in its dust. She spotted a deer across the street, nibbling branches in the cemetery. A few shops down, a silver Honda pulled to the curb. The couple inside was kissing. The whole world felt like that Yeats poem her mother loved— things falling away, the center unable to hold. Mariah hadn't slept well. Sickened by the multitude of cookies and soup bowls and holiday orders she had to prepare, she'd eaten nothing. She pictured Fergus asleep on his back in the berth-style bed. He basically laid down and did not move until morning. Theodora stood by patiently, waiting for him to wake up. Mariah thrashed and got up for a glass of water three times before giving up and driving home. A man on temporary visa, a dog too big for her own good, and a boat called the *Ellen Cole II* named after a brave and selfless mother. There didn't seem to be much room left for a waitress.

When Fergus first told her he was going to Scotland for Christmas, Mariah figured that meant a week, maybe ten days. But the community college had a winter recess that lasted a whole month, which meant five weeks, plus an extra one he added on to his vacation. I'll miss you, she said, but what she meant was here I give you my heart and there you go. She'd been at this bend in this road before. She remembered the pain of being left behind when a man she loved didn't return. Get hold of yourself, she said. You're a capable woman who's proven she can get along just fine without a man. You gave up love to focus on Lindsay. Lindsay had turned out great, but without Fergus, her own life seemed as dry as a gravel gully filled with not very interesting rocks.

The Honda's door opened, and Simon stepped out. As the car drove by Mariah looked in the window and saw the blond cop, Terry, who came by the café every afternoon for take-out coffee and a cinnamon roll.

"Good morning, Simon," she said as he approached the café. "Better not let Gammy catch you snogging in public."

"Snogging?" He stopped on the sidewalk. "I've seen you mashing lips with kilt boy in several public places, not the least of which is Gardener's Alley. At least I make out with a modicum of discretion."

"Guilty as charged. Are you happy?"

He looked at her blankly. "Are you daft? How can anyone be happy in these perilous times? If it isn't war, then it's a certain virus we cannot seem to eradicate, and may I remind you that your mother has leukemia? Honey, the most I hope for is getting through the day, hour by hour."

"Drama queen," she said.

"Harlot," he shot back.

"Harlot? Mr. One-Night Stand is calling me a harlot for sleeping with the second man in my life ever?"

"He's only the second? I pity you, Mariah. Truly I do."

"Why do we do this, Simon?"

"Do what?"

"Snipe at each other. Squabble. I like you. I'm happy for you, for however long things last." She waited for him to reassure her about her relationship, to wish her well, but he did nothing of the kind. "I'm a total idiot, aren't I?" she said. "Kilt boy will return to the land of plaid, marry a bonnie lass, and leave me here with dirty dishes and nickel tips."

He put his hands on her shoulders. "Now who's being the drama queen? It's too early in the morning to be this serious. Let's go cook. With Allegra gone, I've got a few new recipes I want to try."

"Fine with me," Mariah said.

With Simon chopping jicama in the background, and the radio on NPR, Mariah shaped her bread loaves and set them aside to rise. She rolled up cinnamon rolls; cut out, baked, and iced gingerbread men; and then made five dozen blue-frosted dreidels for a Hanukkah order. When she was just about to take the bread out of the oven, she realized she'd forgotten to make the Springerle.

Quickly, she broke four eggs into two cups of sugar and whisked the mixture until it was creamy. Her arms had grown strong over the last four months and she could lift a fifty-pound bag of flour without a whimper. She greased a cookie sheet, scattered crushed anise seed on top, and the faint licorice-lavender smell filled the kitchen, competing with Simon's tortilla soup. Then she measured, added ingredients and stirred until the dough came together, rolled it out and used the wooden owl-and-moon mold to make each cookie.

There were two things to remember about Springerle, and they were the same thing, essentially. Sift. Sift the sugar before measuring, and sift the flour with the baking powder. If you didn't sift, what you got was a heavy cookie. You had to use a firm but light touch when pressing and cutting. Gammy had taught her to make the cookies when she was half Lindsay's age. Mariah had stood on a soda bottle crate, listening. She believed all grandmothers were bingo addicts, and that all mothers got arrested for peaceful protests. Life was one "Schoolhouse Rock" moment after another.

Around three, Mariah began expecting Lindsay. She closed the café, but left the door unlocked, sent Gammy upstairs to put her feet up, and mopped the floor. Simon finished the dishes and changed his shirt, and then presented himself for inspection. "How do I look?"

His black hair was slicked back and his white Polo shirt accented his tanning bar glow and his gym-toned arms. "You look handsome. The cop?"

"His name is Terry, and he prefers to be referred to as a peace officer."

"Okay," Mariah said, "but I have to say, Simon, a peace officer doesn't seem like your type."

"Are you kidding?" he said. "You should see his pension."

Mariah grinned. "Do I have to?"

"It's this place, you know," he said, his voice as dry as a martini. "It's turning you into your mother."

"The hell it is," Mariah said. "This is only temporary until she comes back and I find a teaching job."

"Mariah, please. Have you been beating down doors to look for a teaching job?"

Flustered, she dropped the mop onto the floor. "I've downloaded adjunct pool application forms. I just haven't sent them out yet."

"Sweetie," Simon said, "wake up and smell the latte. As we speak, Allegra's probably eating peeled grapes and looking out onto a private beach. Bess is a mean old stick who needs to retire and go on Catholic Church tours of Ireland. We're it, babycakes. You and me. Chief cook and bottle washer. Think about what this place could become, would you? Unless you've already decided to sell."

"Sell the café?"

"An option worth exploring. Tirrah," he said, poking fun at Fergus, and went out the front door to meet his peace officer.

Mariah wrote out a produce order list. She restocked the to-go packages. They were almost out of string for tying packages. When it was three forty-five and Lindsay still hadn't shown up, Mariah phoned the school.

"Country Day Academy for Girls," the secretary said.

"Hello, this is Mariah Moon, Lindsay's mother. I wondered if my daughter might be staying late to work on her science project," she said.

"Actually," the secretary said, "our records show she was absent today."

"Absent?" It was Country Day's policy for the parent to call and let them know when a student was ill. "That must be a mistake. I never called to approve the absence."

She heard shuffling papers. "Her grandfather called."

Her grandfather! Oh, that galled her. "Thank you," she said crisply and hung up the phone. Heads were going to roll. She paced the kitchen, trying to decide what to do. Call the good doctor at his office? Have him paged? She knew his home phone number was in Gammy's address book. She'd looked it up when Allegra was sick with pneumonia. But what did she say if her mother answered? And why hadn't Allegra called to apologize for the Thanksgiving debacle?

Suddenly all she wanted to do was run to Fergus. She wanted to leave the till money on the counter, rip off her apron, race out the door and drive a hundred miles an hour to Pier Two, past the Harbormaster's hut, skidding on coastal pine needles and oil slicks, jump the locked gate, or swim her way through the gunky water to the *Ellen Cole II*. He wouldn't be home this early. She could pick Theo up from Noah's Bark and take her for a walk. She could have dinner waiting when Fergus came home. Potatoes in jackets. Beans on toast. A tin of treacle and a jar of clotted cream. All his peculiar Scottish favorites were basically heat and eat. She'd tidy up the boat, sit on the gunwale and watch the sun set, and in doing so, turn into every other woman on the planet, which compared to a bingo queen and a middle-aged hippie, sounded normal. But the mother portion of her heart won out, and she sat down at the counter to make the call.

The moment Mariah heard the female voice on the other end say hello, she blurted out, "The only reason I'm calling is to ask where Lindsay is and what makes you think you have the right to keep her home from school without asking me."

"Who this?" the voice said. "Who calling Dr. G and yelling like madman?"

"Who's this?" Mariah said, realizing she'd just gone off like an idiot to a complete stranger.

"This Cricket Kyon Jin, Jin with J, Dr. G housekeeper. Who you?"

Another person to apologize to. Well, get in line. "This is Mariah Moon, Lindsay's mother. I believe my mother, Allegra, is staying there?"

"Mrs. Allegra here. Why you not take more better care of mother? Too skinny, mother. Daughter should tend sick mother always."

"Could I just speak to her?"

"Sick mother asleep. Call back later." She hung up.

Mariah stared at the phone, stunned at the woman's rudeness. She pressed redial.

"Hello?"

"This is Allegra's daughter again," Mariah said. "May I please speak to my daughter, Lindsay?"

"Lindsay not here," Cricket said.

"Do you know where she is?"

"At hospital with Dr. G."

"Thank you so much," Mariah said, and as childish as she knew it was, she hung up first.

The Community Hospital of the Monterey Peninsula backed up to the Seventeen Mile Drive, and had a newly built and sorely needed parking garage. Mariah remembered coming here to see her mother. Every time she visited, Dr. Goodnough had either been there in person, had called on Allegra's phone, or was in the hallway talking to her mother's nurses.

At the elevator, she scanned the directory for Hematology/Oncology. She hated confrontation, but forged ahead, pissed off that this man was making decisions about her daughter. She rehearsed a number of scenarios, yet abandoned them all the moment she caught sight of Lindsay, who was standing on a chair cleaning a fish tank with two magnets covered in scrubbing material, one inside the tank, one outside. Dr. Goodnough stood behind Lindsay, his hands hovering near her shoulders in case she lost her balance.

"Mom!" Lindsay said, looking happier than she had in months. "Does this mean you're coming to dinner with us?"

In that single moment, in a room generally reserved for the worst news a person could receive, Mariah saw how much her daughter needed a grandfather. Her other male role models were Simon, a keg of sarcasm, and Mr. Cashin, of the quarter tips. Dr. Goodnough had given Lindsay more of a healthy role model in one fish tank than Mariah had over the course of her daughter's life. If only for Lindsay she had to make this work. A single missed day of school—what did that matter in the long run? "Sure, I'm up for dinner. Where are we going?"

"Back to my house," Dr. Goodnough said, and Mariah could see in his eyes he was waiting for her to yell at him.

Mariah wanted to say, that's right. You should be worried, pal. Mess with my child and you'll find out just what her mother is made of, but she knew she wasn't all Lindsay needed. For the last two months she'd paid Lindsay's tuition in tips. She bought her own shoes at the thrift store in order to buy Lindsay new ones. She would do anything to help Lindsay grow up and out of her own circumstances. No daughter of hers would wait tables, or be let go after eight years of term appointments and find herself having ill-fated affairs with Scotsmen who didn't for one second intend to stick around. "Sounds good," she said. "Can you draw me a map?"

"Why don't you ride with your mother, Lindsay?" Dr. Goodnough said, steadily meeting Mariah's eyes.

"Okay," Lindsay said. "I know how to get there, Mom. And I know the guard at the gate so we don't have to pay," she babbled, and Mariah was undone just to see her daughter excited about something that didn't reside in a textbook.

"Then it's all settled," the doctor said. "I'll see you both at home."

Mariah's neck was tense the whole walk to the car, while Lindsay chattered on about Cricket, the housekeeper who dusted every single thing each day, no matter if it needed it or not. "She told me this Korean folktale about a frog that wouldn't obey its mother," she said. "It wouldn't croak like everyone else. Instead of saying 'kay-gul,' it said, 'kul-gay,' and the mother was really annoyed but couldn't get him to stop."

"So then what happened?" Mariah said as she unlocked the car.

"The mother frog got sick and made the bad frog promise to bury her by a stream when she died, and then she died, and he buried her, and then there was a big storm and he was worried she'd wash away, so that's why frogs croak 'kay-gul' when it rains."

"Sounds cheery," Mariah said as they pulled out into traffic.

"Get in the left lane," Lindsay said, and Mariah did. They were both quiet after that, looking at the Spanish moss and the costly homes tucked back from the road by various wooden and metal gates and cherished, tall, elegant trees. You couldn't see the ocean, but you could smell it.

"You know," Mariah said, trying to keep her voice even, "I understood you wanting a night with Allegra, but it's not okay for you to take a day off school until you clear it with me."

"I know," Lindsay said.

"So why didn't you call me?"

"Because I knew you'd be mad," Lindsay said, and reached for the radio knob. She tuned the station to Monterey Jack's evening drive time. "This song goes out to my mother," he said, "a real Buffalo Gal, my mom. Ladies and gentlemen, Mr. Bill Frisell, from the CD 'Good Dog, Happy Man.'"

Mothers, Mariah thought. Some locked in, others kept out,

but our children, even when they're mad at us, they can't forget us. Outside the car the sun began its descent into the Pacific. She wondered what Monterey Jack's mother must be like. Maybe they had pet names for each other, family stories they told over and over, or maybe, like the misbehaving frog, his mother had died, and he was memorializing her in the dedication. That alone was reason enough to forgive your mother for being the kind of person who rubbed you the wrong way. Mariah waited until a few more songs played before speaking, but by then they were at the gate and Lindsay was waving to the guard.

"So what were you sick with yesterday? You look like you feel well today."

"My stomach hurt," Lindsay said.

"And this morning? Did it hurt then, too, or were you playing possum?"

Lindsay looked at her, as if stunned. "Mom, my stomach *always* hurts. Some days it hurts worse than others, but it really never goes away."

"Why didn't you tell me?"

Lindsay looked at her, stone-faced, then quietly said, "It was only a stomachache. It wasn't cancer."

Mariah wanted to pull over and cry. How could she not have seen something was wrong with her own child? "But Lindsay, if it doesn't go away then you need to see a doctor. We'll"—she swallowed her pride—"ask Dr. Goodnough for a referral and make an appointment first thing in the morning."

"He already made an appointment for me with a gastroenterologist today. Dr. Caroljean Miller. She thinks I should have a test called an endoscopy. That's when they put a tube with a camera on the end of it down your throat into your stomach. I wish I could stay awake to see it but they give you anesthetic. Turn left here and go to the end. That's Dr. G's house. The one with the circular driveway. I wish I could get a video of my endoscopy. I wonder if I asked if they would give it to me."

"Excuse me, but did it even occur to anyone to clear this

with me? I'm your mother. No one's running tests or taking you to doctors without clearing it with me first." Not to mention the fact that she'd turned in the last COBRA payment late, and wouldn't they just love a chance to deny her claim? With a name like that the test had to cost a couple thousand dollars.

Lindsay gave her the big blinking eyes that always did her in. "The only reason I didn't call you is because Dr. G said he thought he could explain it to you better so would I please wait until dinner."

Mariah shut the engine off and sat there, stunned. Dr. G's house was a sprawling one-story done in the Monterey style, with a courtyard, fountain, and a beautifully landscaped yard filled with twisted cypress and scarlet bougainvillea.

Lindsay opened her door. "Come on, Mom. I want to show you the beach. It's really great. Khan loves it. And there's a separate house, too. Dr. G calls it a mother-in-law apartment, but it's really more like a little house. It even has a fireplace. I wish I could live in it. It's just sitting there empty. Do you think Gammy would like it?"

Mariah followed her daughter up the flagstone steps to a pair of roughly hewn arch-topped oak front doors with hammered copper fixtures and a grated window inset at eye level. The lantern-style light fixture gave off a pearly glow. Simon was right. Allegra would never come back. She'd hire a moving service to pack up her sixties posters and albums. Allegra would live here for the rest of her life, however long that might be.

While Lindsay took her hand and showed her around the house, in Mariah's mind she saw the pie chart in *Society: The Basics* rise up out of its gray 42.7 percent slice—wealth—and come to life. In terms of distribution of wealth, California was worse than most states, and Carmel was the worst of all. The top three occupations of prestige were physician, attorney, and college professor, although Mariah took issue with the last entry. Dr. Goodnough had original paintings, not prints. The nubby rug over the tile floors was thick and white. The kitchen was a monument to fossilized granite.

"This way, Mom," Lindsay said.

Mariah followed her daughter to a beach so private and perfect it seemed like Elizabeth Taylor and Richard Burton should be there performing a love scene that would win them an Academy Award. It was growing dark, but she heard the waves crashing, and knew the peace this place must give her mother. Silence where there was none. Immortality when she'd spent so much time thinking of her own mortality. Serenity, solitude, peace—all things that were missing at The Owl & Moon.

"Dr. G says in the summer, he swims every single morning. Isn't it great, Mom?"

"It's great."

"Race you back to the house," Lindsay said, and Mariah watched her go, that strawberry hair flying behind her.

"Hello, Mom," Mariah said to Allegra, who was sitting on a leather couch, Khan on her lap. She was wearing new clothes—plum-colored lounging pajamas and embroidered slippers. Next to her was a shawl made of ribbon and mohair, and she knew immediately that Dr. Goodnough had picked it out himself and bought it for her.

"Hello, Mariah," she said back, and Mariah could see the tension beneath her silk outfit. "It's good to see you. I've been thinking of you a lot."

"Have you?" Mariah asked. If you've been thinking of me, why haven't you called to apologize for being such an ass on Thanksgiving? Wait . . . what were they mad about, exactly? "I've been thinking of you, too."

Dr. Goodnough took out a CD. "How about some Aretha before dinner?"

Shortly after, "Respect" issued forth from hidden speakers.

"Your mother loves this song," he said. "Way back in 1967 it was like nothing I'd ever heard before, and I'll be damned if it doesn't sound just as good today."

Mariah knew had she not been there, he would have danced. She could see the two of them dressed in suede and denim, sitting on the sidewalk while music poured through the Haight district. Lindsay was off in the guest room having a Jacuzzi bath before dinner. Allegra had said it was her third since she'd arrived. It was just the three of them here in the living room, although the housekeeper was making a racket in the kitchen. Mariah took a breath and charged in. "Lindsay informed me that you made an appointment for her with a specialist without speaking to me," she said. "I haven't given my consent for her to have this procedure and don't you dare pull an end run around me."

Dr. Goodnough nodded, and Allegra laid her bony hand over his. "I understand how you feel," he said. "Ordinarily I'd've gone directly to you, but she was afraid to tell you, Mariah."

"Afraid?"

"Yes, afraid. This doc thinks she has a bleeding ulcer. It's imperative that we get it checked out."

"An ulcer?" Mariah said. "How can she have an ulcer? She's twelve."

Allegra said, "Now, babe, that's what I said at first, too. But Al says age has nothing to do with it. It can be a bacterial thing, not just stress related."

"That's right," he said. "If we do the test, we'll have some answers."

Mariah felt her knees begin to shake. "But isn't it dangerous, putting her under general anesthesia?"

Dr. Goodnough folded his hands in his lap. "It's not a general, just a small amount of a drug called Versed. Dr. Miller's a wonderful G.I. doc. She'll put Lindsay out for a half hour, tops, just long enough to scope her, take samples and pictures, and then wake her right up."

The taking samples part made Mariah feel faint.

"Mariah, I know you're not wild about having a father foisted on you this late in the game. You don't have to acknowledge me or even like me, but Lindsay's a different story."

"What do you mean?"

"She—and again, I don't intend to step on your toes—seems to like having me around."

"She does, Mariah," Allegra said. "She took to him so quick. They talk about science. She's fascinated with medicine. Who knows, with Al's influence, she could grow up to be a doctor. I know you want the best for her, babe. I know I haven't been the best mother to you, Mariah, but I just don't see how Al being in her life could hurt her. Please give it a try, if only for Lindsay's sake."

Lindsay came into the room dressed in slim new jeans and a long-sleeved Gap T-shirt. As petite as she was, she did not look twelve; she looked days shy of leaving her family for college. "What are you guys trying to do for my sake?"

Mariah smiled sheepishly. Gammy would say, You can fight the tide or let it carry you. "To get along with your grandfather."

Mariah watched the way her daughter looked at each person, reading his or her expressions and body language. Ever since she could toddle upright, her daughter could read hearts the way fortune tellers did Tarot cards. Apparently all that time she had been taking the burden of what she learned to her tummy.

"Thanks, Mom," she said, "because I love all of you."

Mariah's heart cleaved in two.

"Dinner ready!" Cricket called from the kitchen.

The dining room had whitewashed walls with the occasional piece of decorative straw poking through. Above their heads natural beams supported an iron chandelier forged to look like branches. The sideboard held Nambe bowls and platters, and a Christmas cactus so enormous and full of buds that Mariah couldn't imagine the stress of keeping it alive. Dr. Goodnough uncorked the wine and poured her a glass. The first sip reminded her of how stupid she'd behaved on Thanksgiving. She pushed her chair back to see if Cricket needed any help serving, and the tiny housekeeper snapped at her with a napkin.

"You, guest. Sit. Serving my job, not yours."

"Might as well cave in," Al said. "My housekeeper makes a formidable opponent."

"Formidable," Lindsay said, "is a word with three different meanings. One that hardly anybody thinks of is 'to inspire respect because of ability.' That's what Dr. G means, Mom. It's not like Cricket would ever hurt anyone. She's really nice."

"Smart girl, Dr. G granddaughter," Cricket said.

Nice or not, this wasn't like being out with Fergus in a restaurant, where the server was earning his or her money, and being extra nice for the tip. This was the pie chart leaping to life again. The stratum was unmistakable. The richest were bluebloods, lucky enough to be born into old money. Next came the upper-upper class, and then the just plain upper, who'd worked their way there. It was miles down the chart before gender, race, people working two or three jobs, those immigrants who left their families in their country of origin and sent money to them while the children grew up without a parent figured in. Mariah's head began to ache. She wanted two aspirin, Lindsay's stomach to be perfectly fine, her mother to stop being nice to her, and Gammy to move to a retirement village that offered bingo tournaments every evening and Mass every morning. She wanted Fergus to forget about Scotland, ask her to get an apartment together, Simon and his cop to work out, and if she could not find a teaching job, then at least she wanted a freaking vacation. She put her head in her hands and the weight of it surprised her. How had she managed all these years to hold it up on her skinny neck?

"What's wrong, honey?" Allegra said. "Are you sick?"

"Just a headache," Mariah said, looking up. "Sometimes I get migraines," she said.

"I didn't know that," Allegra said.

"She gets them once a month," Lindsay said. "When the weather changes or she gets her period."

"Lindsay!" Mariah snapped.

"What? Migraines coincide with hormone levels, at least that's what the medical literature says. If you kept a migraine journal, my data would be much more relevant."

"I can get you something a little stronger than aspirin if you like," Dr. G said, "but you can't drink any more wine, and you'll need a ride home."

"I'll be fine with aspirin and a cup of coffee," Mariah said. Lindsay ran to fetch her both.

Allegra got up from the table and began to rub Mariah's shoulders, and inside her the dam broke. Her always-difficult mother was using what little energy she had to work the knots from her daughter's shoulders. Mariah felt tears slide down her cheeks, and didn't bother to stop them.

"How's that?" Allegra said a few minutes later.

"Good," Mariah managed, wiping her face with her napkin. "Mom, you look so happy."

Allegra smiled. "I could buy a tiara from Tiffany's and never look as beautiful as you and Lindsay. You two are the masterpieces. Thanks for letting her stay over. I've missed her so much."

"Then why don't you come home?" Mariah said. "Why don't you get your butt back in the kitchen and run your business?"

There was a brief intermission while Cricket served them soup.

"Cricket, this smells wonderful," Allegra said.

"Hah," Cricket answered her. "It not only smell wonderful but taste wonderful and you going to eat it all up or I make you sit here all night until you finish."

"Cricket raised four sons," Dr. Goodnough said. "Two live

in Silicon Valley and are computer programmers. The other two are finishing up med school."

"All good boy," she said. "They eat this soup every week. This is good Korean soup. Encourage health."

"What's in it?" Lindsay said.

"Good food," Cricket said, setting the tureen on the table. "Daikon radish, yellow squash, green onion, dry kelp, which also call *dashi,* cabbage, tofu, and one hot pepper. This soup cure cold, mend heart, and encourage will to live. So easy to make you should serve at your restaurant and give me co-mission." She untied her apron and bunched it up in one hand. "Okay. My job done for today. I go home now and feed my birdies."

"What kind of birds do you have?" Lindsay asked.

"You ask too many question, Miss Dr. G's nosy grand-daughter. For your information, my birdies all canaries. Sing good when you feed hot pepper seed. Maybe I bring you picture sometime. You leave dishes in sink, I wash tomorrow."

She left the room, and they all looked down at their bowls at the same time. They smiled like civilized people. They lifted silver spoons that didn't need polishing but would get it tomorrow anyway. They ate. And wonder of wonders, Lindsay helped herself to a second dumpling.

"Remember, no food after midnight," Dr. G said.

"How can I eat when I'll be asleep?" Lindsay said.

"Is business going okay?" Allegra asked. "I imagine with the monarchs' return, you're doing about twenty-five percent above average. I hope you ordered more paper goods. We run out fast when tourists arrive. How are the Christmas baking orders?"

"I'm taking care of it," Mariah answered.

"How's Gammy?"

"She gets tired quickly. I think we need to hire two wait-people," she said, just to see what Allegra would make of it. "Gammy can't stay on her feet that long, and if you're not sure when you're coming back . . ."

Allegra nodded, and took hold of Dr. Goodnough's hand. "I think that's a great idea."

"You do?"

Allegra nodded. "Babe, I've decided to sign The Owl and Moon over to you."

"You're giving me the restaurant? What am I supposed to do with it? I'm a teacher, not a cook."

"Well," Allegra said, "you could hire someone to run it. I'm sure Simon would jump at the chance. You could rename it, change the menu, serve dinner, or you could lease the space and rake in the rent. However, there's a deal breaker. I don't want you to ever sell it."

"I don't understand. If you sold it, you and Gammy would be set for life."

"Oh, I could never do that. Not just because the land is so valuable, but also because it's the Moon women's chunk of the earth. When Myron died, it was the only thing Gammy had left. I had no idea of the details of their marriage until I overheard you talking that day in the café. But what matters is that it's precious to her, just as it is to me, and I hope to you and Lindsay."

Mariah noticed how quiet and pinch-lipped Lindsay had become. "That's a generous offer. Can we talk about it later?"

"Sure," Allegra said.

"If you need waiters," Lindsay said, "can I have a job?"

Both Mariah and Allegra turned to Lindsay at the same time. "You are not going to work as a waitress the rest of your life," they said in unison, then looked at each other, and Mariah thought if this were any other time in their lives they would have laughed.

"How about the Lakers this season?" Dr. G said. "Kobe's amazing."

"What are Lakers?" Lindsay asked.

Dr. G sighed. "I can see I have my work cut out for me."

"Gammy and I were always going to give it to you, honey," Allegra said. "That was the plan from day one. Believe me, we have offers every week to sell the property. We both feel that if you hang on to it, by the time Lindsay goes to college, it'll be worth so much she can mortgage it and go to Harvard, Yale, Juilliard, wherever she wants."

"Mother," Mariah said fighting back tears as she looked at Allegra's hardly touched soup. "You have to eat your dinner."

Dr. G put his arm around Allegra's shoulders. "Mariah's right. Otherwise, my dear heart, you are definitely looking at a feeding tube."

"You're both such meanies," she said, and lifted her spoon.

While Lindsay and Dr. Goodnough fooled around on the computer, Allegra took Mariah outside. "Come sit on the deck for a while," she said. "Take off your shoes and wiggle your toes in the sand."

Mariah would rather have lost another teaching job than have this conversation. "It's too cold for you out here."

"Two minutes won't kill me. Sit. Pretty please?"

Mariah felt the sand slide into her shoes, and hoped the cool air would clear her head enough so she could drive home.

"How's that handsome Scotsman?"

Such a typical Allegra question. Cut to the heart of things without warning. "Going home to Scotland for the holidays. Going back there permanently in May."

"Bummer. That must take the joy out of sex."

Always with the sex. "Well, he'll be back in February," Mariah said. "When he leaves for good, he leaves. I knew that from the start."

"You still have five months," Allegra said. "A lot can happen in that chunk of time. What do you think, babe? Is he the one?"

"The *one* what? I like him. He's smart, but he's a citizen of another country who's leaving here in May."

"So?" Allegra said.

"So what?" Mariah answered.

"Mariah, if he's the real deal, you go after him. Don't make the mistakes I did. Go to Scotland if you have to. Don't let him get away."

"Be realistic. When would I have time to undertake a project like that?"

"Hire a manager to run The Owl and Moon. Al and I will watch Lindsay. Gammy can stay at the apartment by herself, or come here and stay with us. We'll make sure Lindsay gets to school and does her homework. If you see your happiness out there on the horizon, honey, you run for it like hell's hounds are on your heels. Don't let somebody else steal it."

"Sounds like something Gammy would say."

They were quiet for a few minutes. Mariah remembered when her mother excused her from school for the day to hear Noam Chomsky lecture on Middle East policy and the American Peace Movement, which made Mariah miss her world history exam. Cronkite was fussy that day. They rode the bus to Berkeley, and stopped for organic juice. Mariah's solid A turned to a B because she missed that test. "I'm still mad at you."

"I'm still mad at you, too."

"Mother, how can you justify being mad at me? I'm not the one who kept a monumental secret. I'm the one you kept the news from for thirty-four years. I'm the injured party!"

"Oh, Mariah, don't talk to me about injuries. Embrace this miracle," Allegra said. "All your life you've been badgering me for his name. I finally give it to you and what thanks do I get? Screamed at on our first family holiday. Humiliated in front of your father."

"Well, to be fair, you had months to talk to me."

"Maybe I was too embarrassed. Did you ever think of that? Have you no compassion for the stupid sixteen-year-old girl who gave birth to you? Did I make you feel bad when you got knocked up with Lindsay? I opened my arms. Try imagining Lindsay three years from now giving birth to a baby."

"That will never happen."

"How do you know? Are you planning to lock her in a convent? Mariah, life's messy, embarrassing, sometimes everything you know falls to pieces and you pick yourself up, get rearranged, and then boom, you get cancer, and like some kind of cosmic joke the man you love arrives." She threw up her hands. "That's it, the extent of my motherly wisdom. If you want a pithy saying you'll have to go to Gammy."

They sat there in silence, the muted lapping of the waves the only sounds of life. At sixteen, Mariah was this uptight fatherless girl who above all didn't want to attract attention to herself. Five years later, she was pregnant. Her mind bubbled over with the percentages of unwed mothers, how the welfare system didn't help that many get out of it, and added in the minimum wage having stayed frozen for fifty years while politicians siphoned money out of the government for private jets and vacation homes. It almost made her want to, well, protest.

"I forgive you everything," Allegra said. "Now you have to forgive me."

The note from Gammy was taped to Mariah's bedroom door:

It is now eleven PM and I am going to bed. I have no idea where you are, but I suspect you are doing more than playing footsie with the bagpiper. I assume Lindsay is at the doctor's with your mother, but once again I am not sure because no one tells me anything. I am sixty-eight years old and I can't be everywhere at once, which is why I rely on God to take care of you all. However, would it kill you to tell me a few of the details so I can go to sleep without worrying? If you can see your way clear to do that, I will try to stay out of your personal business as much as I can.

In His Name,
Gammy

Mariah left the note where it was, slid into her bed fully clothed, and swallowed another aspirin to make sure the headache didn't find its way back. In a few hours, she would stand in the café kitchen and make bread, cookies, take special orders, and needle Simon until he revealed details of his date with the peace officer. Fergus would be packing for his flight, Theodora following him around morosely because she wasn't going along. Mariah'd relayed Lindsay's offer to dog sit, knowing full well she'd end up walking Theo herself—what the hell, the dog was the closest she could get to being with Fergus.

And in just a few hours, Lindsay would lie down on a gurney while a nurse fitted an I.V. into her hand. I.V.'s were for sick people. Sick like Allegra had been. Poking needles into her little girl's freckled skin. Lindsay wasn't worried; she was excited. Her grandfather promised to stand there while her insides were inspected and sampled. Where is this child's mother? one of the nurses would whisper to another, and if Dr. Goodnough heard he might dress her down. Who accompanied her daughter for the procedure was a practical solution to an impossible schedule upon which so many people depended it was dizzying. It makes sense for us to be there, Al had said. Allegra's will be the last face she sees before she goes under and the first face when she wakes up. Mariah nodded, oh, yes, practical, but all night long all she could think was that even if it meant leaving Simon and Gammy in charge of the café, she couldn't let that happen.

It was six AM, and by now Lindsay was checked into the surgicenter, changed into her paper gown, and a nurse was rubbing her hand, feeling for a willing vein. Mariah could see her daughter pumping her fist, looking at the needle as it pierced her flesh, fascinated. How had she managed to raise this girl who fell in love with dead scientists and would rather pore over her grandfather's medical textbooks than watch MTV?

"I can't believe we're out of shallots," Simon said as he simmered the chicken broth in one pan and the leeks in another. "Even Bess knows I like to caramelize shallots for cock-a-leekie soup," he said. "It imparts a touch of earthiness."

Mariah looked up in wonder. What had happened to Mr. Sourpuss, who could send her mood into a death spiral in under a minute, and who was he playacting for? Oh. The peace officer with the enormous pension was with him. Maybe it was his day off, and he'd tagged along to watch his new beau create culinary masterpieces as part of the afterglow of the previous evening's sex. She was jealous. Fergus didn't venture behind the order counter unless he was on his way to the loo. Given her sorry state this morning—dirty hair, swollen eyes from crying and worrying about Lindsay, and the specter of the headache rattling around behind her left ear— she was glad Fergus had arrived late. There was only time to hand off the dog so he didn't miss his plane. Theo was now upstairs sleeping on Mariah's bed.

"I adore shallots," the peace officer said, smiling. His shoulders were broad, but his frame was thin, just like Simon's. Mariah imagined the two of them sitting on his couch looking through one of the many coffee table books Simon had: *The History of Winemaking, The Amalfi Coast, An Aerial View of San Francisco*. He always told Mariah what to buy him for Christmas.

"Have you ever wrapped them in puff pastry? Divine. Open a bottle of Wild Horse Cabernet Sauv, and you're in heaven."

"Mariah," Simon said. "Terry makes brioche. His Godiva brownies are sin on a plate. And he's on vacation this week."

Mariah slid the challah into the oven, set the timer, and turned to retrieve cookie dough from the fridge. "How are you at peanut butter cookies?"

"I enjoy eating them," he said.

"Trust me, they're a snap." She handed him the waxed paper–wrapped dough. "Roll these out to half an inch. This

330 • JO-ANN MAPSON

spatula is best for making the crisscross design. Don't wax the cookie sheets; use parchment paper. It's on the roll over there. Bake them ten to twelve minutes at three seventy-five. The cooling rack is over here. Use it. When you finish, do the sugar cookies. Use the Christmas cutters." She threw him her apron and he caught it. "If anyone bitches tell them I'll make the goddamn fudge when I get back, that I've gone to be with my daughter at the hospital, and that's more important than anybody's sweet tooth. And don't let Mr. Cashin bully you."

"You told me she was cute," Terry said to Simon, "but you didn't tell me about the Bette Davis eyes."

"Where are you going?" Simon asked, still using his nice voice.

"CHOMP. Lindsay's having a test because she might have bleeding ulcers, and I think it's more important for me to be there than it is to be here."

"Mariah?" Simon whined, "please take Gammy with you. Terry and I can run orders and the register. Please, Mariah, it'd be a huge favor."

"All right." In the café, she pulled her grandmother away from Mr. Cashin, who was in early, and on whom Gammy had chosen to stretch her antagonizing muscles. "Get in the car," she said. "If we can't be there when Lindsay goes under we can sure as hell be there when she wakes up."

"Amen to that," Gammy said, not even batting an eyelash at Mariah's mention of the underworld.

17
Lindsay

LINDSAY WAS SIPPING apricot juice from a box when her mother and Gammy came rushing into the recovery room. Her mother had the pinched look that meant she hadn't slept, and Gammy "rattled her beads," which was what she called it when she prayed in public, like when the pope was sick in the hospital and couldn't do the Easter Mass. "Want to see inside my stomach?" she said, holding out a computer-generated image that showed four views of the places where she'd been bleeding.

But Gammy didn't want to look, and her mother started to cry and then wanted to hug her, which was embarrassing and also seemed overly dramatic to Lindsay since the whole procedure start to finish took about twenty minutes, which wasn't even as long as it had taken Dr. Ritchie to give them their last-minute instructions for how to present on Science Project Fair night. No last-minute surprises, girls, she'd insisted. Everything will go nice and easy, just like we practiced. Ha. That showed how little she knew.

"I'm going to be fine," she said. "All I have to do is take medicine and have periodic blood tests."

"And stop worrying so much," Allegra added.

"Which is not anybody's fault," Dr. G added. "The human body, for all we know of its design and function, is filled with idiosyncrasies. It helps if you think of it in terms of a weak spot. For Mariah, it's migraines. For Bess—"

Gammy pointed the crucifix on her rosary at him. "Enough speechifying. Just tell us our little girl is going to mend."

"Of course she is. Now that we know what's wrong, we can prescribe the right medicine to fix it."

"Lindsay needs to learn to meditate," Allegra said. "Acupuncture wouldn't hurt, either. Krishna Dahvid'll pick out the right meridians and invoke their chi and—"

"Alice," Gammy said, "that is a load of woo-woo nonsense and you know it. The child's going to start attending church with me on Sundays even if I have to pay her ten simoleons to do it."

"Mama," Allegra said, "just because church works for you doesn't mean it works for everyone. Lindsay's smart enough and old enough to choose her own path."

"What other path is there but God's," Gammy said, "seeing as how He blazed all the trails in the first place?"

"Ladies," Dr. G said, "right now we all need to calm down and let Lindsay rest."

Lindsay looked between Gammy and Allegra, feeling like she was watching a speeded up tennis match. Then she saw her mom, her hair clipped up at a funny angle, dark circles under her eyes, flour on her wrist and her shirt sleeves rolled up unevenly. She noticed Lindsay watching her and came perilously close to tears. Then, as she usually did, she shoved them out of the way to some secret location to where they'd build up like a rainy day savings account for the worst storm ever.

"Mom, what do you think I need?" she said, and waited for her to say art lessons or a therapist or a trip to Yorkshire, which she knew all along her mom had been planning until she lost her teaching job.

Her mom touched her right hand to her throat. A floury fingerprint remained when she took her hand away. Her mom looked rattled, the way she did during thesis defense week, when she had to make the pass or fail decisions that allowed a student to get his degree or sent him back to the library. No wonder her mom was happiest when she was in school; school was safer than the outside world. Sure, you had to put up with the Taylor Fosters, and friends like Sally could come and go, but you could know some of the rules. Hold off speaking until everyone else has given her opinion. Go a little wild in art class. Omit certain parts of your science project until the night of presentation because you were going to get into trouble, but maybe, just maybe, you were going to win a scholarship that would allow you to go to SAT camp.

"Lindsay," Mariah said, "I think it's time that you get to decide what will make you happy." Then she hugged Lindsay around the shoulders, the way Lindsay preferred affection, coming in little bits and lightly offered, something you could leave right there or lean into if you needed more of it.

"Mariah," Dr. G said, "you're a wonderful mother."

That undid her. Lindsay studied her mom as she went from a few tears to a choked sob to allowing Dr. G to give her a hug. All she could think was, I guess I won't be spending all my allowance on Pepcid anymore. She'd miss the familiar berry taste. Anything you knew that well was going to be hard to forget.

"Girls," Dr. Ritchie said the afternoon of Science Project Presentation, "get yourselves collected and sit down this minute."

Her voice rose on the last three syllables and the muttering and fretting immediately stopped. Taylor Foster smiled smugly, while next to her Sally looked bored. Avril ran to the bathroom because she needed to throw up, and Dr. Ritchie asked if there were any final questions before they went to the pizza party.

Belva said, "Everyone should be checked for celiac disease

334 • JO-ANN MAPSON

but especially Avril. It doesn't just cause irritable bowel, you know."

"Will you shut up about the freaking wheat thing?" Sally said. Dr. Ritchie must have agreed, because she didn't scold Sally.

"Listen closely, because this is tonight's schedule," Dr. Ritchie said. "At four forty-five the pizza dinner will commence in the cafeteria. The video showing of *The Secret Life of Insects* begins at five. At six-thirty you are all to be in the greenroom backstage from the theater. At six forty-five, there will be a brief introduction, and at seven presentations will begin."

"Who goes first?" Taylor said. "Are we alphabetical by subject or is the order arranged by name? Subject order's the fairest, if you ask me."

Of course she'd say that, Lindsay knew, since she'd worded her project title to come in last in the alphabet. If you went last, you could come up with something to make the judges forget everyone else but you. Taylor deliberately titled her project: "Urchins: The Life Cycle of Monterey Bay's *Allocentrotus fragilis,* aka the Fragile Pink Sea Urchins." She'd win, too, because the Aquarium had a killer exhibit and probably allowed Taylor to work behind the scenes, even if she had to get her dad to make a donation in order for that to happen. Lindsay didn't care anymore. She just wanted Science Fair to be over and Christmas vacation to begin. This wasn't about presents. It was about sleeping with Theodora while she watched New Year's Rockin' Eve. She wanted to burn this whole year in the annual bonfire on the beach, and she wanted to read as many books as she could before school started again.

"Yes, we will be going alphabetical by project title," Dr. Ritchie said. "Now I need you girls to remember—"

"Alphabetical order is archaic," Sally said. "Think about it, Dr. Ritchie. You're condoning the tyranny of twenty-six letters. Suppose my project started with 'zoology,' and then after the colon, I had the subtitle of 'Apes.' Then I'd be last, unless someone else was also 'zoology,' had a colon, and what followed that colon was after my colon alphabetically. We should draw numbers. Leaving things to chance is better than bowing down to whatever dictator invented the alphabet."

Taylor drew back from Sally like a pet snake had bitten her. Once again, Lindsay noted, Sally looked bored, maybe even annoyed. Dr. Ritchie, on the other hand, now looked like she might kill Sally. Her hands shook on the paper she was trying to read and her mouth was drawn so tight her lips seemed to disappear. Lindsay kicked Sally under the table. This was, as Gammy would say, "the eleventh hour."

"Do you want Taylor to tell about the marijuana now, or can you wait a few stupid hours before this is all over?" Lindsay hissed.

Sally looked at Lindsay and said in a monotone, "Sorry, Dr. R. Alphabetical works just fine. Really. Let's go alphabetical. Come on, everyone. Let's hear it for the vowels."

The teacher read on. "I need you girls to remember, should any of you win an award or an honorable mention, to thank the Science Fair's sponsors, who are the State Council for Science and Mathematics, the PTA, and Pacific Grove's mayor elect. Additionally, there will be a short presentation by last-minute sponsors who are giving an additional monetary award for special recognition."

"Another award?" Taylor said. "For how much? Are there any special circumstances? Because to exclude that information until now isn't really fair and could easily be contested."

Dr. Ritchie set her paper down and walked to the window. It was raining. The rabbit was curled around his bedding. Limp carrots lay around him, their green tops nibbled away. Dr. Ritchie didn't say anything for the longest time. Then what she did say was unexpected. "You've all worked very hard and deserve a reward. Lindsay's mother has thoughtfully provided an assortment of cookies, some of which are clearly marked as wheat-free." She opened a bag and took out two familiar pink boxes. "She's also baked brownies for the Science Fair Presentation as well. I think I'll just sit down for a bit. Just sit here and put my feet up. Talk among yourselves, but try to keep it down to a roar, please."

There was a general dive-bombing for the cookies, but Lindsay didn't want any. It surprised her that her mom had managed to get the cookies and brownies to the school without her finding out, but she'd hired a new person a few days ago, an older woman named Esther who Gammy bet wouldn't last the week. Look at her, she said. Skinny as a rail post, and would it kill her to take a few smiling lessons? But Lindsay's mom had started out not smiling, and now she could slap one on her face any old time. She pointed out that Esther was walking circles around everyone, including herself, so Gammy had shut up, and begun planning a weeklong trip to see her friend Dove Lyons, down near San Luis Obispo.

What concerned Lindsay was that Dr. Ritchie had her hand over her eyes, and that her color wasn't its usual porcelain white with twin bright spots of color on her cheeks. Lindsay mentally reviewed all the reasons this could be, which included things as simple as a bad sandwich or stress from preparing for the Science Project Presentation Night to an unplanned pregnancy, which generally started out with nausea. Was it leukemia? Maybe, like Gammy, she needed to take a trip. Scotland was kind of pretty, at least in the books. Theodora, FTF's dog, was beautiful, but had to be on a lead at all times, which meant no running on the beach like Lindsay had with Khan. Theo was perfect for hugging, though, and she didn't mind when Lindsay used her as a pillow while she read. Dr. Ritchie might be getting the flu, like Mrs. Shiasaka had. The flu hit older people harder than it did kids. Maybe a friend of hers had died or her boyfriend had said she was getting in the way of his studies. Lindsay walked over to the desk.

"Dr. Ritchie?" she asked. "Do you need to go to the nurse?"

Her teacher looked up and smiled. "I'm fine, Lindsay. I'm simply nervous about tonight. I want things to go well." Dr. Ritchie pointed to Lindsay's hem. "You'll need to get that let down to comply with school regulations," she said.

"Huh?"

"You've grown at least two inches this semester."

"I've grown?" Lindsay stared at her knees, but of course that just made the hem drop lower because she was bent over. Then she heard Sally call out that the pizza was here, and to step on it or she'd end up eating salad with Belva. "You're my favorite teacher," Lindsay said quickly.

Dr. Ritchie grinned and the spots of red on her cheeks returned. "Go get your pizza. And good luck tonight."

Spicy foods and ulcers—Dr. G told Lindsay that was a myth, that she could eat anything she wanted with the exception of fast food, which he didn't recommend for anybody. Sally had her plate loaded up with the pepperoni and bacon pizza, but Lindsay didn't think she could eat them even if she didn't have an ulcer. It wasn't just the meat, which to be honest grossed her out, but the animals the meat came from. Take the sausage, for example. *Sus scrofa* was naturally lean, unless overfed, and smart, with the verified intelligence of at least a human toddler. One family's pet pig had saved a kid from drowning. Their sense of smell was so keen they could hunt out truffles, the most delicately scented of fungi. Pigs knew enough to wallow in mud to stay cool, which, given the fact that they had no sweat glands, took some thinking. E. B. White had written *Charlotte's Web,* a story that always made Lindsay cry, but he was also the author of the essay "Death of a Pig," which was funny and also sad, but in a way that showed what it meant to be human and tend animals, and she bet that during his life-time, E. B. White didn't eat bacon either. She loaded up her plate with salad and went to sit by Belva, who was alone at her end of the cafeteria table. Carl Sagan probably was a geek at age twelve, too. Anyone could be the next great scientist, even Belva.

"Hi," Lindsay said. "Good luck on your junk-food presen-tation."

Belva looked at her dully, and then pointed to the salad dressing Lindsay had drizzled over the greens. "I bet you didn't know that ranch dressing has wheat in it," she said.

"Good thing I'm not allergic," Lindsay replied. "So what do you use for dressing?"

Belva reached into her sweater pocket and pulled out the tiniest Tupperware container Lindsay had ever seen. "My mom makes it for me. It's just plain vinaigrette."

"Can you chew gum?" Lindsay asked.

"Not unless it's free of starch and malt."

"Toothpaste?"

"Thickeners. I have to buy mine at the health food store."

"Ice cream?"

"Wheat by-products are everywhere, Lindsay."

"Candy?"

"Wheat is the main ingredient in red licorice, the kind Dr. Ritchie eats."

"Next year you should try making wheat-free candy in science. I bet you could. All you need to do is find a recipe and flavors."

Belva stabbed at her salad and chewed a mouthful before nodding.

Lindsay looked down the table to where the two Cheyennes and Avril and Taylor were toasting their pizza slices by jamming them together. Sally came in just a second behind them, but in that second delay Lindsay saw how deeply bored Sally was with the posse. If they hadn't gotten caught, if they hadn't had to pretend, Sally could be sitting with her, and then Lindsay might not be talking to Belva. Somebody was always left out. Why did it have to be like that? She finished her salad, and helped bus the table. Then Sally waved at her and Lindsay knew it was time to bring in the dangerous stuff. She followed her to Gregorio's truck, which was parked across the street from Country Day. He waved, and they hurried across the lane the minute traffic cleared.

He'd agreed to transport the "product," he called it. But

after helping them grow their crop, he'd moved his growing operation elsewhere. "Your mom's been good to me," he told them. "No way do I want to get her in trouble. I vacuumed each piece of gravel in that greenhouse," he said. "You two keep your lips zipped about getting any help from me, *comprende?*"

"Duh," Sally said. "We're not complete morons."

"Remember, this all started because of my *abuelo*'s rheumatism and your blackmail, *chica*. I'm not a pothead. I don't go around selling drugs to anybody."

"Blah blah, blah blah," Sally said. "This is exactly what you told me yesterday. Cross my heart and hope to die, stick a needle in my eye, I will not mention your name even if they drive bamboo under my fingernails."

"Thanks for everything," Lindsay said.

"You're welcome. Now go win that money!"

He drove off, and Lindsay picked up the box.

"Careful," Sally said, picking up the shopping bags.

"Like I wouldn't be," Lindsay said, annoyed Sally would even suggest she wouldn't be. "Omigod, I can smell it from here. There's no way we're going to sit in the greenroom for five minutes before someone figures this out."

"Which is why we're stashing this in the bathroom," Sally said. "Follow me."

They carried the bags and box to the bathroom at the far end of the hallway instead of the greenroom, where all the other girls were congregating.

"This is it," Sally said. "All our hard work and your great paper. All that's left is wowing them on stage. Did you write out the mission statement?"

"Of course I did." Lindsay wanted it to be over, so she could go home and reread *The Dragons of Eden*. Maybe Carl Sagan would talk to her again. She'd like to hear his voice, hear him remind her that the world was very old and human beings were very young. Her prescription medicine settled her stomach, but sometimes a person needed reassurance medicine couldn't provide. It was hard to sleep when your brain was the only part of you that got exercise, and it was hard to relax when all around you were the ways the world could fail you. "Who do you think will win?" she asked.

Sally unfolded the top of the bag she'd carried and Lindsay caught a breath of the cannabis plant, as herby and distinctive as newly mown grass. She wondered if Gregorio would get questioned, but had no doubt Sally would zip her lip at any cost, except maybe if her mom threatened to take away her horse. If that happened, Lindsay planned to take the blame. "*We're* going to win," Sally said. "How can you even doubt it?"

Lindsay was done with playing along with Sally's bravado. "No, we're not," she said. "Taylor's going to win. Did you see her display booth? It must have cost five hundred dollars to build. The letters on it are neon. And excuse me, but an aquarium on loan from Monterey Bay? What good are homegrown marijuana plants against that kind of technology?"

Sally reached into the depths of the bag and pulled out the electric clippers she used to keep Soul Man's mane roached for horse shows. "We're not going to rely *totally* on the plants," she said. "*This* is how we're going to win this stupid competition. We're going to shave our heads in honor of your grandma, to whom, remember, we are dedicating this project. The judges are going to bawl like babies, and then they are going to give us the money."

They hid in the bathroom until show time. Lindsay looked in the mirror, stunned. Her hair was shorn as close as a golf club putting green. She couldn't stop running her fingers over the stubble, wondering what a phrenologist would make of the bump on the right rear part of her skull. Later she'd read that was the area allotted to cautiousness, but right now her heart was thudding in her chest and she was thinking about Carl Sagan's bare head when he was trying to get better, taking chemotherapy or his sister's bone marrow or interferon or whatever last-ditch measure there was to try. No matter what, in every picture his smile seemed happy. Was that because of pot, or did he just love the universe and all its secrets so much that cancer couldn't erase that? In a way, this project had been about his struggle, too. Hair grew back, and who could tell, maybe hers might come in straighter, or she'd discover she liked it short, that it suited her better than the bushy mane of frizz, thanks to Ephraim Cantor, a man she decided she wanted to meet someday.

They heard their names being called and looked at each other and smiled. "This is it," Lindsay said.

"Don't look at anybody until after you've read the mission statement," Sally warned her. "After that, focus on the clock or the light switch or a bug on the wall. Above all, don't look at your grandmother. Promise. Pinky swear."

Lindsay said, "My great-grandmother always says, 'All audiences are dead drunk and fifty feet away.' "

"Maybe," Sally said. "But just to be on the safe side, don't look at her, either."

Lindsay hesitated before the open door. "I really liked being your friend," she said. "I learned a lot from you."

"I am *still* your friend!" Sally practically yelled. "After tonight it'll all be out in the open. I'm telling you, Linds, we can go back to just like before. We'll always be friends. Best friends. Even if I'm researching culture in Bolivia or swimming in the Amazon with white dolphins or writing in my Paris garret."

Lindsay knew Sally meant whatever she said the moment she said it, but they would never be friends like that again. She wanted to try to be friends, but was it possible to make it all the way back to thinking the sun rose and set on Sally DeThomas? Not really. Lindsay pictured herself as a slab of steel that had tempered and turned stainless because the pain of what she'd gone through had so changed her.

Outside the curtain their families waited. Inside the green-room, Taylor was rehearsing her sad plight of the fragile pink urchin, forced to feed in waters polluted by boat fuel and trash and reduced in numbers by the Japanese gourmet food import industry. Sally and Lindsay walked onto the stage with their bags and boxes, and grinned at each other when they heard the collective gasp of the audience as they took in the shaved heads. The girls proceeded to arrange Charlies one, two, three, and so on, poured the baggie of harvested marijuana in the glass bowl stolen from Sally's mom's studio, and laid out the carefully rolled cigarettes. Then they joined hands, and turned to "face the piano man," as Gammy would say.

But neither girl had counted on cameras, or local news station KMSTV 67, or the reporters from *The Monterey County Herald* and *The Blue Jay*. Country Day was Pacific Grove's gem, and people turned out in support for it. Sally was in her element. Lindsay stole one glance at the audience before she began the mission statement, and of course she saw Allegra, and this being all about her almost took Lindsay's voice away. Make me proud, she heard a voice in her head say, and couldn't tell if it was Carl Sagan or Dr. G. Sally elbowed her, and Lindsay cleared her throat, and began to read her piece without so much as a wobble.

"This is our mission statement," she read. "A successful middle school science project isn't about the hardest topic or the most meaningful issue. It's about the willingness of scientists to be persecuted in search of scientific truth. If we could ask Frederick Douglass, Galileo, or Rachel Carson about that, they'd tell us stories of being mocked for their beliefs during their lifetimes. Today they are honored for their contributions. Studying their examples gave Sally and me courage to take on the subject of palliative care in cancer patients, like my grandmother, to whom—" she stopped and cleared her throat again. She didn't dare look at her mom or Gammy, because she knew the shaved heads part was going to be hard for them to get over. She waited for her jaw to stop trembling before she went on. "That's why we dedicate this project to my grandmother, who has leukemia. Statistics show, as our charts will prove, that smoking marijuana helps reduce nausea in a significant percentage of chemotherapy patients. There is a measure on the upcoming ballot to impose fines and prison sentences on people who grow marijuana for personal use, or sell it outside of government sanctions to sick people. Our project asks the question: Whose business is it if a sick person can be made well enough to eat by using *Cannabis sativa?* We respectfully submit it is not the government's, that it is the business of science. Thank you for listening to our mission statement. I will now turn the presentation over to my partner, Sally DeThomas."

Lindsay stared at her feet while Sally quickly explained that nobody had to worry, this was the entire crop and it was going into the trash the second the judging was completed. She made everybody laugh, and Lindsay thought of Gammy, who always said, "You catch more flies with molasses than you do with sauerkraut."

When it was Lindsay's turn to talk about the value of stringent recordkeeping, Sally handed the microphone back to her. "Sometimes the smallest observation turns out to be the most valuable," she said, feeling the many moments of their project add up. "It might happen with any plant, not just *Cannabis sativa*. But if we aren't allowed to study it, we'll never know."

It did seem as if she might go blind from all the camera flashes, but Lindsay didn't really get nervous until the television crew moved through the crowd to get a close-up. The judges' faces stayed stern-looking as they examined the display, and just when Lindsay thought she and Sally were dead meat, one of the judges winked at her, and she knew it, they'd won something, even if it only turned out to be honorable mention. Her heart felt like it had grown wings, which was scientifically impossible, but like something Allegra would say, and she bet Allegra was feeling the same way.

When she and Sally stepped down off the stage, they were surrounded. Lindsay actually felt a little sorry for Taylor, but only for a second. She caught her mother's eye and saw her smile the "I'm so proud of you I can't talk" smile, and she smiled back. Then it was questions and microphones and a couple of angry parents, one of whom had to be Taylor's father, if only for having the whitest grown-up teeth Lindsay'd ever seen. Lindsay stood all that just fine. It was only when the cops showed up that she got so nervous that she felt light-headed, and the familiar crawling inside her stomach began, which meant she might throw up. Dr. G must have recognized that, too, because he rushed in there and caught her before her legs collapsed underneath her, and before Taylor's dad insisted both girls be drug tested and their project disqualified due to its illegality, and furthermore, Sally's mom's farm inspected for breaking the law. Taylor's presentation? Second place.

"Someday this will all be a funny story to tell your grandchildren," Allegra said that Christmas, as everyone sat around the tiny artificial Christmas tree upstairs from The Owl & Moon. "You'll explain how you were forced to take a drug test, and how the ACLU came to your aid, and how that began your lifelong interest in the legal system and—"

"Alice," Gammy said, "enough already. This is Jesus' birthday, and I don't think He appreciates talking about drugs when He started his life in a stable on scratchy animal hay, for crying out loud. Lindsay, open my present next. I knitted you a hat. Put it on. I can't bear to look at your poor, bald head another minute."

Lindsay unwrapped a knitted gray cap that even Belva Satterly would have been ashamed of. "I love it," she told her great-grandmother, and put it on. Why not, if it made Gammy happy for a few hours? Later, she would rub lunchmeat all over it and accidentally drop it in Theodora's bed. Behind them, the deerhound yawned. "Now you open my present," she said, and handed Gammy a heavy box six inches square. Inside was a moisturizer made from rose petals that came from

Sally's mother's farm. It was guaranteed to restore "youthful dew." Gammy peered over her glasses to read the fine print.

"Have to make sure no marihoochie went into this," she said gruffly, and everyone laughed and took another Christmas cookie, and pretty soon Allegra couldn't stand it any longer, and put her new DVD of *Scrooged* into the DVD player, fast-forwarding to the scene when the fairy hits Bill Murray with the toaster.

"Allegra," Lindsay said. "Please open my present."

She did, peeling away tissue paper to reveal a small box, inside which was a single, hand-rolled cigarette.

"I made it myself," Lindsay said, and they all laughed except for Gammy.

"Alice, can you please refrain from toking up until I head down to Dove's?"

"I don't know, Mama. This looks pretty good."

"Lord, God," Gammy said. "Give me strength to get through this night."

Mariah touched her mother's hand. "It's okay with me if you smoke it."

Lindsay could tell that one touch meant more to Allegra than any dozen presents.

Then her mom said, "Does it work on broken hearts? If so, I want a little."

"We'll smoke it together," Allegra said.

Gammy put her hands over her ears. "I am not going to be a party to this."

"Lindsay, this present's for you from Fergus," Mariah said.

Obviously it was a book. Lindsay tore the paper away, and held in her hands a hardcover copy of *The Dragons of Eden*.

"Oh," Mariah said. "You already have that, don't you?"

"Not in hardback," Lindsay said, and then opened it. There on the title page, in turquoise ink, was Carl Sagan's signature. She'd know it anywhere. "Mom, look," she said, taking out an index card that was covered with writing. She read aloud, "Dear Lindsay, I know this book is a second edition, but the seller assured me it was still quite valuable. On Thanksgiving night I drove clear to Crescent City in order to purchase it. I didn't dare take a chance on the post. Many happy returns of the day. Your friend, Fergus D. Applecross."

Lindsay saw her mother's face redden. FTF being so thoughtful, him being in Scotland, she didn't know what to do. "Fergus drove all the way to Oregon to buy that?"

"That's what the card says." Lindsay turned it over. "I guess I'd better write him a thank-you letter," Lindsay said. "I love it. I love you, too, Mom. I'm really sorry about almost getting arrested. And my hair. We were just trying to make a point."

Mariah sighed. "Sally's a bit more of a dramatic influence on you than I would like, but in the end it worked out okay. You won the scholarship."

"Taylor's dad is still contesting it."

"Taylor's dad can afford to pay her college tuition," Mariah said. "Tell me something. Would you have been as happy with an honorable mention?"

"Yes," Lindsay said. "That would have been enough."

"Hand over that devil weed," Gammy said. "Good Lord, it smells like the business end of a skunk. How on earth anyone can smoke this . . ."

With the dorky hat pulled down over her ears and her jacket collar turned up, Lindsay was warm enough to stay out on the beach for hours, but Khan didn't get very far in the sand. She carried him down by the water, and found a sand dollar with only one part missing. It was gray and had probably been tossed around by waves for a long time before it was deposited on the sand. She brushed the sand off, let Khan sniff it, and then put it in her pocket to show to Dr. G when he got back from San Francisco. A little ways down the beach, her mother held on to Theo's leash, standing on the beach looking like one of those sailor's wives Allegra used to tell her about. Just standing there, looking out to sea, waiting.

18
Mariah

THE OWL & MOON CLOSED fifty-two Sundays out of the year plus Christmas, December twenty-sixth, and New Year's Day. But even when the doors were locked, work remained to be done. The Sunday before New Year's Mariah was downstairs early with Lindsay, who was going with Sally to a horse show and then spending the next two nights at her house, including New Year's Eve. Mariah was a little worried—after the pot business, who knew what those girls might dream up next? Sally wasn't the person Mariah would have picked for her daughter's friend, but watching Lindsay apply the Thomas theorem, matching an opponent's wit and endurance often resulted in a desired friendship, was ethnomethodology, a theory Mariah respected, because instead of accepting a perceived reality as already being out there, it showed that you could create and live your own reality.

"What are Sally's parents doing for New Year's Eve?"

Lindsay stopped petting Theo and looked up. "Mom, look at me. Do I look like a girl who would get into trouble?"

"Are you sure you want me to answer that?"

"Her parents will be there, plus her entire family. Not that we would try to get away with anything, but how could we? Plus we are supposed to keep an eye on Savannah, and she is the neediest child in the universe. She won't even go to the bathroom by herself and she is almost seven years old!"

"That must be hard on her mother," Mariah said. Then the horn honked and with a brief kiss, Lindsay was out the door. Allegra was at Dr. G's, and Gammy had taken the bus from Salinas to visit her friend Dove. Simon had offered to drive her to the bus station, and she'd actually let him. Gammy was having no problem letting go. The Owl & Moon, she reminded Mariah, was a business, not a way of life. Though she was still suspicious of the new waitress, she had "bigger trout to fry" since Simon would soon be coming out from behind the stove into the café proper. "It's time for a change," Mariah said, but her comments fell on deaf ears. To say it was hard watching her grandmother transition to retired life wasn't the half of it.

Mariah inspected the cupboards. If she was going to make any cookies for Monday, she needed to restock supplies. The vanilla bottle was dry. They were drastically low on brown sugar, and one of the cookie sheets had been dropped too many times to bend back into the proper shape. "Well, Theo," she said, "looks like it's just us two tonight."

At the sound of her name, the gray dog looked up, her warm brown eyes alert and the pink tongue lolling from her mouth, giving her every appearance of smiling. When Fergus left her with Mariah, she strained at the leash to go with him. "Tirrah," he'd said, kissing Mariah on the forehead. "Farewell for a brief time," he'd told his dog. Mariah watched him go out the café door without a backward glance.

On Christmas night, when everyone was asleep, Mariah invited Theo onto her bed and buried her face in the dog's neck. "I'm afraid I've made a terrible mistake letting your master into my bed," she'd said, "because look what happened next—he wormed his way into my heart. What do you take for that, Theo? Is there any medicine?" While Lindsay could explain the chambers of the heart, and science was always interesting and full of debatable ideas, it was no better than sociology at three o'clock in the morning when you ached to have a man put his arms around you and snore in your ear. The unvarnished truth was that Mariah no longer liked being alone, and in order not to be alone, she had to get in her car and drive to her mother—and father's—house. Mariah would rather cut off her arm than watch her mom live the last five months over again. Gammy would return eventually, but Allegra wasn't coming back. It was stupid to feel awkward with a man who'd saved your mother's life and who just happened to have contributed one half your genetic code. Dr. G was generous with Lindsay. Mariah said thank you as often as the occasion warranted it, but it was difficult to articulate what she felt in her heart. *I want to tell you about the times I skinned my knees, how my third-grade teacher made me do over my paper because she didn't believe I wrote it, and dammit all, I did, and if you'd been there, I know she would have backed off instead of arguing with Allegra.* How did a person condense a childhood into a conversation?

Supply list made out, Mariah began counting the till. Suddenly, Theo's tail began thumping like it did when Mariah announced supper. "What's got you so happy all of a sudden?" she asked, and in response, the dog went to the café windows and began to vocalize, the "roo-roo-rooing" that was common to sight hounds. "Nothing out there except some stupid deer," Mariah said without looking up. "As tempting as that may be to you, I refuse to be a part of the hunt, so you might as well lie back down."

Rock salt! She turned back to the supplies list to write it down. Rock salt was coarse, it made for a better pinch, and she liked to cover the crust of rosemary bread in it. She grabbed a twenty from the till cash so she could buy what she needed and tucked it into her pocket, and started separating bills.

The bell on the café door rang, startling her, and her first thought was, *Oh, no! I forgot to lock the door after Lindsay* left and here comes a robber. What a way to start the New Year. But it wasn't a robber. It was Fergus.

"Come here, you big old funny face," he said to his dog, reaching for the biscuits he kept in his pockets.

"Greet the dog first? I guess I know where I stand," Mariah said, trying hard to sound as blasé as he did, but oh, her knees were shaking.

"Look at you," Fergus said. "Sitting there counting your gains, my adorable little capitalist."

Mariah calmly smiled, though her heart was hammering so loud she was sure he could hear it. "By my reckoning, you're back four weeks early. What happened? Did they kick you out of Scotland because too much California rubbed off on you?"

"I missed the love of my life," he said, and made as if to kiss Theo, but at the last minute, came to Mariah instead.

She swallowed hard and looked into those blue eyes. "Really?"

"Truly. I'm knackered. Done for. A fool in love."

She felt his breath in her hair and didn't want the moment to end.

He pulled away first, as if this day was no different from any other, as if men cut short holidays and told women they loved them all the time. "Come along," he said. "We've a dog to walk. A sunset to be enjoyed, however briefly, and then that holiday thing, yes, we must attend to that, ringing out the auld and welcoming the new, though I must confess, I've forgotten to purchase crackers and party hats, so sorry."

"It's okay. We'll think of something else to use."

When Fergus looked at her, Mariah saw things she didn't want to admit. A little house. Enough fenced yard that Theodora could safely run. A baby crying. Lindsay driving the Subaru to college. These pictures blocked out her ability to detach, to remain the observer instead of the one doing all the living. Did she really, truly want a life that had the potential to hurt her as much as make her happy? But suppose it did make her happy? Life came with no guarantees, whether it was how long her mother would live, or how Lindsay would turn out. "You learn as you go," Gammy always said. "Trust the big guy upstairs to show you the path."

She kissed Fergus, locked the money into the safe, shut off the lights save for the neon "CLOSED," kissed Fergus two more times, and then snapped Theodora's leash to her harness. Fergus took hold of it while Mariah zipped up her winter jacket, and she followed them out the door. As it always did, the bell rang out with its tenor chimes. And just as she always did, Mariah looked up at the sign, the crescent of moon shining, the shabby owl perched there, his wing outstretched, saying *Come in, come in. You are welcome here. We will feed you and we will listen.* But now there was no reason to wonder who her father was. And what her mother had said was true: The sign maker had been just a sign maker. Halfway across the threshold, she cried out, "Fergus!"

"What's the matter, love?" he said as she stood there, finally able to see something so simple it had been in front of her nose all the time."

"Nothing. I'm fine. I'm wonderful. I get it," she said, smiling. "Fergus, I finally understand."

"Well, tell me, then. What is it you finally get and understand?"

"The sign. It's the *Owl* and Moon. All this time I was thinking owl as in bird, but it's not the bird, it's a person. It's my father. *Owl. Al.* They're homonyms! And I even know why she did it. This way, even though he'd left, she kept him close, every single time she walked in or out the door. How could it have taken me all this time to figure it out?"

Fergus handed her Theo's leash so he could turn down Mariah's collar. He pulled pencils from her hastily assembled bun so that her hair fell into his hands. "My number two geisha," he said. "You are clever. Let's talk about that as we walk, shall we?"

Theodora whined, and in that moment, the leash slipped from Mariah's hand. Instantly, the dog seemed to fly from the sidewalk into traffic. Mariah saw it all unfold in slow motion: The car veering into the intersection, the deer across the street in the cemetery. Oh, this was going to end badly. She could not find the voice to scream. She wanted to shut her eyes, but this was her fault, and then Fergus whistled. "Come, Theo," he said. He whistled again. "Come along, girl."

Theodora stood torn between what she knew and what she wanted. Then—who knew why—the deerhound trotted back to the sidewalk and came toward them, her red leash trailing after her. When she was close enough, Fergus crouched down, took hold of the leash, and wrapped his arms around her. He was shaking. In turn, Mariah embraced them both and sighed. My God! The choices life handed you! One minute you had all the time in the world, yet it could be taken from you in a second. Allegra was right. When you knew what you wanted, you had better run after it.

In the distance, the Pacific roared. In a matter of steps they would be on the beach, dog and people safe. But for that one awful moment, Mariah had stood there witnessing an ancient breed move the way nature had intended, which was freely and focused, and yet, she was willing to give all that up for companionship. It was almost New Year's, and this coming year would be good. She slipped her hand into Fergus's. He squeezed it, and the three of them moved on.

Author's Note

I chose to write about the subject of medical marijuana purely out of interest in the complexity of the issues, not to condone drug use, or to use my fiction as a platform. Exploring marijuana fictionally offered me new ways to think about medicine and illness, two subjects that remain fascinating to me. *The Owl & Moon Café* is a story about people, plain and simple, and the everyday trials they experience when illness visits their world. I write this note so my mother won't worry.

Acknowledgments

Marysue Rucci's wisdom, honesty, and generous spirit helped me to locate the novel that lay hidden in my rocky first (and second) draft. I cannot thank her enough for reminding me that every book, be it my first or my ninth, is different from the one before it, and must be approached with humility and respect. I hope we will continue to make many more books together. Thanks too to her assistant, Alexis Taines.

Deborah Schneider, longtime agent and friend, and fellow sight hound enthusiast, remains my pillar of strength, my cold drink of water, my heart's dear friend, my work's fiercest champion, and she is always, always there for me when I need her. Her assistants, Cathy Gleason and Britt Carlson, are continually kind and ever helpful, as well.

Thank you, David Rosenthal and Simon & Schuster, for believing in my writing and continuing to publish me in a time when the industry is tentative.

Major blessings on Pam Cravez, an old soul with a wise eye, for her willingness to read, comment on, and help edit this manuscript. I wouldn't have made it without her.

To Isolde Sauer and Jane Herman, my production editor and copyeditor, thank you for your hard work—any mistakes are mine.

Friend and fellow writer on planet earth Earlene Fowler has gotten me through many hard times, and is a superlative human being I love with all my heart. Sherry Simpson, words fail. Thanks for being my friend. Judi Hendricks and Jodi Picoult, thanks for your abiding friendship and support. Erica Baird turned my office from a total heap into impeccable order, and I still can't figure out how. Erica, I've a feeling that in no time at all your books will be in print. Cat Whitney, house-sitting the Insane Clown Posse is above and beyond the call of friendship. Money will never be enough to demonstrate my gratitude. To the Whine and Dine girls: Jacqui Carr, Ellen Cole, Deborah Fink, and JoAnn Asher, thank you for putting up with my moods when I am remote and strange, which is unfortunately a lot of the time.

This book found its center when I passed by two sociology students selling old textbooks in the Social Sciences Building. Returning to Carl Sagan's words reminded me just how much undiscovered magic still exists. I pray he is up there in the celestial canopy enjoying his reward, and I also hope he knows that it's perfectly possible for a young girl to fall in love with him, even an old girl, too.

To my mom, Mary; my sisters, Lee and Carol; my brothers, Jim and John—thank you for letting me borrow from your lives to inspire my fiction. To my son, Jack, and his lovely wife, Olivia, I couldn't write a word without your abiding love and frequent laughter. To my doggies, Echo angel always missed, Max angel newly winged, Verbena, Cricket, and Henry the goofball, thank you for the privilege of being in your always illuminating lives, for curling up in my lap, for the nudges that remind me there is always time to play ball, for the stinky kisses and the jumps for joy.

Lastly and always to Stewart, thank you for our life together, made all the more precious when I remember how hard we have struggled to hang on to it.